RETRIBUTION

ALSO BY CARRIE MAC

TRISKELIA

The Droughtlanders

✦

The Beckoners

Charmed

Crush

[TRISKELIA BOOK 2]

RETRIBUTION
CARRIE MAC

PUFFIN
CANADA

PUFFIN CANADA

Published by the Penguin Group

Penguin Group (Canada), 90 Eglinton Avenue East, Suite 700, Toronto, Ontario, Canada
M4P 2Y3 (a division of Pearson Canada Inc.)

Penguin Group (USA) Inc., 375 Hudson Street, New York, New York 10014, U.S.A.
Penguin Books Ltd, 80 Strand, London WC2R 0RL, England
Penguin Ireland, 25 St Stephen's Green, Dublin 2, Ireland (a division of Penguin Books Ltd)
Penguin Group (Australia), 250 Camberwell Road, Camberwell, Victoria 3124, Australia
(a division of Pearson Australia Group Pty Ltd)
Penguin Books India Pvt Ltd, 11 Community Centre, Panchsheel Park,
New Delhi – 110 017, India
Penguin Group (NZ), 67 Apollo Drive, Rosedale, North Shore 0632, Auckland,
New Zealand (a division of Pearson New Zealand Ltd)
Penguin Books (South Africa) (Pty) Ltd, 24 Sturdee Avenue, Rosebank,
Johannesburg 2196, South Africa

Penguin Books Ltd, Registered Offices: 80 Strand, London WC2R 0RL, England

First published 2007

1 2 3 4 5 6 7 8 9 10   (RRD)

Manufactured in the U.S.A.

Library and Archives Canada Cataloguing in Publication

Mac, Carrie, 1975-Retribution / Carrie Mac.
(Triskelia; bk. 2)

ISBN-13: 978-0-670-06601-8
ISBN-10: 0-670-06601-X

I. Title.   II. Series: Mac, Carrie, 1975-Triskelia; bk. 2.
PS8625.A23R48 2007 jC813'.6 C2007-900056-8

Visit the Penguin Group (Canada) website at **www.penguin.ca**

Special and corporate bulk purchase rates available; please see
www.penguin.ca/corporatesales or call 1-800-810-3104, ext. 477 or 474

for Jack

~ 1535 ~

Some lives are grievable and others are not . . .
what counts as a livable life and a grievable death?

—JUDITH BUTLER, *PRECARIOUS LIFE*

[ONE]

EXODUS

1

Eli lay still, curled in a tight ball under the thin cover of his coat. He was awake, as he had been off and on for most of the night, and he hurt all over. His bones felt as if they'd been pulled out, rearranged, and jammed back in all wrong. His shoulder, where he'd been shot, throbbed mercilessly. The bullet was still in there but the pain was less today, or perhaps he'd just gotten better at ignoring it.

He was too stiff to get up just yet. It was a week into spring, but the ground was still cold and unforgivingly hard and he'd had nothing to sleep on and only what he wore for warmth. There were a few blankets among the survivors, but Eli wouldn't ask for one, not when so many of the others were injured far worse than he. Aside from the bullet wound he was okay, although his skin felt tight, as if bloated by the effort of pushing rebellious blood through frigid veins. His fingers were swollen and chaffed, his lips so cracked they were bloody and numb.

He closed his eyes again, slipping into a delirious half-sleep induced as much by cold as by fatigue. The nightmares didn't need to actually begin, per se . . . they were always in full swing, a gauntlet waiting for him whenever he slept: the bombs, the bodies, the blood and fire of the massacre they'd left behind.

Through the murky darkness of the nightmares Eli felt a sudden, familiar warmth nuzzling his hand. He woke, but did not open his eyes. He squeezed them shut tighter, willing the sensation to be real and not a dream. When he dared open his eyes he was elated to find see he hadn't imagined it. It was Bullet!

The survivors had been travelling for three long days, but his dog had tracked Eli anyway. Eli put his hand to the silver medallion that his grandfather had made, one each for him, Seth, and Sabine. He shut his eyes again, turned his face skyward, and promptly offered a prayer of thanks to his highers.

Prayer?

Although he wasn't one to pray typically, the instinct had been swift and powerful and had caught him off guard. But times were strange, and stranger still, Bullet had found him. Perhaps his highers had led the dog to him?

Eli shook off his confusion and gave Bullet a long, hearty belly rub. The dog grumbled happily and then curled up in the crook of Eli's knees as if nothing was amiss. As if the world was normal. As if they hadn't left the ruins of a massacre behind, as if they were back home in the warmth of Triskelia and not fleeing its wreckage, sleeping only when they could go on no more.

And where *were* they going? Eli had asked but no one would tell him. All his grandmother would say was that it was best if few knew. She assured him it was somewhere safe, where they could rest, and grieve, and ready themselves.

Ready themselves for what, though? Would they finally take up arms and begin the revolution Eli had been so anxious for? If this is what they needed to finally revolt, it was wretched and cruel and brutally unfair. If this is what revolution required, Eli wanted to give it back. And so much violence! There *had* to be a better way. If fighting meant this much pain and death and suffering he'd forgo the freedom of the millions of Droughtlanders they were supposed to be releasing from Keyland apartheid.

Before he'd left the Eastern Key so long ago, any single aspect of this horrible situation would've sent Eli into a tailspin of panic. But now he was merely numb with hunger and pain and hopelessness. He couldn't see forward and there was no turning back. He was a reluctant prisoner of the moment, and he hated that. He wanted to know what was going to happen next and how they'd manage. Would Triskelia be rebuilt? Were there plans? For anything? But it was just too overwhelming when really all that mattered was keeping themselves alive, even just long enough to get somewhere other than here—a cold, desolate forest with little to eat and nowhere soft to rest their weary souls and aching bones and exhausted hearts.

Eli stood with difficulty, his knees creaking. He put his fingers to the rag covering his wound. No fresh blood. That was good. He rolled his shoulder back a little, testing it. He couldn't move it much, but he had full feeling down to his fingers and was grateful for that. He eased on his coat and stepped carefully around the others who were still asleep.

Bullet gave himself a shake and a wag and then trotted proudly beside Eli as if he'd found a prize. Eli knelt to check him over. The dog was skinnier and had a chunk missing out of one ear, but other than that Eli found no bumps or other obvious wounds. He tried to remember where he'd seen Bullet last on the night it all happened, but he couldn't. In the bunkroom? On the stairs? No matter; wherever Bullet had been when the barrage of blasts began it was a miracle he'd escaped unscathed.

It was still dark. No sign of sunrise on the horizon, and Eli wouldn't be surprised if it never rose again. Why would it bother to shine down on this wretched world? And yet it had. It'd risen three times now. The survivors had walked each day without rest, pushing distance between them and the horrors they'd left behind.

Not all the horrors had been left behind, though. Eli's glance fell to Anya, finally asleep at the base of a tree, lifeless little Charis clutched in her arms. On the first day rigor mortis had set in, Charis taking on the waxy stiffness of a doll, and still Anya had refused to believe she was dead. And when the rigor slowly left and Charis's limbs relaxed, Anya took it as a sign that Charis was getting better. She wouldn't listen to anyone no matter how they approached the subject, with compassion or anger or disgust. And when the bravest among them tried to take Charis from her—for everyone's sake, for the preservation of what little human-ity remained to them—Anya went wild with protest, lashing out and screaming to be left alone.

She got her wish. No one could bear to look at her, let alone speak to her or even come near her. Everyone turned away from the macabre tableau of mother and child. Beyond sad and deeply unsettling, it was also a terrible reminder of the monumental loss they'd all suffered.

Celeste, in her makeshift position as leader until Zenith's whereabouts and safety could be confirmed, was the only one who felt obliged to persevere with Anya. Over and over she tried to make Anya understand, tried to take Charis from her, until soon, even if she spotted Celeste in the distance, Anya would shriek and run in the other direction, little Charis flopping lifelessly in her arms.

It could not go on. Celeste knew that Charis had to be put to rest, not only for Anya but for them all. The presence of the dead child rattled emotions and strained already beleaguered hearts, but soon the rot would worsen and it would be too horrible for any of them to endure. Already there was a smell no one wanted to acknowledge. Anya vowed not to sleep so that Celeste couldn't take Charis from her. Exhaustion now added to her grief. She stumbled around, mumbling to herself, frightening the children even more with her blank stares and gaunt cheeks.

As much as Celeste wished Anya could take all the time she needed, it just wasn't fair to make the others bear witness to such primal grieving on top of their own private and collective anguish. The night before, as they set up camp, Eli and Sabine had watched their grandmother sneak up on Anya as she finally succumbed to slumber. But as she'd gently lifted the baby's body out of her arms Anya had awakened with a violent start and staggered into action.

"Don't you touch my baby!" She'd shoved Celeste to the ground and grabbed Charis back. "*C'est la mienne!* I won't let you take her."

"Nana!" Sabine and Eli rushed to help Celeste.

"I'm all right." Celeste took their hands and eased herself up.

"What are you doing, Anya?" Sabine turned her eyes to Anya, despite having to see poor Charis so desecrated, the smell worse this close. "This is insane! You have to realize that she's dead. Can't you see it? Charis is dead!"

"What a terrible, cruel thing to say." Anya glowered at her. "Why I was ever kind to you, *je ne sais pas*. Your maman would be ashamed of you, treating me like this."

"Oh, Anya. Why can't you realize what's happening?" Sabine felt tears coming. Tired, frustrated, sad tears.

Eli put his arm across his sister's shoulders. "It's okay, Sabine."

"Don't be ridiculous." Sabine twisted away. "It's not okay. None of this is okay! Nothing will ever be okay again. Not ever." She turned to Celeste. "We have to do something, Nana. The others can't even stand to look at her! She's making all of this that much worse!"

"Leave her be." Celeste took Sabine's hand as Anya fled into the dark forest. "One more night. I will take care of it tomorrow. I promise."

Celeste left Eli with instructions to keep an eye on the edge of the clearing for Anya's safe return. Sabine kept him company but eventually went to help settle the children for the night, leaving him alone. It was a grim task, waiting for the dishevelled pair to emerge from the dark woods like ghosts.

Would Anya ever be the spirited joy she'd been before? Not likely. Maybe she was crazy now. Maybe this was the end of the Anya who'd mothered them all, who'd brought Eli to Triskelia and kept watch over him. Something had to be done to break the spell, to bring Anya back, or she'd be lost to them. And where was Trace? Had he even survived? Was he dead? Or worse, dying slowly, trapped under rubble, bleeding out, gangrene setting in like an evil army? Either way, it was the end of that beautiful little family. But now was the end of so many things, so what was one more loss amid an endless sea of grief? What was left, really?

Hours passed before Anya emerged from the forest. Eli squinted. Her arms hung at her sides and for a brief moment he thought maybe she'd left Charis behind, buried her in the woods, sparing the others any more gruesome chores. But no. She'd only tucked the toddler into the folds of her knotted shawl, carrying her as if Charis were merely sleeping. She walked past Eli without so much as a glance, found herself a tree to settle under, and shifted Charis around to her front so that she could cradle her in her arms. All was lost, Eli was sure of it. Everything that was ever good would never be theirs again.

ONLY IT WAS a new day now, and Bullet had found him. That was good. And his sister and grandmother were alive and uninjured, and that was good too. So there was some hope, even if it was nervous and shy. Sometimes Eli wished he were more pessimistic. That way, he could just give up and let his life happen to him instead of always trying so hard to make things better.

He stretched, his bones cracking, his muscles protesting the cold, damp air. Everyone was still sleeping, or trying to. The most elderly and the worst injured rested in the caravans under what few blankets and spare layers they had between them or had managed to grab as they'd fled, but everyone else had just the earth for a bed. The majority of the group were children who'd been hidden when the ambush began and had survived unharmed, albeit traumatized and terrified beyond description. Because the caravans were filled with the wounded the children had to walk, despite their protests and blisters and the cold, and so they were quite miserable and exhausted on top of it all.

They were all still asleep, in a heap like puppies, limbs tangled together. Last night Sabine had tried to calm them with a fairy tale, and the children had listened, but more because there was nothing else to do. There was no fire for fear it would be spotted. There was nothing to eat except the tiniest portions of dried fruit and the smallest strips of jerky. They were tired and scared and full of grief, too stunned to play. So they sat and listened to the story about the mermaid and the prince.

Sabine had taken unofficial charge of the children, with Althea's help. The girl was eager to be put to work. The ten-year-old's only wound was a jagged slice along her arm, and with a piece of ripped-up jersey covering it, it seemed to be healing well, although Sabine kept an eye on it, watching for the red streaks or dangerous heat of infection. As she started the tale, Althea gathered the children. A little boy climbed into Sabine's lap and another had his arms around her neck, his pudgy little body pressed against her back. When Sabine finished the story the children had asked for another, so she told the one about the juniper tree, and when that was finished they asked for a third.

"We must sleep some time." Sabine yawned, pulling Toby into her lap too. He hadn't said a word since Gavin had dug him out of the rubble as the gunfire rat-a-tatted just metres away. His arm was broken, encased for the moment in a splint made of two sturdy branches and a length of greasy twine.

"Don't you want to sleep?" Sabine hugged him, careful not to press on his arm. "Aren't you tired too?"

He ignored her and played with her medallion instead, catching his fingers in the Triskelian triangle, tracing her name carved on the spiral inside.

"You must be tired, Toby."

He gave the medallion a little tug and emphatically shook his head.

"He means the nightmares," Althea said. She'd taken to interpreting the children's silences. Sabine wasn't sure how much of it was empathy and how much her own fears, voiced on behalf of them all.

Toby gazed up at Sabine, his eyes a glaze of fatigue and sadness.

"We must try to sleep, pet."

He shook his head again.

"He means where," Althea said. "And how? We still have no blankets and nowhere to lie down. We don't like the nighttimes at all."

"We'll be each other's blankets," Sabine said. "We'll be each other's pillows and teddy bears too. And," she hugged Toby again, "we'll be each other's good dreams. Okay?"

Toby still shook his head, but his eyes drooped with exhaustion.

"He means maybe that sounds all right," Althea said. "Come on." She brought the children closer, tucking them in like dolls.

"Hold tight," Sabine urged, linking the filthy hands of the children. "That way we'll share our dreams and be sure no one gets lost in the middle of the night. Make sure no nightmares take you away."

Eventually the children fell asleep like that, all in a hand-held huddle. And as the night crept into dawn with the reluctance of a thief coming into the light, they slept like that still.

ELI WATCHED THE CHILDREN SLEEP. That made his heart slow a little from its panicked pace. Children sleeping. Despite the circumstances it seemed peaceful, and normal. Almost sweet.

Someone whistled for him across the camp. Eli peered into the indigo dark and headed toward the sound.

It was Gavin, standing guard at the far end. He scowled as Bullet bounded up to him, tail wagging, looking for affection from someone who'd always been generous with it back in Triskelia. When Gavin ignored him Bullet leaned against his shins, gazing up expectantly until Gavin kneed him hard, sending the dog scurrying back to Eli, tail between his legs. Eli made a quick and wise decision to say nothing about it. He knew better than to criticize anyone right now, especially Gavin, who had little tolerance for Eli at the best of times.

"When did your dog show up?" Gavin's tone was filled with disdain.

"Just now." Eli grinned and tousled Bullet's ears. The dog pressed against his legs, growling happily. "Amazing, isn't it?"

"Huh," Gavin snorted. "Whatever."

"What?" Eli's ire got the best of him. "It's not like he's going to take someone's rations or anything, not that we hardly have any anyway. He can fend for himself."

"It's not that," Gavin muttered. "It just pisses me off that the highers would help a friggin' dog find its way to us, and yet we have no idea who we left behind or what's ahead. What about Jack? And Zenith? She might be dead back there and we don't even know it! And there're three in the caravans who won't make it another day. Yet your dumb dog shows up? It's stupid, that's all."

"I can't argue with that," Eli said. Not that Eli would choose to argue with Gavin at all, given a choice. They'd never really gotten along, and now, while it seemed to matter less, it still mattered. And he wasn't about to suggest that if the highers had brought Bullet to him they must've had a good reason. Maybe Bullet had a larger part to play in all of this. Sure, it sounded ridiculous, but it was possible. "I can offer to take over the post though, and that'll make Bullet useful. He almost took Trace's leg off when I sicced him on him before I knew who he was."

"Trace," Gavin murmured. "Zenith, Jack, Nappo . . . everyone. All the others . . . we have no idea how they are or if they even survived. But no, it's your damned dog that shows."

Eli's heart dropped to the cold earth at the mention of his best friend. He stared at the ground, almost as if his heart really was lying at his feet, pumping blood onto the dirt.

The two of them said nothing for a long while, and that was fine by Eli. He wouldn't apologize for Bullet showing up, even if only to shift their attention away from the endless pit of grief that opened up before them at the very mention of the names of those still left behind. Instead, he said, "Why don't you go get a little shut-eye before we pack up?"

"I'll stay put." Gavin shook his head. "I wouldn't be able to sleep anyway. I was just curious about the dog."

In other words, he didn't trust Eli to stand watch. "I'll stay with you then," Eli offered, determined to be useful.

"Whatever." Gavin yawned.

Eli sat himself on a stump. "Do you know where we're going?"

"North still."

"How much farther?"

"Never gone there this way." Gavin shrugged. "I don't know."

"Never gone this way to where?"

"Cascadia."

So that was their destination. Eli felt that pleasing rush that came when he was just about to know more about something he'd been desperate to understand.

"What's Cascadia?"

"Weather station."

"Who's there?"

"What does it matter to you?" Gavin glanced at him. "You won't know any of them."

"But where is it?"

"I told you, it's north of here."

"But is it hidden, or near a market, or by itself, or what?"

Gavin's glance narrowed. "Why do you want to know?"

Eli paused before saying, "I cannot believe you're actually looking at me like that after everything we've been through, Gavin."

Gavin looked away and shrugged again. "And I cannot believe that you can't believe it. After everything we've been through, Eli."

Eli pushed down the urge to defend himself. He was too tired, and why bother? Gavin would never like him, and right now Eli couldn't honestly care less.

"Well, I hope at least one of us knows how to get us there."

"Celeste does."

"Just Celeste?"

"Look, I don't know who knows or doesn't know. It's best that way, in case we run into Guardies."

"So you might know exactly where we're going, how we're going to get there, and how long it will take, but you won't admit to it in case I'm a spy."

Gavin grinned. "You're catching on."

"Well, unless it's only a couple hours away we won't make it like this, with nothing warm for the children and hardly any food at all. And not enough horses."

"There's a market not far from here. We have sympathizers there. We're hoping they'll have enough to kit us out better. And there's a life-minder there for the injured."

"We?" Eli bristled, ignoring the obvious, that Gavin had been this way after all. Had they, whoever *they* were, been talking without him? "Who's we?"

"It doesn't matter, Eli." Gavin yawned again.

"It does matter." Eli kicked the dirt, startling Bullet to his feet. "I want to help! And I can't help if no one will tell me what's going on. I've earned my position here. I have. I went through hell to find Triskelia and now it's my home and its people my people."

"Your *position?*" Gavin gave him a withering look. "You've got a hell of a lot more to learn about us, Eli. And as for you wanting to help, here's how."

Eli waited for it.

"Take over for me after all. I've suddenly realized I *am* tired. Very tired." Gavin stood. "Especially of your company."

Eli took a deep breath and let it out slowly while he chose his next words. "There's a very good reason I'm not sleeping with the children." Gavin or not, he was ticked off and wasn't going to keep quiet about it forever. "I'm not a kid! I've been across this continent on my own and survived! Have you? Have you ever had to make it on your own? You haven't, have you? You've always been looked after in Triskelia. Seth is right."

Gavin rolled his eyes. "Oh, do tell."

"He says Triskelia is no different from the Keys."

"Careful who you share that theory with, my friend. The Keys just slaughtered us." Gavin handed him the rifle. "Or had you forgotten?"

"I was there too, Gavin." Eli took the gun. The last time he'd held one was just as the ambush started. He hadn't known how to use it though, and so he'd been given a machete instead. "I still don't know how to use this."

"Right." Gavin gave a bitter laugh. He grabbed the rifle back, snugged the butt of it against his shoulder, cocked his finger at the trigger and lowered his eye to the scope. "Pow." He handed it back to Eli. "Like that. Just be sure to use your good shoulder, of course. It's got quite the recoil. Consider yourself taught."

Eli let the gun rest on his boot as Gavin walked away. Part of him wanted to go after him, make Gavin tell him everything he knew, even if it meant putting the gun to his face to make him do it. But that was the half-starved, crazed-with-fatigue part of him. Which, he thought as he glanced down into the barrel of the gun that was staring back at him like two blank eyes, was the same part that made him do such a stupid thing as rest a rifle so it would remove his whole head should it go off accidentally. He gingerly repositioned it at his side and thought better about chasing after Gavin for answers.

Now Eli was alone with his thoughts. Eli hated his thoughts. He wished he could shut off his brain for a while until things settled, if they ever would. The moment he had nothing to do, no task, no pressing anxiety, his thoughts crowded to the front of his head and wrestled there, giving him a constant headache from the worry. About everyone who wasn't here.

Especially Nappo and Teal. The two brothers and Eli had crossed the Droughtland together and had lived through peril upon peril. Nappo was his best friend and Teal was like his own little brother. Where were they? Had they survived every sick only to be gunned down in an instant, caught in a battle that wasn't their own?

And where was Zari? Eli's heart leapt. She'd looked so beautiful the night of the feast. If he closed his eyes he could imagine kissing her, smelling the rosewater she'd dabbed on her neck. Would he ever see her again?

And Seth. Of course he wondered about Seth. How could he not?

Eli hadn't seen his brother since the night of the massacre, up in the dorms, when they'd fought. Would Eli care if he were dead? He would, he guessed. But not as much as if Nappo was dead. Or Trace, even. The friendships he'd built in his time at Triskelia were so much stronger and more meaningful than anything he'd ever had with his brother.

Maybe it'd be better if Seth were dead. Especially if he'd had anything to do with giving away Triskelia's location. Had he? Eli searched inside himself but found no answers. Instead, a strange sensation caught his attention. It was like . . . a voice. Only it wasn't. It was more like an echo.

Pray, Eli.

Eli obliged without question. He closed his eyes and moved his lips silently, praying to his highers for some answers, for some direction, for a few moments of peace at least.

He snapped his eyes open and glanced around, suddenly embarrassed. Thankfully, no one had seen him. What had just happened? Why pray to the highers? What had they done for anyone lately? What had they done for anyone, ever, come to think of it? Other than the Keylanders, all snug and warm and fed and with weather like clockwork and not a worry in the world except for what to wear to the Chancellor's next ball. And was any of that privilege a result of the highers' deciding who was deserving and who was not, or was it the Keys' own muscle and manipulation that ensured their ease? And why did Eli care what the highers had to do with any of it? These were their circumstances, no matter how hard he prayed for them to be different.

Hunger and grief and fatigue were making his brain soft, Eli decided. This strange urge to pray would pass and then he'd be back to normal, believing only in the certainty of what he could see, and feel, and touch.

He'd never been one to pray to his highers, despite his mother's steadfast belief. When he and Seth were very small she'd have them kneel at their bedside, hands together under their chins, and say their prayers. He and Seth considered it a chore, and when Edmund found out he put a stop to it, much to the boys' delight. There was a worship hall in the Key, at the south end, near the complex that housed the workers, and it was mostly labourers and Keylanders of a lesser stature than the Maddoxes who ever attended worship there.

"The stuff of voodoo and sentimental drivel," Edmund called it. "A house for make-believe and hocus pocus."

Lisette didn't argue with him. She rarely did. But each night she'd ask the boys if they wanted to say a prayer together, and every night after Edmund had dismissed the ritual they'd said no. Eli added that nightly slight against his maman to his list of regrets and lost opportunities. What had she prayed about every night? To be reunited with her family? For the safety and health of everyone she loved in Triskelia? For Eli and Seth? Had she really believed in highers, or was she just clinging to something familiar, some stray hope that still survived after being separated so long from her people?

The sun was rising now, shifting the indigos into lighter hues and revealing the lush damp forest for all its mean coldness. Sabine approached, pulling the sleeves of her sweater over her hands.

"Bullet found you!" She sat beside him on the log and let the dog jump up. "Wow." He could hear it in her voice, the same sentiment as Gavin's. "What are the odds?"

"He's a dog. Tracking is what they do, Sabine."

"What? What did I say?"

"It's not what you said." He passed her the rifle. She knew how to handle it better than he did. "It's that you think the same as Gavin. Why should a dog survive when thousands of our people didn't, right?"

"Whatever, Eli." Sabine shook her head. "I can't say I'd given it any real thought."

"Well I have," Eli said. "And my conclusion is that it's pointless to blame Bullet for surviving, dog or not. We might as well be pissed off at ourselves, if you follow the logic. We should be mad at ourselves for surviving when so many died."

"And who's to say that's not the case?" The question hung there like a breath suspended in the crisp morning. "If you're looking for a fight, you won't get one from me, Eli. I'm tired and cold and hungry and I don't care if Bullet lives or dies, to tell you the truth."

Eli didn't reply. What was the point? Everything seemed rhetorical, or up for debate at the very least.

"If only it wasn't so cold," Sabine offered as a new subject. Under her sweater she was still wearing her gown from the night of the feast. The ambush had begun as the partying wound down, so most of them were still in their finery. Eli had been back to the dorm and had changed, but he was one of just a few who weren't still dressed up. With the start of day four the group looked like hungover revellers from a party, which was exactly what they were, only they were hungover with grief and fear instead of spirits or dust.

"Did you sleep?" Sabine laid the rifle across her lap.

"A little. You?"

"Not really." Sabine checked that the rifle was loaded properly. Eli stared dolefully at her deft hands manipulating the gun. He had nothing to offer this resistance. He couldn't fight, nor did he want to. He knew nothing about weapons. And furthermore, if he was being honest, guns frightened him. "Not enough. Too cold."

"We'll all get sick if we have to go on much farther."

Sabine offered him a weak smile. "It's not much farther to the market."

"So you know too?" Eli scoffed. "You must be one of the chosen few. Lucky you."

Sabine's smile vanished. "I don't think now's the time to be petulant."

But Eli did feel petulant. And on top of that he *was* feeling guilty that his dog had lived when thousands hadn't.

"They have a lifeminder there," Sabine said when Eli didn't answer. "And a herbminder, and a bonesetter. And we'll be able to get proper clothes and sleeping rolls and food. That's what matters."

"What matters is that we left countless people back there. Injured, hurt, dying, lost, orphaned. We should've stayed. We should've helped. We should've done more." Eli thought of Nappo again. Scrappy and determined. Had he made it? And little Tealy? He felt a swell of grief but managed to keep it in its place by giving over to the hot rage that pushed behind his eyes. He squeezed his brow between his fingers and growled. "We're cowards. Seth is right."

"Seth." Sabine breathed out his name. "I pray to my highers that he's okay."

"You go ahead and pray to your stupid highers, as if that'll do any good." Eli stood. "If we'd stayed, even just long enough to wait for more survivors to join us, we might know a thing or two instead of having to pray about it."

"Prayer helps."

"Helps what? There are no highers. No higher being would sanction this life. It's mean and cruel." Yet even as he said it he struggled against the thought. He *did* believe in something greater, and he didn't believe this mess was their fault. It was humanity, making a sewer of everything.

"There are lessons," Sabine sighed. "Even in all of this."

"That's bullshit." Eli backed away. "You can keep watch. I'm no good at it anyway. I don't even know how to work the damn gun."

"Where are you going?"

Eli stalked off without answering. He stormed a little ways into the dense forest, stumbling over tangles of moss and rotting, fallen trees.

SABINE LOST SIGHT of him, but she knew he wouldn't go far. She shut her eyes and tried to summon Seth. She longed for the feeling they'd shared back in Triskelia, when they could tap in to each other, know where they were, and more importantly, how they were. She sensed nothing now, and wasn't surprised. She and her brothers had shared a connection, true, but that had been in Triskelia. In the sixteen years she'd been separated from them she'd never been able to summon them psychi-cally no matter how hard she tried. But she'd hoped that after their time together something had shifted, that they remained spiritually connected somehow. Had it been so fleeting? Or had they shared nothing special at all except a mutual delusion?

Seth. *Seth. Where are you?* She sent the question out, pushing it far, far back the way they'd come.

She gasped as she caught a flutter of sudden, unmistakable pain that wasn't hers. Was that *his* pain speaking to her? It was gone in a moment. It could've been her own pain, she supposed, even though she was sure it wasn't. Or it could've been the pain of any number of wounded souls they'd left behind. It was hopeless. She had no idea where her brother was or if he was even alive at all.

AS THE OTHERS in the camp woke and were able to keep watch, Sabine left her post and returned to the children. They were starting to stir, one by one peeling off each other and stumbling bleary-eyed into morning. They'd have to get moving soon. If the children went too long with nothing to do the crying would start again in earnest. And there was nearly nothing to feed them, and only water from the frigid stream when all any of them wanted was a simple, hot cup of tea or apple cider. What Sabine would give for a mug of hot apple cider and a plate of breakfast. Toby wandered over, eyeballing the gun still slung over her shoulder.

"It's okay." She put it down and opened her arms to him. He climbed into her lap and wrapped his good arm around her neck. "How's the evil arm of badness?"

He smiled, just a little.

"Should we get going? Warm ourselves up with a walk?"

He nodded.

"Will your evil arm of badness come along?" She gave it a gentle kiss. "Or should we unscrew it at your shoulder and leave it behind to catch up on its fingertips?"

Toby smiled again and shook his head fiercely, playfully, so hard he almost toppled off her lap.

"All right then." Sabine set him on his feet. "Tell the others to get up out of their comfy beds and rise and shine. Mind they put on their slippers and housecoats."

Toby screwed his lips into a moue and then finally spoke the first words he'd said since leaving Triskelia. "There's no comfy beds."

"That's right." Sabine grabbed him in a hug, careful not to make a big deal about his speaking at last. "I just wanted to make sure your thinking cap was on."

"I don't have a cap," Toby said. His tone was weary and sad, as if he'd said he didn't have a family or a single hope left. "Or slippers. No housecoat neither."

"It's an expression." Sabine explained it to him as she got the children ready, just so that she didn't have to think about what to say.

MOST OF THE GROUP started out right away, with Sabine and Althea and the children marching at the front, one-two, one-two—enough of a game to get the children moving for now. It wouldn't last, but she'd work it until it didn't.

As soon as Eli noticed the group pulling themselves to their feet he started off ahead up the trail, but Celeste called him back. "Come." She took his hand. "I need your help. It is time to deal with Anya." She'd kept Gavin behind as well. They gathered around Anya, who was still asleep on the cold, hard ground, in the grips of the deep slumber of grief when it finally takes you.

"Anya?" Celeste knelt, her gown from the feast muddy and torn. "Anya, my dear, wake up."

Anya didn't stir. Eli stood a little ways back, arms folded tight across his chest as if to keep his heart in check. He couldn't look at Charis, but he couldn't help but look, either. Her skin was the colour of the dawn, a dusty bluish grey. Her cheeks were puffier than they should be and her belly was bloated, pushing against the embroidered bodice of her party dress.

Gavin knelt too. He put a hand on her shoulder. "Anya?" When she didn't stir he shook her and said sternly, "Anya. Wake up!"

She opened her eyes. It was brief, but Eli knew that for a moment she had no idea where she was. As she focused on Gavin her eyes hardened. She clutched Charis to her.

"No!"

"She's dead, Anya." Celeste reached for Charis. "Your child is dead. It is time to lay her to rest, please. It will ease your heart, and ours. It is so very hard to see you like this, to see her like this. I know you understand. I know you do. *Ça doit être fait.*"

"No. No, no, no, no, no!" Anya shook her head but, miracle of miracles, she let Celeste take Charis from her arms. Then, to his horror, Celeste handed her to Eli so that she could gather Anya in an embrace. Eli adjusted Charis's limp little body in his arms and shuddered, breathing through his mouth to avoid the smell. She felt wrong, too heavy, too plump, and so very cold. His stomach flipped and he silently prayed he wouldn't vomit. This was all so grotesque, but necessary, he knew that.

"It's time to bury her so that her soul can go to her highers." Celeste pulled away from Anya's desperate hug. She offered Anya her hand instead. Weeping anew, Anya took it. Gavin helped them both to stand.

"Not without Trace."

"Anya," Celeste began. "We don't even know if he—"

"Je sais." Anya put up her hand. "I know."

Celeste led Anya to a towering cedar tree on a little plateau above the creek. Eli followed, Charis limp in his arms. Her eyes were closed. Eli understood how Anya could believe she was sleeping, or just sick. He wished she wasn't dead. He tested his highers, asking them to wake her up now, to bring her back to life if they were so almighty. He'd count to ten, and if she didn't stir there was no such thing as a higher power of any kind. He counted to ten. Charis remained still, lifeless.

The highers couldn't, or wouldn't, bring her back. Or they didn't even exist to hear his plea in the first place.

Let her ascend, Eli.

Eli looked around. Who said that? Or rather, not said, but *sent*. It was as though he'd received a message, only how was that possible? The words resonated in his gut and heart and head all at once, as if suddenly comprehending something he hadn't before.

He shook his head to clear it. Of course he'd be affected. He'd loved her very much, and now he was carrying her, three days dead, to her grave. It was a delusion, or an auditory hallucination. Conjured out of grief. Perfectly explainable.

But instead of clearing his head memories rushed in, fully formed and full of colour. Charis and Anya when he'd first met them in Triban, Charis with her shy little grin. Charis climbing all over him in the nursery, nimble as a monkey. All the times he'd watched her drop in the gym, with the glee and confidence she was entitled to by having the parents that she did.

Let her ascend.

There it was again, this time as clear as if Eli had said it himself. But he hadn't. Again, he put it down to circumstance. They'd all go mad if they didn't get a proper meal, a decent rest, some peace from the constant onslaught of grief. Perhaps they'd go mad anyway. Perhaps Eli would be the first. Perhaps he was already crazy.

Gavin had dug the hole earlier, and had lined it with cedar boughs.

"Not like this." Anya shook her head. "She should be washed and dressed, and laid in a painted box with her toys. Her father should be here. This is all wrong."

"Yes." Celeste nodded. "All of this is wrong, and so we do what is best nonetheless."

Anya wept, the tears streaming down her face. She trembled, not only from the cold but from the effort of crying, too, when she had so little energy in the first place. Gavin held her tight in his arms as the sun rose higher over the hills.

Anya took a deep breath and swallowed. "It will be a beautiful day, and Charis will be lying under cold, dark dirt. I can't let her go like this."

"You must." Celeste hugged her. "Let her ascend."

Celeste's words shook Eli's bones like a great clap of thunder. He felt at once crazy and eerily content. What had just happened?

As grim as it was, Eli had gotten used to the weight of the toddler in his arms. He didn't want to say goodbye to Charis, despite the message that seemed to come from on high. It all seemed larger than the sum of one mother's grief for her child—a kind of goodbye to everything he'd come to know and love . . . Triskelia, comfort, happiness, peace. When Gavin lifted her from him Eli could still feel her weight as his muscles adjusted to the terrible nothingness. Gavin set Charis in the middle of a silk shawl someone had donated for the baby's makeshift burial shroud. He started to wrap her, but Anya pushed him aside.

"No!" She fell to her knees. *"Je vais le faire."* Weeping silently now, she kissed her daughter one last time before folding her into the silk. She covered her face last and then lowered her into the grave as gently as if she were laying her down for a nap. As Gavin and Eli piled the dirt back into the hole the sunrise crowned the hill, drenching the horizon and the sad little party on the plateau with the indiscriminate sunshine of a brand-new day.

2

⤜⤛⤜

The first thing Seth noticed was the pitch-black dark, and then the dust. He coughed, feeling around him, finding jagged, creaking debris on all sides and a wide, heavy chunk of masonry wedged above his head. He could barely move, and he couldn't stretch his legs at all. He was buried. Trapped! He steadied his breath from careening toward panic. Could he even feel his legs? He tried stretching his toes, and sure enough they obeyed, if somewhat sluggishly. Think. *Think.* What had happened?

He'd stormed out after the fight with Eli. He'd been in the courtyard when the first cannon blasts broke the night. He'd stayed in the clearing long enough to see uniformed Guardies rush the Colony, cresting the hill en masse from the south first and then from all directions, and then he'd run for cover. Another blast had levelled the archway in front of him; he remembered looking up as it crumbled. He remembered crouching, covering his head as the wall collapsed. And then nothing.

And now this.

He had to get out! He tried pushing, but the stones wouldn't budge. He pushed and pushed, putting his shoulders into it until there was a low rumble and it all shifted dangerously, sending a rain of stone and dirt onto his cheeks. The masonry above his head dropped an inch. If it dropped any more he'd be crushed. He sucked in his breath and put his fingertips to the cool stone, as if anointing it with his fear and thus willing it to stay put.

"Help!" He coughed again as another trickle of dirt powdered his face. He reached blindly around him, his fingers finding no purchase, nowhere to begin to dig himself out. He was in a grave of rock and ruin. Narrow and deep and dark and forever. His fingers found a short length of rebar. He worked it free slowly, in case it was integral to the stability of his rubble prison. He tested the debris for the firmest stone and started hammering it with the metal. "Help me! Somebody? I'm here!"

He hammered and hollered until his hand cramped and his throat grew hoarse. He had no idea how much time had passed, but he was too tired to carry on. He was just going to take the smallest rest, but he must've fallen into a deep, necessary sleep, because the next thing he knew he was waking with dirt crusted at the corners of his eyes and caking his nares. He was thirstier than he'd ever been, even in the driest regions of the Droughtland. He checked his legs, still stuck and completely numb now, but if he concentrated hard he could still move each toe.

He assessed the rest of him as best he could, sliding his hands down each leg as far as he could reach. Wet gashes at the knees, but no broken bones. And no major bleeds as far as he could tell. Hips and ribs intact. Chest expanding equally. Collarbone and . . . his fingers found the medallion at his throat . . . he'd forgotten about that. No matter; he moved on, finding a sizeable bump on his head and then nothing more. He was in one piece. His legs were stuck, but not being crushed by anything, thankfully.

Using his fingers, he explored his confines once more. Rocky, cold, jagged. Splintered wood, crumbling brick and stone, and then something with give. Canvas? Clothing? If only he had some light! Even the smallest nub of candle would be a comfort now. He followed the smooth fabric to the end, where he felt the unmistakable outline of a cool, lifeless arm. Revolted, he recoiled, knocking his head against the rock above him. Fortunately, it didn't shift this time.

He collected himself, found the arm again, and gave it a poke.

"Hello?" he whispered. "Are you alive?"

There was no answer. Was it even attached to anything? Correction . . . any*one*? He yanked his own arm away, disgusted again. He gave himself another minute to calm down, and then he found the arm one more time. Forearm. Wrist. Fingers. And then rubble. He pulled the arm. The rubble shifted. More dust and chunks of rock rolled onto his lap, but his precarious ceiling stayed put. He cleared stones and wood and dirt away from the arm, carefully checking the stability of the masonry above him as he did.

Then he heard a moan. Clearly from whomever the arm belonged to. "Hello?"

Another moan.

"Can you hear me?"

Nothing.

Seth kept digging. As he pulled debris away, he tucked it behind him. He'd cleared up to the shoulder now. He was afraid of what he'd find if he kept going, but now there was the tiniest sliver of daylight. And voices!

"Help!" Seth banged his metal chunk on the rocks. "I'm right here!"

"Who's that?"

"Seth!"

"You Guardy or you one of us?"

He didn't recognize the voice. What a stupid question. Even if he were still Guard he'd know well enough to say he wasn't. But he wasn't Guard. Not any more. Not for a long time now. And especially not after this. The ambush on Triskelia and the Colony of the Sicks was a cowardly move, not an honourable act of war.

"I'm Triskelian."

"Are you hurt?"

"I'm stuck, but I don't think I'm actually hurt. But there's someone here who is. They haven't said anything, just moaned. All I've got cleared is their arm."

"Well, hang on, son!" The debris shifted, sending rocks into Seth's lap. "We're getting you out."

"Wait!" He explained about the masonry above his head. The diggers slowed their rescue and carefully dug around him without disturbing his precarious roof.

SETH DIDN'T RECOGNIZE any of the four men and two women who pulled him out. They might've been Triskelians he hadn't met, but were more likely from the Colony of the Sicks. That they might be diseased did not even occur to him. He gratefully took their hands and sucked in the fresh air as they helped him away from the rubble. He wasn't able to stand yet, not after so long with his legs pinned. They were okay though, just asleep, tingling awake with painful pins and needles.

"Thank you! Thank you." Seth gulped back the offered water and looked himself over in the light of day. Then, as the rescuers turned to dig out whoever was attached to the arm, he tried to stand. Wobbly, but not too bad. And his knees hurt. His pants were torn there, and they were both scraped and bloody, but intact.

Suddenly he felt dizzy. He staggered back and then sat himself down before he could fall, setting his head in his hands and closing his eyes. When the dizziness passed he looked around. There was nothing left. Broken bodies and broken buildings. Nothing more. Dazed survivors wandered about, shell shocked and delirious, calling out for their loved ones, pulling weakly at piles of rubble or sitting in the middle of it all, clutching each other, crying. Screaming. Smoke and fog and misery mingled in thin sunlight.

"Got him!" The rescuers lifted out the man who belonged to the arm. He was alive, but just. They set him down beside Seth and told him to take care of him while they moved on to the next mountain of debris. Seth looked down at him, not recognizing him at first. But then he did.

It was Ruben. One of the twins who took care of Zenith. The arm that Seth had been trying to free was blue and bloated. Death was not far away for him. His arm had been pinned for so long that it had started to die ahead of him, and now that it was freed the dead and dying cells would rush into his bloodstream and send him into toxic shock. Crush syndrome. He'd learned about it in basic training back in the Guard.

He pulled a lace out of his boot and tied it tight just below Ruben's shoulder. Not that it would help much. Ruben's forehead had a great big dent in it and his ribs were sunken all down one side. When he breathed only the uninjured side of his chest moved. Seth stood.

"Hey!" he shouted after one of the women rescuers. "He needs a life-minder." He started to explain but she just shook her head, hollered an apology, and joined the others as they clambered up an incline of rubble and started digging into it.

Seth looked down at Ruben. He was ashen. And unconscious, thankfully. Seth undid the makeshift tourniquet and backed away. He wasn't about to chop the poor man's arm off, especially when the head wound indicated brain injury. He'd be better off dead sooner than later. And sooner would be the case now that those dying cells were rushing poisons to his heart.

It would be a terrible death though. Sure, he was unconscious, but what was he actually feeling? If Seth were in this condition he'd want someone to do what he was considering doing to Ruben. *For* Ruben, he corrected himself. Doing *for* Ruben.

How is it that humans had come to terms with putting a lame horse or a blind arthritic dog out of misery yet wouldn't do it for their own, especially when a person was so clearly suffering?

Seth looked around. No one was paying attention to him. He looked around again, this time for something to do it with. A little ways away he spotted a blanket covering a body. It was a thick, colourful quilt with stars stitched across it and tassels at the corners, its cheeriness an insult to the surrounding palette of death.

He made his way slowly to the heap and then stood over it for a moment, afraid that he might know the person beneath the makeshift shroud. Taking a deep breath, he pulled the blanket off. He did recognize the dead woman, but didn't know her name. She was in Nappo's clown troupe. Seth gathered the blanket in his arms and walked slowly back to Ruben, who was twitching now, his moans louder.

Sahara? Was that her name? Sheila? It was something like that. He was furious that he couldn't remember. The names of all the others slipped past in his thoughts like flotsam on a river: *Sabine, Eli, Zenith, Jack, Toby, Teal, Celeste.* He growled, pushing the names out of the way and choosing a blank void to concentrate on instead. He could not think about the others, where they were or if they were alive even. He had to do this right now. Just this, and then he could move on to the next thing. Right now, this was all that mattered. It was the right thing to do. The only thing to do, ethical debate be damned.

"Sorry, Ruben. It's for the best." Seth bunched the blanket over Ruben's head and then pushed down, suffocating him. Ruben's twitching sped up at first, and his legs thrashed briefly. Seth pushed down harder and started to cry despite himself, even bypassing the usual tears that start things off and heading straight for gut-wrenching, nearly tearless sobs instead.

Finally, Ruben was still. It had taken more strength and more time than Seth had anticipated. And he hadn't thought it would hit him emotionally. He'd thought he was more of a soldier than that.

Seth left the blanket covering Ruben's face and stood up, his knees shakier than when he'd first been pulled from the rubble. He understood the ethical dilemma completely now. He felt like he'd just murdered someone. But that simply was not the case, he argued with himself. It was a merciful act. It wasn't murder.

Still, he looked around furtively. If anyone had seen him kill Ruben they didn't act as though they had—or if they had, they didn't act as though it mattered.

And why should it? He hadn't killed Ruben . . . he'd put him out of his misery. It was a noble—if conflicted—thing to do and Seth did not regret it. He would've wanted someone to do the same for him. He would, he was sure! Or at least, that's what he told himself as he backed away from Ruben's body.

Prayer had not occurred to him at any point. Not while he was trapped, not while he was doing what he'd done to Ruben, and not now that Ruben was dead. Seth stumbled backward, wanting to put distance between him and Ruben but not quite ready to take his eyes off the poor man. He tripped over the dead woman, and as he stumbled he remembered her name, as if disturbing her deathful rest had released it from her body like a spirit. Sharia. And he remembered that she had a son called Morris, who was close to Teal's age. Had stuttering little Morris lived? He was wee for his age, and a timid child at that. Where was he now? Where *was* everyone?

Seth strained to push the thoughts from his head. He would focus on the now, he told himself. He would help. He would do whatever was needed of him. He looked from Sharia's exposed body to Ruben's covered face. He thought he should maybe return the quilt to Sharia. Maybe it had been special to her. Or maybe she'd made it for little Morris, stitching on each shimmering star by hand. Maybe their last shared moments were wrapped in that quilt. Maybe Morris had covered her with it when she'd died.

Seth growled out loud, frustrated that sentimental indecision was paralyzing him at a time when he needed his wits about him, sharp and fierce. It might not be Sharia's quilt at all. "Forget it," he said out loud. "It doesn't matter now."

He forced himself to turn and walk away. He headed for the clearing by the river, where he could see that the bodies pulled from the rubble were being stacked up in crude rows. As he neared he noticed that there was no separating the Colony of Sick population from Triskelians now. In death, they were piled together like so much cordwood. Those still living worked in a macabre bucket brigade, or body brigade, he imagined, heaving bodies from hand to hand onto the piles.

There must be thousands dead. Guardies among them too; he could tell by the uniforms. If this had been reversed and it was Guard dealing with the dead, they would've left the Triskelians and Droughtlanders and taken care of only their own. But here were the survivors of the massacre handling the Guardy corpses no differently from their own kith and kin, and even if it was with no fanfare and no ritual, at least they weren't left to rot.

But that was why, likely. To prevent the spread of sicks that crept from corpse to corpse as they decomposed and then leapt to the nearest host, be it beast or boy, spreading from there, taking entire villages out in a matter of days. Making quick business of dealing with the dead was preventative medicine out here. It really all did come down to science.

It took only another minute before Seth's head cleared and he began to see it all rather mechanically. The bodies blurred into numbers and potential pathogens needing to be extinguished. There was much to do, and he was grateful for this shift into a kind of automated version of himself. He strode into the fray with a singular purpose: to help.

"Seth!" It was Trace, calling to him from near the incinerator.

"Trace!" Seth headed straight for him, his shoulders loosening in anticipation of the bear hug he was sure Trace would assault him with. "Am I ever glad to see you!"

Trace's arms weren't opening for a hug, or even so much as a hearty pat on the back. Instead he tightened his grip on his shovel in a way that made Seth wonder if he was going to beat him about the head with it.

"How dare you show your face here." Trace punctuated his sentence with a plug of spit aimed at Seth's feet. Seth took an involuntary step back. Trace's face was in rough shape, cut and bruised, and with his glowering frown he looked quite menacing.

"I was just dug out." Seth gestured meekly behind him at the ruins. "I came to help as soon as I was free."

Trace shook his head and spat again. "We don't want your help."

Seth wanted to ask about Anya and Charis, and then he wanted to ask about everyone else. Where were they? Were they all right? But by his look, he knew Trace wouldn't give him any answers. The realization set in that Trace must blame him for the massacre, if not entirely, then in part.

"I'm not responsible for this, Trace." Seth felt the colour draining from his cheeks. He felt dizzy again, and suddenly scared. "I didn't tell anyone!"

"Why would I believe you?" Trace took a step forward, shovel steadied in front of him like a bat, his expression darkening even more. A long cut sliced from his forehead down across his cheek and his left eye was blackened and swollen so badly it was almost closed. "This has all happened since you came. You were Guard once. Who's to say you weren't still Guard this whole time, eh? Who's to say this isn't some grand set-up with you, the little rotten prick, in the thick of it all?"

"I don't know what to say to make you believe me, but I swear I'm not Guard and haven't been since the day they left me to die in the Droughtland."

Trace stared at him, his one-eyed glower filled with hatred. Seth really didn't know what else to say, and furthermore, he didn't know what to do. Should he stay put and try to convince Trace of his innocence, or should he just make a run for it? Running, though, would imply a kind of guilt. In basic training Seth had been taught to shoot at any Droughtlander who ran. No questions asked. The point had been reiterated during his early days with the West Droughtland Regiment. He remembered the words of Commander Regis as clearly as if Regis were saying them now. *You can be sure that if the suspect is not guilty of the specific infraction you are pursuing him for, he is most certainly guilty for something equally heinous or worse. That is why he runs, because he knows we will catch him and punish him. That is why we shoot. Especially when they run.* Seth could hardly believe he'd ever been a Guardy. But he had, and he couldn't change that now.

"If I were Guardy, I wouldn't still be here," Seth tried to reason. "If I were Guardy, I'd have fled already. Don't you think?"

"Not if you still had reason to have us believe you were on our side."

"I am on your side!"

"Then where the hell have you been since the ambush? Huh?"

"I told you," Seth said gently. "I was buried this whole time. I was out of it. I don't even know how long it's been since it happened."

Trace didn't tell him either. He let his shovel rest on the toe of his boot and held it with just one hand now, while he used the other to scratch at the dried blood along his cheek.

"You got someone to vouch for that?"

Seth nodded. "I can get my rescuers to tell you where they found me."

Trace peered at him with his one good eye.

"I swear on my mother's grave." Seth clasped his hands together. "I had nothing to do with this."

"I have no reason to believe you." Trace picked up the shovel once more and turned back to the pile of damp sand he was loading against the incinerator wall where it had cracked during the blasts. "And if I were you, I'd make myself scarce."

"Look Trace, if I'd had anything to do with it, I would've fled right away, right? Or I would've left before it happened. Why would I risk my life like that if I had a choice?"

Trace kept shovelling.

"Let me help. I'll prove I didn't have anything to do with the ambush."

"I don't trust you." Trace glanced over his shoulder at him. "I never did. I never will."

"Okay. I can accept that." Seth opened his palms in a gesture of offering. "But do you need to trust me to let me help shovel sand or stack bricks? I'm a set of hands, innocent or not. You need hands, right?"

Trace shovelled another load against the wall before turning to look Seth full-on once more.

"Well, you can't possibly do any more damage than has already been done. If you insist, you can stay to help get the incinerator up and running, and then you will go and never return." There was not an inch of room for protest in Trace's tone. "You will not come back here. You will not be welcome wherever Triskelia rebuilds. You will never be forgiven for your part in this. I will personally make sure of that."

Trace might as well have beaten him with the shovel after all, his words landed so hard. "But I'm innocent," Seth murmured once more. "I swear it to you."

"There's bricks need stacking on the other side. Put in a couple hours then go, or go now. Just get out of my sight before I do something I might, and I mean *just* might, regret."

"Is Anya—"

"I don't know!" Trace roared, raising the shovel. "Now go!"

"I'm innocent," Seth blurted again, as if saying it over and over might make Trace believe him. "I am. Trace, I'm telling you, I'm innocent."

"Boy grows up in the Keyland." Trace levelled him with a look of pure odium before starting in on his shovelling with renewed vigour. "Boy joins Guard. Boy loves Guard. Boy hates brother. Boy wants to kill brother. Boy sets out to do just that. Boy gets the skineater and is supposedly abandoned by Guard. Boy finds his way to Triskelia to kill hated brother. Oh, but wait, boy has sudden change of heart and wants to become a rebel too. And then Triskelia is destroyed shortly thereafter. Quite the story."

"I'll prove it," Seth said to Trace's broad back. "It wasn't me."

SETH WORKED PAST SUNSET, until the orange glow of the incinerator shone bright in the night. The few survivors who hadn't already fled assembled around campfires at the river's edge, too exhausted to work through the dark. Seth wandered down, desperate to wash up. He was squatting on the shore, scrubbing the dirt out of his bloody knees, when he heard a familiar voice behind him.

"So, you're alive."

It was Amon. His eyes racooned with bruises, his lip cut.

"And so are you."

"Yeah." Amon squatted beside him. "You seen anybody else?"

"Besides a million dead bodies? Not really." Seth scooped another handful of water over his knees. "They're probably all dead. Except Trace. He's alive. And he thinks this is all my fault."

"They're not all dead. A bunch left right away."

"Who?"

"Gavin wouldn't say."

"*He* made it, anyway."

"A bunch of others did too, but he wouldn't let me go with them, and he wouldn't let me even see who was leaving. He was too busy beating my face in."

"What'd you do?"

"Nothing. He thinks I brought the Guard."

"Do you blame him?"

"I didn't!"

"But do you blame him?"

Amon shrugged. "I guess not."

"It wouldn't be that far-fetched, Amon." Seth regarded him. He was barely recognizable as the same boy he'd met in Triban, the boy who'd gladly led him to Triskelia so that Seth could kill Eli. He'd been kited on dust, had been off and on for years, committing various slights and betrayals against Triskelia. Clean now, there was no denying that Amon loved Triskelia and had a particular fondness for Zenith, who'd forgiven his trespasses so often. Seth didn't really think Amon would do such a thing. But it was possible. "You're sure you didn't hear any names? Or see anyone we know in the group? Eli? Sabine? You must at least have a clue about where they were going."

"I would if I could have gone after them, but Gavin had some muscle from the Colony hold me back. I don't even know what direction they went in. There were a bunch of children, that's all I saw, but I wasn't close enough to see who." Amon eyed him. "Why're you so interested?"

"What, you think I'm some heartless asshole who doesn't care who lived or died?" Seth snorted. "You think it was me too, don't you?"

"Do you blame me?" Amon's tone mocked Seth's own question.

"More likely would've been you." Seth thought it through with a groggy logic born out of hunger, exhaustion, and the pain he'd worked so hard to ignore all day. His legs hurt and his head throbbed, and right now, although Amon might be the closest thing to an ally, he hated his cousin with every ounce of his blood. If he had any energy at all he would've pummelled his already ruined face into an unrecognizable pulp.

"Wasn't me though."

"Why should I believe you? You never really made your amends—"

"And you did?"

"We're not talking about me," Seth countered. "You could've been in the back pocket of the Guard all along."

Amon glared at him. "You sure we're not talking about you?"

"Maybe you told them about the compound, and the feast. You did, didn't you? What're they paying you? Or did they say they'd let you serve in the Guard? They didn't just stumble onto us, Amon. They had intelligence. They *knew* things. Information only a traitor could've provided. Was that you? All for an empty promise?"

Amon stared at him, mystified.

"If that was your bargain with the devil," Seth continued, unfazed, "you're the fool for it. They'll just hang you and then you'll be as dead as the rest of them."

"You know what?" Amon scooped a handful of river water over his face. "You can go fuck yourself." With that he stalked off, but as he disappeared into the dark he yelled over his shoulder, "I don't need shit from you when I'm getting it from all directions as it is. A fucking shit storm, that's what this is. One big fucking shit storm."

There went the only person who'd deigned to speak to him all day, and as much as Seth wanted to rip him apart, he forced himself to acknowledge Amon's potential value.

"Wait!" Seth stood, his knees protesting. "Amon! Come back!"

Apparently Amon wasn't so stupid as to walk away from his only ally either, because a short moment later he reappeared with a scowl. "What?"

"I'm sorry, okay?" Seth limped toward him. "We're in the same boat here."

He had another look at Amon's face in the moonlight. His injuries weren't as bad as Trace's, but they did look incredibly painful. "Gavin did that, eh?"

"Yeah." Amon touched his face and winced. "He did it to make his point. Told me if I followed he'd do worse." He paused. "It wasn't me, Seth." Amon's eyes were wide and pleading, just as Seth's had been when he was talking to Trace earlier. "I swear."

"And it wasn't me either." Seth sighed. "Maybe the Guard knew all along about Triskelia, and all the secrecy was for nothing. Maybe they were just waiting for the right time."

"I don't know."

"Me neither," Seth said. "But I'm going to find out. Or else Zenith will never let us back."

"Back where?" Amon laughed. "Look around, Seth. And who says Zenith even survived?"

"You know what I mean."

"Yeah," Amon murmured. "I guess I do."

THEY TRIED JOINING a couple of the fires, but word of their supposed guilt had trickled from survivor to survivor and soon it was clear that they weren't safe amid the ruins of Triskelia. They'd already decided to leave, but they wanted to warm themselves first and have a bit of a rest, especially Seth, whose knees only hurt worse as the night wore on. They started their own fire but it was quickly doused by a livid man with a bucket of river water.

"Traitors!" He hurled the empty bucket. It narrowly missed Amon, clattering to the ground instead. "Get out of here or we'll gladly lynch the both of you!"

"Just back off, all right?" Seth brandished the piece of rebar he'd kept from earlier. "It's a terrible misunderstanding. We didn't do anything! And you can tell anyone who thinks we did that they're only cheating themselves if they keep at us instead of hunting down the real traitors. Don't you see?"

The man punched his fist into his palm over and over, each time marked with a menacing smack. "Leave now, or we'll see you're run out."

"We have every right to be here," Amon said. "This was our home too."

"No." The man shook his head. "Not you. And not him. You will never belong here. Not after what you done."

From all around people crept out of the dark to join him. Seth and Amon backed away from the steam and sizzles of the fire's dregs.

"Shame!" the man hollered, and then the others joined in too, chanting. "Shame! Shame! Shame!"

"We didn't do anything!" Seth yelled. "We didn't know about it! Neither of us did. We're telling the truth! You're being fools!"

The insult did not go over well. The crowd surged forward, armed with weapons of all sorts. Some of them clutched Barlow knives, some sticks, bricks, stones, or jagged metal. They needed someone to punish for what had happened, and Amon and Seth would fulfill that need.

"They're not going to listen." Amon shoved Seth into motion. "We have to get out of here. Let's go!"

They ran, stumbling over rubble and roots. At first Seth didn't think he could outrun the mob. It was as if a knife was dug deep into each knee, twisting in deeper still with each lift of his leg, but his fear took over and extinguished the pain long enough for them to get a precious gain. The mob gave an enthusiastic chase, but soon petered out. Everyone was tired, and starved, and wracked with devastation, and so didn't have it in them to run far or fast. Amon and Seth, ignited by the energy of the hunted, finally lost them.

The boys stopped to catch their breath only after they'd climbed to the top of the ridge behind what once had been the Colony of the Sicks. From up there, in the strict, flat light of the approaching dawn, the remains of Triskelia and the Colony that had hidden it successfully for so many years looked even worse than when they'd been among the ruins. The perspective was overwhelming.

"Now what?" Amon said, wheezing.

"We find the others and explain ourselves." Seth stared at the razed expanse below. It looked as if wicked giants had rampaged through the settlement, setting fires, crunching buildings underfoot like so many twigs, scooping up handfuls of life and crushing it in their fists before tossing them aside. It was a miracle any of them had survived. For the first time since coming to, Seth realized just how close that rubble prison had been to being a rubble grave. He'd very nearly died, and only now was that sinking in.

And he'd killed Ruben. Mercifully or not, he'd killed him with his own hands. Seth sat himself down on a rock, stunned, while Amon blathered on.

"But how can we find them? Maybe there's more than one group. Then which one are we supposed to go after? And we don't even know if Zenith is alive, or if she's already left, or if she's dead down there and no one's found her. We need to know who was in that first group and which way they went. But no one will tell us."

"We take a guess then." Seth squeezed his eyes shut against the terrible headache that was shoving its way to his temples. "What else can we do? We'll find them eventually. Or they'll find us, if they really think we're to blame." He stood. "Come on. We're not that far behind them, are we?"

"You're kidding, right?"

"How long has it been?"

"They left right away," Amon said. "That morning. As soon as the Guard retreated."

Seth's stomach lurched. Just how long *had* he been buried in the rubble? "And when was that?"

"It was four days ago, Seth."

"Still . . ." Seth pushed aside the panic rising from the thought of his being buried for that long, and with no recollection. He backed away from the vista of the destroyed valley. "Still, we'll catch up eventually."

"But we don't have anything!" Amon followed him, whining. "No horses, no guns, no food, no water. No nothing, Seth. How are we supposed to survive?"

Seth turned suddenly and gripped Amon's shoulders. "We've already survived the worst!" He gave Amon a rough shake. "Be thankful you're not dead, you idiot. Look around you! Do you even comprehend the level of destruction? Do you have any idea how many people died down there?"

Amon blinked at him.

"You don't, do you? Now, enough whinging. You can either come with me and we'll make do, or you go on your own, or you go back. I don't care."

Seth wasn't expecting an answer. He'd just wanted Amon to shut up, which he did. He started walking again and Amon followed, as he knew he would. A little farther away from the cliff Seth stopped suddenly.

"What is it?" Amon looked around, panicked. "You see something?"

Seth squatted, against his knees' better judgment. He put his hand to the flattened grass at his feet. This had been where the Guard had waited.

All around him and for as far as he could see the earth was trampled down, with depressions in the dirt from the cannons and munitions carts and Guardy horses. They'd been up here, lying in wait, and he'd been ignorant to it all. If he'd known, it all would've happened differently. They would've had a fighting chance. Or would they have? Triskelians weren't prepared to fight, and most of the Colony of the Sicks were in no shape. Not then, and certainly not now.

He picked up a cigarette butt and gave it a sniff. The stale tang of Guard-issue tobacco. What had happened here? And was Regis behind this? Had he followed Seth? Had it been a set-up all along? In that case it *was* his fault. Seth needed to know and, at whatever cost, he'd find out.

"We're going to find the people responsible for this, and see to their punishment ourselves."

"Sure," Amon said. "Great idea, Seth."

"I *will* find who did this," Seth growled. "I'll prove it wasn't us."

"And then what?" Amon shivered. "What would we do then?"

Seth turned slow circles in the clearing, imagining the moments leading up to the ambush. The Guardies would've been waiting, anticipation and fear gnawing at their guts, the sweat of an uncertain future drenching them despite the cold. It was only short months ago that he was one of them; the camaraderie of men at arms as strong a bond as they came. Or so he'd thought. And then they'd left him for dead.

How his life had changed.

"Then what?" Amon asked again. "We take on an army of thousands?"

"Sounds good to me," Seth said. He tossed the butt, grinding it under his boot, wishing it was Regis's face he was smothering in the dirt instead.

3

Honestly, Sabine hadn't thought they'd make it this far without running into a Guard checkpoint. She and the others didn't talk about it, but there was no doubt it was odd. They hadn't seen one single Guardy since they'd left. Where were they? Had they retreated en masse to strategize, or did they really think they'd killed them all?

Still, it was an enormous relief not to have to deal with the Guard just now, what with everyone in such a state. Their absence was almost as chilling, though; it made Sabine wonder if they really were all dead, just ghosts, not even worthy of Guardy pursuit.

The exhausted group kept trudging through another morning. Mountains loomed up on all sides, the sky was a low-slung layer of storm, and the path ahead was straight uphill, as it had been since they'd left Triskelia. Toby stopped in his tracks, pulled his hand out of Sabine's and looked up at her, his cheeks red, his nose snotty, his eyes wet-rimmed.

"Are we there yet?"

"No, sweetheart," she answered. "But we're getting closer."

"You always say that and it's never true!"

The rest of the group slowed. This was bad. It would be hard to get everyone moving again if they stopped.

"But it is true, Toby." Sabine gestured at Eli to keep the others walking. "We are getting closer."

"I want to stop now!" He flung himself onto the ground and started to wail. "Let's live here. I don't want to walk any more! I want Jack!"

So did Sabine. Was their dear friend dead? She'd tried so hard not to dwell on the who and how of those who'd perished, but as she grew more tired it became harder to keep them out of her thoughts. Her best friends, Zari and Lia. Where were they if they'd survived? Sabine felt a swell of grief threaten to derail her completely.

"I know, Toby." She spoke slowly, willing the sadness out of her voice. "But we must keep going for now. We simply must." She took his hand, intending to start walking again, but he was having none of it.

"I want Jack! I want to go home!" He pushed her away and flung his head back to let loose a heartbreaking wail.

At first the other children just stared at him, but then they joined in, crying and complaining until they were all a squalling heap of misery lumped together on the cold, wet ground. Sabine wiped tears from her own eyes as she tried to coax the children back onto the trail while Althea stood beside her, quite useless, her own cheeks drenched with tears.

The adults, all just as tired and hungry and stunned, stood around, not sure what to do despite Celeste's urgings to keep moving.

Finally, with Gavin and Eli at their heels like herding dogs, the adults and older children started walking again, but the younger ones would not.

"It's no use, Nana," Sabine said. "They're just too tired. I'll stay with them." She lifted one of the littlest into her arms. "The rest of you carry on. There's not much farther to go."

Althea suddenly stopped her crying, as if she'd just reminded herself that she hadn't wanted to in the first place. "I'm staying too."

Celeste put an arm around each of them. "Are you sure?"

"Yes." Sabine turned into her grandmother's embrace, allowing herself the briefest moment of comfort. "You'll make much better time without us."

Gavin sent the others ahead with Eli and then dropped back to give Sabine his gun. "I can stay if you want."

Sabine shook her head but took the gun. "The others need you. We'll be fine."

"We'll come back for you." Gavin kissed her on each cheek and then offered the same salutation to Althea, who puffed up with pride. "As soon as we get to the market, we'll come for you."

NEWS OF THE MASSACRE had already reached the market. They'd set up a makeshift hospital, and tents with cots and blankets, and a field kitchen with a great big vat of rabbit stew bubbling over the fire. Eli had never been so happy to see a settlement in all his life. The assault of smells and sounds was like a bear hug, and the sight of so many people, healthy and well, made him almost want to cry. *Give thanks.* That voice again . . . or not really a voice, but that sense. Again, and stronger . . . *give thanks.*

Eli hardened. Give thanks for what? "We thank our highers for the massacre that has brought us together in grief and pain and community"? Not likely! But he felt compelled nonetheless, and so he offered up a silent prayer of appreciation for getting them to the market safely. He couldn't help but add "albeit tired and hurt and hungry." Then, when it came to deciding which line to get in, the one for stew or the one for first aid, he was torn. He was hungry, and perhaps a bellyful of real food would put a stop to his highers' interrupting his thoughts, or maybe it was just the pain in his shoulder that was giving him auditory hallucinations. That was just slightly more likely, so he got in line to have his shoulder looked at.

Meanwhile, after Gavin scarfed down a bowl of stew without even sitting down, he went about arranging carts and horses and drivers to go back and collect the children. The market elders wanted to meet with Celeste right away to discuss the group's plans. Anya and the others were helped to cots and food and treatment from the life- and boneminders. Eli swooned with pain while a lifeminder's apprentice dug out the bullet and packed the wound full of a foul-smelling poultice. She bandaged it up, remarked on his luck, and then left him to go on to the next injury. *It's not luck . . . you are blessed. You are all blessed and it is up to you to tell her so.* Eli gritted his teeth, trying to ignore both the voice and the hot, throbbing pain. How he had hoped he'd stop hearing voices once his shoulder had been treated. He was beyond thankful when Gavin came to ask that he drive one of the carts back with him. Injured shoulder or not, Eli was grateful for the distraction.

BACK IN THE FOREST, Sabine and Althea tried to keep the children's spirits up, an admittedly impossible task. After a few attempts at circle games and campfire songs they all just huddled together, crying and whimpering and wondering where their mothers and fathers and siblings and friends were. Were they okay? Were they dead?

Sabine didn't know what to tell them. She wondered the same things herself. And who had betrayed Triskelia's location to the Guard? Could it have been her own brother? She loved Seth, even though she'd been separated from him for so long. She couldn't believe he'd do such a thing. But then, their father murdered their mother, didn't he? And Seth would've killed Eli if he hadn't found out the truth about Edmund. Maybe their blood was tainted—maybe all three siblings were capable of terrible things? Maybe Seth's amends had been an act . . . maybe he'd planned this all along!

Someone had betrayed Triskelia. *Someone* had told the Guard where to stack their men, where the best access and egress was, where the few weapons were kept. She was certain of this, sure that there'd have been more survivors if the Guard had come in blind with no inside information. It hurt her heart to think that someone had broken such a long-lasting trust.

Oh, what would happen now? It was all so desperate and awful. How could Triskelia ever recover? Sabine squeezed her eyes shut, willing herself not to cry again. Not when the children were as fragile as a slip of ice over a pond.

Althea tugged at her sleeve. "They're coming!" She pointed to a short convoy of carts coming toward them down the trail, Gavin and Eli in the lead.

"You've been so brave, Althea." Sabine took a deep breath and put an arm around the thin little girl. "You've been such a help. I'm so proud of you. Now, see if any of the children need to pee before we go, okay?"

"Okay, Sabine."

"Thank you." Sabine straightened Althea's mangy hair and then smoothed her own dirty locks, mostly fallen out of the elaborate braids she'd worn the night of the feast, and tried to look like a leader. "Have the older ones help with the babies. Come on, let's go." She took Toby's hand. "There'll be food and warm beds when we get there."

"What about Jack?" Toby asked. "Will he be there too?"

"I don't think so, love."

Toby yanked his hand free. "Then I'm going to wait here for him."

"You can't, Toby." Sabine picked him up, and as she did he started thrashing. "You'd freeze to death."

"I want Jack!" Toby screamed as Sabine handed him over to Gavin.

"Me too, kiddo." Gavin hugged his little brother to him until his tantrum subsided into plain, tired tears. "Me too."

As Sabine helped the other children into the carts she watched Gavin and Toby. If Jack was dead they'd still have each other. And even if Jack was alive they'd all be bonded in a way they'd never been before. When the last child was seated Sabine climbed up to ride with Eli and finally let herself weep, for her friends, for the fear of what lay ahead, for her own shattered dreams.

"Come here." Eli patted the bench beside him, the reins gripped in the hand of his good arm. Sabine wiped her eyes and sidled up beside him. He draped his bad arm across her shoulders and held her as best he could while the voices babbled on in his head. *Pray for her. Pray that she will find peace. Pray to help soothe her grief.*

LATER, WITH EVERYONE as settled as they could be, injuries tended to, the babies cleaned up, fed, and put to bed, the children bathed and given fresh clothes donated from the market kids, Eli and Sabine finally let themselves take a moment to sit down for a mug of strong dark tea in a quiet corner of one of the huts cleared for the survivors to bunk in.

"Do you think Seth's dead?" Sabine sipped her tea slowly, wanting it to never end.

"No." Eli was emphatic. "He's alive." He'd decided this after thinking about it since fleeing Triskelia.

"How do you know?"

"I just do."

"Do you sense it? Like we did before?"

"It's nothing like that," Eli said. "It's logic. He's stubborn. And proud. And strong. He'd never let himself die at the hand of the Guard."

"Who says he had a choice in the matter?"

"*Has*. I just know. And if he had anything to do with leading the Guard to Triskelia, you can bet it was part of a larger scheme he had all along."

"You can't really believe that. I know you two don't exactly see eye to eye, but he's still our brother."

"Who very nearly killed me, don't forget."

"But he did the Trial. He made his amends."

"Or pretended to. Think about it, Sabine. He gets credit for exterminating the rebels . . . that way, Father would have to take him back, even with the sick scars. The Keyland government knows the scars aren't contagious. They just tell the people that so they'll stay afraid of anyone who's had it. Father knows that. He could convince the Key to let Seth back despite the scars. I just know it—he'd go back there on his knees, begging. 'Look what I did for you, Father,'" he simpered. "'Please let me back, please. I beg you. Have mercy on a son who's done such a magnificent thing for you and the Group of Keys.'" Eli shook his head. "That's what he'd do. If he had anything to do with the massacre."

"Right, *if*. You can't know that he did."

"Well, I know for sure he's not dead. The world would feel different. Lighter. Relieved. He very well could be to blame for this, Sabine. Trust me."

She gazed into her mug. "I don't know, Eli."

Eli stared at her. How could she still be so naive? How could she not see that he might've duped them, and at the cost of thousands of innocent lives? "No, Sabine." Eli's lip curled in a slight, involuntary grimace. "Clearly you don't."

"Well, *Eli*," Sabine bristled, "neither do you, not really, not if you don't have the feeling. So don't act all high and mighty. We don't know it was Seth. It could've been anyone."

"Sure." Eli laughed, and then he said, with such conviction that it resonated in Sabine's gut, "But it was Seth. I know it was." He wanted to tell her that while he wasn't experiencing the feeling, he sensed it nonetheless—only differently, as if it were on another frequency. But that would sound far-fetched, and Eli still hoped the messages would stop after a good night's sleep. "It's no coincidence that he came and then this happened."

"So? You came not long before he did."

"You can't think I had anything to do with it."

"I'm just saying." Sabine shrugged. "If you're talking about coincidence, don't be so sure some of the others aren't going to factor you into the equation."

The prospect shattered Eli. "Let's just drop it, okay?" They were the only words he could muster.

"Fine."

The lively noises of the market danced in the awkward space between them. Children laughing, dogs barking, the raised voices of friendly bartering. They were normal noises, everyday noises, but they made Sabine mad. She wanted silence. Blessed, respectful quiet.

"Do you think everyone else is dead?" Eli asked.

"I don't know." Sabine shrugged. "I pray to my highers there are others."

There are others. Eli shivered. "There are others," he echoed. The voice had been so certain, and comforting too. He wanted to share it with his sister. "But who?" He was asking himself, or the voice, or his highers, just as much as Sabine. "What about Zenith? Do you think they'll find her?"

"I don't know." Sabine stood, her eyebrows furrowed. "I don't know anything you don't. Okay?"

"But they tell you things," he murmured. "No one ever tells me anything."

"There's no conspiracy against you, Eli." Sabine shook her head. "You think it's all about you. It isn't. Got it? No one gives a shit about you right now."

Eli shrank. "That's not what I meant."

Sabine's tone softened. "You have to remember that you're still new here."

"Here?"

"Yes, here." She nodded. "With us. We are Triskelia. Wherever we are. It takes time to trust."

"You don't trust me?"

"I trust you." Sabine touched his arm. "I do. But I can't speak for the others."

"What about Seth? You trust him? Now, after everything?"

Did she? Had she at all? Would she ever, now that she might never know if he'd been responsible for the massacre?

Maybe it was the thought of so much death, but suddenly Quinn came to mind, and her heart swelled with pain.

Quinn.

He'd been Sabine's very best friend in all the world. Their birthdays were only three weeks apart. She couldn't remember a time without him. Except for now, since his death. She shut her eyes. She missed him so much. The memories didn't so much flood back as drop out of the sky, hitting her like fat, hard raindrops. They were four, fighting over a game of jacks, then seven, building forts out of chairs and blankets. Ten, chasing each other up and down the towers of Triskelia. Twelve, rolling on the floor in fits of laughter. And then fifteen, sitting on his bed, serious about everything, their futures spread out before them like a spill of stars.

Why couldn't she leave it behind? Why, after all these months, did it still pain her so much that she could hardly breathe sometimes? Even with the thousands dead, left behind in the rubble of her home, it was Quinn's death that hurt the most, even now. Here she was, with her life in a mess of wreckage, and all it took was the briefest thought of him and she was right there watching his horrific fall over again.

But this time it was different. Usually when her heart and mind dragged her back to that awful night in the Eastern Key, she only remembered him tumbling through the air like a rag doll, spinning and falling and no net in sight to catch him. She'd seen the whole thing, from the pigeons dive-bombing him to the horrific thunk as he hit the concrete. But now she remembered more.

Jack had told her that she'd screamed up at the Chancellor, that the Guard had moved in, and that the clowns had dragged her away before she could start a riot. But now she actually remembered it. She remembered more too. She remembered looking up from the wings as she was held back by the clowns, and seeing . . . seeing . . . *Seth*! It had been Seth at the railing in the Chancellor's box, laughing. Pointing. Demanding that they turn Quinn over so that he could see his crushed-in skull better.

"Quinn," she whispered. "My Quinn. And he enjoyed it!"

"What?" Eli stared at her. Sabine looked as if she was floating away, her eyes distant, her jaw slack.

"The night he died." She blinked slowly, the memory thankfully receding. "Seth was *happy* about it. He was laughing!"

And so Eli told her the truth. That Seth and his friend had caused Quinn's death by setting loose the pigeons.

"Why didn't you tell me this before?" Sabine's voice was shrill with dismay.

"I wasn't sure." That was the truth. He hadn't been sure, not until that last night in Triskelia. "Seth admitted it the night of the massacre."

"I hate you." Sabine stood. At first she gripped her mug with both hands as if she'd never let it go, but then she wound it up in one hand like it was a ball and hurtled it at the wall where it smashed against the stone. "I hate you, and I hate him. Both of you!" The tears came in a rush, along with a sudden, passionate rage. "You should've told me, even if you weren't sure. I would never have let him stay in Triskelia. And that means, if he *did* have anything to do with the ambush, then it's all *your* fault too!" She stalked off.

"That's not fair," Eli called after her. "Wait! Let me explain!" But what else was there to say? She was probably right.

Sabine hesitated at the doorway. Then she held up one dismissive hand and started running. She wanted to be far, far away from all this. She wished she'd never been reunited with her brothers. They'd brought nothing but grief and destruction with them. Nothing good had happened since they'd come. Nothing good at all.

4

The next three days passed quickly. There was much to do, tending to the wounded, taking care of the children, planning and resting. On the fourth day another party of survivors arrived. They'd managed to catch a few horses and to cobble together some carts and a couple of caravans out of the wreckage, and had barely stopped along the way. The good news was that no one in the group was on foot. The bad news was that many were gravely wounded.

"There's Trace!" Althea yelled as she ran with the others to see who was among them. "And Jack too!"

"Althea!" Trace was driving the first cart. He pulled to a stop, jumped down, and lifted Althea into a quick hug. "You okay, kiddo?"

She nodded.

"Where're my girls?"

Althea bit her lip and started to cry.

"But I was told they'd left with you." He frowned at her. "Didn't they?"

"I . . . I . . . I don't . . ." she stuttered. "Anya's here."

He scanned the crowed, his face going pale. "Anya?" he hollered. "Charis?"

Amidst the tearful hellos and the devastating realization that so, so many were not among the raggedy group, Sabine stepped forward and put her hand on his arm.

"I'll take you to Anya."

"She's okay?"

"She's not injured." Sabine took his hand. "But Trace, Charis didn't make it. She died in the attack."

"No!" He wrenched away from her and started running toward the tents. "Anya! Charis!"

GAVIN RAN TO FIND JACK, who was driving the caravan that carried a very weak but alive Zenith.

"Jack!" Gavin hugged him. "I didn't know if you were alive or dead. All this time, I had no idea if I'd ever see you again."

"I'm okay." Jack kissed him hard. "I went with the group that secured the western ridge after the Guardies retreated and when I'd got back you'd already left. I stayed behind to help." He squeezed Gavin's hand and then brought it to his lips. "I'm so glad you're all right. I heard Toby went with you, and he's okay?"

"Yes, yes, he's fine. He stayed put with a bunch of children in the cellar below the pantry. They're all fine, that bunch. You've got Zenith with you?"

"Yes."

"Thank the highers she's alive!" Gavin moved to open the flap to the covered cart, but Jack held him back.

"She didn't fare so well, Gav. She lost a lot of blood and she's very weak, but thankfully she hasn't gotten any worse since we left."

"Shall I fetch the lifeminder?"

Jack nodded. "Tell her to come quickly."

"Of course." Gavin turned away.

"Gav!" Jack called after him. "It's so good to see you. I was so worried. I love you, you know that?"

"And I you, Jack." Gavin backed away, his and Jack's eyes locking for another long second before he turned to sprint to the lifeminder's tent.

"JACK!" SABINE RACED across the clearing and threw herself into his arms. "You're alive! Zenith's in there?"

"Yes, but we're going to wait for the lifeminder before we move her."

"I must see her."

"I don't think anyone should see her until the lifeminder checks her over."

A knocking sounded from inside the caravan. "That's her," Sabine said, sure of herself. "She wants to see me too."

"All right, but only you."

"Thanks, Jack." Sabine hugged him once more. "I'm so glad you're here!" She climbed in quickly, not wanting Jack to have even one second to start telling her who was dead.

Inside the dim caravan a young girl Sabine didn't recognize was helping Zenith sit up. The frail old woman's skin was nearly translucent and she had great grey half moons under her eyes and bandages on her arm. The girl tucked the blankets around her and stuffed a pillow between her and the caravan wall so that Zenith could rest against it.

Sabine was taken aback. This woman was not the Zenith she knew, elderly yes, but sure and wise. This woman looked like a remnant of her hero. A shadow at best.

"Oh, Zen Zen!" Sabine started to cry. "I didn't know if you were dead!"

"I'm fine," Zenith said as Sabine fell to her side and hugged her, bawling with relief. "Tell me, child, who is here with you?"

Sabine told her who was with the first group. Zenith started to tell her who was with her group, but she was weak and mixed up names of the living with those Sabine knew for a fact were dead. Sabine told her to be still until the lifeminder came. She bade the other girl to go help with the others and stayed with Zenith herself, holding her thin, cool hand.

OUTSIDE, THE REUNIONS and the sorrows continued.

"Anyone seen Nappo?" Eli ran into the crowd. "Or Teal?"

Teal popped his head out from one of the covered carts. "Eli!"

"Tealy!" Eli lifted him down in a hug. "You okay, pal?"

"Yeah."

"Where's your brother?"

"Back there."

For a brief, gut-wrenching moment, Eli thought he meant back in Triskelia, dead, but then Nappo climbed down from the last cart and waved, his face grim. "Taking care of the babies," Teal added.

Nappo lifted a toddler down, and then another.

"Who didn't—?" Eli stopped himself. Teal's expression was glazed. He wouldn't ask a little boy for the roster of dead. Instead, he took Teal's hand. "I'll take you to the kitchen. There's hot soup."

NAPPO MET THEM there. He didn't help himself to food though. He just sat beside Eli and said nothing, the expression on his face unreadable but clearly pained. Eli got up and fetched his friend a bowl of soup.

"Thank you." Those were the first words Nappo had spoken.

"I have to ask," Eli said. "You understand?"

Nappo nodded, his eyes on his soup.

"Lia? Zari?"

Nappo shook his head as a tremendous sigh left him. Beside him Teal silently munched on a hunk of bread, his eyes on his brother.

"What happened?" Eli asked.

Nappo lifted his eyes, levelling Eli with an incredulous look.

"I mean, where were they, or how do you know?"

"Later, Eli." Nappo pulled Teal onto his lap. He was really too big for that, but Eli didn't think it odd. Who knew what horrors the brothers had seen?

Eli helped get the brothers settled into the tent he was bunking in and then went to find Zenith, who'd been moved to the makeshift hospital and was being watched by the lifeminder herself. He wanted answers, and of anyone, Zenith was the one who'd have them. She was sleeping, her thin white hair plastered to her head with sweat, her face pale and drawn, her mouth slacked open, each breath dragging a nasally snore behind it.

"She's not to have visitors," the lifeminder said.

"Can I just sit here while she sleeps?"

"I suppose that would be all right." The woman pursed her lips. "But just for a moment," she added before leaving him to attend to someone else at the other end of the tent.

Eli stared at Zenith. With her mouth open like that and her skin waxen she looked dead, or very nearly. He was almost surprised when one breath lurched after another; each one seemed as if it were finishing her off. This was their leader?

"What happens now?" Eli whispered. He reached for the old woman's hand. "What do we do? We can't keep going on like this!"

Beneath the blankets, Zenith stirred. Her mouth gawped closed, but she didn't open her eyes.

The lifeminder hurried back. "You!" she whispered harshly. "Out! I said you could sit with her and that was all." She ushered Eli out of the tent. "She might not be busted and broken, but she must rest and regain strength or risk death."

"I'm sorry. It's just that—"

"*Just* nothing!" The lifeminder tsked-tsked him. "Leave her be."

Yes, leave her be.

Eli blinked in the sunlight and squeezed his head between his hands. Was he going crazy? He didn't think he'd mind, really. But he did want to know either way, just so he could make sense of it all as best he could, considering.

He was going to tell Zenith about the voices. Like everyone else in Triskelia, he wanted to bring her his troubles, his hopes, and his questions most of all. Zenith was the only leader they had. Neither the Droughtland nor Triskelia was like the Keyland, with its formal appointments and clearly designated government structure. But despite the apparent anarchy beyond the Keyland walls, an unspoken but unmistakable hierarchy prevailed. Zenith was the leader. And not just of Triskelia, Eli was discovering. Her reach extended much farther than its now ruined walls.

She had never been officially appointed, or even elected. Maybe that's why Eli had always thought she was just an old matriarch. But there was no doubt. She was all they had, and everyone out here considered her their leader too. They spoke of her often and with great respect, referring to her as *Auntie* to hide her identity when in the company of acquaintances or strangers, and especially in the clean markets, in case Guardy spies were in their midst. She was the people's hope, their focal point for the revolt they dreamed would one day topple the Keys.

What if she didn't live? Who would guide them? Who would be their anchor? If she died there really would be anarchy beyond the Keyland, and then what? Is that what it would take to set things in motion, to bring about real and meaningful change? The thought gave Eli the chills. He glanced at the skies above him, half expecting the voice to weigh in on the matter. Nothing. Sure, he thought, just when he needed it, there was only silence, leaving him alone with his fears.

SABINE SEARCHED THE SECOND EXODUS for her friends. Of the dozens who'd come, there was no Zari, no Lia, no one she was very close to except Zenith and Trace and Jack. Was that it? She went through the motions, helping the others get settled but all the while feeling a terrible numbness slip over her. A few were heading off to friends or family elsewhere and a few more coming on foot, Jack had said. Not Seth or Amon though; he told her about their being run off. Other than that, everyone was dead.

With the last child changed and happily noshing on bread and jam, Sabine made her way out of the big tent, wondering about Seth's role in all of it—if he had one, that is, other than being an easy, if false, scapegoat to those who'd chased him away.

Just then Eli was wandering by, Bullet at his side, eyes on the sky again, waiting for the voice. The siblings crashed into each other.

"Sorry," Eli said. His sister's face was pale. "What's wrong?"

Sabine pulled the arms of her sweater over her hands and folded her arms. She opened her mouth to speak but nothing came out. She stared at the ground, muddy from the rainfall during the night.

"Sabine?" Eli put a hand on her shoulder. He hadn't seen her since she'd stormed off, but he didn't think she'd still be mad. He couldn't be sure though. He felt none of the bizarre but comforting connection the triplets had had back in Triskelia. In fact, he felt about as estranged from his sister as when he hadn't even known of her existence. "Are you okay?"

"What?" Sabine kept her eyes on the ground while fury crept up her legs as if from the very earth she stood on, a nasty creeping vine. It heated her up from the inside, roiling her guts and sending spikes of fire through her spine. She grimaced from the taste of it. Metallic and bitter.

"How *dare* you ask me that!" She shoved him, which so surprised Eli that he staggered back. The fur along Bullet's back ridged and he lowered his shoulders, readying to pounce.

"No, Bullet." Eli put him at ease with the signal to sit—just as Sabine shoved him again and down he went, ass first into the mud, stunned. Bullet whined but did not break his sit. Eli held onto his collar just in case.

"This is all your fault!" Sabine cried. "If you and Seth had never come, none of this would've happened!" She kicked him and he yelped, shocked more than anything. She drew back to kick him again, but one of the nearby stallminders hauled her away.

"That's enough, missy! We'll have none of that here."

"Let go of me!"

"Calm down!" The stallminder wrestled her until she acknowledged his strength and gave up. "Highers be, girl, get a grip."

"Do you know who I am?" Sabine yelled at the man as Bullet barked at her, confused. "Let go of me at once!"

"Don't care who you are. No violence here." The stallminder held her arms for another moment, until Gavin appeared and told him he'd keep an eye on her.

As soon as the stallminder was gone, Sabine spat at Eli. "This *is* all your fault. Everyone is dead because of *you*! I meant what I said earlier. And I still mean it. Doesn't matter that Seth's alive."

Seth was alive? Eli's mind rang with confusion. What did that mean?

"Go, Sabine." Gavin gently pushed her away. "Nana is looking for you. She's with Zenith. She's awake now and wants to see you."

"Don't talk to me, Eli." Sabine jabbed a finger at her brother. "Don't even *look* at me!"

Make peace.

"Come on, Sabine." Eli felt tears coming. He didn't want to cry in front of Gavin, but the idea that Sabine wanted nothing to do with him was just too much to handle. "Don't be like this, please. Please don't."

"Don't be such a pussy." The way she said it reminded Eli so much of Seth that it caught his breath in his throat and he suddenly couldn't swallow.

"Sabine!" he choked out as she took off down the lane of stalls. "Please!" She didn't so much as look back.

Gavin helped Eli stand. "She get you hard?"

Eli shook his head. "Surprised me, that's all. Coming from Sabine."

Gavin laughed. "Shows how much you know her. She's got a temper. You just haven't seen it."

"I think I'm getting a pretty good view of it now." Eli wiped the mud off his butt as best he could while Gavin explained what had happened between Seth and the survivors back in Triskelia. Eli listened without comment and then skulked off toward his tent, keenly aware that if he were a dog his tail would be meekly positioned between his legs. Bullet, still confused, followed behind him, his own tail at half mast.

WITH HER ANGER so hot that she broke out in a sweat and had to yank off her sweater, Sabine reported to Zenith. The moment her gaze found Zenith's kind, tired eyes, the anger thinned into nothing and she forgot all about her brothers.

"Oh Zenith!" She knelt at the old woman's bedside and enveloped her in an awkward, careful hug. "I'm so glad you're feeling better."

"There, there, child," Zenith said as Sabine was wracked with sudden, enormous sobs. "All will be well."

"No, it won't!" The anger was back. She pulled away from Zenith. "Everyone's dead! There's nothing left, and it's all Eli and Seth's fault!"

"You can't know that." With Celeste's help, Zenith pushed herself up a little in the bed. "And not everyone is dead. We have two hundred survivors right here with us, and who knows how many more are seeking safe harbour elsewhere."

"You know what I mean!" Sabine shouted, and then felt suddenly ashamed as the lifeminder shot her a stern look from across the tent. She'd never raised her voice to Zenith before. Not ever. "Thousands died, Zen Zen," she said, her tone reflecting her shame.

"And still," Zenith said, "we must carry on. The survivors need us. They need you, child."

"Me?" Sabine turned her eyes to Celeste, looking for some explanation, but her grandmother just looked at her evenly, revealing nothing. "Why me?"

"For now, let's deal with the details." Zenith reached for a pencil and gave it to Sabine. "We're going to have a ceremony. Something to help the others move on, or else we'll be stuck here forever, in a mud puddle of grief."

"Nothing's going to change that." Again, Sabine surprised herself. She'd never contradicted Zenith. But perhaps things were different now. She felt no shame about speaking her mind, and she was being respectful, so she continued. "No ceremony is going to make any difference to everyone's grief."

"We perform ritual as a means to heal, not as instant healing." Zenith shivered. Celeste rearranged the shawl across her shoulders and went to fetch another blanket from the warming cupboard. "Now. Let's get started."

THE PLAN WAS to have a ceremony honouring those left behind in mass graves and those lost, whether they'd fled or were dead and hadn't been found. When the list was finished and the ceremony clear, Sabine said, "But you can't even stand. How are you going to address everyone?"

"Not me." Zenith reached out a frail, bony hand. "You. You will speak for me."

"No." Sabine tossed down the paper and pencil. "Absolutely not."

Zenith gripped Sabine's hand. "You will."

"No!" Sabine shook her head. "I'm so angry I just want to scream. I would. I'd get up there in front of everyone and just start yelling my head off like a madwoman!"

"You won't," Celeste said.

"You'll do just fine," said Zenith. "Your anger will pass."

"No, it won't!" Sabine's cheeks flushed. "I'm going to stay this mad forever."

Zenith patted Sabine's hand. Sabine held herself in check, shocked by the sudden urge to slap the old woman's hand away. She was patronizing her! How condescending!

"I won't do it."

"You will." Zenith pulled her hand away, sensing Sabine's brimming aggression.

"I won't." Sabine stood. "And you won't make me. You never make us do what goes against our beliefs. Well, this goes against my beliefs. I believe there is nothing you or I can say or do to make any of us feel any better. We have all failed. And you're responsible. You're our leader, and you let this happen!"

"Sabine!" Celeste half stood from her perch at the edge of Zenith's cot. "You can *not* talk to Zenith like that."

Sabine levelled a chilly glare at her grandmother. Celeste bristled and sat herself back down. She'd never seen such an expression on her grand-daughter's face. What was becoming of them all? Were they fraying at the seams? Never to be repaired?

"It's all right, Celeste." Zenith patted her knee. "It's okay. Take your thoughts, Sabine, and go sit with them in silence, then come back to me and tell me your decision."

"I don't have to think about it," Sabine said. "I know my decision. The answer is no."

"I have room in my heart and in my logical mind for your defiance, just as I know you have the respect for me to do what I ask of you. I am not demanding you address your people, but I *am* demanding that you go away and think it over before you give me an answer about whether you will or won't."

"I'm sorry, Zenith." Sabine's eyes brimmed with tears. She was so confused and sad, and didn't know where to put her anger. "I'm so sorry. I'm behaving terribly, aren't I?"

"Go. Now."

"Zen Zen . . . I wish I hadn't . . . I-I-I can't—" Zenith looked so wasted and crumpled up. Sabine swallowed. She backed away from the cot. "I'm just so sorry, Zen Zen. I didn't mean what I said."

"Yes, you did." Zenith nodded. "Now, go and be still with your thoughts."

"But I am sorry! It's not really your fault!" Sabine started to cry in earnest. "I'm sorry, Zen Zen!"

"It's true, Sabine. You're only voicing what so many are thinking." Zenith held up her frail hand. "I'm responsible. I accept that. Now go."

As Sabine backed out of the tent Celeste bent over the old woman, straightening her pillows and bringing a cup of water to her lips. Zenith looked older than ever. Ancient. Barely of this world, as if she were occupying the blurry space between the world of the living and whatever lay beyond. And Sabine had just told her off. Celeste glanced up as Zenith took a dribbly sip of water. She shook her head at her granddaughter and then looked away, eyes downcast with disappointment.

NAPPO SAT ON A BENCH with Teal asleep beside him, his head in Nappo's lap, while Eli rearranged the cots so that the three boys could be side by side. The tent was mostly empty, with everyone lined up to eat down the lane. There were a couple others, napping, but it was quiet and dim, the sunlight outside sliding sideways into sunset. When the beds were sorted Nappo laid his little brother down and tucked him in, pulling the thin blanket right up under his chin. He laid a hand on Teal's brow and sighed.

"It was his birthday yesterday. He's six now." Nappo sat beside Eli, the two of them perched on the edge of the next cot. They stared at the little boy, afraid to move on to darker topics. "He doesn't know it though. I'm going to make up a new birthday for him. After."

"When's after?"

Nappo shrugged. "I thought he was dead, you know. We didn't find him until two days later. I must've dug out a hundred bodies and I didn't care. Check for signs of life, drag them to the pile, keep going. I didn't sleep, didn't eat, didn't even take a shit. Just kept digging until I found him."

"Where was he?"

"With a group of kids who'd hidden in the crawlspace under the stairs at the far end of the dining hall. They should've been with the bunch that left with you, only Teal and his buddies had been raiding the kitchen when it happened and so no one knew where they were. They weren't in any of the spots where the children were hidden."

"Where was Zenith?"

"In her room. In a tiny wedge of space created beside her bed when the beams fell. She'd fallen onto the floor with the first blast. Riva went to help her up, but then another blast caved the roof in, and Riva was killed." Nappo closed his eyes.

"Charis is dead," Eli offered, as if they were trading corpses.

"I heard."

"Trace left with Anya this morning. He's making her show him where we buried her. They're going to miss the ceremony."

Neither of them wanted to bring up the subject of the sisters they'd been so fond of. Nappo's Lia and Eli's Zari. They talked about everyone else they could think of, right down to those whose names they didn't know, until they ran out of people to talk about. They settled on silence instead, until Nappo could stand it no longer.

"Let's just get it over with, Eli," he said. "Okay?"

Eli nodded. "Okay."

"Trace's team found them."

"Where were they?"

"Clinging to each other."

Eli paused. "But *where?*" he pressed. He wanted to place them. He wanted to know exactly where. That night he was going to meet Zari in the bell tower. They were going to climb up to the top to watch the sun rise, and to get up to who knows what else. Eli had only gone back to the dorms to get changed into something warmer. Then the fight with Seth, and the explosions, and since then life had kept lurching forward to the very place he found himself now.

"I guess it would've been the courtyard." Nappo closed his eyes again, squeezing them tight. He nodded. "Near the bell tower."

Eli sucked in his breath. If she'd stayed at the party, would she still be alive? Most of the survivors had been the last at the feast. If they hadn't had plans to meet, would she be here with him now?

No. There was nothing you could do. It was her time, as it was the time of so many others to meet their highers.

"You know how some dead people look?" Nappo said, his eyes fixed on the floor now. "Like they're sleeping?"

Eli said nothing. He was remembering Zari that night. She'd worn a dress that made her look like a princess, her hair plaited with silver ribbons woven through, as if she were wearing a tiara. That's how he wanted to remember her. Or asleep in the arms of her sister. That would be okay too. But Nappo kept talking, ruining both images forever.

"Not them. They just looked dead." Nappo rubbed his face. He dropped his hands in his lap and looked at Eli with bleary eyes. "There were maggots in their eyeballs, Eli."

Eli felt a surge of nausea prickling his skin and constricting his throat. Zari had been so beautiful.

"Stop, Nappo." It took all of Eli's energy to stand. He teetered, steadying himself against the taut canvas wall of the tent. "Please."

But Nappo couldn't. It was as if by talking about it he could relieve himself of the tiniest portion of the horror, but only to bestow it on Eli, who could stand no more. They were both full up with death. "And the soft bits of their hands had been eaten by rats, and they'd chewed through their clothes and into their bellies. There were so many maggots crawling all over, it almost looked like they were still alive, kind of moving, you know?"

"Stop!" Eli clamped his hands over his ears. "Enough."

Maybe it would've been better if they'd all died. Being left behind was worse. Far worse than death. Eli stumbled to his cot and collapsed. He pulled the blanket over his head, the weight of so many deaths dragging him into a dark, thick sleep from which he hoped never to awake.

5

⚶

Seth and Amon were on foot for the first two days, with nothing at all to eat until late the second day, when they came upon the remnants of someone else's camp and found one bread heel and half an apple, brown and mushy. They brushed off the bugs and split the apple and bread. The third night out they came upon a tent set up under the forest cover. Seth hadn't seen it at first, but Amon had. Or rather, he'd spotted the horses and put two and two together. A couple of sad old mares tied to a tree, staring at them with rheumy eyes.

Seth assessed the situation. "We'll untie the reins and walk them out, saddle up once we get back into the clearing."

"We should take their food too." Amon's belly rumbled so loudly Seth could hear it as clear as if it were shouting. "The cache. In the tree." Amon pointed.

The plump sack hung high up out of the way of bears and raccoons, swaying slightly.

"Too risky." As hungry as he was, Seth shook his head. "We might wake them. Best to take the horses rather than push our luck."

"I've got to eat, man."

"The horses are more valuable. There'll be other food."

"More wormy apples and mouldy bread?"

"Keep your voice down!" Seth whacked him.

"Ow!"

"Well," Seth whispered harshly. "Shut up then. You go first."

They left their meagre belongings at the edge of the forest and crept toward the horses, who snorted puffs of air into the frosty night and stamped their hooves in anticipation. Amon held out a reassuring hand.

"Easy," he whispered. "Easy."

They untied the reins and led the horses as quietly as possible into the small clearing, where they mounted them with just the slightest jangling from the stirrups and bits. Seth grinned from atop his horse. He felt more powerful already. He jerked his head, gesturing for Amon to follow.

"Nice and slow," Seth whispered to the horse, who bobbed his head as if agreeing but then lurched off at a nervous trot, snapping branches and brush. "Whoa!" Seth whispered, louder. He glanced behind him.

Amon wasn't following. He pointed at the food cache as he headed back toward it. Worse, whoever was in the tent was stirring. There was the unmistakable strike of a match, and then the glow of a lantern.

"Let's go!" Seth yelled. "Now!"

"Who's there?" The flap opened and an old man stuck out his head, fumbling to get his glasses on.

"Amon! Let's go!"

"No way!" Amon stood up in the stirrups, stretching up toward the sack. "Not without the food!"

The old man disappeared briefly. Seth could hear him rouse someone else. When he came back to the flap, an old woman came too. The two of them stuck their heads out and shook their fists.

"Stop! Thieves!" the old woman screamed. She pulled at the man's sleeve. "Henri, do something!"

The old man stumbled out of the tent, barefoot and pyjamaed. He thrust a rusty old knife into the air as he shoved his feet into his waiting boots. "Stop, or I'll gut you!"

Amon had hold of the food sack now and was pulling, the branch creaking down, threatening to snap.

"Stop I said!" The old man lurched forward, swinging his knife. "I warned you!"

"Unbelievable." Seth shook his head and sighed. He trotted up behind the man and clubbed his temple once, hard, with a closed fist. The old man dropped flat onto his face without so much as a gasp.

"Henri!" The old woman pulled a blanket over her shoulders and tripped over herself to get to his side. "*Vieux foux*, my love!"

"Not a move, or you're next." Seth didn't like saying it, although he had to admit he wanted what was in that bag too. He wasn't going to hit her, but she grabbed a stick and reared up with a sudden shrill scream.

"You beast!" She swung at him, missing grandly. "*Tu est fou et misérable!* Stealing from old people. What kind of lowlife scum are you?"

Seth actually considered the question as she jabbed him hard. He was no lowlife. He was full of life to be lived, unlike these geezers who would've been tucked away long ago if this were the Key.

"Got it!" The branch snapped and Amon swung the bag triumphantly. "Let's go!"

"Give it back!" The woman jumped for the bag, swinging at it with her stick like it was a piñata.

Seth felt his patience peak and then vanish entirely. "Back off, you old cow." He clenched his fist again and landed it hard on her temple as if he were banging on a door. She fell backward and clutched her head.

"May the highers curse your every breath!" she said, her eyes squeezed shut in pain. "May your blood run thick with sick!"

"Desperate times, old lady." A calm came over Seth. He smiled. "I'm sorry."

"You're not!" she cried. "Or you wouldn't leave us like this!"

"You're old." Seth followed Amon out of the bush, calling behind him. "No one cares about you. The world is for the young. There's no room here for those who can't take care of themselves. You'd do us all a favour if you'd just bloody well die!"

They left the old couple clinging to each other and rejoined the trail south. Amon handed him a fresh apple and a hunk of dried rabbit meat. The two of them ate in silence as they rode.

"Stop," Seth said when he was finished eating and his head had cleared. "Wait a minute. We have to get something straight." He dismounted as Amon slowed to a stop beside him.

Seth gave his apple core to his horse, his back to Amon. "What you did back there was unacceptable."

"How can you say that when you've just eaten the first real food for days?"

Seth turned. "You disobeyed me."

"You're not the boss of me, Seth." Amon laughed. "Disaster is the great equalizer, or hadn't you noticed, big man?" He tightened his reins and clucked at his horse to get him trotting again. Seth reached for the bridle and held it tight.

"It's not going to work like that."

"What isn't?"

"Look, we part ways now, or you agree that I'm in charge." Seth's tone was even, his gaze cool and level. "It's that easy."

"Fine. I don't need you. I'll head west. You carry on south, and we never have to see each other again."

"All right." Seth let go and mounted his own horse. "So be it." He snugged the reins and dug in his heels. "It's not like you could be trusted to do what I need you to do anyway, so it's just as well." With that, he started down the trail.

"Wait!" Amon caught up. "What are you talking about?"

"I have a plan, and you could have a part in it, but only if you acknowledge me as sole leader."

"A plan to what?"

"Take down the Keys." Seth stared at him, daring Amon not to laugh.

Amon met his cousin's eyes, but could not hold his stare long. It made him uneasy, and a little scared, truthfully. Plan or no plan, ridiculous or not, he did not want to travel alone. And truth be told, he didn't really mind if someone else wanted to be in charge. That only meant that he wouldn't have to shoulder any blame himself should something go wrong. Let Seth have his ego trip. Let him have his grand, impossible schemes. What did he care?

"Fine," he snapped. "Whatever. Okay. Happy?"

"I mean it." Seth's stare hardened. "You answer to me, and only me."

"All right, Seth." Amon laughed nervously. "I get it."

"You think this is funny? I'm talking about overthrowing the Keys and you're acting like it's some childish game."

Because it was! Just a stupid, impossible pipe dream! But Amon wasn't going to tell him so. And besides, he still wasn't sure if Seth had had something to do with the massacre. Maybe all of this was a cover. Maybe he was still in with the Guard. Time would tell, and either way, being with Seth was about as safe as it got at the moment. Seth's motivations might be suspect, but he had ambition and stubbornness to equal Amon's laziness and doubt, and so he'd at least be in the company of someone with a mission in mind, which was more than he could say for himself.

There was an undeniable allure to being part of something, even if it never got off the ground. Left to his own devices he'd find the nearest dust den, get as high as he could and stay that way. But what he really wanted, deep down, was to put things right for Triskelia. To finally do his part for a community that had shown him such forgiveness and understanding despite his wayward past, years lost to dust. He'd do right by Zenith. Whether she was dead or alive, he owed her that much.

"I'm in, Seth."

"All right, then. Let's get going."

Sabine tossed and turned all night, and in the morning nothing was any clearer. She got up before the others, fetched a cup of tea, and then wandered out of the village with it into the cool, clinging mist of the morning. She wanted to feel the cold in her bones, anything that might distract her from the pain in her heart and the confusion plaguing her mind.

She parked herself on a boulder under a tree some distance from the market. Despite the beautiful day, the blue sky and birdsong, horrible images came crashing back. She'd been celebrating her return to the circus with Jack and Gavin when the first blasts hit. They'd been warm and cozy by the fire in the great hall, halfway through a bottle of wine. The blasts shook the building, sending the wine bottle to the floor where it broke, pooling red on the slate as if it were an omen of what was to come.

And Quinn. She missed her dear, dear friend more now than she ever had and she could not understand how that was possible. She wanted him here, now, to tell her what to do, to hold her hand, to make her laugh, to bring some life back into all the death. But he wasn't here. She was suddenly angry with him too. How dare he die and leave her all alone? How dare he abandon his best friend like that, after they'd promised to be there for each other forever, no matter what?

Oh, the anger was back in full. Sabine could hardly stand the crashing swings between anger and grief. It was like being on a trapeze swing, and wanting off, and feeling sick.

Her anger swung over to Seth now, to his part in Quinn's death. All this time she'd thought it had been her fault, because she'd made him perform even though he was miserable that Jack had dumped him, a secret she had kept to herself all this time.

And to think that it had been the pigeons! She would never have known. They were used to birds roosting above them in the gym, but not birds trained to go after them. How could Seth live with himself? He was no better than their father and his part in their mother's death. How could she ever forgive him?

She crossed her arms tight and scowled. Who said she had to forgive him? She could blame him forever. She *did* hate him. This notion struck her hard, so hard that she sat up straighter, as if she'd been smacked. But she hadn't hated anyone until now. Not even Edmund. Hate and she did not have anything to do with each other. It just didn't hold any value in Triskelia. Is this what hate tasted like? Bitter and hot, yet satisfying in an unnerving way?

She forced herself to move past the feeling, as seductive as it was. She turned her thoughts to Zenith. She should never have said those things to her. It really wasn't Zenith's fault. None of this was anyone's fault. Except for whoever revealed Triskelia to the Guard. And if that was Seth, then it was entirely his fault. And he would pay for it.

Everything was so confusing. Sabine stood, took a deep breath, and shook her arms, willing the thick paste of misery to slough off. She didn't like feeling this way. She wanted to feel light and easy, but doubted she'd ever feel that way again. She glanced at the tree towering over her, dotted with the bright green of spring growth. She backed up, took a run, walked up the trunk a few steps as if she was going to somersault away from it but then caught the lowest branch instead and swung herself up, bark scraping her hands and bruising her knees as she climbed. To feel something other than grief and anger and guilt was miraculous. She monkeyed her way up to the tallest crook that would hold her and straddled the branch.

This was better. Up here the world reclaimed some of its perspective. She could see the market, with the people bustling about doing normal, necessary things. It was both frustrating and comforting. Frustrating that the world just went on, as normal as you please, while so much injustice festered around them. And yet comforting too, in that some things would always be the same. Babies needed feeding, food needed cooking, laundry needed washing.

The sky above boasted a procession of plump white clouds. They were close enough to the cloudseeder camp and near enough to the ocean and mountains that the weather here was almost normal. The Guard left this corner of the world alone, mostly. It was too rugged for one thing, but more importantly, it was populated with healthier Droughtlanders. The Guard knew not to meddle here; they might incite an uprising among the only segment of the Droughtland that could put up a real fight.

Sabine bristled at the thought of an uprising. The Guard had slaughtered thousands. An uprising would surely result in even more deaths. But how else would those responsible be punished?

Retribution.

Like hate, it wasn't of any value where she came from. But times were different now, and rage was an undeniable power that could fuel a lot of good.

But would it?

And what of grief? Born out of violence, what did it fuel, but more of the same?

Sabine turned her thoughts to the ceremony she'd so adamantly refused to speak at. An idea came to her, a way of helping the others leave their grief behind. She *would* speak to her people, just as Zenith had probably known all along. She wasn't sure what she'd say yet, but she knew what she'd have them do.

6

⁓✲⁓

Seth was feeling more like himself now. It was all in the power he commanded over others. By taking what he needed and getting what he wanted he grew metaphoric inches until he felt taller than anyone and capable of just about anything. He needed to feel that way if he was going to meet the challenges he'd set for himself. And when he had to steal or cheat or lie he just reminded himself that it was for the greater good. He had rules, though: no stealing from orphaned children or the sick, no violence unless it was absolutely unavoidable. The people he stole from now would thank him later when the Keys fell. They'd brag that they'd "donated" to the cause by not resisting when Amon and Seth helped themselves to their chickens or candles or axe or horse.

Now, he had his eye on a bigger prize.

Before them a tiny cottage sat tucked away in the forest, a delicious plume of smoke promising warmth inside.

"Showtime," Seth said as they approached the door, the knives they'd acquired in their last mission out and at the ready. On cue, Amon flung open the door and they strode in as if they were coming home for tea after an easy afternoon ride.

The shocked family was halfway through supper: father, mother, sister, brother, and an infant in the mother's arms. Seth grabbed the boy in a chokehold and pressed his knife to his throat. He was maybe ten, or twelve. Perfect.

The mother screamed.

"Papa!" the boy croaked, his eyes tearing. He tried to stand, but Seth shoved him back onto his butt.

"Get off of him!" The father pushed his chair back and set up for a punch. Seth pressed the blade harder against the boy's pale skin. A bead of blood appeared. The father hesitated.

"Don't move, mister." Seth was getting used to this. The screaming wife, the defiant husband, the squalling children.

The mother screamed again. She threw a jug at Seth, hitting his shoulder.

"Not smart, missus." Seth dug the knife in a little more. The boy yelped as a line of blood trickled along his collarbone.

"Don't hurt him!" The father lunged for Seth. Amon stopped him with a quick left hook to the jaw.

"He said, don't move!"

"Okay!" The man reeled back. "Just go! Take whatever you want! Take everything!"

"Why thank you, mister," Amon said, playing as if he were shopping. "I'd like a loaf of bread." He plucked it from the table and dumped it in his sack. "And I'd like a new coat. This one will do nicely." He slithered into one he lifted off the hook and slung another over his arm for Seth. "And another knife, and these apples, and a sharpening stone, and a couple of blankets." He stopped, arms laden. "I seem to have run out of room."

"Just hurry up," Seth growled.

Amon went to pack the stuff he'd gathered so far onto their new cart, leaving Seth alone with the family. The boy wasn't struggling much, which struck Seth as more than a little pathetic. The kid was trembling, his teeth chattering loudly. And he could not believe that the father, after only one punch, was just sitting there letting this happen.

The little girl on the other side of the table started to slide out of her chair, her eyes on Seth for permission. He winked and nodded, and so she left her seat and climbed into her mother's lap and buried her face in the folds of her shawl. She'd be worth something to the childtraders, especially if she was bright. She was maybe four, so had a decade of hard labour ahead of her. If things went his way, by the time they'd want her for babies, the Keys would be toppled and she would be free.

Seth blinked. What was he thinking? She was just a little girl! And what if his plan failed and the Keys stood? His thoughts hurried back to the Droughtland girls in the villages he'd passed through with his Guard regiment. The lives they had, what they were forced to endure at the hands of the Guards. No. He wouldn't take the girl. He'd stick to his original plan. No girls.

Only boys. An army of boy soldiers.

Amon came back inside now. "Ahh, so nice and warm."

"Just hurry." Seth kept his knife at the boy's throat. With his free hand he grabbed the back of the boy's neck as if he were a kitten and stood him up for inspection. The scrawny kid came up just to his shoulders but he had clear, bright eyes and a healthy look to him overall, not too skinny and with no telltale signs of recent sicks, only old skineater scars that meant he was immune to it now.

As Amon packed up more of the family's possessions, careful to leave behind the things they never took—food stores, cooking pots, means to hunt—Seth gave the boy a wink and shoved him back on his seat. The boy looked up at him, perplexed but curious, and not all that afraid considering the circumstances.

"Please, please, please don't hurt us." The mother clutched her daughter to her and wept. "We've done nothing. I beg to the highers, just take what you want."

Amon laughed. "Open your eyes, bitch, we already did."

"No need for such language." Seth shot him a withering look. "Sorry, missus."

The mother looked at him, as equally perplexed as her son.

"Will you go now?" The father's glare was angry, but resigned too, as if this had happened before, and it likely had.

"Why do you live out here?" Seth moved the knife away from the boy's skin but kept it at his neck. He grabbed a piece of meat from the platter. He addressed the father before taking a bite. "It's not very safe out here, as I'm sure you realize now if you hadn't already."

"Where else would we live?" the father grumbled.

The meat was rabbit, Seth guessed. A little chewy, but marvellously spicy.

"Well, not Triban . . . I wouldn't want to raise my kids there either. But the markets." Seth wiped the grease off his lips and helped himself to more meat. "Or one of the villages on the other side of the mountains. Definitely not all by myself in the woods. That's just asking for it."

"In the Droughtland proper, you mean." The man gave a sharp, bitter laugh. "So we'd die from sicks? We came here because of the sicks. After we lost our eldest to the skineater, and almost the other three too. I'd rather take my chances with you miserable night bandits."

"We have a gun you know," the boy began, but he stopped as soon as Seth turned an amused look on him.

"Go on, kid," Seth said. "Keep talking. I'm curious."

"We usually take turns on watch, but we was only taking a break for supper and that's why you got past us." The boy's chin lifted just a little, in the smallest act of defiance. "We'd a shot you deader than a rabid dog!"

"Is that right?" Seth respected the boy's boldness. He actually liked the little kid. "Well, lucky me, then."

"And then we'd gut you and bleed you and roast you and have you for supper!"

Amon snorted. "Yeah, right." But he did not bring the chunk of meat he'd just grabbed to his lips.

The father folded his arms across his chest. The mother let an odd-looking smile appear, despite her despair. The father grinned triumphantly at them both.

"Go on. Help yourself."

Seth felt the blood drain from his face. He glanced at the bones he'd tossed on the table.

"Tasty, isn't it?" the father said.

Seth's breath quickened but he didn't move, even though he wanted to bolt out the door and throw up.

"You're lying."

"Are we?" The father tried to wipe the smile off his face, but was failing.

"Let's go." Seth nodded at Amon.

Amon stared at the meat in his hands as his thoughts charged across his face. Eat it? Don't eat it?

"Some things are just plain wrong," Seth said. "Have you no morals?"

"We do what we need to in order to meet our highers in good time, my friend." The father was relaxing a little, which angered Seth. He had the upper hand here, no matter what. "What I do to feed my family is between me and my highers, and when the time comes, I will be redeemed."

"Maybe now would be a good time to meet your highers, eh?" He snugged the knife back at the boy's throat. "Where's the gun?"

"Beside the door, under the curtain," the mother blurted. "Don't hurt him!"

Amon fetched the gun, cocked it, and rested the muzzle over the father's heart.

"Would you like to meet your maker now?"

The father shook his head, all earlier bravado gone. Out of the father's vision, Seth shook his head.

Amon jabbed the gun. "Or how about now?'

"We have men surrounding this place," Seth said as he let go of the boy. The boy's hand went to his throat, to the blood coming from the little cut. "They'll see to it that you don't follow us. I'd advise you to stay in your seats, unless you'd like to die tonight after all."

He turned to the boy. "What's your name?"

"Orin." His face flushed with colour. "Ori. For short."

"You're coming with us," Seth said.

The boy's mouth went slack and his eyes went wide. It wasn't a look of terror though, not at all. It was excitement.

"Seth?" Behind him, Amon raised his eyebrows.

"No!" the mother cried, but she had the baby in one arm, and the other clutching her daughter, and no third arm for her third child. "Do something, Menno!"

"Please, leave him." The father opened his hands in a gesture of peace, or offering. "He's just a boy."

"On your feet, Ori." Seth nodded at him. "You can pack a bag, if you'd like. Amon will go with you." Again he felt that strange calm he'd felt only the few times he'd been in absolute control, with no doubt about it. "Don't worry," he said to the father. "We'll treat him well. He'll come back to you. We have a job for him."

"We do?" Amon muttered as he followed the boy, whose hands shook with fear as he packed a few things into a thin pillowcase. A book, a sweater, a shirt. He started to add a little carved horse to the sack, but after a long hard stare at it, he gave it to the little girl instead.

"Don't go, Ori!" She clutched the little horse to her and wailed. "I'll be good, I promise!"

"Ori." His mother thrust the baby at the father and gripped Ori's hand tight. "You are not leaving. I won't let you go."

"Missus." Seth pried the boy away.

"No!" she screamed. "I'll die before I let you take my child. You'll have to kill me first!"

"Missus!" Seth shook her shoulder. "Look at me!"

"I won't let you." Pushing out great sobs, she raised her teary eyes to him.

"I won't hurt him." Seth nodded at the boy. "I promise you. Now don't make me do something I don't want to do here. Just let him go. He's a big boy. He'll be fine."

"It's okay," Ori said. His lip trembled. "I'll be okay."

"Oh, Ori!" The woman sobbed and sobbed, but said nothing more.

"Now." Seth put a hand on the boy's shoulder. "Say goodbye to your family."

Ori cried fat, silent tears, his gaze fluttering between his distraught parents and Seth. Finally, he hugged his father and whispered something in his ear. The father held his son tight and would not let go, even when Ori tried to pull away.

"That's enough." Seth took the rifle from Amon and levelled it at the boy. "Let him go."

The father slackened his grip, letting Ori go to his mother and two sisters.

"My boy, my lovely boy." The mother wept. *"Je t'aime!"*

"I love you too, Maman."

Maman. Seth bristled. An image of his own mother flashed across his sights. He quickly shut her out. The feelings were too big. There was no room for them right now. He grabbed the boy's ponytail and yanked him away. He shoved him out the door ahead of him.

"Remember. Don't follow," he said to the parents. He winked at Ori out of his parents' line of sight. "Or your son will see the rest of you hanging in the trees." Seth put a hand on the knob and looked at the family one last time. "That's not the memory you want to leave him with now, is it?"

The parents shook their heads.

"Well, we have an agreement then. Good." Seth pulled the door shut.

HE AND AMON and their first boy soldier stood alone in the cold, damp night. Amon stared at Seth, mouth agape, while the boy cried silently.

"What did you just do?" Amon smacked the back of the boy's head. "What the hell are we supposed to do with this brat, huh? What the hell are you thinking? Was it because of the meat? Maybe they were bluffing."

"Were not," Ori said, putting a hand to his head where it smarted.

"Leave the thinking to me, Amon." Seth's look extinguished any other questions Amon might've asked. "And if you touch him again you will be very, very sorry. Let's go, both of you." Seth strode toward the horses, feeling taller with each step.

Amon and Ori hung back, glowering at each other.

Seth looked over his shoulder. "Now!"

"Don't talk to me," Amon said to the boy. "Don't ask me to help you, don't even look at me." He shoved his hands deep in his pockets, already feeling the cold. "Understand?"

Ori nodded, copied Amon's stance, and said nothing.

"Maybe you're not so dumb after all," Amon said, and then the two of them followed Seth.

IT RAINED SOLIDLY for the next two days, chilling the trio to the bone. Was it a Guard storm, brought in to soak the people into submission, or was it a natural front, in from the ocean they were close to now? Seth had never paid much attention to the subject of weather modification. He'd never been interested, thinking it a science for those too scared to take on a real job, like politics or warfare.

Now he wished he could tell the difference between modified and real weather, both of which were plentiful this side of the mountains. It was easier on the other side, where the largest stretch of Droughtland never saw real weather, but here, in the coastal regions, the proximity of the mountains and the ocean created their own weather no matter how hard the Keyland cloudseeders tried to claim it.

Seth knew that Triskelia had cloudminders too, and a weather station up one of the mountains, although he had no idea which one. As they neared a roadhouse outside of Triban he turned his face up into the rain. The closest Key lay several days' ride to the northeast, so it could be their doing. Well, no matter whose rain it was, it was cold and cruel and he could not wait to get out of it.

The roadhouse beckoned them with smoking chimneys and steamed-up windows. They were going to dry out and have a proper meal there before they tackled the wretched city. Seth took Ori aside before they went in.

"Don't try anything." He jabbed a finger at the boy's chest. "Got it?"

Ori nodded. Seth let him go in ahead of him. He wasn't worried that he'd try to escape. From what he could tell the boy was actually excited to be travelling with them. He seemed to think it was some kind of adventure, like something out of a storybook. Perhaps he was a bit daft. No matter, he had two arms and two legs and seemed to quite like being told what to do.

There was no table to be had in the crowded pub, what with all the travellers seeking refuge from the deluge. A few Seduce games were in progress and so Seth joined one, putting Ori up as his collateral. Ori didn't protest because he didn't know it was happening. He and Amon were across the pub, drying themselves in the crowd jockeying for space in front of the lone woodstove.

It was a short, brutal game, the Queen of Hearts circling the table only twice. Seth managed to keep Ori and gain himself another boy. He was scrawnier than Ori, and was maybe twelve, even though he puffed himself up and claimed to be fourteen.

"I got muscles to prove it!" he said when Seth gave him a doubtful look. "Grrr." The boy flexed his arms like a wrestler. He danced around like that, little prizefighter he thought he was. "Finn." He introduced himself when he was finished posturing. "What's your gig?"

"My gig?"

"You got a farm?" The boy flashed him a smile and cocked his head at him. "You a pimp?"

"No! No." Seth grabbed him by his shirt collar and shoved him through the crowd to the other boys. "Nothing like that. Get your mind out of the gutter, you little pig."

"Oink, oink." Finn shrugged. "I don't make no judgment. So long as I get fed."

"Let's go," Seth snapped at Amon and Ori. "This is Finn."

"Another one?" Amon shook his head and followed Seth outside to where the rain had mercifully dulled to a light shower. "How you gonna feed us all, huh?"

"Hey." Finn bobbed and weaved, fists up. "I don't get food, I'm outta here. Pop! Pow! I'll beat all of you up, just watch!"

Seth pulled out the pistol he'd bought from a shifty dealer the day before. He shoved Finn so that he stood shoulder to shoulder with Ori. He put the gun to Ori's head. "If one of you tries to escape . . ." He dragged the gun across Ori's forehead and pressed it to Finn's temple. "I kill the other one. Understood?"

Ori nodded solemnly, his face pale.

"So?" Finn threw his shoulders back and huffed. "I don't know him. What would I care if—"

"No cheek!" Seth knocked him upside the head with the butt of the gun.

Finn stumbled back, one hand at his head, the other balling into a fist.

"Why you—" Finn rushed him. Seth grabbed him easily and shoved him against the wall of the pub. With a flourish, he set the gun between the boy's crusty eyes and cocked it, pushing the metal into Finn's spotty forehead.

"I mean it."

"And I get it! Okay, okay." Finn moved his head away. "Geez."

Seth let him be. For now. He'd left his mark, in more ways than one. The tip of the gun had left a red dent, but more than that, Seth could tell he'd broken the boy, if only just a little.

7

⁓

The day of the memorial ceremony dawned with a clear blue sky. Sabine carried a large reed basket so full of strips of cloth that they spilled out as she led the procession of survivors up to the tree. A gaggle of children followed her, collecting the strips as they fell. Under other circumstances they would've made a game of it, but as it was, they just slipped the rags into their pockets and kept their eyes to themselves. It was a beautiful day—warmer than it had been—with a spring breeze that brought pink to everyone's cheeks.

Behind her, Jack carried another basket, also filled with colourful strips of cloth. Eli had offered to carry it, but Sabine had ignored him and pointedly handed the basket to Jack instead. She still hadn't spoken to Eli since she'd shoved him into the mud.

Eli and Gavin pushed Zenith up the craggy path in a rickety wheelchair, easing over roots and rocks and slicks of mud. Celeste came next, with a walking stick to steady herself. She smiled, but it was a pained smile. She was tired, and this small climb up the hill caught her breath in her chest. She waved away help, though, wanting the others to think she was stronger than she felt.

The rest of the Triskelian survivors followed behind, forming a raggedy, slumped-shouldered line trudging up the hill. Sabine stopped at the base of the tree she'd climbed the day before.

"Everyone take a handful of cloth," she said as they gathered and passed around the baskets. Jack and Eli parked Zenith's chair beside

Sabine. Sabine glanced at Eli, not offering him a smile but not glaring at him either. He wished she'd either spat or smiled. The indifference was worse. It made him feel invisible, the way he'd felt growing up with Seth. He helped himself to a fistful of cloth and backed away into the crowd.

"Do you want to explain it?" Sabine asked Zenith when everyone had their share of cloth strips. Zenith, tired and cold despite the thick wool blanket across her knees and the wrap over her shoulders, shook her head.

"This is yours, child." She gestured at the fractured group in front of them. "They've come up here for you."

Sabine beheld the faces staring at her, waiting. Exhausted and drawn, with grief weaving through the crowd like a wicked, airborne sick. How would any of them recover? Sabine sighed. Maybe this was a dumb idea. Zenith reached for Sabine's sleeve.

"Carry on," she said. "We all need this. Very much."

Sabine nodded. She lifted up a strip of cloth.

"Each of these will become a goodbye for someone we've left behind." Sabine felt the lump of sadness in her throat that always came before tears. She swallowed hard. "We have lost sons and daughters, mothers and fathers, aunties, uncles, friends, lovers, and strangers too."

The crowd murmured a rumble of agreement.

"We have buried some bodies, but not all. We have said goodbye to some, but not others. But we have to move on from here, or we will become our grief in all its jagged coldness and bitter wind." Sabine wasn't sure she believed her own words, but she carried on. "So we will bless each strip of cloth, and then tie it up in the tree, and this tree will bear the weight of our grief, freeing us just enough to keep going. This tree has the strength and shoulders to do that for us. This tree will be our memorial . . . our grave for our loved ones and lost ones. We will leave our grief here."

At the back of the crowd, Eli fingered his handful of cloth. One was sky blue, another was a scratchy beige, there was a red strip with tiny pink flowers, and a green one, and a slithery black one.

It was a stupid idea. Praying over strips of cloth. For what? To what? Anyone who actually believed in highers was stupid.

But you believe.

Himself included then. "Not that I want to," Eli muttered, almost used to conversing with the voice now.

"Me neither." Beside him, Nappo gave a short, sharp laugh. "Like this'll help at all."

As much as Eli agreed, he felt compelled to defend his sister.

"Got a better idea?"

Nappo shrugged.

"Then shut up."

Nappo harrumphed, took Teal's hand, and moved them both away from Eli. No matter; Eli didn't care. He felt suddenly proud of Sabine for doing *something* when it was so obvious that they needed this, whatever it was, and whether it worked or not.

Around him, people were stepping forward with their colourful little flags. Surviving and uninjured Night Circus performers swung up easily into the tree, just as Sabine had. Others who could helped themselves up. Jack and Gavin locked hands and boosted up the children and those who just needed a hand. The rest climbed a little ladder that leaned against the tree. Soon the tree came to life as if so many spring birds were perched in its branches. The mourners murmured their blessings and prayers as they tied the cloths to the branches. There were tears, enough to water the tree for a year, but tears of a different sort. Not just tears of grief, but tears of catharsis, tears of movement.

Something was happening. Maybe it was the act of climbing a tree, so innocent and basic, or maybe it was the stretching of unused circus muscles, or just the simple proximity to the heavens, but when they came down people seemed lighter, or at least more peaceful, contemplative. Eli stepped forward, clutching his cloth strips tight in his fist.

He used the ladder, and then, with his one good arm, he climbed past everyone to the highest branch that would hold him.

"For Zari." He tied the blue one. "For everything that never was and won't be now."

For peace. For an end to the violence. For love.

For love? This voice, or sense, or insanity—whatever it was that was speaking to him—had pushed too far. Why should he pray for peace when there was so much retribution to be had? There is no peace in revenge. And revenge is all that mattered now. Wasn't it? Justice had to win on behalf of all those lives lost.

He would not pray for peace. "For Charis." He tied the red one. He gritted his teeth, so furious that she was dead he couldn't say anything else about her.

No, Eli. Think bigger. Pray for peace.

"Rather than for a little girl who was murdered?" he said out loud, eyes up to the sky. "Never! And this one is for Saber." Eli stroked the beige strip, remembering his horse with such clarity that he caught himself glancing at the ground, just in case he was there, waiting for him. Maybe he was alive, taken by the Guard. He could hope.

The green one he tied for everyone else, murmuring name after name under his breath until he almost swooned with the gravity of it all. So many hearts, brought violently to a halt. He would pray for them, but he would not pray for peace, voice or no voice. And certainly not for love. Love was dead. It had to be, for so much violence to find room to flourish in the world.

Why do you fight your own sense of right and wrong? Why do you struggle against what you believe?

Eli ignored the voice. Below him the tree danced with the vibrant cloths tied along its branches. There was Sabine, just a couple of branches below him. She was watching the others, clutching her strips of cloth against her chest. She didn't notice him. He watched as she closed her eyes, her lips moving. In prayer, Eli figured. Was she hearing voices too? They'd shared the feeling back in Triskelia. Was this like that? He wanted to ask her, but he was afraid of the answer, and besides, she wasn't talking to him. Eli fingered the last cloth he had. The black one.

A prayer for peace.

Again, the voice! Eli remembered a story of Cook's. Her cousin's son had started to hear voices. It got so bad that he went mad and ended up driving a stake into his ear to make them stop. "Worse," Cook had explained, her tone hushed, "worse was that he didn't die right away, but lay comatose for a year before he finally went to his highers."

Eli gritted his teeth. He was not crazy. Surely this would pass? He was suffering, that's all, along with everyone else. Grief, trauma . . . it changed you. Eli knew that from his mother's death. But this, this was a scarier kind of change. He didn't like it. Not one bit.

Then a prayer for your brother, at least. A prayer for your blood. For family.

Worse, he had to admit, was that the things he was sensing, the things he was giving credit to some invisible, omniscient voice, actually resonated as truth. And not truth as in fact versus fancy, but deep-down profound *truth*.

He knew he should give the last strip of cloth to Seth. He'd survived the massacre, according to Trace. But he and Amon had been run off by other survivors, so who knew if he was still alive, or if they'd killed them?

Pray for him, dead or not.

Part of him felt compelled to, but a greater part fought the urge. No. He wouldn't. He searched within himself but came up with the same answer. He could not, or simply would not, give Seth any kind of blessing. Not while he wasn't sure of his brother's role in the ambush, if he had a role in it at all. And if he was dead? Did Eli care? After everything? After so many bodies what was one more dead?

Damn the voices, the sense, whatever it was. He wasn't going to be its slave.

Eli pocketed the black strip and started climbing down. He didn't feel any lighter. He didn't feel any better. He felt like he'd been shattered into a thousand pieces after the massacre and glued back together incorrectly.

He passed Sabine, who had to move a little to let him go by. She didn't look up at him. Eli paused. He wanted to say something to her but held himself back. It wasn't the time, and certainly not the place, here as they were in the middle of a tree now dressed for a carnival, the rainbow strips catching the wind, practically dancing. It seemed wrong, as if the cloths should be heavy instead, soaked with grief, weighed down with death.

WHAT SABINE WAS UTTERING when Eli saw her lips move wasn't a prayer. She had no urge to pray, and a dying trust that it amounted to anything anyway. She was reciting names.

First she'd tied a cloth for Charis, and then one for Zari and Lia, and with the next she'd started reciting names. This was a collective one, because so many souls had been lost that the survivors would each need a tree to fill with strips of cloth. She whispered as many names as she could remember, all the Triskelians she could think of, and then the names of the few people in the Colony of the Sicks whom she'd known, even if she'd only known their first names, even if she'd only met them once.

The one name that weighed heavily on her mind and heart was Seth's. Trace had told her what he'd said, his denials. And although she shared Trace's skepticism she felt compelled to tie her last cloth for her brother. Perhaps he'd died since and she could sense it? Had those who believed he'd betrayed Triskelia beat him to death? If he was still alive and had anything to do with the ambush, then he was as good as dead to her anyway. Perhaps that explained why she felt she should tie a cloth for him. She tried to open her heart to her brother, knowing that that's what Zenith would want her to do. She tried to let go of her anger but it had talons and it was fierce and proud of its grip. She glanced down at Zenith who was handing her strips up to Althea for her to tie. Let Zenith use one for Seth. Let Celeste. Sabine would not. She would tie the last one for herself instead.

"But I'm not dead," she whispered out loud, just to be sure. Or was she? She felt her face, blew a breath into her palm. Surely she wasn't dead. But then, she didn't know what death would be like. Could this be it? The same, only different? No. She shook herself and smiled. "Silly." She was alive. But parts of her were not. The part that had never known hunger, and only a fraction of the fear and grief she knew now. The part of her that had never hated anyone, not even Edmund for keeping her mother from her, not even Lisette for choosing to stay away, for choosing her brothers and the Key over her.

The Sabine who was dead was the innocent Sabine. She squared her shoulders. She would've thought that Sabine had died along with Quinn, but apparently not. She'd thought that was the worst experience of her life. But this, *this* was a million times more difficult.

Was this all life was? One hard thing after another? One grief easing just as another one careens out of nowhere to floor you anew? Grief upon grief, until your own death?

She'd do better to die right now and be done with it.

The idea found a place in her heart where there had been none for it before. She could kill herself. Then it would all be over. The fear, the pain, the grieving. The danger, the unknowing. All of it would be over. That would be better than becoming like Anya, all arms and legs, just mechanics. She had no soul left. Perhaps it was buried in the rubble back in Triskelia. Would Anya ever get better? Would any of them? Or would they be just so many zombies, lurching toward their own demise?

She tied her last strip to the bough.

She knew what they were supposed to do. She wished she didn't, but she did.

Relief and retribution. Relieve the suffering of the survivors as best they could, while avenging those who'd razed their home and murdered their loved ones. Justice. That was what she had to live for, and so she would.

Before, when she was sure of some power higher than herself, some godlike spirit of goodness and strength, she might have chosen death. To know infinite peace in the company of Quinn and Zari and Lia, and most of all her mother. But now she didn't believe in anything like that. What higher would have orchestrated this? Not one she wanted to spend eternity with, that much was certain.

"Blessed be," she said anyway, out of habit more than heart, as she touched each one of the cloths one last time before climbing down.

IT WAS ANOTHER WEEK before the survivors were ready to leave the market and carry on northward to the cloudseeding camp. They couldn't stay in the market; it was already stretched for resources, and wasn't safe, should the Guard come looking for survivors. And if word got to the Guard that the market was harbouring them it would put the good

Samaritans at risk after all they'd sacrificed and provided. They would go to the cloudseeding camp, and there they would devise a plan about what to do next.

The survivors couldn't pay the kind people of the market any money, nor could they give them goods, for they had none but what the market folk had donated. The one gift they left behind was the prayer tree.

Nothing had magically changed since the ceremony, but it was starting to. The ritual had given a little something to everyone who'd tied a cloth to the tree. For some it was something to hold on to, for others it was a means of letting go. And the power of the prayer tree itself had grown. At first it was the people from the market who tied their blessings to the tree. And when that first tree was dripping full of colour still more people came, from away, travelling especially to visit the tree. Ribbons started blossoming in the trees neighbouring the first one. It became a kind of pilgrimage.

The morning they left, Sabine rode beside Zenith in the cart at the front of the line. The two of them kept their gaze on the grove of prayer trees until it was just a spray of colour behind them.

"You should be proud." Zenith patted Sabine's arm. "You've given everyone something very special."

"I know, Zen Zen." She adjusted Zenith's blanket across the old woman's lap. "I know."

And while she did not believe in the power of prayer, she did believe in the power of community. Some might say the two weren't so different, but Sabine knew they were. Prayer relied on the highers. And what were they? Some amorphous hocus pocus to make people feel better when bad things happened. What strength was there in that? Strength lived within the people themselves. Community found its power in the real live strength of its members, in beating hearts and sharp minds and strong, able limbs.

8

꿎

The triplets' father was beside himself with fury. This was not unusual. He spent a great deal of his time being mad; he'd always been like that. What was unusual was the scope of his anger. It was massive. He wanted to hurt, either himself—just to feel something different from this suffocating rage—or something or someone else, so that he wouldn't be alone with it. He wanted to maim animals, break windows, punch a mirror, slam a fist into the wall. He'd like to plow his guest's head into that wall, as a matter of fact.

Instead he'd thrown a mug of tea and then yelled at Francie who'd been sent in to clean it up. She'd scuttled around, sweeping up the broken ceramic as fast as she could, blotting at the tea stain on the heirloom tapestry while the other man, young and hulking, had sat stone-faced and quiet.

Until Francie glanced at him on her way out. Then he'd winked at her, not a friendly wink but a lecherous one that made her stomach lurch. She hurried down the hall with the broom and dustpan full of broken bits, the rag stuffed in her apron pocket. As she wrung out the rag in the sink she told the kitchen staff about Chancellor East's dour mood and the strange man he had in his office.

"So what news you reckon this stranger brung?" Cook set aside the Cornish hen she'd been plucking. "What's he gone and said that's got his Master's panties in such a knot?"

Francie and the other maids giggled. They had a great big pile of vegetables in front of them and were chopping and peeling and dicing.

"I don't know what he said." Francie picked up a carrot and attacked it with the peeler. "And I don't know who he is. He looks like Guard. No uniform, but he's got that look to him. In his eyes, you know? He's not that old, maybe eighteen? But he's big and oafy and has hair creeping out his collar. I bet he's that hairy all over, his back and all. Like a smelly bear."

The kitchen staff giggled again.

"Well, in he comes and rattles it all up, after we'd just got it down to a dull roar. After everything," Cook muttered. "Got the nerve, hasn't he?"

Francie shrugged. "You think it's about the boys?"

"Rest their souls." Cook touched her heart, kissed her fingers, and offered the gesture up to the highers. "May they rest in the heavens, poor boys. Loved them like they was me own."

A silence flooded the kitchen. The maids eyed one another, not sure what to say. They were thankful when Cook broke the sad reverie. "Well, all's I want to know is if the bear is bloody well staying for supper or not. He'd probably want six of these all to himself!"

Once more, the girls tittered.

"I don't think he's going anywhere in a hurry," Francie said. "Better pluck a couple more cocks!"

This sent the maids and Cook into a fit of laughter, but they quickly shut up and curtsied as Allegra waddled into the kitchen, steadying herself along the wall, her other hand bracing her enormous pregnant belly.

"What's going on in here?" she asked, breathless.

"Nothing, ma'am." Cook took her arm and helped her to a chair. She eyed the others harshly.

"Something is going on, and by the sounds of it, it's not work." Allegra gestured at the pile of unprepared vegetables. "Not by the looks of it either."

"Oh, it's not what you think, ma'am. Some of these are for the staff's supper." Francie caught Cook's frown and shut up.

"Now, ma'am." Cook wiped her hands on her apron, clasped them together, and flashed a generous smile at Allegra. "Can I make you a cup of tea? A pickle sandwich?"

"No, no." Allegra grimaced. She held up a hand. "No more pickle. Definitely not."

"Oh?" Francie piped up. "Cravings changed? I heard about that, you start wanting chocolate or garlic or whatever—"

"Enough!" Allegra cut her off. "I take exception to your familiarity. It is entirely inappropriate." She winced, rubbing her tummy. "The only reason I'm sitting here at all is that your incessant cackling drew me in, and I wanted to be sure that dinner was well on its way and not falling prey to your little hen party."

Francie bristled, but she kept her mouth shut. She chopped the carrot in front of her into tiny, decimated pieces much too small to be good for anything.

"Sorry, ma'am." Cook dipped into another curtsy. "Can I get you anything at all?"

"No. I'm fine." Allegra pushed herself out of the chair and started toward the door. "I've already said no. If you people would only listen. Is that asking too much?"

Cook and the girls kept their eyes to themselves, heads bowed.

"Well?" When no one answered Allegra asked the question again. "Is it?"

"No, ma'am." The staff said it in unison, but the girls shared cool, knowing glances between them. Cook returned her eyes to the floor and prayed Allegra didn't notice their defiance.

"Let me, ma'am." Cook reached for the door.

"I'm docking your pay," Allegra said. "All of you. A week each. I'm tired of having to come in here and oversee matters that should not require my attention at all."

"Yes, ma'am." Cook held the door, eyes down again.

Francie hated seeing Cook so cowed when she was normally such a sharp, vibrant woman. Francie slapped her knife down on the marble countertop with a bang. "You can't just—"

"And you, little miss insolence." Allegra eased herself up the steps into the hall. "You, two weeks docked. You're getting a mouth on you. I suggest you shut it."

The kitchen staff listened for Allegra's steps to fade into quiet before they spoke again.

"Two weeks' pay!" Francie fumed. "That's just plain rotten evil! And who's she calling little miss? She ain't but a few years older than me!"

"I remember when she was such a nice girl." Cook shook her head. "Before she moved in here. Before the real missus died, bless her. Before Allegra's grandfather died. Before the boys . . . before they—" Cook sniffed, her cheeks reddening.

"There, there, Cook." Francie patted her shoulder as Cook wiped the tears from her eyes with the handkerchief she kept tucked up her sleeve. "We know how much you loved the twins and the dear first missus."

"I don't know about Seth," one of the girls muttered as she chopped. "Always crashing through here, ruining things, pinching bums, and bossing us around like he was the master himself. And so mean to Eli!"

"Oh, you leave him be!" Cook blew her nose. "Don't you speak ill of the dead. He was a good boy. In his own way. He was. Edmund's what made the bad parts, but he had his mother in him too. She is the light to Master's dark. Or was. Poor dears, the whole lot of them dead and I have half a mind to blame Sir for it all."

BACK IN THE STUDY, Edmund paced, his breath shallow, lines of sweat trickling down his neck.

"Sir?" The visitor stood, shoulders squared. "Chancellor East?"

"Thank you, Nord." Edmund held out his hand in acknowledgment. "I do appreciate the truth, as hard as it is to hear."

"But at least they're alive, sir." Nord knew full well that Edmund had concocted death stories for both his sons and by now probably wished they were true. "Thousands got slaughtered in the ambush. They're very lucky to be alive."

"And therein lies the complication," Edmund growled.

"Well, I thought you should know." Nord stood, making as if to leave. "And about your wife's treason too. I'm sorry to have been the bearer of such bad news. It must be a terrible shock."

"Sit." Edmund lifted his hand again, this time in a gesture for him to stop. "You're not going yet."

"But sir, I . . ." This was going exactly as Nord had planned.

"We need to come to a mutual agreement, you and I."

"Of course." Nord settled back into the chair.

Edmund had him go over it all again—how Nord had met Seth in basic training, how Commander Regis had arranged for Seth to catch the skineater sick and then left him for dead, how he'd survived, albeit grossly scarred, and made his way to Triskelia where he'd met up with Eli. To kill him in defence of Edmund's title before Eli could ruin him. But instead his son, his favourite son, had betrayed him by joining the rebels.

Edmund had already known that Seth had survived the sick. His spies had told him as much. They'd been on Seth's trail all the way to Triban, but had lost him in the city. He'd ordered Regis to find both him and Eli and to get rid of them for real this time, and this is how it had turned out. He was surprised that Eli had made it to Triskelia unharmed, an unlikely accomplishment of his weaker son. He felt a small surge of what could almost be described as pride.

Details proved that Nord had indeed been at the battle at Triskelia, and had seen the boys there. But this prisoner he'd referred to, this informant . . . when Edmund had demanded to know who he was Nord had said little, except to say that, other than Regis, he was the only one who knew who he was.

Edmund could find out, and would, but it would take some time. He set aside his curiosity for now.

"Perhaps Seth is spying for us?" Edmund was desperate for this to somehow turn in his favour. Eli wasn't a threat in the way Seth could be, especially if Seth had switched sides and was aligned with the rebellion now. "Maybe his loyalty is still with us. Perhaps he'll return with valuable insider information?"

"It's possible." Nord worked on a pensive expression, as if he was actually giving the remark some consideration. "I suppose."

"But you don't think so."

"No, sir. I doubt he'll try to come back. Especially with the scars."

"And you're sure they both survived Triskelia?"

"Yes, sir." The time was right. Now he would deliver the zinger. "There is one more thing. I wasn't sure if I should tell you or not. But I believe you have a right to know."

"What?" Edmund was frustrated with Regis's lies. He'd reported that there were no survivors, and now, to find out that there were and that his sons might be among them, was news he was not prepared for. He'd already done whatever mourning he was going to do, and had acted as though they had been dead for months now anyway. What was he supposed to think about the two of them out there, together?

What he didn't know was that Nord wasn't certain that either of the boys had survived, but it suited Nord's plan to act as though they had. The next bit of news would make mincemeat of whatever was left of Edmund's composure, and Nord knew that at least this news was true.

"Regis's prisoner claims there was a third child." Nord watched Edmund's expression. "They were not twins, sir, as you'd been led to believe. Your wife bore triplets."

"Say again?"

Nord repeated himself. "Triplets, sir."

Edmund thought that's what he'd said. He groped his way to his chair and collapsed into it, his head pounding, the overwhelming confusion attacking him with an instant, pulverizing migraine. "I don't understand."

So Nord explained and Edmund struggled to listen despite the thick haze of his headache. Lisette had borne three children. The third, the girl, had been secreted away at birth, before the boys could go with her. They were never meant to be his. Lisette's plan had been to fake her death with the childbirth and then take the children back to Triskelia with her. He'd foiled the plan when he walked in and saw the boys while Lisette was struggling with the difficult birth of the third child—the triplet who was then whisked away to be raised in Triskelia.

Edmund's first clear thought was that maybe that meant Lisette had faked her death so many years later and she was alive too, that all three of them—four if there was this other child too—were out there somewhere, out of his control and getting up to who knew what in the name of bringing him down. Maybe she hadn't died in the bombing. Maybe she was alive. If the Group of Keys ever found out about her true identity . . .

Lisette. The room slipped away and he was back in the ballroom the day he met her, his arm around the slender waist of the most beautiful woman there. Who had she been, really? Had she ever been his? Even for a moment?

Out in the hall, her ear pressed against a glass held to the door, Francie sucked in her breath. He knew everything now. Or at least, everything she did. She would have to get word to the others. She wished she could tell Cook that the boys were alive, but she couldn't. Cook was not a rebel. Francie slipped the glass into her apron pocket and knocked lightly on the door.

The memories from that first, sweet dance collapsed, crashing Edmund back into the present. "What is it?" he hollered at the heavy carved door.

"Excuse me, Master." Francie opened it just enough for her to pop her head into the room. "Dinner is ready."

"We're not eating." Edmund dismissed her with a glare. "Leave us."

Nord's stomach rumbled in protest, but he said nothing. Food could wait. He'd find the kitchen after and help himself, perhaps to the maid as well as to supper. Right now he had to concentrate on keeping his grin to himself.

After leading his own subregiment in the ambush he'd gone AWOL and come straight to the Eastern Key, not getting off the express carriage even once, with what little he'd packed ahead of time as his only food and drink. This scheme was really and truly brilliant. Hands down, the best idea he'd ever had. He could see power forming in his favour as he spoke, building something between him and this political powerhouse. Never mind the Guard; he'd have everything he needed right here in the luxury of the Chancellor's estate.

"And now, sir . . ." Nord really had to work to keep the smile off his face. "I'd like to discuss the worth of this information, and the price of my loyalty to you."

"Ah, of course. It all comes down to a price, doesn't it?" Edmund rubbed his temples, the pain pounding between his ears. "Never mind *loyalty.* You mean the price of your silence. For what you know about my wife. My children."

"Semantics," Nord said.

"This is all so absurd!" Edmund scoffed. "Semantics? That's what you call it?"

"Call it what you will," Nord snapped. "You know full well what we're dealing with here."

"Indeed." Edmund squinted through his headache at the young man. "I'll call it blackmail, then, given that blackmail is exactly what this is. Cheap, cowardly blackmail."

"I don't know about cheap." Nord couldn't help it any more. "Imagine how swift your fall from grace would be once everyone knew about the traitors you harboured in your very own house. Your very own bed!" He steepled his fingers under his chin and finally allowed a great big grin to spread across his face. "I know the value of indiscretion, and I intend to make you pay for it."

[TWO]

CASCADÍA

9

The survivors headed away from the market in carts, on horseback, and on foot, travelling north once again, this time with provisions donated from sympathizers far and wide who'd made their way to the market to visit the prayer trees and to bring much-needed blankets and food preserves and shoes and pots and pans. Word had spread fast about the massacre, and the rumble of anger and grief was getting louder. The Triskelians would retreat and make a plan, Sabine told those who came looking for Zenith to serve quick justice on behalf of them all, and when the time came, justice would indeed be served.

Eli held back, watching the lines of Droughtlanders who'd come to see Zenith. They called her Auntie, a term of affection used to address all older women in the Droughtland. The term had also maintained Zenith's anonymity whenever she travelled outside of Triskelia, but now, what with hordes of the angry and the grief-stricken, there was no hiding who she was. Few were the Droughtlanders who hadn't lost a loved one either in the Colony of the Sicks or Triskelia itself. The remaining Triskelians could only hope the Guard wasn't on their trail. Just in case, though, Jack and Gavin were armed and had the task of protecting Zenith at all costs.

The group finally left behind the fervent masses and travelled comfortably for a couple of days, the weather mild, the nights cool but not too cold. And then the terrain grew increasingly rugged, until they had to leave the carts and continue on horseback and on foot. Zenith had regained enough strength by then to sit up on one of the horses. Sabine sat right behind her, steadying her when she dozed off or when she couldn't balance herself as the horses stumbled over the scree.

At times the path was so narrow that Eli had to inch along with his back pressed against the rocky cliffs. Even thinking about the severe drop made him lightheaded and dizzy. He'd never experienced anything like this, not even when he and Nappo and Teal had crossed the mountain range after the Foothills Market.

"It's not that bad." Nappo followed behind him, holding Teal's hand and carrying a heavy pack. "The horses can handle it, and me and Teal can stand side by side, so it ain't as narrow as you think."

"I don't fancy the thought of meeting my maker right now," Eli said. "And if I so much as sneeze, I might just fall over."

"You're afraid of heights, aren't you?" Nappo grinned, but he kept the jokes and ribbing to himself. "Even after the trapeze?"

"That's nothing compared to this, Nappo, and you know it." Eli crept forward, willing logic to prevail over terror. Why did he always seem to choose fear over bravery or even just plain, beautifully simple indifference? Everyone else was managing the trail well enough. Why not him? It seemed that just when he'd conquered one fear another cropped up to keep him in his place.

Trust that you are not alone.

Eli was becoming accustomed to the voice, and was beginning to trust its messages. Testing this, he dared a glance over the edge. The cliff cut straight down. He could barely see the tiny river snaking along the gully far below. This mountain had teeth and a bad attitude, and would pull him over and eat him up and leave his bones on the ground thousands of metres below. He teetered back and caught his breath.

"See? I'm not afraid." He took another breath. "I'm not."

"Okay, Eli." Nappo shared a grin with his little brother. "Whatever you say."

"Let's see *you* get that close to the edge then."

"Nuh-uh," Nappo said as he and Teal shook their heads. "We're not crazy."

"Oh, sure." Eli carried on up the trail, Bullet at his heel. He felt a little more confident, and, blessed be the highers, a little less afraid. "All talk and no action. What a surprise."

He hadn't told anyone about the voice. And it wasn't a voice, not really. It was a sense of things. Almost like he was psychic or something. He'd tried to talk to Nappo about it, but had stopped himself. It sounded crazy, and he didn't *feel* crazy, so he'd keep it to himself a while longer. Maybe he'd had a head injury during the blasts back in Triskelia? Or maybe he was tapping into something he'd just never be able to explain. But increasingly it brought him peace and calm, and he was glad for that.

THEY CAMPED IN THE MOUNTAINS, with the thin air and remnants of the last spring snow. They were comfortable though, kitted out in their donated sweaters and thick sleeping bags and woollen blankets. And they could have fires too, now that they'd left any possibility of a Guard ambush long behind them. With a mountain cliff cutting up one side and dropping hundreds of metres straight down the other, the Guard would have nowhere to hide.

On the second night Anya joined Eli at the fire, and along with her arrived the dank smell that always accompanied her now. She rarely washed and was always tugging at her clothes, as if she wanted to tear them off and run screaming from a life that had turned so cruel and unforgiving. Eli shuffled a little away from her and her ripeness, but then he felt bad.

Simple kindness, Eli.

He breathed through his mouth, put an arm around her, and pulled her closer to him, feeling suddenly very old and fatherly.

"Your mother loved bonfires." Anya stared at the flames dancing against the black night. "Any kind of fire, actually. *Elle aimait jouer avec le feu.* She could spin it and breathe it, and just watch it for hours. She loved fire." Since Charis's death, Anya was rarely in the present. She spent most of her time reliving a past well before Charis was even a possibility. Her stories were long and elaborate and hard to listen to, what with all the various players and meticulous, somewhat mundane adherence to detail. "She always smelled of smoke. Like a perfume. We'd sing songs and bang drums and dance, as if we were pagan goddesses at Beltane."

Lisette? His mother? Eli had a hard time picturing her dancing with abandon, let alone banging on a drum like some kind of savage. His mother could execute a flawless waltz and could play the daintiest of minuets on the piano. But Eli valued Anya's stories and listened despite the mostly tedious ramblings about dresses and meals and who said this and who said that.

"Your mother and I would howl at the moon and spin ourselves dizzy under the stars until we collapsed on the grass." Anya closed her eyes and smiled. "And then we'd lie there, staring up as the galaxy spun above us." She opened her eyes and locked her gaze on the flames, as if she were watching the stars all over again. "*C'est encore si claire.* Your mother and I were so young then. Just girls. Lisette was no older than Sabine."

Across the fire, Sabine looked up. She too valued Anya's recent babblings. She was gleaning more information about the stranger who was her mother than she ever had through Nana's or anyone else's stories. She cast a glance at Zenith, sitting statuesque beside her as if she were holding court in her cozy Triskelian quarters and not here on a cold, rugged mountainside.

"Are you all right, Zen Zen?" She topped up the old woman's mug of tea and tucked another blanket over her lap.

"Yes, child." Zenith patted her hand. "I'm fine."

Celeste nodded at her from the other side of Zenith. "We're fine, dear. Go join the other children."

But she was not going to join the "other children." She didn't even feel like a child any more. The real children were all asleep, piled into one huge tent, which is how they liked it. The orphans especially couldn't bear being separated from the other children, not ever. They held hands as they hiked up the mountain and would cry miserably if one of them was out of sight for even the time it took to go pee behind a tree.

No. Sabine was not a child any more. Had she ever really been? Was any motherless child ever truly a child? The orphans in her care seemed like children, but she knew how their hearts had aged since their parents' violent deaths.

She didn't correct her grandmother though. She circled the fire instead and sat on the other side of Anya, the log cold and damp and lumpy on her bottom, the smell tickling her nose. She waited for Anya to acknowledge her, but she just kept her gaze on the flames, transfixed. How Sabine wanted the old Anya back. The mother one, the playful one, the disciplinarian and adorer.

"Anya?" She took Anya's hand. *"Ca va?"* Her wedding ring knocked loosely against her knuckle. She'd lost so much weight, more than the rest of them.

Eli leaned forward and looked across Anya at his sister. They hadn't spoken since before the day of the ritual. He missed her but was angry with her too, and wasn't quite ready to work for her forgiveness, which is what she seemed to want.

Sabine squeezed Anya's hand until Anya turned her blank stare on her, and it quickened just enough for Sabine to know she was as present as she could be.

"Tell me more about my mother," Sabine said.

Eli leaned forward. *"Our* mother."

"Tell us more, Anya." Sabine resisted the steam of anger she felt rising. "Tell us about when she was young."

"I will tell you how your parents met, *oui*?"

"Yes, please." Eli sucked in his breath. He'd heard bits of the story, but it wasn't something anyone freely talked about, either because it opened old wounds or because it was old news. He bit back the flurry of questions and prayed that Anya's narrative would be easier to follow than some of her ramblings as of late.

"It was the Doomsday Vault that brought your parents together," Anya began.

Eli knew about the vault. The brainchild of the Global Agriculture Diversity Trust, an independent body at the time, the vault was meant to be a kind of Noah's Ark for seeds from over ten thousand different crops, to preserve them in the face of global catastrophes such as nuclear war and climate change. When the vault was ready to accept the seeds the planet was hotter than it had been in four hundred years. It was a brilliant idea, and had been actualized just in time. Seed donations came from across the globe, packaged in foil and stored at such cold temperatures that they could last hundreds, even thousands, of years. The vault was safe on a tiny island in the Senechal Archipelago, not far from the North Pole, behind reinforced concrete walls and electrified fences, and was further protected by the island's generous population of roaming polar bears.

"There were other seed banks around the world," Anya continued. "But the Trust had designed this one to avoid the pitfalls that had shut others down—lack of funding, war, waning electricity, natural disasters. *Des choses comme ça.*"

Eli's hope thinned as Anya droned on about global agriculture and seed stock preservation. He'd be lucky if his parents even made a cameo. He warmed his hands at the fire and concentrated on Anya's voice, just in case it got interesting.

He'd read about what she was telling them, in the books from the rooms under the gardens. The arctic seed bank, once stocked and locked, was an international news curiosity at first. But as decades and then centuries went by and all the things it had been built to withstand wore down the world around it, the Doomsday Vault was forgotten—the fences long rusted, the electricity long since failed, the polar bears nearly extinct. The seeds were still okay, with the vault kept just cool enough within the surrounding permafrost, but its security was at risk should anyone think to raid it, and it was only a matter of time before the thought would occur to someone. And so the Group of Keys organized an expedition to open the vault and claim possession of the precious seeds. Dignitaries came to the tiny island from all across the globe, both to celebrate the opening and, more importantly, to ensure their stake in the vault's contents. Triskelian spies were there too. Eli perked up as Anya neared this part of the tale. Spies!

"It was so cold outside, the wind like ice. A woman stood at the back of the crowd, one hand on her hat, the other holding her cape together at her throat." Anya arranged her own hands just so. "That woman was your mother."

"How did she get there?" Eli asked.

"Ah, yes. Two years earlier she'd gone undercover. Oh, your *grandpère*, he was so mad. He did not want her to go. '*Non! Jamais!*'" Anya's imitation of Pierre was uncanny. Her eyes took on a faraway look as she lowered her voice. "'I won't allow it. It is all too quick. It is all *ainsi mal!*' But your maman, she insisted. And there was no time to argue. The family that ran the bookshop in the Southwestern Key were Triskelian sympathizers. They were moving to the Northwestern Key for the father's health, but the daughter, she died from the skineater. The parents, they were thinking. Even though they are so sad, they invite Lisette to come in place of their daughter. She looked just like her, like you two." She furrowed her brow, taking on Pierre's grumbly voice again. "'*Non!* I won't allow it!' But your mother. She is stubborn. She went anyway. And he was so mad."

Anya pulled her eyes from the fire, as if finished. Both Eli and Sabine were sitting forward, leaning into her every word now. They desperately wanted her to keep going. The siblings shared a glance, not sure if they should urge her on or just be still and see if she'd pick up the thread of the story again, stitching it together seamlessly as if it were one of her elaborate circus costumes. Eli and Sabine each let out a careful breath as she started again.

"Your mother, she met her new *famille*. She travelled with them to the Key, she worked in their shop. The family was francophone, so it didn't matter that she spoke French, but she was no Keylander, so it took time before she could talk their way. She kept to herself and made their little plot in the community gardens beautiful with vegetables and flowers. Everyone noticed it—and a botanist from the Key gardens hired her on as an apprentice. Oh, how Lisette wanted to go home, but it was a chance to go further, find out more. Another three years pass, she is now lead botanist too, equal to the woman who trained her. And then the Doomsday Vault trip was planned, and she was chosen to go when the other woman fell ill.

"On the day of the opening ceremony your maman, she couldn't hear the speeches for the wind, and so she watched the crowd instead. A young man behind her caught her glancing over her shoulder, looking at everyone. He held her gaze, flirting with her, and then he pushed his way through the crowd until he was beside her and he says to your maman, 'I am Edmund Maddox, Chief Regent, Eastern Key.'"

Eli nodded. At last, here was his father.

"Your maman knew the custom. She held out her hand, palm down, fingers together like a Keyland lady, and gave him her name. He did not leave her side. He crowded her that night, swept her onto the dance floor despite her protests. But he was a good dancer, *très beau* . . . charming, attentive, *and* he was a Chief Regent.

"Back on the mainland the next day, he helped her from the boat and invited her to dine with him at a gala dinner for the Chief Regents. She accepted, *bien sur,* and that evening, while the dinner conversation fluttered around her and she smiled and she laughed and commented at all the appropriate times, she could not believe she was in the company of the upper echelon of the Keys, and with no one having a clue about who she really was. It was thrilling for your maman, and pleasing, and terrifying. This was the sign from her highers, she was sure. She was meant to keep on. It wasn't time to go home just yet."

Anya stopped there. She folded her hands in her lap as if she'd set the story aside, as if it had been an embroidery she was working on. She lifted her face and looked clearly at Eli and Sabine. "That is how they met."

"Thank you, Anya," Sabine said. Eli thanked her too.

"I am not crazy," she added, which made no sense at all.

"*Je sais.*" Sabine took her hand. "I know."

Eli wasn't so sure. Something had come over Anya as she told the story, and now it had gone. A spirit, or a current. Something that had fuelled her.

"I miss your maman," Anya said.

"Me too." Sabine patted Anya's hand.

"She was smart like you. And so good at the circus arts like you too. She would help me on the trapeze. I wasn't as good at it as she was, and I was so mad. She was good at everything, and I was not. Only sewing. But still, she would help me, because we wanted to do an act together, even though I wasn't very good. I was clumsy, not graceful like she was."

"I'm sure you were better than you think," Sabine said.

Anya shook her head. "Not me. I was awkward and always in a rush. But your maman . . . she could fly. She had wings. She was a bird. She was a beautiful, rainbow bird, with wings of silk, and taffeta feathers."

Anya abruptly sucked in her breath, pulled her hand away from Sabine, and stood. She levelled the siblings with a cool glare.

"What are you doing?"

Eli shrank. "You were talking about my mother."

"*Our* mother," Sabine mocked. She stood too, taking Anya's hand back in her own. "It's okay, Anya. Shall I help you to your tent?"

"Is Charis asleep already? I don't remember putting her to bed."

Sabine and Eli looked at each other, their discomfort momentarily bridging their differences.

"Yes, she's asleep," Eli finally said, because what else could he say?

And suddenly their differences were back. "No, Anya." Sabine frowned at him. She took Anya's other hand too, grasping them both. "Charis is dead." Anya started pulling away, mewling like a kitten, but Sabine held her firmly. "She's not asleep. She died. You buried her. Remember?"

"*Oui. Oui, d'accord.*" Anya nodded. "If she wakes she'll wonder where I am. She'll want a cuddle. And Trace is playing cards." She laughed, but it was unsettling, and odd. "I'm sure he's winning. He always does."

"Definitely." Eli sighed with relief to be back on solid ground. "He's an excellent player."

Sabine let her go. She and Eli watched her make her way into the dark, toward the tents.

"Aren't you going to go with her?"

Sabine shook her head. "Would you want to be there when she finds an empty tent?"

"Good point."

The two of them sat on the log again, stretching their hands toward the warmth of the fire.

"Maybe she *is* crazy," Sabine said after a stretch of silence during which they both tried to shake off the macabre shivers. "Although Maman *was* a bird in her trapeze act. Anya made her costume. I've seen it. She keeps it in the closet in her sewing room. Or used to, I guess."

"Oh." Eli tried to imagine his poised, regal mother soaring through the air in a bird costume. He knew she would've been graceful, but it seemed almost comical. He was more comfortable thinking of the botanist side of her, because that's what he knew.

"I'm sorry." Sabine directed the words at the fire, but Eli knew they were meant for him. "I don't really blame you for everything. Not really. I'm just so mad. And sad, and tired."

"Me too." He slung his arm around the sister he barely knew. "I'm sorry too." His triplet, and he understood next to nothing about her. "Hey."

"What?" She glanced at him out of the corner of her eye, her chin down, head tilted just so, in the exact way Lisette did. Along with her medallion she was still wearing their mother's pearl choker, the one Eli had brought from the Key and given to her the night of the feast.

"What's your middle name?" he suddenly wanted to know.

"Claire." She looked away from him. "Yours is Edmund."

"I didn't choose it." Eli hadn't given it any thought before, but now he did. He hated the name he shared with both Seth and their father. "Why Claire?"

"After Maman's little sister, who died."

There was so much Eli didn't know. If he did nothing but ask questions for the rest of his life, would he ever know everything?

"How'd she die?"

"The skineater sick," Sabine said. "She worked with Trace, collecting orphans. They were always so careful. No one's sure how she got it."

They were the only ones at the fire now. One by one, everyone else had either headed off to bed or joined the other fire, where a new game of Seduce was about to begin.

"Tell me more." Eli prayed for time. More of it. The return of time lost. New times with no struggles. But if all he had was right now, he'd make the most of it.

So Sabine told him about when she was a little girl, when she and Zari and Lia were in the tumbling troupe. It wasn't the kind of story Eli wanted, but he knew it was exactly the kind of story Sabine needed to tell, and so he listened, until the fire crumbled into embers and they stumbled to their tents, already half asleep.

10

꩜

The next day, after several hours of hiking and just when the children were starting to grumble about wanting lunch, the trail ended and in front of them a tall, wrought-iron gate crossed the path. It was rusty and ornate, and reminded Eli of some of the older estates in the Keys. It struck him as very odd to see something like that at the top of an inhospitable mountain in the middle of nowhere. A fence of similar wrought iron reached away from the gate on both sides, forming a stern perimeter, the edges of which Eli could not see.

The children clambered at the gate, trying to scale it, but it was tall and had jagged, unwelcoming tips making spearheads of the tops. Two armed boys—a little older than Eli maybe—ambled toward them from a watchtower, offering greetings and broad smiles, guns slung over their backs. Beyond them an even narrower path carried on, straight up to what looked like a fairy-tale castle perched on the very tip-top of the mountain. This was Cascadia, the weather station and their destination.

"Friends! *Amis!*" The shorter of the two young men unlocked the gate and swung it open while the taller one, red-haired and gangly, headed straight for Zenith, who'd been helped off her horse and was steadying herself with a walking stick in each hand.

"Zen Zen!" He embraced her in a tight hug, lifting her off her feet. "You are looking regal, as usual. *Si belle!* And so young!"

"Yvon! *Mon petit choux.*" She swatted him playfully. "You are blind."

"I'm not. I know a timeless beauty when I see one. Gavin!" Yvon set Zenith down, making sure she was firm on her feet before opening his arms again. "It's great to see you, brother. It's been too long."

Gavin came forward and embraced his younger brother whom he hadn't seen in over a year and a half. His mouth at his ear, he muttered, "Turn it down, Yvon—think of what they've been through. Kill the cheery chum act, would you?"

"Sorry. Of course." Yvon helped Zenith step aside and let the others pass. He gawked at Eli, and Eli could only imagine the questions he had swirling in his carrot top. Toby caught up then and clamped himself onto Yvon's leg. Without taking his eyes off Eli, Yvon swung Toby up into his arms.

"Little fox." He put his nose to Toby's in their private greeting.

"Big fox," Toby said as they rubbed noses. "Everybody's dead," he blurted matter-of-factly.

"That can't be right." Yvon hugged him tight. "You're okay."

"But there was a bomb. People died all over. Dead, dead, dead." He turned his palms up to the heavens, his broken arm in a proper cast now. "It's all gone."

"I know, little fox." Yvon nodded. "But now you're here. Where it's safe."

"He's right," Zenith said. "We'll be safe here while we make a plan."

Toby shrugged, unconvinced.

"Do you want to ride up on the horse?" Sabine asked Zenith, more for the opportunity to change the subject than anything else.

"No. You go on ahead, child." Zenith reached up to touch a hand to Yvon's cheek. "Yvon will see to it that I arrive in one piece. We will take our time and have a visit."

Sabine frowned. "It's still a long hike up the hill."

"It will be good for me."

"No, it won't." The others had gone ahead now, and it was just Sabine and Eli hanging back with the horse Zenith had just climbed off. "You're weak, and tired. Why won't you let me help you back onto the horse?"

"You'd be up there in two minutes," Eli added. "It would take you forever to walk."

Annoyance flashed briefly across the old woman's face. "No. Thank you."

"I don't mind, Zen Zen." Yvon gestured at the horse. "I'll walk beside you. We can still have our visit."

Zenith stabbed the earth with one of her walking sticks. "No!"

The three others each took a tiny, involuntary step back, surprised.

"I'm sorry, Zen Zen." Yvon put a protective arm around her thin, bony shoulder. "I didn't mean to start anything."

"And you didn't, child." Zenith started up the hill, placing her walking sticks firmly in front of her as she did. "I simply want to walk on my own."

Eli and Sabine stood with their hands on their hips as Yvon and Toby hurried after Zenith.

"You feel as old as I feel?" Eli asked.

"A million years old," Sabine said, clucking for the horse to follow her as they made their way up the hill, the ragtag end to the group. "Galactically ancient."

THE CASTLE HAD TURRETS and towers and a courtyard, even a moat and a drawbridge.

"Langdale Gibson built it long before the Keys. He was some crazy eccentric who fancied the place as a refugee camp for books," Sabine said as they neared. "When people started burning books for fuel he saved as many as he could and brought them up here. When he'd amassed them all he never left the mountain again."

They stopped midway across the lowered drawbridge. "Have a look." She pointed down at the dark waters. Eli looked. It took a moment, but his eyes adjusted to the murk, and he could see plump rainbow trout slipping through the water. "Farmed. To eat."

Eli's stomach started grumbling immediately. He could practically taste the salty meat now.

Once inside, Eli endured the customary oohs and aahs as everyone greeted him. It was on a much smaller scale here though, with only about a dozen new faces giving him the awed looks and ceaseless comments about looking so much like Sabine. After the hellos, he and Nappo and Teal were led to their quarters along with several others: first through the great room, lined floor to ceiling with books, then down a wide hall, also lined with stuffed bookshelves, up an expansive staircase, and finally down another book-filled hall to a great big box of a room at the end. That room was also floor-to-ceiling books, the musty age of them a little bitter to the nose. Diffused daylight eked through the windows, stretching columns of sunlit dust to the floor. Nappo drew the heavy curtains and the three of them each chose a bunk and flopped down for a much needed rest.

Eli lay in the dark, the sudden quiet turning the volume up on his thoughts. The castle with its winding corridors and many staircases reminded him of Triskelia. He knew they were here only to devise a plan, but honestly, he wanted to stay. He was tired of moving, and tired of being afraid that the Guard would resurface to finish off what they'd started. Eli wanted nothing more than peace.

Peace. It was a small word, with soft edges and a hopeful halo. He wanted it not only for himself but for the world around him too. Why was he the only one who didn't want to take up arms? He'd had a taste of it the night of the ambush, when he'd lashed out at the two Guardies about to attack him. It made him ill to think that he might've killed a man, even in self-defence, let alone two.

He wanted nothing more to do with any kind of violence. The more he saw of it, the more he abhorred it. At first he'd thought it was cowardice. But the more he contemplated the implications of any kind of bloodshed the more it made no sense at all. When would it end? Would it ever, so long as aggression always led to revenge?

SABINE SLEPT IN that first morning. She woke slowly, stretching her arms out into the cold room and then pulling them back into the warmth of the duvet. She snuggled lower in the bed and shut her eyes, trying to recapture the blissful nothingness of sleep. It had been the best sleep since they'd left Triskelia, even though the beds at Cascadia weren't as thick, the pillows were smelly and flat, and the blankets smelled of mould and wood smoke. It was luxurious nonetheless and she wanted it to never end. She shuffled to the edge of the bed and glanced at the floor. As soon as her feet hit it, the painful, confusing world would be in her face again. Everyone wanting something from her, needing her to do something, decide something, *be* something. She flopped back into the centre of the bed and pulled the duvet up over her head.

The door to the room opened and Toby barrelled in ahead of a girl who looked much older than her seventeen years. Just inside the room, she hesitated.

Mireille.

Quinn's sister.

They weren't twins, but they were only ten months apart and looked unnervingly alike. Sabine hadn't seen Mireille since that fateful Night Circus tour had returned to Triskelia after Quinn's death.

"Look!" Toby jumped onto the bed, knocking the wind out of Sabine. "Look who I found! I brought her for you."

"Some present." Mireille stayed at the doorway, her arms crossed, a small, cautious smile on her face. "Hi."

"Hi." Sabine didn't know where to start or what to say. Mireille resembled Quinn so closely that even just glancing at her made her heart hurt. She grabbed Toby instead. "Oh, you great big monster!" She pulled the covers over him. "I'm going to bury you under the sea!"

"I heard about Zari and Lia." Mireille took a tentative step toward the bed.

Sabine sat up and nodded. Toby popped his head out.

"I told Mireille. About the bombs." He nodded, the expression on his face befitting an old man and not a small child. "All the dead people."

"It's over now, baby." Sabine pulled him to her and hugged him. "How about you go bring Mireille the rest of the way?"

"That rhymes!" Toby hopped off the bed and took the girl's hand. "This way, Mireille. I'll save you from the sharks."

Mireille smiled and let him lead her across the room. "You don't even know what a shark is, Toby."

"I do!" Toby let go of her hand and went behind her and pushed. Mireille resisted, but only for his sake. "It's a big fish with teeth and it will eat you up!"

"No, don't feed me to the sharks! No, please!" Mireille rolled her eyes at Sabine, until Toby, with much grunting and heaving, had shoved her all the way to the bed. Sabine patted the comforter.

"Come aboard?"

"Oh, Sabine." Mireille sighed as she sat. "It's been too long."

"And it still hurts," Sabine murmured. She helped Toby climb back onto the bed.

"I'm a pirate! This is my ship!" He stomped along the length of the mattress, stepping on Sabine's calf.

"Ow!" Sabine grabbed him. "Ahoy, matey. Time to walk the plank." She set him back on the floor. "Give me and Mireille a minute, okay? We have to talk grown-up stuff."

Toby frowned but then swung an imaginary sword at the two girls. "I'll get you!" He backed out of the room, brandishing his sword as he went. "Argh!" he hollered as he disappeared into the hall.

The girls stared at each other for a long moment, then clutched each other and wept.

"I'm sorry!" Sabine cried. "I am so sorry."

"No, no." Mireille shook her head. "It wasn't your fault."

"But Quinn didn't want to perform that night, and I made him! And then he fell and I just know it's because he wasn't feeling up to it. Those birds should never have bothered him. It is my fault! It is!" Sabine wished she could tell her everything, but she'd made her promises and so she would keep them.

"My brother would not have climbed that ladder unless he wanted to." Mireille wiped her eyes and pulled back enough to look Sabine in hers. "You know how stubborn he was. I was upset. I just needed someone to blame, and it should've been the Chancellor, I know, but then it would've been pointless. He doesn't care. I wanted someone to hurt for what happened. You were his best friend. His circus partner. You were the easiest target to attack, so I did."

"Well it did hurt." Sabine's tears fell freely. "And I still hurt. I think about him all the time."

Mireille had literally attacked Sabine, screaming at her and pummelling her with her fists as she stepped down from the caravan that first night back. Sabine had simply taken it. It felt good to be hurt. After all the sympathy everyone else was dishing out it felt right to be punished for something she felt responsible for. But that was before she knew about Seth and the trained pigeons. Should she tell Mireille about that now? And about Jack's part in it?

"I should've apologized before I left," Mireille said.

"No. I understand. If I were you I would've done the same thing."

Mireille was to begin her training as the cloudminder's apprentice before the Night Circus's return. When she heard of her brother's death, though, she postponed her trip to be home for the memorial. Although Quinn's body had been burned on a pyre their first day back in the Droughtland, Sabine had personally carried the small wooden box of his ashes across the continent to Triskelia for the ceremony.

"Still. I'm sorry I left still so angry."

"Really, Mireille. I understand."

"I should've stayed. We both loved him the most, and we should've been there for each other."

"I don't know if we could have," Sabine murmured. "We all deal with death in our own separate ways."

"Like Jack?" Mireille frowned. "Quinn's ashes hadn't even cooled before he hooked up with Gavin."

"We all cope in different ways," Sabine said again.

"Some are more right than others."

"No, Mireille." Sabine shook her head. "That's not fair. You don't know what anyone else goes through." If ever there was a time to tell her everything, it was now.

But she didn't want to tell Mireille the truth: that Jack and Quinn had broken up the night before the fall, as they set up camp outside the Eastern Key. That was the reason Quinn felt so miserable. He hadn't slept. He'd barely eaten. He'd wandered around all day in a daze. And

Sabine had bullied him into performing. *Come on, Quinn. You knew it was bound to happen. You said so yourself.* Quinn had shaken his head. *But why now? Why here? Why couldn't he have waited for a better time?* Sabine stared at him, her arms crossed. *And when is a good time to dump someone, exactly?* Quinn shrugged. He offered her a slight grin. *When you can do it first. I was going to, you know. After our last fight. Bastard beat me to it.* They'd laughed. Quinn never swore, and so it sounded funny coming from him. *Come on, it'll get your mind off him.* Sabine handed Quinn his costume. *Don't make me go out there all alone.*

And then he'd fallen, when that pigeon swooped him.

Mireille shrugged. "Still."

"Don't be mad at Jack." There was so much more to say. Jack had asked her not to tell anyone they'd broken up. He'd said he didn't want anyone to think Quinn had jumped, even though he and Sabine both knew that wasn't even the remotest possibility. She'd agreed, and hadn't told anyone. Not even Mireille. Should she tell her now? She'd promised Jack, so no. "We've lost so many," she said finally. "We've got to hang on to everyone who's left."

The door opened again. It was Toby, with an old leather patch over his eye now, a handkerchief taming his curls, a stick for a sword, and a posse of fellow pirates. They'd raided the dress-up trunk in the playroom that hadn't seen much use since the last time a young family had worked at the station.

"Grrr! Ahoy!" He and the others stormed the bed. "This is our ship!"

They climbed all over the girls. Mireille and Sabine locked eyes for a moment and then dug in with the children, tickling and tossing them around, putting aside their own grief to give the children a respite from their own.

ELI WANDERED THE BOOK-LINED HALLS of the castle, getting his bearings. It was a labyrinth, not as sprawling and complex as Triskelia, but still daunting. He climbed a steep staircase with worn stone steps, around and around, up and up, exiting off into another corridor with yet more shelves stacked with books. Eli wouldn't be surprised if the castle contained a copy of every single book ever published.

The sound of children playing, screaming happily, caught him short. He hadn't heard the sound of joy since the night of the feast, and it beckoned him down the hall. The door to the room was open. In each corner was a four-poster bed with a canopy, just like the ones back in the Key. Each bed had a gang of children jumping and wrestling upon it.

"My ship'll bomb yours!" Teal yelled. He had a patch over his eye, as did all the others. They had hats and capes, and swords of all sorts, some toy ones, but mostly sticks and rulers and canes. The children leapt from one ship to another, fencing each other. In the centre of the biggest bed, Sabine's bed, Mireille and Sabine sat back to back, hands bound, the two girls tied together at the waist. Sabine saw him standing in the door, gawking.

"Oh! Help us, Captain Eli!" She struggled playfully against the scarf tied sloppily around her wrists. "We are two brave pirate queens, but we were outnumbered by these evil sea bandits. They have captured our ship and are stealing our gold! You must do something!"

But Eli wasn't looking at his sister. He was looking at the other girl. Her cheeks were pink from laughing, her lips rosy and plump, her olive skin pale against her long black curls. She did look like a pirate queen. She was beautiful, her slender shoulders pulled back, her knees folded under her.

There she is. In that moment Eli knew they would have a future. What kind he wasn't sure, but he felt as if he'd known her forever. *That's her.* It was the voice, it was him, it was the entire universe in agreement.

"Eli?" Teal pulled him into the room. "You okay?"

And then Toby was hanging off him, claiming him for his ship. Teal plucked Toby off. "Eli?" Eli could not take his eyes off the girl.

"There you are," she said. Eli felt his knees weaken. Did she feel it too?

"My brother Eli." Sabine let the scarf loosen around her wrists. She pulled free while the children protested and scrambled to tie her up again. "Eli, this is Mireille. Quinn's sister."

"Hello," Mireille said as Sabine freed her hands too. Mireille offered one to him. Eli took it, and felt again that deep sense of fatefulness. He didn't want to let go.

ELI STAYED IN THE ROOM for a while, playing the good captain while the children leapt from bed to bed *yar*-ing and *ahoy*-ing and growling, brandishing their makeshift swords. They played with a dedicated vigour, having gone so long without any kind of play at all. Eli tried to talk to Mireille a couple of times, but when he opened his mouth only gibberish came out. He was awed by her. There was something special about her, something more than what he'd ever seen or felt with Zari.

He almost slapped himself after that thought. Zari was dead! And here he was falling over himself with a brand-new crush. He threw down his walking-stick sword and fled from the room, horrified. He'd actually forgotten Zari was dead. He'd forgotten her altogether. How was that possible?

"Eli?" Teal ran after him, but Sabine grabbed his arm.

"Not so fast, Blackbeard." She hauled Teal onto her ship and started tying him to one of the posters. "Let him go, hon," she whispered. "He'll be okay." She kept her eye on the door though, wondering if Eli would reappear. Something had just happened. She wasn't sure what, but something. It wasn't any shared sense that told her so either. It was obvious. The children saw Eli's abrupt, troubled departure, and their swords faltered and their play slowed as they tried to understand. Sabine knew she needed to recapture their abandon.

"You're my slave now." She turned her attention back to Teal. He watched her, his expression unsure. She touched his cheek. "It's okay, Teal. Really."

"He doesn't look okay."

"He'll be all right. We all will." Sabine winked at him. "Help me get the game going again, okay, pirate?"

"Okay. I guess."

Sabine leapt to the floor, claimed Eli's sword, and poked Teal with the blunt tip of it. "I've got you now! You're going to walk the plank! Ahar!"

The children glanced at each other, still wary. Sabine thought all was lost, that the tears would start again and the sadness return. But the urge to play, the *need* to play, won out, and within seconds they were all back on the high seas, fighting feuds and imaginary swells aboard their four-poster pirate ships.

11

❦

After only a week in Triban, Seth's army of boy soldiers was now one hundred strong. He'd set them up in a warehouse gutted by fire. There'd been other squatters there, but one gunshot into the roof and they knew he was serious. Seth invited the boys among them to stay, and the rest took off. And so the boy soldiers moved in.

Only a few boys had dared ask him what their army was actually *for*. Seth's reply was always the same: "All in good time, kid. You'll see." For the most part, though, the boys simply didn't care about the whys. They were just happy to have a roof over their heads and the promise of a meal when it could be scrounged up.

Seth had paired them all up, letting the boys choose their buddy and telling them that under no circumstances were they ever to separate. The children thought this was great: they got to hang out with their best friend, or new best friend anyway. Seth watched the bonds form as the boys returned after each day of thieving and bullying. He let them go each morning. He knew they'd come back. The boys were like dogs—they'd go where the food was, and despite their wild time on the street they did want direction, however foreign and awkward it felt at first. Seth was their meal ticket in a city where food was almost as scarce as potable water. Best of all, he was their protector too, keeping them safe in a city where children were bought, sold, and consumed, then tossed aside with no one to look for them if they went missing.

By the end of the first week they were all coming home to him, for food, for shelter, for safety.

ON THE SECOND NIGHT in their new quarters, Seth sent Amon to summon the boys for a meeting. He ordered them into neat lines in front of him, even if that was the only thing neat about them. They were a filthy, snot-nosed bunch, some kited on dust and probably half of them riddled by some kind of sick or another. What did it matter though? Sicks were everywhere. There was no point trying to avoid them. They'd get you in the end, no matter what. The scars that covered Seth, including his face, were a reminder of his own battle against the skineater sick. It was a reminder of Rosa too, the Droughtland girl who'd nursed him away from the lure of death. He pushed her out of his mind and strode between the lines of seated boys, one hand behind his back, the other gripping a carved walking stick Ori and Finn had brought back for him the night before. It had a skull carved out of the wood at the top, with grooves for his fingers.

"I said hands palm down on the ground at your sides!" He caught a boy's arm with the stick.

"The floor's slimy," the boy murmured. "And there're bugs."

Seth stopped. He squared his shoulders. The boys tittered with quiet, nervous chatter.

"Silence!"

He jabbed the boy's scrawny chest with his stick. "Get up."

"I'm sorry, mister!" The boy stood. "I am! I shouldn't a said anything!"

Seth placed the tip of his stick in the small of the boy's back and walked him to the front of the group.

"You don't want your hands to get wet. Is that right?"

"I'm sorry, Mister Seth." The boy's shoulders slumped forward as he tried to make himself smaller. "It don't matter. Really!"

"Put your hands up!"

The boy slowly stretched his hands above him, and managed between the tears to say, "Are you going to shoot me?"

"No." Seth smiled. This was so easy. So simple. So cheap. "You are going to stand there with your hands in the air until I say you can move. Amon will watch you, see that you do it right. Understood?"

The boy nodded, a look of relief betraying his attempts at modest respect.

"Good." Seth left him and resumed his inspection of his boys. "Who is this boy's comrade?"

The boys looked at one another, not knowing what the word meant.

"Your buddy," Seth explained. "You will call them your comrade from now on. Now. Who is it?"

The boy who'd been sitting beside the first one raised his hand and lowered his head as if he might get whacked just for admitting to it.

"Get up."

"But I didn't do anything." The boy still sat, his cheeks pale with fright. "I been good. Honest."

Seth strode back to the first boy and before anyone could've known what was about to happen, Seth hit him hard across the back with his stick. The boy crumpled to the floor with a yelp.

"Get up!"

Amon hauled the boy back onto his feet.

"Hands back in the air!"

The boy tried to stop his tears, and did what he was told.

"You!" Seth pointed his stick at the second boy. "Get up here and do as he's doing."

The second boy joined the first. The first boy's arms were starting to quiver with the effort of keeping them up. Tears rolled down his face but he remained motionless, arms up. The second boy did the same.

Once more, Seth began his survey of the boys. A plump rat scurried across a counter along the wall. A steady trickle of rain pattered onto the floor from a leak in the corner. The warehouse smelled of rot and damp and piss. He would have better someday. A real army, and real barracks. But for now, this would do.

He surveyed the decrepit boy soldiers for a long moment, and then began. "I have fed you, housed you. I have kept you safe. Correct?"

"Yes, Mister Seth!" they responded in unison.

Seth bristled. He badly wanted them to use *sir*, but as it was a verboten word outside the Keys, he had to make do.

"You each have a partner you have chosen, correct? Your new comrade."

"Yes, Mister Seth!"

"All of you, if you are not sitting beside your comrade, find him and stand at attention in your pairs."

He let them have more time than Commander Regis would ever have given. He was not like Commander Regis. He was a much more generous leader. He earned their respect by taking care of their needs and by being firm. Seth had his own ideas about war and a soldier's loyalty.

The boys stood, chatting and jostling. When they were at attention and silent again, Seth continued.

"Now, stand back to back with your comrade."

The boys laughed as they shuffled into yet another position. Seth kept still, his anger rising. They thought this was a game. An adventure! They had no idea what was at stake. They had no idea what he had planned for them. He tossed a fierce look at Amon.

Amon blew his whistle and hollered, "Silence!"

The boys shut up, their chatter still echoing in the damp, crumbling warehouse.

"Your partner, whom you have selected, will continue to go everywhere with you." Seth paced in front of the lines. "You will not be separated at any time, for any reason. If one of you has to go pee in the middle of the night, your comrade goes with you." A few of the boys snickered. "He will watch your back. You will watch his."

"Well, I ain't going to watch his front!" someone dared to pipe from the ranks.

Seth stopped. He did not turn his gaze into the group, but instead shook his head slightly, his eyes on the floor. He summoned Amon to his side with a single curl of his finger.

"Move Ori and Finn up to the front."

Ori and Finn stood back to back at the far end of the group. They'd had the chance to pick whomever they wanted as partners, but they'd picked each other. They knew they were special, the very first boy soldiers chosen by Seth, and they'd grown tight despite their differences.

Amon hustled the pair to the front, beside the first two boys who were still standing side by side, arms in the air, faces strained with the effort of holding their limbs up for so long. Their whole bodies were trembling now.

Finn and Ori stood beside them, having perfected the "at attention" pose for some time now. They glanced at the two boys with their arms up and then grinned at each other. When he was sure neither Seth nor Amon was watching, Finn dared roll his eyes. He mouthed *Stupid idiots* at the two. Ori grinned, stifling a laugh. Seth turned to them and saw only the middle-distance stare of military respect.

"From now on, not one of you is to be without your comrade. Not for any reason, not at any time." He shoved Ori forward then bent over him and yelled into his ear like a drill sergeant. "If you disobey me, if you don't return to me at the end of the day, if you lie to me, if you keep something from me . . ." Seth slid his gun out of the holster on his belt and released the safety. He looked at it, and then up at the rows of silent boys who were hanging off his words, waiting to see what he'd do next. He raised the gun as if to put it to the back of Ori's head. Instead he shoved Ori aside and held the gun to Finn's head. "If you betray me in any way, I will kill your comrade. And you will watch."

Finn trembled. He forced himself to stand tall and still, his breath quick and shallow, making him dizzy. What was Seth going to do?

The two boys with their arms up in the air gawked at Finn and Seth, their arms, now heavy and so tired, starting to drift, down, down.

Seth tapped the back of Finn's head. "Understood?"

"Yes, Mister Seth."

Seth raised the gun just slightly, but not so much that the others could see the barrel was now clear of Finn's head. He pulled the trigger. The bullet shot into the rafters, startling the pigeons. The boys screamed and ducked for cover as bits of plaster fell.

Finn held his ground, his jaw clenched so hard he wasn't sure if he'd ever be able to open his mouth again. He would not be afraid.

"Quiet!" Seth yelled at the panic-stricken gang of boys. "Fall in line!" They scrambled into place, the younger ones' faces streaked with tears, the older ones trying for cool looks of indifference, as if they'd known all along Seth was going to fire at the ceiling and not blow out the back of Finn's head. These were children who'd seen so much, experienced worse, and committed their own horrors, some lesser, some greater, some unthinkable. There were murderers among these boys. The warning had to hit hard and to terrify.

Seth swung his gun at the first two boys, whose arms were now at their sides. They stared at him, wide-eyed, and shot their arms back into the air.

"And keep them there." Seth holstered his gun, careful to buckle it in. He would never trust these boys, these ruffian throwaways and vagabonds. "Until I say otherwise."

AFTER SETH HAD RELEASED THE GROUP, newly subdued with fright, he charged Finn and Ori with the responsibility of watching that the two boys being punished kept their arms in the air. They sat on a rusting metal cabinet, sharpening their knives. Normally they wouldn't get a Barlow knife until they turned thirteen, but in Seth's army, once he decided you were worthy of belonging, he gave you one no matter how old you were. Ori was eleven, Finn twelve. They were very proud of their knives.

"What's your name?" Finn waved his knife at the brown kid, the one who'd kept his hands in his lap in the first place.

"Bal." The little boy had his hands clasped together above his head, hoping that would help keep them up. Sweat ran down his face from the effort. It'd been almost an hour. He silently dared either of those two know-it-all showoffs to do the same.

"What're you? Eight?"

"Nine. I think." He counted silently. "Yeah. Nine."

"Nine, *what*?" Finn jumped down, knife drawn.

"Nine, Mister Finn!"

"That's better." Finn lowered the knife. "And who's he?"

"George."

Ori leapt down too, not wanting to be left out. "How old are you, George?"

"Eight?" George sniffled. He'd been crying for the last twenty minutes. His arms felt as heavy as tree trunks.

"You sure about that, George?"

The boy shrugged, his arms flagging a bit. Finn glared at him. He straightened his arms again, the tears starting afresh. His shoulders felt hot, as if his sockets were on fire and his arms might sear off. He actually worried that they would, and then how would he scavenge for food? And what kind of pickpocket has no arms? That just made him cry harder.

"He's my brother." Bal shrugged too. It was one of the only gestures he could think to do with his arms stuck up as they were. "We think he's eight. Not sure."

"But he's white," Ori said. "How can he be your brother?"

Finn shot him a disbelieving look.

Bal shrugged again. "We got the same mum."

"Duh," Finn said and then, "You sure about that? You sure he's not some other whore's kid your mom took in out of pity?"

With a roar, George dropped his arms and rushed Finn, grabbing his waist and bowling him over onto his back.

"You can't say that about our mum!" He tried for a punch, but his arms were too tired to lift his fists. "Take it back!"

Finn grabbed the boy's wrists and punched George with his own fists.

"Oh! I hit myself!" Finn laughed, pummelling George's face as he struggled. "I must be a retard!"

Ori held back Bal, who was trying to get to his brother. He broke free, and soon it was the four boys in a dogpile, splashing in a puddle of fetid water. They rumbled for a moment, until Ori pulled away and leapt to attention. Seth stood nearby, his arms crossed. Amon stood a couple of steps behind him, his arms crossed too.

"The little ones are free to go." Seth turned slightly and nodded at Amon. Amon hustled forward and pulled Ori and Finn away. George and Bal fled from the room. Amon stood Ori and Finn in front of Seth. "Is this how you demonstrate responsibility? You think this is how to earn my respect and trust, let alone the other boys'?" He shook his head. "I'm disappointed in you two. I expected more."

"Mister Seth, we're sorry," Ori began. "The boys were mocking us and trying to leave—" He spoke fast, trying to get his words out before Seth could cut him off. Seth just shook his head.

"I don't want to hear it." He turned and walked away, chin high, shoulders squared, his hands clasped behind him in a way that anyone who knew Commander Regis or Edmund Maddox would recognize. "You disgust me. Come talk to me when you are worthy of some respect."

And so Seth left, leaving Amon with Ori and Finn.

"Way to go, idiot!" Finn punched Ori's shoulder.

"What?" Ori hit him back. "You started it!"

"Shut up, both of you." Amon slapped each of them upside the head. "Go on. It's getting dark. Get out there. See what you can scrounge up tonight. Maybe that'll help. If you bring back something special for Seth."

Edmund stood at the far window in the study hall, hands clasped behind his back. He hadn't been in this room since the night after the bombing. Eli had sat in this very window, with that wretched dog that never had anything more than a snarl and a growl for Edmund.

There was an unobstructed view of the gardens from here. They were nearly rebuilt now, or the buildings were at least. It would be a long time before they were restored to their former glory and the Eastern Key a strong agricultural force once more. They'd brought on three new botanists, recruited from the other Keys. Supposedly the best. But then, Lisette had been one of the best, and look what had happened there.

What nonsense! Lisette had said the night before the bombing. They had just retired to bed, she as far as possible to her side, he so far away he might as well be sleeping on the floor. It was an enormous bed, but still did not feel big enough. Lisette sat propped up against a pile of pillows, a jar of night cream balanced on her knee. She worked the cream into her hands. *It's ridiculous, the garden is just that, nothing more, nothing less. You are wasting your time on this conspiracy theory. Rebels in the garden! Listen to yourself.*

I am tired, Lisette. Edmund swung his pyjamaed legs over the side of the bed. *Tired of your distance, your coolness, your lies.*

Lies? Lisette set the cream on her bedside table stacked with books on plants and flowers, research suitable for the Key's master botanist. *You accuse me of lying, yet you will not tell me what I am supposedly lying about! Mon dieu. Well, I am tired too.*

I bet you are, Edmund muttered viciously.

Oh, Edmund. Lisette plaited her hair so it wouldn't tangle in the night. *We are strangers to each other, always have been, always will be. It is too late for us.*

Edmund slipped his feet into his slippers and pulled on his housecoat. *I'm going to sleep in my study.*

Lisette said nothing as he headed for the door. This was when she was supposed to stop him, pull him back, tell him she was sorry. But she said nothing. By the time he got to the door, his resolve was granite.

Stay home tomorrow, he said. *You and I must have a serious talk. We cannot go on like this.*

No. Lisette spoke, but to her hands, not to him. *I have work to do. I am needed there. You don't need me.*

He was going to give the order for the bomb! She knew it. She'd lived with him long enough to be able to interpret the subtle tones and not so subtle determination. But she needed just one more day to get everyone out.

I cannot stay home tomorrow. Perhaps the next day.

No. Tomorrow. I insist. Edmund considered talking to her as his wife, using language from his heart, but it had been so long since she'd stirred his heart that he gave up the idea. He faced the door as he spoke, one hand on the knob, gripping it so tight he could've ripped it from the door with little effort.

As Chief Regent, I command you to stay in this room until I send for you. Is that understood? The bombing would take place in the morning, and as conflicted as he felt, he didn't want her there when the gardens exploded. *You will obey me, or you will face the consequences.*

A short, sardonic laugh sounded from the bed. *Oui, monsieur. D'accord.*

Edmund hesitated.

Yes, sir! Lisette laughed again. *Is that better? In English? After all these years and you have learned not one word of French. Good night, Edmund. Get out.*

Did love matter? Was it wrong that they'd never truly loved each other? Was it wrong that he had married her because it was the proper thing to do, because she was pregnant and he needed a wife to bolster his image as Chief Regent and eventually as Chancellor? Should he have waited for love? Or had he loved her, and it had been so long ago now that he couldn't remember? All he remembered is that she was the only Keyland girl who would have him. There was much he regretted in his life. So much that he wasn't sure where to begin.

Bon nuit, he said as he left the room.

That night Lisette didn't sleep. Surely he wouldn't bomb the gardens knowing she'd be there? She'd have to get everyone out. She couldn't keep refusing to obey him; she sensed terrible things on the horizon. He'd never ask for a divorce. He wouldn't allow it! Would he send her away? Make up some story to get rid of her? Before he did anything like that she had to make sure the rebel cell was cleared, that everyone was out safely. Then she'd agree to stay home, and he could give the orders for the bomb.

EDMUND HADN'T THOUGHT TWICE about Lisette the next morning while he read his papers over breakfast. She wouldn't dare leave their bedroom. She wouldn't dare defy him like that. As strained as their relationship was, she was still his wife, and therefore must obey him. He hadn't even checked on her before he left.

And so he had no idea she was at the garden when the bombs exploded.

Horrified at his blunder, he'd told the Chancellor that she'd left him for another man, more ready to admit to marital difficulty than to her blatant disobedience. He even hoped it was true; after all, he was sure she'd been sleeping with the stableminder. But when the man himself had shown up Edmund could no longer maintain the ruse, and so it was accepted that she'd been at the gardens and was dead. The guilt soon slipped away and he felt nothing but relief. He was almost happy.

Yet he was supposed to love this woman! His disgust at himself was short-lived though. It was a blessing, he decided. He would not blame himself. He knew he should feel worse, but he just didn't. Sometimes, when his mood was both dark and fragile, he wondered at his humanity, at the state of his very soul. Did he even have one?

Conceivably—if not—women might sense this deviance—perhaps that was why he'd been accepted by no other Keylander woman, except for Allegra now, who had possibly settled with him out of duty, or respect for her late grandfather's wishes. If he were being honest with himself, he knew part of his difficulty in romancing Keyland girls reached back to his adolescence, when he'd punched a girl after she'd spurned his attempts to woo her. He knew she'd spread the story around the Key, advising the other girls to stay away. Perhaps that's why he lowered his standards to marry Lisette, the daughter of a lowly bookseller from another Key. But then, she wasn't even that. She was just some rebel bitch who'd used him for all those years.

When it came right down to it, he had no idea who it was he'd been with for the last seventeen years. Truth be told, he hadn't spent much actual time with her. With such a sprawling estate and such divergent pastimes they could both be home for days at a time and see each other only when they sat down to supper. It was a poor excuse for a marriage, if it could be called that at all. That she'd been a rebel all this time didn't, in the end, surprise him. If anything, he found himself respecting her determination.

12

⌘

Zenith let the survivors of the Triskelian massacre take a few days to settle into Cascadia. She herself needed the time to collect her thoughts, and so hadn't left the chambers Rainy had prepared for her since they'd arrived. But now it was time to summon Sabine.

"Are you sure?" Rainy paced the room. He was an old man, older than Pierre, older than Zenith even, but physically spryer than either of them. Only the elders knew his real name, Maurice. He'd been called Rainy for so long that almost everyone thought it was his birth name, as if he was born to be the master cloudminder he'd become. "She is so young, Zenith."

"Everyone is so young, Rainy." Zenith lifted a hand dismissively. "Because we are so old."

"She is younger than Mireille, and I could not imagine giving Mireille that much responsibility."

"Mireille is a different child."

"A *child*! Exactly!" Rainy turned and started pacing in the other direction. "And so is Sabine, then. You agree?"

Celeste had been quiet so far, but now she felt compelled to speak.

"Yes, she is a child. But she is Lisette's daughter, and Lisette was special." Celeste felt a flutter of grief as she spoke. What had happened to her family? Dear curmudgeonly Pierre had taken off in a huff and hadn't been heard from since; her grandchildren were estranged from each other; and Lisette was dead. Brilliant, brave, beautiful Lisette. She did miss Pierre—of course she missed her husband of fifty years—but her longing for her daughter was far more painful. "Lisette was a leader herself: she was able to sacrifice, she was strong, she was compassionate. Wise. Sabine has these same qualities. They are a gift. I believe she can do it."

"But resting the fate of an entire population on the shoulders of a *child*?" Rainy shook his head. "It's impossible."

"On the shoulders of *children*," Zenith said. "This revolution belongs to them now. We are old. Our ways are old. Our job now is to let the children carry out what we failed to do ourselves. It is happening already—small, scattered uprisings in villages and markets. Who is leading them? Who is making them happen? Who is finding their identity in small acts of defiance? The *youth*, that's who."

"Sabine will not bear the responsibility alone." Celeste took the job of pacing, now that Rainy was still. These were worrisome times and they were all plagued by worrisome thoughts, and it seemed only right that someone should be pacing. "She has Eli. And Seth, wherever he is. There is power in their trinity."

Zenith and Rainy shared a private look. Was there a place for Seth in Triskelia now, after everything? Celeste believed in Seth's innocence and could not be swayed. But Zenith wasn't sure. She had confided in Rainy alone about her doubts: that there was something about Seth, that he possessed a darkness that made her believe he could be capable of the treason that brought the Guard to Triskelia. At his core burned a hot, dark force, and Zenith knew she'd be grateful if it was extinguished. She briefly closed her eyes, humbled by her own hard feelings. How could she harbour such ill will toward Lisette's own child? Ah, but he was Edmund's child too.

"What about Trace?" Rainy broke Zenith's uncomfortable reverie. "Why not him? Or Jack?"

"Trace is not a leader." Zenith shook her head. "He is a loner. And now with Charis dead, his place is with Anya. She needs him."

"Well, so do we! So does all the Droughtland!"

"Anya needs him more. And Jack isn't much older than Sabine. He too is not a leader. He does what is best for himself first and foremost."

Zenith nodded. "I am sure of this, Rainy. I have watched Sabine over the years. I have helped raise her. She is the one. And Eli will support his sister, I am sure. He has his place, and he will find it, but right now, we must turn to Sabine."

"You haven't convinced me." Rainy's tone was firm. "And if you of all people can't convince me, how can you think you can convince anyone else?"

"I won't need to convince anyone." Zenith smiled. "Sabine will do that. And Eli will help her. It is time. It's been time for many years, and now there is no reason to wait any longer. Send for her."

"This does not feel good." Rainy sighed. He tugged on his scraggly grey beard and sighed again. He removed his glasses, puffed on them and wiped them on his shirt, and sighed once more. And then he nodded, slowly. "But I'll go along with it for you, Zenith. Because I trust you." He replaced his glasses on his nose, magnifying the lines at the corner of his almond-shaped eyes. "I'll go get her."

SABINE WAS WITH ELI AND MIREILLE in the gym that had been set up decades earlier in the east tower. Most of the bookshelves had been cleared out then, leaving only the shelves by the door filled with relevant tomes on circus arts and physical fitness and the like. A haphazard array of circus equipment, carried into the mountains in pieces or devised out of spare bits, had been rigged up and now the room looked like the raggedy cousin of the Triskelian gym that had been sprawling and magnificent, gleaming from care and attention and use.

Eli stared up at the girls as they slowly let themselves down two lengths of wide cloth, as light as fairies, their arm muscles taut. The cloths in Triskelia had been red silk, but these were just strips of bleached-out parachute material, with the odd patch job that Sabine insisted was sound but that did not win Eli's confidence. He couldn't hear what they were talking about, but he hoped it was him.

Mireille, Eli had learned, was the cloudminder's apprentice, a job that Jack told him was very important. She worked with Rainy reading the skies, setting the ground generators beneath updrafts, mixing the careful concoction of silver iodide and acetone that resulted in the plume that would seed the clouds and bring the rain. It was like magic to Eli, and that she could do it made her a beautiful, wondrous sorceress of the skies. What would it take for a piece of perfect like her to be interested in a piece of nothing like him, one who heard voices no less?

"What?" Sabine wound herself down the bottom metres of cloth and dropped lightly to the floor.

Eli shook his head. "I didn't say anything." But maybe he had? Oh highers, had he said that last thought out loud?

"You were mumbling something."

"No, I wasn't."

"You were." Sabine reached for a towel and wiped the sweat from her brow. The girls made it look easy, but it was one of the more physically challenging feats of the circus, requiring every single muscle group in the body to keep from falling and to properly execute the graceful moves that made the act as beautiful as it was.

"I heard you," Mireille said as she dropped to the floor too. Sabine handed her a towel, and then the girls stared at Eli.

"I don't know what you're talking about." Eli's face flushed a deep red. "What did I say, if you heard it?"

Mireille helped herself to a glass of water. "I didn't hear the words, just mumbles."

Eli opened his mouth and then shut it and then opened it again, gawping like a fish.

"Mireille." Rainy appeared in the doorway just then. "We have to reset the generator at the base of the west peak before that system moves in."

"Okay, Rainy." Mireille pulled on a thick hooded sweater and a pair of wool pants over her leotard.

As she did Rainy kept his eyes on Sabine, her cheeks flushed and her hair damp with sweat from the workout. She looked younger than her years, but then she'd been through enough to be as old as Rainy, who'd led a sheltered life after arriving at the castle almost sixty years before. He could count on his fingers how many times he'd been off the mountain

since. What did he know of the world? This girl had criss-crossed the
continent on tour with the Night Circus. She'd lost her parents, she'd lost
friends and family in the massacre, and now she was here. A girl child
with the eyes of an elder.

"Rainy?" Mireille laid a hand on his arm. "Are you okay?"

"Yes, yes, child." He patted her hand. "I'm fine."

"I can reset the generator by myself." She looked into her mentor's
face for signs of fatigue or sick. He'd had a stroke the year before, and
ever since had had a lopsided smile and a slight shuffle. "You could have
a rest, and then join me in the lab when I get back."

"I could go with her." Eli tried to sound casual, as if he couldn't care
less either way. "Carry stuff, you know. Learn a thing or two."

"Are you telling me to go to my room like a child, Mireille?" Rainy
pulled his arm away. He was about to tell her to mind her own health
and not take such a keen interest in his, please and thank you. But then
he thought about the west peak, and the craggy hike to get there, and at
that moment he wanted nothing more than to sleep, just for a few
minutes or maybe an hour. Blessed sleep.

"No! Not at all, Rainy. I just worry about you sometimes. That's all."

"Well, I may be an old man, but I'm still in charge of myself, and you
for that matter."

"Of course, Rainy."

"But you're right. I am tired. Take Eli with you, and reset the two generators for the incoming front. The updraft should be adequate for two
plumes, by my calculations." He reached into his pocket to give her his
notes, but they weren't there. He fished in his other pants pocket and then
flustered through every pocket of the half dozen or so of his engineer's vest.

"You won't find them," Mireille said, embarrassed for him.

"How do you know what I'm looking for and how important it may be?"

"You're looking for your notes, right?"

Rainy stopped rooting in his vest. "Why, yes."

Mireille pulled a notebook from the bag slung over her shoulder. "You
gave them to me at breakfast."

"Oh." Rainy tugged at his beard and looked at his feet. His brain just wasn't doing its job as well any more. He was forgetting things and losing things almost every day. "I suppose a rest might be in order." He turned and started for the hall, and once out of sight he stopped to catch his breath. He leaned against a shelf of books, his eye catching one in particular— *The Science of the Highwire: Applications and Innovations.* He used to read a book like it was a meal, in one sitting and with a flourish of appreciation for something that had profoundly nourished his brain and soul. Not any more. He could hear the children talking. He shuffled a little closer to the doorway to listen.

"He's changed," Sabine was saying.

"I'm so worried about him." That was Mireille. "It's gotten much worse." There was a quaver in her voice, as if she might cry. Rainy's heart clutched itself.

"I'm sure he's fine," Eli said.

"How would you know?" Mireille snapped. "You don't even know him, so how can you say that?"

And then silence. Rainy's shoulders slumped as he remembered the reason why he'd been sent to find the children in the first place. He pulled himself together and strode back into the room as if he was the confident, brilliant cloudminder he'd been for so long. His mind was slipping; he could no longer deny it, with each day foggier than the one before. It was getting more and more difficult to hide.

"Sabine?" He stayed near the door. "Zenith is looking for you." He suddenly felt like a child sent to collect an older sibling for supper. "She wants to talk to you."

"Oh." Sabine looked from Eli to Mireille, confused. "Okay. Should I come with you?" She pulled her long hair into a fresh ponytail as she spoke.

Rainy tugged at his beard as a wash of panic filled him. He couldn't remember. He couldn't remember if Zenith had wanted him to bring her or if she was to go on her own. He couldn't even remember why Zenith had wanted to see her in the first place! He was so alarmed at his mind's failure that he didn't say anything at all. He held up his weathered, liver-spotted hands as if conceding defeat and walked away.

SABINE GOT CHANGED and went to find Zenith, leaving Eli and Mireille alone. They looked at each other like a couple of puppies scoping each other out. Mireille grinned.

"What are you looking at?"

"Absolutely nothing." Eli grinned too.

Mireille's hands went to her hips. "Is that right?"

"Yup." Eli felt about six years old, like he'd just as soon find the nearest table to hide under, or poke her and call her stupid and run away.

"Well, if that's the case, let's get going." She tossed her towel into the laundry and headed out the other end of the tower, to the door that opened onto the path that took them up the hill to the laboratory. Eli just stood there. He looked at his feet, expecting to see cement blocks instead of the weathered boots that had carried him so far.

"Are you coming?" Mireille held open the door. There was no fog today, just glorious sunlight opening the day behind her and illuminating her dark hair, crowning her with light.

"Yeah, I'm coming." Eli jogged across the room. "Can I take your bag for you?"

"That's sweet, but no." Mireille laughed. "There's lots to carry. Don't worry. I'll put you to work. You'll have your chance to prove how big and strong and capable you are, Eli." And with that she stepped out into the sunshine.

"That's not what I meant!" Eli ran after her, still feeling six years old to her proper seventeen. "I was just trying to help."

"Okay, Eli." Mireille had to raise her voice over the wind whipping across the top of the mountain. "Whatever you say. Come on, we've already lost a good chunk of this updraft. We need to set the generator pretty quick or we'll blow it entirely and lose the front altogether."

13

For as long as he could remember, Seth liked to destroy things. He'd spend hours in the garden, around back where Cook's husband kept the old herb pots and crumbling statues and piles of spare bricks. He'd smash Gardener's pots on the cobblestone, take a hammer to the broken statues, chuck bricks at the stone wall of the little garden shed. He could use up an entire afternoon doing that while Gardener puttered around, repotting new herbs and tinkering with this or that, pretending not to mind Seth's flurry of destruction but wanting to stick close should he start after the important breakables. Afterward, out of breath and with a pile of rubble before him, Seth could only describe his feelings as deep satisfaction and elation. As if he'd conquered something. He'd go back to the main house for his tea as if he were returning from war, puffed up and exhausted and proud.

So it didn't surprise him much that his gang of boy soldiers spent all their waking hours ripping up stuff, bashing it to bits, pummelling each other and demolishing anything in their path. They were like a pack of wolf cubs, teething on the world before them and then collapsing with exhaustion in the safety of their den each night. Most of them were asleep now, in whatever corner they'd claimed for themselves and had managed to hold on to. He and Amon had pulled a couple of stools up to the fire barrel and were warming their hands over the flames. They were thinking up names they might call their army of boys.

"Maybe The Wolf Army," Seth mused out loud. He didn't really want Amon's opinion, but having him around was better than talking to himself, or worse, keeping all his thoughts in his head, filled as it already was with myriad logistics as befitting the Commander of a large force. How to house them? Feed them? Train them? And most of all, how to discipline this unruly tangle of boys and instill in them the unquestioning respect that he required?

"Yeah." Amon's eyes darted back and forth in the light of the fire. He couldn't concentrate on the task at hand and could hardly sit still, his knees bouncing, his head jerking now and again. "Sure. That's good." So far he'd offered The Boy Bandits and The Demons of Triban, neither of which Seth had acknowledged beyond a dismissive glance.

"Doesn't matter really. Whatever." Amon wiped his nose. "Oh." He blinked. "I got a good one."

"Yeah?" Seth was inspecting three guns Ori and Finn had brought back a couple of days earlier. They'd offered them up pale faced and wordlessly, and so Seth hadn't asked any questions. Those two were doing well despite their attitude. They worked hard, and stayed away, fending for themselves unless they had something particularly valuable to bring back for Seth. "What is it?"

"The Midnight Molotovs." Amon nodded. "Like the bombs, right. And how we're out all night, right." More nodding. He blinked fast. "Explosive. Ninjas. Hey. That'd be good too. The Explosive Ninjas. Ninjah. Ninnnn-jaaaaa. That's a weird word. Say it, like, four times, and it starts to sound weird. Maybe not explosive though. Makes you think of diarrhea, don't it?"

Seth stared at Amon for a second. "You're on something other than dust, aren't you?"

"Dust, crank." Amon shrugged. "What does it matter?"

"You sound like an idiot," Seth said. "You're bad enough when you're kited, but all wired up on some nasty upper you're downright useless. If the boys saw you now they'd laugh you out of the room. How are they supposed to look up to you when you're like this? And you're filthy. When's the last time you washed up? Hmm? You want to get a sick?

That's the best way, stop washing. Or go shag more whores. You're headed for a sick either way."

"Don't call me stupid." Amon stood, wobbling a bit. "I'm just helping you pick a name for our army, that's all, and you're sitting there calling me stupid? What kind of friend are you anyway?"

"That's just it." Seth went back to fiddling with the guns. They were in surprisingly good condition, and would've been very expensive to purchase. "We're not friends, Amon. I am the leader. And you are supposed to be my right hand man."

There was a pause. Amon tried to hold still.

"I am?"

"Well, who else?" Seth said. "But only if you could at least follow the rules I have for the boys. No drugs, for example."

"No problem." Amon sat down again, using his hands to steady himself and the tottery stool. "I'll lock myself in my room for a week. I've done it before."

"Uh-huh. Sure."

"I will, Seth! After all we've been through, come on. Let me prove it."

Seth shrugged. "Why should I?"

Amon grinned. "Like you said, who else you got?" He took Seth's silence as the reluctant concession it was. "So then, if you get to be the Commander, what am I?"

"I'm not making any promises, Amon. Not until you show me that you're up to it. But, when or if . . . and I do mean *if,* you get clean, you can be my sergeant."

"Sergeant Amon." He tried it out. "I like the sound of that."

The rusty metal door creaked open and they turned their heads, Seth with swift alertness and Amon with the slow pull of his high. It was Ori and Finn, heading for them at a run.

"The Guard is here!" Finn shouted. "Keyland Guard! In Triban!"

Some of the boys stirred from their sleep. Seth put a finger to his lips.

"Sorry," Ori said for them both when they got to the fire. "We shouldn't a yelled." They stuck their hands toward the warmth. "Only it's big news. The whole city's talking about it!"

"They got here tonight," Finn continued. "They're setting up at the edge of the city, with a line of mounted Guardies with guns all around, like a wall!"

"There's probably a million of them." Ori's eyes were wide with fright.

"Doubt it," Amon laughed.

"You do?" Seth plunged his hands into his pockets and started pacing. "How many do you think annihilated Triskelia and the Colony of the Sicks, huh?"

"Dunno."

"At least twenty thousand," Seth said. "They'd need three times that to even attempt to take down the city, if that's what they're trying to do."

"What're you gonna do, Commander?" Ori asked.

It had been a week since the boys were instructed to call him that, and still, every time one of them did he swelled with a quiet pride.

"Why would I tell you?"

"Sorry, Commander."

"Leave us."

"Yes, Commander," the boys said in unison.

When they were halfway to the door, Seth sent Amon to bring them back.

"What regiment was it?"

"Huh?" Finn gave him a blank look.

Seth whacked him upside the head. "What did I tell you?"

"Sorry." Finn trembled. "Pardon me, Commander?"

"That's better. Now, tell me what regiment it was."

"But we can't read, Commander Seth," Finn admitted quietly.

"I can read," Ori offered. "You mean what it said on their caravans?"

"Yes, Ori." Seth grinned. "Thank you."

"West Droughtland Regiment, 54632." Ori beamed. "Commander Seth."

The words might as well have been bullets. In an instant Seth was back in the cloud of dust, abandoned by that very same regiment after the most horrific day of his life.

"Seth?" Amon squinted at him. "Is that the one you're looking for?"

The heat. The pain. The unrelenting sick that had scarred him for life. The humiliation of Rosa seeing him shit himself and cry for his maman in a fevered delirium. His weakness. How close he'd come to death. All because of Commander Regis setting him up to sleep with a Droughtland girl who he knew was in the first stages of the skineater sick.

Seth rubbed his face and cleared his head with a shake.

He was a soldier again now. A different kind of soldier, with an army of his own. He had five hundred boys now, seventy-five guns, two hundred machetes, and a cache of smaller knives and the odd homemade contraptions the wastes of life in Triban used to take each other out for a sniff of dust or a couple of coins or a Seduce game gone bad.

"Yes, that's the one." Seth pulled his hands from his pockets. He'd made them into fists without realizing it. Ori and Finn stared at him, slightly awed and more than a little nervous at Seth's transformation. He unclenched his hands and clasped them behind his back. "Thank you, Ori. Good work."

"You're welcome, Commander Seth."

"All of you, leave me alone now." The fatigue was obvious in his voice.

As Ori and Finn scuttled off into the dark corners of the warehouse, Amon teetered.

"You too, Amon," Seth said. "You have a lot of work ahead of you."

"But we got to name the army, Seth." Amon sat down. "Don't we?"

"It can wait." Seth shook his head, his hands in fists again. "Leave."

"Well, okay." Amon backed away. "So, I'll see you in the morning."

"No. Come find me when you're clean."

"But I was supposed to run the obstacle course downstairs."

"As of now, you are relieved of all your duties. Until you're clean," Seth said. "And also as of now, you will call me Commander as well."

"But Seth—"

Seth held up his hand. "What did I just say?"

"Sorry. Commander Seth," Amon said from the shadows. "Never mind."

"Good luck." Seth settled into his chair by the fire. "And good night."

Wisely, Amon didn't argue, and as his footsteps faded into the quiet, Seth was left with his thoughts.

Commander Regis. Again, Seth's hands balled themselves into fists. He lifted them in front of him. Lit by the firelight now, they cast a menacing shadow. Seth wore a gun at his hip and a Barlow knife in his boot, but Commander Regis would die by his fists. He would beat him to death with his bare hands, and he would take great pleasure in it.

The thought of smashing Regis's face in brought a kind of peace. Seth steepled his fingers and settled back in his chair, an ankle resting on one knee. He closed his eyes. It was quiet, or as quiet as Triban ever got, which meant random screams from the streets below, and the clatter of horses and carts, and people shouting, and the odd creaks and clanks from this old, crumbling warehouse. And the coo of an owl, which had been there when Seth had moved his boys in and had remained, despite how crowded the warehouse was becoming.

Each night the owl perched in the same window whose glass had long since been smashed out. It was a high window, near the ceiling, and Seth imagined the owl could see most of Triban from there. Perhaps all the way to the edge where Commander Regis and his men were right now establishing themselves. If only Seth could fly. He'd find a perch in the Guardy camp and then calculate the perfect time to kill Regis. But he couldn't fly, and so he'd have to choose his time as best he could.

14

❧

If the owl perched in the window above Seth had been at all interested in humans, it might've noticed a rather pregnant and rather young girl hurrying along the boardwalk below. She passed the warehouse none the wiser that an army of boys resided there, and that she had, in fact, once seen their leader. She clutched her Barlow knife in one hand while the slender fingers of the other curled around a crude knuckle-duster.

Tasha, the breadminder's daughter from the Foothills Market, had been in Triban for a month now, desperately hoping to find Nappo. She'd met an older girl, Pilar, the first night, and Pilar had invited her back to her room to stay while she looked for the father of her baby, the love of her life, her future husband and provider. That first night Pilar had listened to her story of Nappo with the attention of a longtime best friend, and so Tasha, despite her market savvy and in her loneliness, had warmed to her immediately. She'd stayed on, letting Pilar pay for her food and accepting her offer to bunk in her room for free. And then! And then, this very night, she'd revealed herself to be a traitor of the highest order.

Tasha had been napping on her thin mattress on the floor when Pilar came teetering through the door in her high heels. She yanked at her short skirt to keep it from riding up and then knelt beside Tasha and shook her awake.

"Tasha." Pilar shook her harder. "Wake up."

Tasha had been asleep on her side with her knees pulled up—the only way she could make herself comfortable now that her belly was so big, and even then her hips always ached when she got up.

"What is it?" She pushed herself up and crossed her legs, blinking at the couple who stood arm in arm in the doorway.

They were tidy and well dressed, which was unusual for the city. The woman's hair was carefully plaited and arranged with pins and the man's pants were pressed and his shoes were in good shape and had a shine to them.

"Do they know where Nappo is?" She couldn't think of any other reason why Pilar would bring someone to see her.

"Don't be silly." Pilar squeezed her arm. "Why would they?"

"Who's Nappo?" the woman asked, a nervous smile playing at her modestly rouged lips.

"Never mind." Pilar dismissed the question with a flap of her hand. "No one."

"Don't say that!" Tasha grabbed Pilar's bed frame and heaved herself onto her feet. "He's the—"

"Hear these nice people out, would you?" Pilar smiled at her through gritted teeth. "For me? Please?"

"About what?" Tasha eased her backside down until she was perched on the edge of the bed. Pilar brought the couple in. There was nowhere for them to sit, so they stood, very near to each other, holding hands. Tasha did not have a good feeling about this, or them. "Who are they?" She gave the couple a calculated glare.

"Cletus and Rachel Shea," the man said. "Pleased to meet you."

"Huh." Tasha narrowed her eyes even more. "And why's that?" They smiled down at her like someone gazing at a wishing well just before they threw in a coin. When they hesitated to answer, Tasha let her glare wander to Pilar. "And what the hell are Cletus and Rachel Shea doing here?"

"Are you sure that she—" Rachel began.

"I'm sure!" Pilar barked.

Tasha blinked and looked at Pilar again. Something had just shifted. In that moment Pilar stopped being the kind, generous friend and now stood before her as the kited whore she was. What was she up to? Were these people her clients? Did they want to—?

Tasha didn't even want to think about it.

"Well, whatever you're all going on about, *I'm* not sure." Tasha crossed her arms protectively over her belly. "Someone tell me what the hell is going on."

"Tasha." Pilar sat beside her and put a hand on her knee. "This nice couple wants to adopt the baby."

"No! The baby is *my* baby." Tasha scrambled backward on the bed as the couple took a united step toward her. "Me and Nappo's."

"We run a roadhouse a two-hour ride from here," the man said. "We have a five-year-old boy, and he has a safe yard to play in, and all the toys and friends he could want."

The woman reached out a tentative hand, as if willing to snatch even the idea of the baby away from Tasha. Tasha turned her face to the wall and curled up into a ball.

"Go away!" She turned back and slapped at Pilar. "I'm not going to give away my baby!"

"Pilar, you misled us." The man's tone was chilly now. "Have we come all this way for nothing?"

"She'll warm up to the idea," Pilar said. "Tell her about the money."

"Yes, of course," Cletus said. "Go ahead, Rachel."

"We'll bring you home with us, Tasha." The woman sat on the bed too. She stroked Tasha's hair, which actually calmed her down a little. "We'll feed you and clothe you. You'll see a proper birthminder every week." Rachel's voice was soothing. "And of course, we'll pay you for the baby. Pilar had said a thousand. We paid less than that for our boy, but the circumstances were different. He was almost one."

The look in Pilar's eyes at the mention of the boy gave it away.

"He was *yours*!" Tasha was horrified. "You gave away your own baby?"

For the briefest of moments Pilar's eyes glazed over with sadness. Then she steeled herself and sneered at Tasha. "Oh, shut up! Don't pretend you're some innocent little bitch." She pulled off her stilettos and threw them down. "I did what was best for him! I knew he wouldn't be safe in

Triban. I knew he'd be better off with them. I know what you're going through, Tasha. I've been there, honey."

"How *dare* you compare yourself to me!" Tasha grew four feet in her anger. She became as big as the room, as powerful as a storm. She reached for Pilar's bedside table with its jumble of makeup and envelopes of rubbers, grabbed an empty ale bottle and threw it at the couple. It smashed against the wall above the man's head.

"Cletus!" the woman cried.

"I'm okay." Cletus brushed the glass from his hair and smiled wanly at his wife. "We should go." He took her hand. "Clearly, this is more complicated than we'd like."

"No!" Pilar grabbed Rachel's other hand.

"You can keep the finder's fee." Rachel pulled away. "Let go."

"I can make her change her mind!"

"No, you can't!" Tasha scrambled off the bed and started shoving her few things into her pack. "You stay away from me and my baby!" She pushed past the trio and into the hall.

"Tasha, stop!" Pilar yelled. "We need the money!"

She turned back. "I can't believe I ever thought you were my friend."

"I *am* your friend, Tasha." Pilar's eyes teared up. "I am."

"No, you're not." Tasha shook her head. "You wouldn't even *know* how to be anyone's friend." Her mother had taught her to trust her gut about people, and she always had. Until she'd left home. By the time she got to Triban she was so desperate for a friend she made one out of a lying, thieving whore, she was that lonely. She'd just wanted one person to turn to in the foul city. One friend. Tasha turned her eyes up to the stained ceiling and asked her highers what she'd done to deserve a life like this. Then she turned her eyes back to Pilar. "You're just a filthy whore who wanted to sell my baby all along. How does that make you any different from a pimp, huh?"

Pilar could only stare.

"That's right," Tasha said. "The truth hurts, doesn't it?" She hiked her pack onto her shoulders and took off.

"Wait!" Pilar ran after her. "Tasha, I'm sorry!"

"Pilar, stop," Cletus called out. "Just stop now! Let her go."

Pilar slowed as Tasha disappeared down the stairwell and then out into the night.

Outside, Triban slapped Tasha like an angry mother. Momentarily stunned by the layered stench and the cacophony of the streets, she braced herself and took off at a run. She didn't get far before she had to stop, but she'd gained enough distance to put Pilar behind her.

And now she hurried along the boardwalk in the middle of the night, past Seth's dark warehouse, the hustlers on the corners, the drug dealers and kited maniacs up to no good. She would leave this wretched city and carry on searching for Nappo. Where *was* he?

The irresistible smell of fresh loaves and hot teacakes beckoned her into an all-night breadminder's. How she missed her parents. How she missed the market! She checked her pockets for coins even though she hadn't had any money for weeks. She loitered in the warmth of the shop, filling up on the smells at least, until the crowd thinned and the breadminder shooed her out. When she stepped back out onto the boardwalk it was raining. Tasha found an empty doorway, put on every stitch of clothing she had, and settled in for a long, sleepless night.

15

❧

The rain that fell on Triban was the tail end of a system that dumped mostly on the north side of the valley in which the city was situated. It was a weather system manipulated by Mireille, with Eli's help. He was getting good at setting the cloudseeders. Mireille had taught him how to mix the silver iodide with the acetone, taking care not to burn himself in the process. That part was easy.

Reading the sky was much harder, and he could see how it would take years of training before graduating into the role of cloudminder. He'd pull the cart with the seeders set and ready to go while Mireille walked ahead, eyes up, watching the sky. She knew the network of trails so well that she never needed to watch her footing. Not once did she trip on a root or stumble on a rock. It was as if she and the planet were one, especially in the way she communicated with the sky, talking to it as if it were a live creature.

"Come on, honey. Bring it down," she'd murmur, and Eli swore the wind dropped for her. "That's it. Where should we play today?" And then she'd look to the west, or east, or wherever, as if she'd been personally invited by the clouds above. "There. Thank you."

Eli would set the seeder where Mireille pointed. And she was always right. The plume would catch the updraft and be carried up into the sky, and then a couple of hours later the rains would start.

THE SYSTEM THAT brought rain to Triban was a massive one, so large that as it passed it brought rains to most of the northwest. By dusk the rain had reached the mountain, pounding on the slate roof of the castle like an angry stranger banging to get in. Sabine, Mireille, Eli, and Nappo were playing a round of Seduce in Mireille's turret room. It had windows all around, providing a huge view of the skies she needed to know so intimately.

Sabine stared intently at her cards. Eli stared intently at Mireille, who had an eye to the window, watching the rain. As for Nappo, he was playing a particularly good game.

Despite her apparent concentration, Sabine wasn't thinking about her cards. She couldn't care less that she was holding the Queen of Hearts and needed to get rid of it. She was thinking about what Zenith had asked of her. Well, not asked of her so much as informed her. She'd kept quiet about it but planned to tell the others tonight. She'd needed the time to think, and now she needed her friends.

You will be leader, Sabine, Zenith had said. *It is time. My era has passed, and I have failed.*

Sabine had argued, but even as she did she knew it was right. Ever since the massacre she'd wanted to break free, to storm the Guard, to seek justice for all those murdered at the hands of the Keys. She didn't care what might happen to her as long as she was fighting for Triskelia.

I think you know this to be true. That you are the next leader of Triskelia.

Sabine had eventually stopped arguing, replacing her fearful rebuttals with a simple, solemn nod.

Now she looked around the table at her brother and her friends. Playing a game of Seduce should be an ordinary thing to do on a rainy night. But it was calculated rain, and they were together at the castle only because their people had been slaughtered, and it was that fact that kept Sabine's core hot with the desire for revenge.

You have always been a leader, Sabine, and now you must accept the responsibility that accompanies your nature. And you have a passion that I was never blessed with. A passion for action. A passion to start the revolution. You will lead the Droughtlanders to their emancipation. You and your generation will be the ones to liberate us all. It will not be easy. This is war. There will be much bloodshed.

There already had been. Sabine's cards trembled as she shook with the memories of that night. The bodies, the screaming, the blood.

I had hoped for a more peaceful way, and I have spent my lifetime working for that, but perhaps violence is the price of freedom. Perhaps this new, massive grief will be our path to liberation at last. It is true that I could have been more insistent, more forceful, but it is also true that the people have not had a will like this in all my lifetime.

Sabine understood the anger that grew out of grief. She understood the resulting compulsion to act, or react, with equally devastating force. She understood the need for blame. She understood that for Triskelia to be born again it needed justice for wrongs done. Most importantly, she understood that now was the time—the time to harness the people's grief and mobilize them into action. The Droughtland was ready now when it had never been ready before.

But how can I lead that many? she'd asked Zenith. *Why would they listen to me? How will I know what to do?*

Zenith put her cold fingers to Sabine's forehead and then moved them to her heart. *The momentum will be so powerful that you will have little effect on the how, but you will be essential afterward, when it is time to rebuild.*

Sabine glanced at the rain-streaked windows of the turret room. She could open one right now, leap out and fall to her death and be done with it. She'd go to her highers, reunite with her lost loved ones, and bear no responsibility for the state of the world. There was an alarming allure to the idea. That's how she knew it was time to talk to the others and alleviate her isolation.

"Guys?" Sabine set her cards down. "Stop the game."

"No way." Nappo fanned his cards with a flourish. "I got a hand straight from the highers here."

Eli felt a sudden familiar chill. It was the feeling he'd shared with Sabine and Seth back in Triskelia. One glance at his sister confirmed it. He took Nappo's cards and shuffled them back into the deck. "Game's over."

"What are you doing?" Nappo pushed away from the table. "You two got that psychic thing again? You knew I had the winning hand and you just couldn't let me play it out? Some friends!"

"Nappo, sit," Eli said.

"Fine." Nappo sat. "But this better be big."

And it was. Sabine told them everything that had been said behind Zenith's closed doors. That the revolution that had already started in the streets was hers, and theirs too, that it was up to them to shape it into a lasting freedom for everyone.

And that she'd been chosen as leader.

"No disrespect, Sabine. But why you?" Nappo crossed his arms and stared at her with slack-jawed disbelief. "Or is this some kind of joke?"

"No." Sabine shook her head. "I wouldn't joke about this, Nappo."

"But how?" Mireille paled. "I mean, just think about it, Sabine. A revolution? The entire Droughtland?"

"It's already begun." Sabine hardened her expression, hoping to lock out her own fears and doubts. "We just have to play our part."

"Oh yeah?" At last, Eli spoke. "And what part is that exactly?"

Sabine bristled at his tone. "I didn't ask to be made leader, Eli."

"Not surprising, considering Triskelia has never had any proper way of establishing its leadership." Eli laughed. "No, I guess the honour just fell from the highers and landed on your shoulders, huh? Your *destiny.*"

"So Zenith says, as a matter of fact."

"And what does she know about destiny?" Eli was gripped with a sudden bitterness. "She's sat on her ass all her life, living the easy life on high while millions struggle for survival, and she has the gall to talk about destiny?"

"That was then." Sabine shrugged. "This is now."

"How convenient," Eli muttered. He wanted to ask what Zenith had said about him. He wanted to know why he hadn't been chosen, or at least been in the room. He and Sabine were practically the same person. They came from the same parents, the same birth, yet she was chosen and he wasn't? And how could they just "make" her leader, without any pomp and circumstance? Sure, there'd likely been endless discussion, just not with him participating. What was he worth to these people? Why had he sacrificed so much, his life even, just to find himself holed up in a musty castle turret surrounded by mouldy books and a lousy hand of cards? He shuffled his own cards back into the deck and then slammed the deck onto the tabletop. "What a crock of shit."

"So . . ." Nappo's glance flitted between the siblings. "What happens next?" He wanted to give Eli a moment to collect himself so that he wouldn't say something he'd regret. Nappo knew Eli well enough to know he'd thank him later for it.

As Sabine started to explain, Eli quietly stewed.

"First, we'll have a fundraiser." Sabine pulled a notebook and a pencil from her satchel.

"Some revolution," Eli spat. "What, a bake sale and silent auction?" That made him think back to the Eastern Key and the annual Fall Fair with its cake walks and raffles, homemade pies and races through the laurel labyrinth in the gardens. Had he ever really had it so easy? Even the homemade pies and cakes were made by the staff. The only thing the Keylanders had to do was show up and drink tea with their pinkies stuck out and make polite conversation about who was donating how much. It had been so easy. So peaceful. Why the hell had he ever left?

"No." Sabine wrote *To Do* at the top of the page in her neat, blockish printing.

"A revolution organized by a *To Do* list?" Eli barked out another laugh. "Way to instill faith in your minions, Sabine."

Nappo kicked him under the table. Eli glared at him but shut up.

"Then what?" Mireille asked for him.

"A circus gala in Triban. We're going to advertise it as a fundraiser for the victims of the Colony of Sicks Massacre, but really it will be a way to bring people together so we can get the word out. It'll be an epicentre of sorts."

"That's a good idea, Sabine." Mireille grinned at the boys. "Isn't it?"

"Yeah," Nappo said, excited already by the prospect of the circus.

"I guess," Eli conceded. It felt so long since he'd thrilled to the exhilarating high of the trapeze. If he were being honest he'd have to admit he craved it, but he wasn't being honest, not with himself and certainly not with his sister.

He felt as though he were a child back in the Keys, left out and useless while Seth steamed ahead organizing games and playing war, toppling pretend rebel factions, storming villages made of blocks with his vast army of tin soldiers. And there was Eli, his arms around his mother's slender waist while she had tea with the other mothers, his head in her lap, skittish of the other children's pushing and shoving and yelling. Only now it was ten years later and Seth was probably out there somewhere still pushing and shoving and yelling his way through the world while their sister calmly and gracefully stepped into the surplice of leadership. What did Eli have to offer? He was just a coward. No wonder Zenith hadn't chosen him.

"I'm going to bed." Eli stood, utterly done with it all.

"But it's hardly dark yet," Mireille said.

"I'm tired." Eli pushed his chair in and left the room before he could say anything else. He felt powerless and small, but his thoughts were cumbersome and huge. He didn't want to fight. He didn't want any more violence. And to be honest, the last thing he wanted was the obligation and pressure of being in charge. Where was the voice now when he could actually use a little direction?

THE NEXT MORNING Sabine found Eli in the mudroom as he was donning his layers to hike up to the lab to join Mireille, who'd gone up at dawn.

"Why are you mad at me?"

Eli stabbed his arms into his sweater sleeves. "I'm not mad."

"I don't need some triplet psychic superpower to tell, you know."

"Well, you're wrong."

"Am I?"

"What do I care, Sabine?" Eli rooted through his pack, pretending to look for something. "Better you than me, obviously."

"You think I want this?"

"I don't know." Eli shrugged. "My triplet psychic superpowers are on the fritz."

"Well, I don't." Sabine tucked her hair behind her ears and sighed. "I wish we could go back in time. All the way back to the day we were born, so it could've unfolded differently. Better."

"You'd have grown up in the Key too, like me. None the wiser and all the more ignorant. Like that would be any better?"

"I meant if we'd all left. You, me, Seth, and Maman. Like how it was supposed to go."

"Oh." Eli adjusted his pack on his shoulders and reached for the door. "Well. You can't change what's already happened. And so here we are."

"Right, but that's not what I'm worried about." Sabine chewed her lip. "I'm worried about what's going to happen."

"Good thing you're in charge then." Eli's eyebrows shrugged up. "You can make it happen however you want. The elders seem to think so anyway. So what are you complaining about? You're the boss of it all. The whole thing. Doesn't that feel good?"

Sabine stared at him. "Why are you being mean?"

There was a knock at the open door behind them. Nappo hesitated there, Teal at one side, Toby at his other.

"Hey," Nappo said. "We interrupting?"

"Thankfully," Eli said.

"Trust me, Eli," Sabine said as Eli pushed past her on his way out of the room. "You wouldn't want the burden."

"What would you know about it?" Eli took a step out into the cool morning. He stopped and looked over his shoulder at his sister. "Maybe it's about the honour, ever think about that?"

And then he took off. Not at a run, because that would be immature, but at a determined pace, a pace that warned against anyone following.

Back in the mudroom, Teal looked up at Nappo. "I thought you were going with him today."

"Yeah," Nappo said. "But I think he wants to be alone right now. I'll find something else to do."

"How about we find Anya and see what she's up to?" Sabine shook her unease off. "Maybe she's helping Nana make cookies in the kitchen." It was unlikely, given that Anya spent most of her days wandering the halls and corridors of the castle, clutching a quilt over her shoulders, the length of it dragging on the floor. But Celeste *was* going to make a huge batch of cookies, though, enough for everyone, and she'd asked for help. Sabine wanted to leave Teal and Toby with her so that she could talk to Nappo alone. About Eli.

They found Anya on their way down to the basement kitchens. The quilt was filthy, as was Anya. Her hair was stringy, her face pale and spotty. These days Teal and Toby were the only ones who could lift her spirits even a little. Toby was oblivious to Anya's state and ran for her, expecting the same warm open arms she'd always had for him. And something in her would not deprive him of that, and so she stretched a tired smile across her face and let him into her smelly, quilted cocoon.

"You can't see me!" Toby's laugh was muffled from behind the quilt. "I'm invisible!"

Teal sensed the difference in Anya, though. He approached her cautiously, taking her hand in his and sidling up close.

"What're you doing, Anya?"

"*Je ne sais pas,* kiddo." She looked at him, but with blank, watery eyes. "Nothing, I guess." Teal looked to Sabine, unsure of what to do next.

"How are you, Anya?" Sabine put her arm on Anya's shoulder as she spoke, but Anya didn't look at her.

"Teal, did you get taller overnight, *mon petit chou?*"

Teal shrugged. He didn't like this Anya so much. She smelled like dirty feet and said funny things, like she was talking in poetry instead of real-life words.

"I think *I* mighta." Toby peeked out from the quilt. "Are you coming to make cookies with me and Nana and everybody?"

"I don't . . . I think maybe no, or yes—" Anya started to turn in a confused little circle. Toby thought it was a game, so he laughed and hopped with her while she shuffled about. But Teal backed away, closer to Nappo.

"Something's the matter with her," Teal whispered.

Nappo kneeled so he could whisper in Teal's ear. "You know that, Teal. Her kid died."

"Well." Teal stared at the floor. "All our family died and then bunches more died, and I don't smell bad like she does. And I don't wander around like some ghost haunter thing. I seen more dead people than she has. I'd bet money on it."

"Give her time," Nappo said.

"I'm only six." Teal held up as many fingers to illustrate his point. "She's a grownup."

"Give it a rest, Teal."

"Nana's making cookies downstairs." Sabine took Anya's hand. "And I know she'd love your help. You're a master baker, Anya."

"Cookies! Cookies! Cookies!" Toby popped out from the quilt to do a jig. Anya stopped her circling and watched him as if he'd just appeared out of thin air.

"Why, yes." Anya patted his head as he circled her again. "Of course. What a good idea. Cookies!" She said it as if she were reading from a cue card that had also appeared out of thin air.

As Toby dragged Anya downstairs toward the kitchens Teal flatly refused to go, and frankly, Sabine couldn't blame him. "At least it's an improvement," she said to Nappo. "At least she's making a bit of sense now and then."

"I just don't understand why she's acting like a zombie," Teal muttered.

"She's sad, Teal." Nappo squatted to let Teal ride piggyback. "You've been sad before. When Mom and Dad died, and Talia. And your friends back in Triskelia."

"I know." Teal rested his cheek on his big brother's back, as if he were three again, as if he might fall asleep like that. "But we didn't die. We're still alive."

He felt as small as Toby. He wished he *were* as small as Toby. Maybe if he was, listening to Sabine and Nappo talk about the revolution and strategy and weapons acquisitions wouldn't make him so afraid. He was only six, but he felt like his life might be over soon. He didn't think he'd ever get to be grown up. Especially if they were going to war. This *revolution* just sounded like a fancy word for war. Guns and knives and blood and death, and always the sicks lurking around like ghosts. He for one had had enough of such things for one lifetime, if not ten.

16

✧

Edmund glanced at his watch. It was almost noon. He'd be summoned for lunch at any moment, and then he had a meeting with the comptroller to discuss the budget surplus left over from the waves of donations after the garden bombings. After that he was to meet with the chair of the Star Chamber to go over a ream of new anti-terrorist policy. And then he had to endure tea with Allegra's pinch-faced mother and her scabby lap dog. And then to the Weather Lab with a very pregnant and understandably crabby Allegra in tow for a ribbon-cutting ceremony at the new wing. And all this on a day when the rains were coming early. They were due to start any minute and, if all went according to schedule, should clear up by the time he and Allegra stepped out for the ceremony. There'd been talk about postponing it for a drier day, but there was something poignant about holding a function at the Weather Lab just after a rain, when the earth smelled fresh and the foliage glistened with damp and the world seemed slick with possibility and growth. Even Allegra, in all her pregnant glory, was a fertile window dressing to the occasion. She didn't want to go, but Edmund was insisting.

Edmund crossed his office and opened the French doors that led out to his private balcony. He stepped out into the midday. It was muggy, the air bloated with humidity. Almost instantly the sky darkened just a hue and the first tentative spits of rain fell, splotching the slate at his feet with satisfying dark spots.

He watched the rain for a moment, while a strange urge built up inside him. He wanted to feel the rain, really *feel* it. He fought the silly notion until the compulsion was too much to ignore. He stepped out from under the eaves and let the rain fall on his face. The first cold drops felt sharp against his warm cheeks. And then, as he turned his face upward, it just felt gloriously *clean.*

The last time he'd felt rain on his skin had been so many long years ago.

Oh come, Edmund. Lisette had pulled him from their bed in the middle of the night. *Come outside, just for a moment. The thunder, the moonlight, the rain . . . it's all so magical!*

He hadn't wanted to. He was wary of uncharted weather, as that storm had been, but his new wife was so enthusiastic it was a little catching. She tugged at his arm.

Vite, vite! She was barefoot, in a white linen nightgown, her dark hair flowing over her shoulders, her skin aglow with silken moonlight. Another crack of thunder.

No, Lisette. It might not be safe. It might be enemy weather, tainted even.

Come, Edmund, she said, but she let his hand go. *There is so little joy in planning everything.*

He'd watched her for a moment, beholding this strange, wondrous beauty who had come into his life. They'd rushed the wedding when they found out that she was pregnant, and ever since she'd been behaving oddly. Sad, even melancholic. Maybe if he played along with her it would raise her spirits. A woman expecting a baby should be joyful. Against his better judgment he'd pushed aside the blankets and reached for his shoes.

Non, non, coco. Lisette grabbed his shoes and held them out of reach. *You must at least once feel wet grass underfoot and the open skies above, raining down. Sois pas si bouclé.*

English, Lisette. Please . . .

Come, come.

And so she'd pulled him outside like that, he in his pyjama bottoms and she in her nightie, the swell of the baby already showing. She'd pulled him out into the middle of the back lawn where she spun around and around, her arms outstretched, head flung back, offering her cheeks to the rain until she toppled over onto the grass. Edmund shivered, the rain streaking down his face. She patted the grass beside her, and he sat. She pulled him to her and kissed him, their wet faces warming with touch.

"Sir?"

Edmund did not need to turn to know the owner of the voice. The only person who would enter his office uninvited was Nord.

"I would rather you knocked."

"I have a wire here you might be interested in."

Edmund took cover under the eaves again. "What does it say?"

"The Guard is set up at the edge of Triban now. Commander Regis is waiting for word from you."

Edmund had sent Regis to Triban, but he didn't know what to have him do next. It made sense that any survivors of the attack on Triskelia would congregate there. He wanted them finished off. He wanted his children brought to him. All three of them. He wanted to *finish*. But what was he finishing? His first family, the one that had grown so twisted with secrets and lies? Or was he finishing himself in a way, sealing his own downfall? And what would that look like? Not killing his own children, surely? He *had* to see the girl. He needed to. But why? Acknowledging her would ruin him.

"Tell him to hold his position."

"Until?" Nord knew Commander Regis well. He was a man who needed direction, somewhere to go. A goal at least. He was not a man to just stand there with his hands in his pockets.

"I said, tell him to hold his position." Edmund pulled the balcony doors shut, closing out the rain. He took a seat at his desk and dried his face with a handkerchief. He picked up his pen and perched his reading glasses on his nose in a manner he hoped would be dismissive to the brute who stood before him. "Send in Phillip."

"What do you need Phillip for?" Nord let the paper fall onto Edmund's blotter. "What's he gonna do that I can't? We have an arrangement, sir. I don't want to have to keep reminding you."

"Phillip is my Chief Regent." Edmund glanced coolly over his glasses. "You are not. Need I keep reminding you of that?"

Nord's rage coursed through him as if it had been injected right into his veins. He held his breath, taking care not to say anything stupid.

When he finally spoke, he practically growled the words. "Maybe that should change, all things considered."

"I don't see how that would ever happen." Edmund did not lift his eyes from his work this time. "Even *with* all things considered."

Nord tugged at his tie, which seemed suddenly tighter than usual around his thick neck. How had Seth endured any of this? Sure, Nord was a Keylander, but low Keyland, from a family that didn't have much to do with the Keyland elite. He hated the pomp and circumstance that came with a position within the Maddox household. Having to bite his tongue, play nice, follow rules, when a solid punch to the face would get so much more done so much more quickly. Nord let a long breath out through his nose. That sometimes helped in steeling himself against his rage.

"I'll find him. I think he's already in the dining room."

"Tell Francie to bring our lunch here." Again, Edmund didn't look up.

"Mine too?"

Edmund snorted back a laugh. "No, Nord. Not yours."

Nord scowled at him. It was definitely time for another talk. Time to remind Edmund of the power Nord held, just by having the knowledge he did. Or maybe it was time to let his fists do the talking. Not with Edmund. Of course not. But he did have an idea. He would let it cook for a bit. He'd learned at least that much during his time in Edmund's circle. Think before acting. He'd get Phillip. Oh, he'd definitely get Phillip.

17

Seth hadn't ventured out of his makeshift army compound in weeks. After Amon had emerged from his self-imposed exile to get clean, Seth had put him in charge of taking over the buildings on either side and constructing walkways between them. It had been a test, and he'd done surprisingly well.

Now that Amon was clean, for the time being, Seth cracked down on his no-drugs rule with the boys. He wanted his soldiers to have healthy minds and bodies, and if they dusted that would never happen. He'd been rotating the boys into a detox wing and so far the results were pretty good. It was harder if they used needles. The withdrawal was worse than if they sniffed or smoked, and some of them had the bloodsick from sharing needles or from the sextrade.

It was an awful sick, leaving them stick thin with waxy yellow skin and cloudy eyes and blisters head to toe, progressing to a dementia that particularly unnerved Seth. The first time he'd found one in his troops he'd sent him away and the boy had died in the alley at the end of the block just hours later. He hadn't wanted to turn him out, remembering all too well the terror he'd felt when Commander Regis had done the same to him. But he'd thought it was the correct thing to do. It was what Edmund would do. It was what Regis did. And so Seth had done the same, all the while fighting the unease and guilt that churned in his belly.

Afterward there'd been rumblings among the boys. He didn't hear anything specific, but Seth knew they disapproved of his sending the sick boy away, just by the glances and murmurs that trailed behind him like a wake wherever he went. They all knew someone, if not many, with the bloodsick, and they'd all been sick at one point or another, Seth included.

It was then that he'd realized he wasn't the kind of leader his father or Commander Regis was. He was his own brand of leader. Kinder, more compassionate, and by being so, the kind of leader whose men were truly loyal. Firm, but humane. So the next time a bloodsick boy was discovered among his ranks he was moved to a section of the attic detox wing converted into a sick room.

For the longest time there was just the one boy. Seth assigned Dache the task of watching him in addition to the beds of boys withdrawing from dust. Dache was tall for his fifteen years, with long, lanky limbs and a neck to match. He wore glasses, with one lens cracked across, and was always reading a book. The other boys taunted him, called him four-eyes and spider legs and sissy and faggot. He might be bent, and then again he might not, but Seth didn't particularly care. He knew that a lot of the boys hooked up with each other, and after his time in Triskelia he at least knew to keep his opinions to himself on the matter. He'd chosen Dache because he was smart and calm and had a stomach of steel.

When the boy died Dache sent Ori to bring Seth to the sick room. Seth and Amon had their heads bent over a stack of maps a couple of boys had brought back the night before. As far as they could make out, the rat-chewed, mouldy maps showed tunnels and ancient dried-up water mains that ran beneath the city, as if it were a shadow metropolis lying quietly asleep beneath them.

"Quiet?" Amon shook his head. "I don't think so. I bet a million people live down there."

"Then why wouldn't we have heard of it?" Seth tapped one set of intersecting lines. "This is the brothel. Up behind the old city hall. I bet you no one has a clue that three tunnels intersect below."

"Doubt it." Amon glanced up. "There's no way no one knows about it. I bet it's even worse than up here."

"You've lived in this city off and on for years and you've never heard of it."

"Seth—" Amon corrected himself. "Commander Seth, if you think you're the first one to discover these underground tunnels, you're off your nut. And if you go down there, take half the army, because you'll probably need it."

Seth opened his mouth to respond, but Ori was at the door. "Commander Seth?"

ORI LED HIM UPSTAIRS to the attic room. Seth slowed as the smells hit him. The puke and piss and shit was one thing, but the waft of medicinal treatments Dache had procured at the lifeminder stalls was what hit Seth like a slap to the face. *Rosa.* He'd looked for her, had given his entire army her description. He was determined to find her and hire her to run the sick room, now that it had six patients and just awkward, weary Dache to run the place. Seth had provided him with a stack of books on lifeminding and herbminding and bonesetting, so now with each arrival Dache dug into the books first, researching while the new boy writhed in pain or puked his guts out. Seth wanted Rosa. He wanted her to come work for him, but more than that, he just plain *wanted* her.

Where was she if she wasn't in Triban? Had she gone back to her village with some lie so that they'd take her back? Was she out there on her own? Or worse, not on her own? What if she'd hooked up with another guy? Seth squeezed his eyes shut for the briefest moment. That usually worked when Rosa saturated his thoughts, and so it did this time too. Seth nodded, signalling Ori to lead him into the sick room where Dache stood at attention beside the dead boy's bed.

The boy's name was Edgar. He lay there, his head arched back as if his last moments had yanked his muscles taut with pain. His eyes were wide and opalescent and his skin was stretched thin over his bones, his ribs sticking out as if they were the only things holding his human shape. He was blotched with sores and his hair was thin and patchy on his dry scalp. Beside Seth, Ori stared at the floor, not wanting to look.

Seth stood with his shoulders squared and swallowed back his nausea. There was plenty of inspiration too, in a bucket beside the bed and on the sheets by Edgar's head. Seth felt his face pulling into a grimace, and so he forced himself to take a breath, through his mouth to avoid the smell, and to relax his face into a neutral, thin-lipped stare.

"Why have you brought me here?" Seth was startled by his own voice. He sounded so much like Edmund just then that he had to take a few seconds to recover.

"He died." Dache folded his arms and hunched his shoulders a bit. "I figured you should come. Say a few words or something."

Seth wanted to ask Dache why the hell he'd think that. Like Seth had anything to say to his highers ever, let alone now? As if there even *were* highers?

"Dache." Seth turned to him. Dache straightened a little but did not unfold his arms. There was an unspoken agreement between them: that although Dache was just another one of Seth's soldier boys he held a unique position, especially as he gained skills and knowledge from his books and experience. "There's no need to call for me every time one of them dies. Make a note of it, deal with the body, and carry on. Understood?"

"Won't happen again, Commander. Sorry."

"Never mind." Seth nodded. "Start a log, in case someone comes looking. Record their names, any identifying marks, tag their belongings, that sort of thing."

"What about a service?" Ori piped up.

"Not yet."

"What're you going to do with his body?" Ori asked. "Can I have his watch?"

"We'll let you get to it, Dache." Seth put a firm hand on Ori's shoulder and steered him to the door. "Let me know if you need anything from me."

"I'll send out one of the boys to see if they can find his sister." Dache walked them to the stairs. "He said something about her working at the brothel, so maybe she's still there. Her name is Eugenie."

"I'll see to it," Seth said, an idea forming. "Leave it to me."

Beside him, Ori snickered. Seth glanced at him. Ori made a face, suggesting one of the various things on the menu at the brothel.

Seth wanted to whack him upside, but he was experimenting with his leadership style these days. Edmund had rarely hit either him or Eli as children, and yet they'd been respectful and somewhat terrified of him. Seth tried a stern look instead.

"Sorry, Commander Seth."

"I appreciate your apology." Seth grinned to himself. "Now, go."

"But should I walk you back?"

Seth shook his head. "I don't require your company, nor do I want it."

"But I said I was sorry."

Seth nodded. "Go, Ori."

And so Ori slunk off ahead of him down the stairs.

Seth turned to Dache. "Wait on the service until I get word back to you about his sister."

Dache nodded. "If I move his body down to the cellar he should keep for a couple days without stinking up the main floor too bad. I'll make sure he's rat proof."

"Thank you." Seth started down the stairs, grateful when the smells faded and his head cleared. He stood in the dim corridor for a while, enjoying the quiet. Most of the boys were out scavenging. Then he walked slowly on, forming his plan. He would go to the brothel and look for Eugenie, and while he was there he'd find the entrance to the underground tunnels. Through those tunnels he'd make his way to Commander Regis's camp. And then he would kill him with his bare hands for leaving him to die from the sick. And for what he'd done to Triskelia.

Word had also reached Cascadia that the Guard was encamped just outside Triban. The messenger added that most of the city believed they'd come to put down any potential uprising resulting from the Triskelian massacre. And that, oddly, the Guard had already passed up a chance. Two makeshift rebel groups had attempted to storm the Northwestern Key, whose military was the weakest of all the Keys. The Guard at Triban had done nothing, letting the Key's own troops annihilate the sad Triban rebels as they rushed its walls.

"The Guard obviously has larger things in mind," Zenith said. "Like us."

"What would they care if we want to put on a circus?" Sabine said.

"They know now that Triskelia is the Night Circus," reasoned Zenith. "Therefore, wherever the circus is, there are the rebels."

"We'll be unarmed as far as they know."

"Ah, but they'll know that's what we want them to think."

"Perhaps we should consider a different plan." Sabine hoped her voice sounded more confident than she felt. She didn't want to have to come up with a whole new strategy, even if it meant bringing the circus to the city under the threat of a Guard attack. Thankfully Zenith was shaking her head.

"No. It only means we must move quickly, before they can do any damage in the city while they wait. Triban must not fall to them. If they want us, they shall get us. We'll leave for Triban in the morning. If we arrive ahead of schedule we may catch them even just slightly by surprise."

"But we're not ready! We weren't going to leave for another week. We're still waiting on the two shipments of weapons—they won't get to the village in time and we'll miss them. And there's the circus to put together, and the costumes. We *can't* leave yet," Sabine insisted even as Zenith directed Gavin and Jack to get the others prepared to depart at once.

Later, when they were finally alone, Sabine added, "I'm supposed to be giving directions now, Zenith."

"Leadership is not an instant transformation, child." Zenith shuffled around her quarters, collecting her things. "I will be your mentor and advisor for some time to come."

"But I'm telling you, we're not ready!"

"That was always my excuse too," Zenith said. "We will start for Triban as soon as possible. We can arrange for the weapons to find us along the way somehow. We can still move into the city under the guise of the circus; the Guard might think we're not yet prepared for battle—"

"We're not!"

"We must move out now, Sabine. End of discussion."

AS THE OTHERS RUSHED ABOUT, packing in a flurry of disorganization, Eli wrestled with himself. They'd been told to get ready to leave, but he didn't want to go. He'd offered to stay behind and look after the children who'd be remaining at Cascadia, but there were enough among the wounded survivors to take care of them. Mireille wasn't going. Why couldn't he stay with her, with the crew that ran the weather lab? But he knew he wasn't skilled enough to warrant leaving behind a perfectly able-bodied person.

Furthermore, he did not want to fight. Not ever. It was wrong.

Peace is the way.

And the voice did not want him to fight.

You must not take up arms.

Then why go? If he didn't want to fight, what was the point of his going at all? It wasn't likely that the circus would perform, not if the Guard was lying in wait. And so that meant one thing. That Sabine was leading them to slaughter.

Well, Eli didn't want to die either. He wanted to stay with Mireille in Cascadia, forever if he had his way.

But neither Zenith nor Sabine would accept his reasons for staying behind. And when it was clear he'd lost that battle he tried to convince Mireille to come with him at least. Despite the danger, he wanted her with him.

"I'd be gone at least a month!" Mireille shook her head. "It's impossible. I can't leave Rainy."

"But don't you want to go?"

"Of course, Eli. It's all so exciting. I do want to." Mireille sighed. "But this is my life, up here on the mountain. My destiny."

"I am so sick of that word."

Everyone was talking about destiny, or Sabine's anyway, ever since Zenith had announced her as the new leader of Triskelia.

18

༺✦༻

At the Maddox estate the staff was busily preparing for Edmund's trip to the annual legislature, set to meet in the Western Key in two weeks' time. The Chancellors weren't due to meet this early in the year, but with the Guard set to strike Triban and the two brazen attempts to take the Northwestern Key, they had agreed to convene as soon as they could all arrive.

There'd been talk of moving the legislature to a Key farther away from the trouble brewing in Triban, but that would send the wrong message. This way the Chancellors would demonstrate that they'd considered the problem and concluded it was a mere nuisance rather than a threat. Edmund wasn't convinced it was wise to gather in one of the closest Keys to Triban, but with each Chancellor accompanied by a heavily armed Guard contingent, and still more poised outside of Triban, surely they'd be safer there than anywhere.

The timing was problematic for Edmund at home, though. Allegra was due to have the baby at any moment and didn't want him to go.

"Please, please stay." She'd been bedridden for a week now, by order of the birthminder. She was alarmingly unattractive as of late, and getting worse each day. Edmund perched uncomfortably on the edge of the bed, all too aware of her body odour and lank hair falling across her puffy cheeks. She clutched his wrist. "I need you here. The baby needs you. We need you, darling."

"I must go." Edmund offered her a thin smile. "There's so much turmoil right now, and all kinds of rumours since Triskelia fell. Talk of retaliation and rebellion. The risk of terrorist attack is as high as I've ever known it to be. These are dangerous times, my dear. The Keys must strategize in order to keep us all safe. You want a safe home for our child, don't you?"

"Of course." Allegra pouted. "But I also want you home with me right now."

"I can't be here and there at the same time."

"Then choose *me*. Choose your baby. Send Phillip on your behalf?"

"Perhaps if he'd been in the position longer. But it wouldn't be fair to send him alone. He'd be in far over his head. He's not ready."

"I know." Allegra sat up to receive the tray of tea and toast Francie was bringing into the room. "But I'm scared. I just want you here, with me."

"I have to go." Edmund waited until the maid had backed out of the room, head bowed, before he continued. "I know you understand. Don't you?"

She nodded.

"All right then. Good girl." Edmund placed his hands on his knees and made to stand. "That's settled."

"No! Not just yet." Allegra pulled at his arm. "Stay with me for another little while? Everyone is still packing, so you can be with me just for another minute."

"I'm to meet Phillip to go over the itinerary." Edmund read his watch. "Now, actually."

"He can wait, darling." Allegra put her hand over his and brought them both to her belly. "The baby is restless. Can you feel that?"

Edmund nodded.

"Stay with me just now," Allegra whispered. "Phillip can wait."

"Just a few minutes." Edmund pulled his hand away. Feeling the baby's kicks and turns made him uneasy, queasy even. It seemed grotesquely primal for one, and served as a reminder of the last birth he took part in, which he did not look back on with fondness now. But certain things must be done, if only because it was the proper thing to do. "Another minute or two, and then I must be off."

IN EDMUND'S OFFICE, Phillip glanced at his watch. Edmund was late. He looked over the itinerary, blocked out by the hour and beginning with their arrival in the Western Key, which would take the full two weeks, travelling constantly, stopping only to quickly change horses and drivers. It was the best way to avoid the night bandits and any other Droughtland filth who might try to take down a Keyland caravan. That happened only rarely, what with all the Guard they travelled with, and the guns. Thankfully, the idiot, dust-crazed Droughtlanders at least had a healthy fear of guns. Phillip grinned to himself. He crossed one leg over the other and bounced his foot. He was going across the continent with Chancellor East! And as his Chief Regent! Had anyone told him as a boy that he'd grow up to live this life he would've laughed until he peed himself. He stopped kicking his foot. He didn't like being reminded of the times when he'd wet himself. He'd peed the bed for ages, and even his pants if he was particularly nervous. Like his first kiss. Oh dear. Not a pleasant memory at all, her laughing and he scurrying away with his hands covering his damp crotch. But that was all in the past. He'd just been a boy. Well, fourteen, but still. He couldn't even remember the girl's name now, or at least that's what he told himself. He shored up his mood with a cheerful sort of nod and resumed his kicking. That was then and this was now and life was a delicious buffet laid out before him to enjoy indefinitely.

Nord watched him from the hall, the door cracked just enough for him to see Phillip murmuring to himself and pumping his leg like a nervous twit. In his jacket Nord had a blank piece of paper and Phillip's treasured pen, which he'd lifted from his shirt pocket the day before without his even noticing. Phillip had dug in all his pockets over and over again, frantically trying to find it, working up a sweat and even ripping right through a pants pocket until Edmund had yelled at him to stop. Nord had almost laughed but managed to hold it back.

Now he opened the door, the grin still on his stubbly face. "Sir—"

Phillip whipped around, his smile flattening when he saw it was Nord. "Oh. What do you want?" He didn't bother to keep the disdain from his voice. Nord was just some oafish interloper after all; a nobody Edmund had taken a shine to for some inexplicable reason. He was just some Guardy. Phillip didn't see whatever it was that Edmund saw in him.

But Edmund must have some reason to keep him about. Perhaps he was undercover? Or perhaps his sheer size simply made Edmund feel safe. Whatever the reason, Nord was always around now, like a mutt who'd wormed his way into a fine home with no one caring about his breeding or the fact that he might be riddled with fleas and insufferably stupid as well. If only Edmund would explain to Phillip why Nord was there at all. If only he'd give the oaf a title of some kind, one that would firmly park him well below Phillip in the hierarchy. Chief Bodyguard, for example. Or Page.

Nord pulled Phillip's pen from his pocket. "Look what I found."

"Oh!" He warmed to Nord suddenly, despite himself. The gold-plated pen had been his uncle's, the previous Chancellor East's, and had been willed to him specifically. "Thank you!" He reached for it as Nord approached.

"Uh-uh. Not so fast." Nord placed the blank piece of paper, still folded into thirds, on the desk in front of Phillip. "I'd like you to write something for me first."

Phillip pulled his chin to his chest, confused. "Whatever for?"

Nord stared at him. "Humour me."

"I don't have time for this." Phillip tidied his pile of papers and tucked them back into his attaché case. "I'm a very busy man."

"Trust me." Nord glared at him. "You have time."

It was something in the way he looked at him—his jaw tensing, the darkness in his eyes combined with his daunting presence—that made Phillip afraid in that moment. He would do what he said, right now anyway, and then he'd tell Edmund to get rid of him. Before they left for the legislature. Phillip was the nephew of the deceased dear Chancellor East, blessed be the highers, and he did not have to put up with this silliness. He was an important man! Chief Regent no less, and Nord was just some hulking dunce.

"Fine." Phillip snatched the pen. "Let's get on with it."

"Thank you." Nord took the seat across the desk.

Phillip scowled at him. "That's the Chancellor's seat."

"Edmund won't mind."

"He'd certainly mind your using his first name like that."

Nord pounded a thick finger at the exposed third of paper. "Write."

"Write what?"

"What I tell you to. Word for word." Nord started dictating. "Chancellor East . . ."

Chancellor East, Phillip wrote in his careful, scholarly script, not bothering to unfold the paper, which felt satisfyingly spiteful, in a way. He smiled at the words. His penmanship really was exquisite.

He continued to write as Nord dictated what Phillip assumed was a letter to the Chancellor from Nord himself. Maybe the idiot couldn't even write. Dumb nitwit. Whatever, Phillip was enjoying himself. The letter was turning out to be rather interesting. He might not have to talk to the Chancellor about Nord after all. By the sounds of it Nord was leaving, and by his own volition. For all his bullish nature, he was just a ninny underneath. My, my, this was turning into quite the excellent day.

> *Chancellor East,*
>
> *I am sorry, but I just can't take it any more. I have thought long and hard about what I am about to do, and still, I can see only one way out. I am sorry to disappoint you, and I am sorry to leave you and my responsibilities this way, but I just don't see any other solution. I am a coward.*

"Coward?" Phillip looked up, a sudden chill slicing through him as he completed that sentence. "What are you getting at with this?"

Nord grinned. "Keep writing."

"I won't." Phillip capped his pen and pushed the paper across the desk. "I won't have anything more to do with whatever it is you're up to."

"Okay." Nord shrugged. "Have it your way." He left the paper where it was and came around to Phillip's side of the desk as if to make his way to the door. When he was safely behind him, Phillip let out a sigh of relief. And in that moment Nord pulled Phillip's gun from his holster and shot him in the side of the head, careful to aim up from below so that the wound would be convincing.

Phillip had only just got the gun, and only after Nord's urging. After all, he'd argued, these were dangerous times. Surely the Chancellor's Chief Regent should be armed so that he could do what was necessary if the situation demanded it? No doubt, he'd insisted, there would be occasions when force would be required, either to keep the peace or protect the Chancellor.

During that discussion Nord had sat back, knees spread, shirtsleeves rolled up, his thick, muscled arms folded, his own gun tucked snug in its holster. He'd looked every bit the protector, and Phillip had not. Edmund had given him an appraising glare from across his desk. Phillip received the message loud and clear: get a gun. And so he had. But he hadn't even had the chance to learn how to use it yet. He'd only got as far as learning how to clean and load it.

The gunshot hurt Nord's ears. A wide splatter of blood dripped down the wall behind Phillip's chair. As the shot echoed through the house and startled shouts erupted from the staff, Nord tucked the gun in Phillip's hand and unfolded the paper, careful not to get any blood on it. It was a piece of Phillip's own stationery, with his signature at the bottom. He'd signed them stacks at a time, enjoying scrawling his signature with a flourish, especially since acquiring his new title and his uncle's pen. *Phillip Walsh, Chief Regent, Eastern Key.*

As the footsteps drew closer and the shouts louder, Nord slipped out the balcony doors and dropped over the railing onto the grass with a stealth that no one would associate with his bulk. By the time Francie entered the room with a horrified scream Nord was making his way up the back stairs so that he could hurry down from his rooms to see what all the commotion was about.

He ran into Edmund on his way down, a delicious bonus.

"What's going on?" Edmund flew down the steps two at a time.

"Let me go ahead, sir." Nord drew his gun and popped the release. "Just in case it's some kind of ambush or something."

"Do you think it's about the legislature?" Edmund yelled after him as Nord ran down the hall, his gun leading the way.

Two Guards were already in the room. Edmund could hear them as he neared.

"Check if he's breathing!" one hollered.

"And what would he be breathing through?" the other shouted, a manic laugh punctuating his remark. "His neck?"

"In there!" Cook screamed at Edmund, clutching a wailing Francie to her, the two of them huddled against the wall outside his office door. "It's the Chief Regent! He's been shot!"

Edmund stopped cold in his tracks. Nord glanced back at him just before he entered the room. They shared the briefest of looks, but the mere second was all it took for Edmund to know.

This was Nord's doing. He might never know how, but he knew it was him.

Edmund slowed, his feet suddenly leaden. The next thing he was aware of was standing at his desk, looking down at the bloodied mess that had been Phillip. He read the note. He asked the appropriate questions, made several appropriate remarks, and then he let one of the Guards escort him to the dining hall, away from the horrific scene.

What mattered to him was not Phillip's death, but how to stop the investigation into it. It shouldn't be too difficult. Nord had covered his tracks nicely, and the suicide note was an exquisite seal on the whole matter. Edmund had to admit that perhaps Nord was not as stupid as he seemed.

"Have it cleaned up," Edmund said to the Guardy. "Immediately."

"But the investigator is coming."

"There is no need. Clearly, and sadly, it was a suicide. Have it cleaned up."

"Yes, Chancellor," the Guardy said. "Right away."

EDMUND HAD BARELY A MOMENT to collect his thoughts before Allegra's screams broke the silence. Edmund shook his head. He was tired and his head was spinning.

Would he ever have peace?

Cook popped her head into the dining room, Francie still teary-eyed under her arm, clinging to her.

"The Lady's bedside bell is ringing, sir." Cook petted Francie's head as she spoke. "I can send one of the girls up, but I'm guessing she's wanting you, sir. After all. Likely frightened. We all are, at that. What with all that's just happened, and the baby coming. She'll be wanting you."

Edmund sighed. "Do you not hear her screams?"

"Yes." Cook was taken aback. "Sir?"

"Then do you think I need you to tell me that she's ringing the blasted service bell? Do you think I'm stupid?" Cook, of course, stayed mum. Edmund put his fingertips to his temple. "I'll go."

"Yes, sir." Cook backed into the hall. "Sorry, sir."

Edmund stood, fingers still at his temple. He went out the back way to avoid his office, taking the service stairs up to his and Allegra's floor. He'd have to tell her that her beloved cousin had shot himself in the head, unable to deal with the pressures of his position. He would have to lie to his wife. But that was nothing new. She would wonder why he'd choose Nord as his Chief Regent, but she'd know better than to ask, and for that Edmund was thankful.

This was a household of secrets, the Maddox house. As Edmund climbed the final stairs and stepped into the hall he took a moment to swoon from the magnitude of it all. Loss. Betrayal. Grief. Deceit. And now murder.

THREE

TRIBAN

19

~✦~

Tossing and turning on the hard cold earth in a tent halfway down the mountain, Eli was thinking about his father, a particular memory that hadn't visited for a long time. He'd been small, maybe four or five, and he and Seth were dressed for Halloween. Eli was a clown, with a red nose and a rainbow yarn wig and long pointed shoes Lisette had made out of papier mâché. Eli clomped around, tripping over his feet, laughing each time he fell.

Seth was dressed as a soldier. That was the first year they didn't match. Before that they'd been twin puppies or cowboys on their dusk strolls from estate to estate. But that year Seth had begged Lisette to make him a Guardy uniform. She'd argued at first, saying she wouldn't know the first thing about making such a costume.

Eli remembered her protests. She hadn't wanted Seth to be a Guardy at all and had tried to convince him to be something, anything, else. A wizard, a magician, a lion, a pirate. But Seth had his heart set on being a Guardy. When Edmund heard he encouraged it. Lisette had given up, but she didn't make the costume herself. She had the family's tailor do it, even though she was a gifted seamstress and it would not have been much of a challenge for her. It made sense now, of course.

It was the first and only time Edmund displayed any enthusiasm about the boys' Halloween costumes. He bought Seth a toy gun, something Lisette had never let them have, and he got him real badges and epaulettes. When he helped Seth put it all together on Halloween Seth had been thrilled, and so very proud.

As they got ready to go out, pillowcases in hand, Seth met Edmund at the door with a sloppy but energetic salute. Edmund always walked them from door to door. It was a tradition in the Keys that the fathers accompanied their children on Halloween, but it wasn't something he loved to do. It was a duty. That year he was a little more into it though, now that he had a miniature Guardy to show off to the other fathers.

Seth had marched ahead to Edmund's enthusiastic "One two, one two!" and Eli had stumbled behind, tripping on his clown shoes. He loved his costume, but the falling wasn't funny any more.

At some point Eli's memory slipped into a dream as he finally fell asleep in the tent on the mountainside.

In the dream, when Eli fell Edmund stopped and scooped him up from the ground. In the dream he'd kissed Eli's scraped hand and helped him collect the sweets that had spilled from his pillowcase. In the dream Edmund perched Eli on his shoulders and they walked the rest of the way like that, together. In the dream they arrived at the Key's bonfire, father and son, Eli proudly atop Edmund's shoulders.

Eli sat up, rubbing the sleep from his eyes. He yawned. It was just dawn, the light flat and grey in the little tent he shared with Nappo and Teal, who'd refused to be left behind on the mountain. They were fast asleep, Nappo with his sleeping bag pulled right over his head and Teal curled up with his hands clasped under his chin, as if he still clutched his scrap of precious blanket between them and had not lost it when they fled Triskelia.

Eli lay down again and burrowed into his sleeping bag, but he couldn't fall back to sleep. The memory of that Halloween was loud in his head, like a clanging song that would not stop. The fireworks, the singing, the crackle and pop of the bonfire as it spat huge embers into the pitch-black night.

Bullet stirred from the foot of the tent as Eli pulled on his coat and toque and shoved his feet into his boots. He slipped quietly out, Bullet following closely. He'd hike up to the ridge above the camp and watch the sun rise. That was a better way to start the day. Better than thinking about what had really happened that Halloween, or what lay ahead for him and the others.

That October night he'd kept tripping over his clown shoes until finally he just stayed down and cried for his father to wait while Seth and Edmund marched neatly ahead.

"Father!" he'd wailed. "Wait for me! Please stop? Father!"

Edmund kept going. He didn't even look back. Who knows why? Because he wanted to teach Eli a lesson? Because he'd told Eli to take off the silly shoes and Eli had refused because he loved them so very, very much? Because he hadn't heard him? Because he hadn't cared?

Eli had lain face down on the cobblestones, bawling and sniffling, until he felt a hand on his back. It was Allegra, dressed as Little Bo Peep with her puppy as her sheep. She helped him stand and then hugged him until he stopped crying.

"There, there," she said. "You can come with me and Phillip, Eli." She dabbed at his teary, grease-painted cheeks with the hem of her petticoat. "We'll take you to the bonfire. Never mind your father."

Allegra's father was dead, and her grandfather—the Chancellor himself—had a bad hip, so Phillip was the one to walk her around the Key every year. Eli liked Phillip, and after that night he liked him even more, because he'd let Eli ride piggyback the rest of the way. He wasn't in costume, given that he was a teenager and took himself very seriously. Other adults wore a mask, or a funny costume even, but not Phillip. He was dressed in tailored slacks and a collared shirt with a tie squarely knotted at his throat. There was nothing fanciful about him in the least, but he was kind.

WATCHING THE SUNRISE did make Eli feel better. He loved being out of doors, here where the weather was near to natural rather than harnessed exclusively by the Keys like it was on the other side of the mountain range that divided the west from the plains. He felt an unmatchable peace when he was alone in the forest, a contentment that he and his guiding voice agreed on. But it was time to get back to camp. They'd be packing up and heading out soon.

Stay. The voice had been quiet for some time, until now.

"Where?" There was only forest and rocks and cliffs all around.

Be still. Meditate. Let the others go ahead.

Eli laughed out loud and headed back to camp. He would not be bullied by a faceless sense. Not yet, not while he could still think for himself. Although he had to admit it was getting harder to argue with the seemingly random observations and advice. He needed to talk to someone about it. Zenith, of course. But she was always busy these days, and Eli didn't want to worry her about his psychological mess. He still hoped it would pass, that it was a symptom of trauma and would slowly lessen until it was gone entirely. But did he really want the voice, or whatever it was, to go away? He did find comfort in it, and would miss it if it ended. It made him feel occasionally sure of himself, something he'd rarely felt before.

Back at the camp everyone was up and Sabine was already meeting with Zenith. She was always with Zenith now. She didn't have time to hang out with Eli or the others. Eli walked past them seated at the fire with blankets over their laps and mugs of tea in hand. He kept his gaze distant, as if his mind was on important things.

SABINE LOOKED UP and watched her brother. She wanted to confide in him, she wanted him as part of her inner circle, but he was so closed lately, and so angry with her. And for what? He should be relieved he wasn't the chosen one. She'd trade stations with him in an instant.

No, she wouldn't.

The truth was that she was excited by all of it. The future lay ahead, uncharted and there to discover and claim with the flags of freedom.

She turned her attention back to Zenith, who was setting down her mug and helping herself up with her walking sticks. "Where are you going, Zen Zen?"

"I will send Trace to you now." Zenith shuffled away from the fire. "He has several ideas about firearms, and has arranged to have the two shipments meet us partway. I'm going to lie down before we head out."

Sabine and Zenith had since developed their plans. The circus—if they succeeded in mounting it before the Guard struck—would be a way to get the word out, but it would also bring in funds. They'd spend the money on building an arsenal. Guns, bullets, cannons even, if they could afford it. While it was strange to funnel monies toward weapons rather than food, times called for it, just now anyway. Thankfully, Trace knew a thing or two about procuring such things. He'd been the one to organize the first shipments and now he'd help her arrange for more, should they end up with the means to purchase it.

"The best market for weapons is on the eastern seaboard," Trace said as they discussed the matter. "That's where seized arms arrive from the Middle East. Now there's a civilization that's been warring for centuries, Sabine."

"You think this will go on that long?" Sabine could not comprehend centuries right now; she could barely handle a single day.

"I don't know," Trace said. "I hope not."

Despite his words, the excitement was obvious in his voice. He'd been so very low, but now—with a focus that drew him outside his grief and catapulted him into action—he was bright-eyed and determined and eager to get started. Sabine worried about Anya, that Trace had essentially abandoned her, but she couldn't dwell on that for long. There was so much to do.

"We won't be able to send a group east. Not right now anyway. We need everyone here."

"No, I know," Trace said. "We'll start with the two shipments we're meeting. And once we're in Triban we'll just have to deal with the arms traders there."

"What if they tell the Guard?"

"They might." Trace shrugged. "You can't count on any sense of secrecy at this point. I'm certain they know exactly what we're up to. We have to do it anyway. Don't you think?"

"But we need the element of surprise if we're even going to attempt this."

"What's 'this' exactly?"

"I don't know yet," Sabine admitted.

"Well, when the time comes for 'this,' let's hope we have the entire city of Triban on our side."

A boy, old enough to come along with the group, brought Sabine some breakfast. She took it, thanked him, and then stared at the bowl of quickly cooling porridge. She was hungry but could not bear to eat. She should— they had a long day's hike ahead—but she was thinking so hard that her body had no interest in fuel. Every ounce of herself was dedicated to assessing what should happen next, and who should do what, when, and how. It felt good, concentrating this hard, and so she left the porridge untouched.

THAT AFTERNOON THEY REACHED the wider part of the trail where their carts were waiting. After repacking and rearranging the group they set off again, this time with Zenith and Sabine in a caravan, with cushioned seats and shutters to block out the cold wind.

Now that Zenith wasn't on horseback her energy sparked and she was more talkative than she'd been for the last couple of days. Sabine tried to pay attention, but her thoughts wandered back to her own ideas and concerns, and as much as she respected Zenith, or thought she did, the old woman's rhetoric was becoming increasingly tedious. Furthermore, she was hungry now and wished she'd eaten breakfast when she had the chance.

"We must harness the ire of the people," Zenith was saying. "Use it to our advantage. Set them on the course to freedom, at whatever cost."

Sabine opened a shutter and watched the trail pass. She wanted to ask Zenith why she hadn't taken up arms before. Why now? Why not earlier, when so much devastation could have been avoided?

It would have been bloody and countless innocent lives would've been lost, but perhaps they would've succeeded and the weather would've been freed by now and the Keys would've toppled decades earlier.

But if that had been the case, would Sabine even be here? If Lisette had not had reason to infiltrate the Key?

Zenith had fallen quiet.

"Are you okay?" Sabine gave herself a little shake, as if it would slough off her heavy thoughts and allow her to concentrate on what Zenith had to say.

"You weren't listening." Zenith kept her eyes on her embroidery. She was so adept at it that the rocking of the caravan was no hindrance. She hardly had to look at it even; the stitching was second nature to her.

"I'm sorry, Zen Zen."

"No mind, child." Zenith shrugged. "Why should you have to suffer the ramblings of an old woman who's done little for the greater good?"

"No! It's not that! And you have done so much."

"For Triskelia, yes. But not the Droughtlanders. With the west blessed with weather no matter how hard the Keys try to keep it from us, it's been easy to ignore the struggles of everyone in the east."

"You haven't ignored the Droughtlanders! Many of them end up in Triban, and while it might not be as weather-starved as the inland, it has its own mess of strife and we do a lot of good for the people there, bringing food and providing clinics. We kept the Colony of the Sicks going, and brought intelligence into the Keys. Every Key! The circus has kept up the flow of information and goods for almost a hundred years. No small feat, Zenith." Sabine listened to herself leap to Zenith's defence, but she didn't actually believe much of what she said. "Don't be so hard on yourself," she finished half-heartedly. "Really."

"I've come to a certain kind of peace," Zenith said. "I have kept my people alive, fed and healthy, so that we could come to this point as strong as we are."

Strong? They weren't strong. Sabine turned to look out the window so that Zenith couldn't read the doubt and confusion on her face. And what of the devastation back at Triskelia? What of the bodies rotting beneath the rubble? They weren't alive or fed or healthy. And the fact of the matter was that the privileged west, blessed with weather, was just the tiniest slice of a continent that was dying of drought and had been for all of Zenith's lifetime.

"You don't understand." Zenith lifted her shoulders in another slow, achy shrug. "That is all right, my child. You will. With time."

"Time?" Sabine didn't feel there was any time to be had. None whatsoever. The world would simply flatten around them, suffocating them all if they didn't fight back and get the justice they so deserved.

"Yes." Zenith smiled, her wrinkly face pulling up at the corners of her mouth and the edges of her eyes. "Time."

"I hope you're right." Sabine's cheeks flushed with the colour of everything she wasn't saying out of respect. She reached under the seat for the folio of maps she'd taken from the castle. She spread them across her lap and tried to look occupied.

But Zenith kept talking. "The people will enjoy freedom because of your actions, and in time you'll be recognized for your efforts. For now you'll be the quiet cog that sets it all in motion."

Sabine didn't feel like a quiet cog. She felt like a very squeaky wheel. She didn't want to orchestrate small acts of rebellion or the first trickles of defiance that would grow into a bigger, lasting uprising. She wanted to punish.

She wanted to capture and execute the ones responsible for the massacre, and if they couldn't be captured, she would assassinate them in situ.

Executions.

Assassinations.

Kidnappings.

Hostages.

Revenge.

Her hunger was suddenly gone. It was as if she'd discovered a new source of nourishment. Retribution was all the sustenance she needed right now. She would not be hungry again until she'd avenged the murders of her friends and family.

Once they were finished with Triban, if she was still alive, she'd move the rebel forces out into the Droughtland like a righteous scourge. They'd take each Key, one at a time, until they reached the Eastern Key, where she'd deal with Edmund herself.

Sabine's thoughts rushed ahead. Was it possible to hate someone you'd never met? Did she want him dead? Would she kill him herself if she had the opportunity? She tried to picture it, coming face to face with him at last. What would she say? What *could* she say? What if—instead of hate—she felt nothing but affection for him? Was that possible?

Suddenly she was very tired. She put away the maps. She yawned, and then yawned again.

"Why don't you try to get a little sleep?" Zenith handed her a small pillow.

"Thank you, Zen Zen." Sabine rested her head and closed her eyes. She didn't think she'd sleep, not with such enormous thoughts clunking around in her head, as rhythmic as the wheels of the caravan turning. *Revenge. Retaliation. Retribution. Revolution.* She fell asleep like that, those daunting words her only lullaby.

20

❧

BAT—the Boys' Army of Triban, as Seth's soldiers were now called—was four thousand strong and running somewhat smoothly, despite Seth's shock that the numbers had grown so fast. Mind you, if he were a boy alone on the streets of Triban, he'd want to join too. It was the one safe harbour in the dangerous city, and there were three squares a day, or as close to it as Seth's cooks could manage with what the boys brought home to work with. Finding enough food was the greatest challenge, far harder than any other aspect of being in charge of so many souls.

BAT had taken over a section of the city comprising fifteen square blocks, each building housing a regiment headed by one of the older boys or young men who'd demonstrated their leadership skills and been hand selected by Seth, with Amon's help.

Within their regiments the boys rotated in and out of training and patrols and cycled through the canteen and bunkrooms in shifts. At any given time three thousand BAT soldiers were on the streets, still paired with their comrades, manning strategic corners, scavenging for food and supplies and information, and generally keeping tabs on the goings on of the city and more importantly the Guard, which was still set up on the outskirts and hadn't made a single move except to secure a fence around the camp.

The Night Circus was coming. Despite the unrest rippling across the city like shock waves the circus's imminent arrival was the subject of choice wherever two or more Tribanites congregated. Since the massacre there wasn't a soul who didn't know that the Night Circus was Triskelia's cover. If the Night Circus was coming, that meant the rebels were coming. The city was aching to rise up but shared a collective understanding, enforced by BAT, that it was best to wait to see what the Triskelians had in mind.

When Seth first heard the news his plan had been to offer up BAT's services to Zenith as a way of making peace and proving he'd had nothing to do with the massacre, at least not intentionally. If he'd inadvertently led Commander Regis to Triskelia he hadn't meant to and he was sorry for it. But the sheer mass of his army and his uncontested power had set his mind off in another direction.

Perhaps he could do better.

Better than what?

Better than anything the peace-loving, playful acrobats of Triskelia could possibly cook up to defeat the Keys. He had a hard time believing that any plan of Zenith's would enjoy lasting success. Seth, on the other hand, with his smarts and his army, could overthrow the Group of Keys himself. But first he had one more thing to do.

NOW THAT BAT was organized and Amon had proven himself capable of being in charge, the time had come for Seth to confront Commander Regis.

He didn't tell Amon his real reason for leaving. He didn't want anyone to know. He told him he was going to find Edgar's sister. Edgar's body had long since rotted into muck and bones in the basement, but he simply hadn't had the chance to leave before now.

"I should go with you," Amon said. "It's not safe to go alone."

"Even still, I'm going by myself."

"What if you get hurt? Or lost? Or kidnapped?"

"I won't." Seth cinched his small pack tight over his shoulders and secured the belt around his waist. If someone sliced the shoulder straps he'd still have the belt, and vice versa. But if someone, anyone, tried anything there would be hell to pay. Seth had a gun at each hip, a knife on his belt, another strapped to his ankle, and fists that were more than happy to pummel the life out of any bastard who mistook him for an easy mark. "I'll be back, no matter how badly you might want to be in charge, Amon."

"Trust me, Commander Seth, I wouldn't want your responsibilities."

"I'll be back. I'm just not sure how long it will take."

"Look, Commander Seth. If you want a field trip to the brothel, you could just say so. There's no judgment in wanting a little holiday. It's a little late for Edgar to have a proper burial or anything now, don't you think?"

"I'm going because that's where the dead boy's sister is, that's all. She should know that he's dead, if nothing else."

"Uh-huh," Amon said. "What a noble cause."

"I don't sleep with whores." Seth buttoned the snap over his pistol. "They're diseased. Sure way to have your dick fall off."

"Funny." Amon glanced at his own crotch. "Still got mine."

"For now, maybe." Seth started for the door. "Until one night you'll wake up and your dick will be on fire and it'll hurt so bad you'll want to chop it off yourself."

"Got some experience you want to share, Commander?" Amon called after him, laughing.

"You won't be laughing if it ever happens to you, my friend," Seth said. "I don't know when I'll be back," he added. "Maybe tonight, maybe not. Don't let the boys know I've gone. Tell them I'm in my quarters."

"Done." Amon said. "I'll keep an eye on all the barracks."

"If I don't come back—" Seth opened the doors that led to the street.

"You will, though."

"I'm trusting you with over four thousand soldiers."

Amon nodded. "I get the magnitude, Commander."

"Good," Seth said. "I'll see you when I return."

"Take care." Amon saluted him.

Seth offered him the same gesture back, plus a grin. "Don't do anything I wouldn't do."

"Same to you," Amon grinned. "They've got some fine honeys up the hill."

"That's not what I'm going for."

"Whatever you say, Commander Seth."

"You know what, Amon?" Seth considered what he was about to say. "Yeah?"

"You don't have to call me Commander. Not any more. Not when the boys aren't around."

"Yeah? Really?"

"Really. I'll see you when I get back."

Amon grinned. "Well, good luck, Seth . . . whatever it is you're up to."

Seth pushed the door open to the street and was immediately assaulted by things no weapon can defend against: the stench of rot and piss and shit, the screeching pleas of the barterers, the beseeching catcalls of the street corner sextraders. The city was a gauntlet of filth and crime, but Seth was inured to it by now and prided himself on his strength. He headed westward to the brothel, pushing through the crowded bustle of just another night in the forsaken city. He'd been going to tell Amon that if for some reason he didn't return he should hand BAT over to Zenith. But Seth would return, because he'd see victory on his own terms, and it wasn't an option to die trying.

THE BROTHEL WAS, in fact, a village of houses in what had once been a gated community atop a gently sloping hill on the western edge of Triban. The city had swallowed it up and bulldozed past it as far west as the eye could see, so now the brothel was practically in Triban's centre. It was still fenced, the perimeter monitored by a private security firm that was an offshoot of the city's feeble attempt at policing. Triban boasted no real police, but rather a bunch of poppy-eyed control freaks who carried a tin badge and a billy club. They had guns once, but they'd had them taken away after shooting them willy nilly into crowds, or had them stolen, or sold them off themselves for drug money.

Seth paid his way out of a weapons search at the gate, with a further fee to have them leave his backpack untouched. He wandered into the compound, glancing up at the glow from storey upon storey in house after house of candlelit windows with shadows lurking beyond. Fake cries of ecstasy serenaded the night along with the farmyard grunts of men pounding away at women they couldn't care less about. None of this stirred Seth's loins. Not in the least. Not any more.

When he thought back to having his way with Droughtland girls he felt only shame. There was nothing sexy in screwing someone who was afraid to say no.

Rosa had changed him. He missed her. He missed lying with her in the dark afterward, as they had so many times, talking about the world, the future. Life. She fit with him so perfectly, her head nestled in the crook of his arm, his other hand resting on her slender hip. He'd messed up and lost her, perhaps forever. He could not imagine any other girl now. She was the one. He knew it deep down. He would always be looking for her.

He pushed the ache of longing out of his mind and took stock of his surroundings. At the centre of the boulevard was what once would've been a small park. It was litter-swept, hard-packed dirt now, with three mangy dogs in the middle ripping apart something that from this distance looked like a pillow. The houses that lined the park had once been grand but were in no better shape now than the rest of the shacks in the city only bigger. Roofs slumped dangerously toward the eaves, and balconies and porches and stairs and railings had suffered hard at the backs of brawls that had spilled out the doors into the open air. Windows were cracked at best and jagged shards at worst, the glass glimmering with the meagre light cast by the candles and lanterns inside.

"Eenie meenie minie mo," Seth muttered to himself. He'd committed the maps to memory back in the barracks, the ones of the underground watermain system below this section of Triban. He sorted out his directions until he was facing predominantly west and slightly south. According to the maps, the house there stood atop a crucial underground junction.

But first he'd try to find Edgar's sister Eugenie, as promised. He strode confidently past parties of merrily drunk and dusted men teetering on the edge of brawls and bawls, past porch steps and open front windows draped with young girls with their slender legs crossed and backs arched or with shoulders pinched to make cleavage where there was none and wouldn't be for years. They stared at him, doe-eyed, as if they knew he wasn't interested. He approached a knot of them, hanging off each other like slips of lingerie.

"Not tonight," he said before any of them could inquire. The trio untangled themselves and lit each other's scrawny stubs of cigarettes, eyeing him from behind heavily painted lids.

"So?" said the fattest one, her cleavage generous and genuine and practically leaping out the top of her bustier.

"I'm looking for a girl called Eugenie."

The fat one shrugged. The two others followed suit, sucking on their cigarettes.

"I can pay."

"So?" the fat one said again. "Who says this 'Eugenie' would want to be found by you, huh?"

The two others giggled.

"Her brother died." As the girls' homemade cigarettes waned, he pulled out a fresh pack and took one from it. The girls gazed at it hungrily. "I came to tell her."

"Where'd you get them?" the one with the dreadlocks asked.

"I have my sources." He handed them each a cigarette and then lit them, one by one.

"A gentleman." The fat one left a red smear of lipstick on her filter. "We can take you to Eugenie. But you're gonna have to pay like you want to do her."

"Not a problem."

"Ah, you *do* want to do her, don't you?" Dreadlocks said, her eyebrows climbing up her forehead.

Seth glanced over his shoulder. "Look, if you don't want to help me out, I can go."

"Hang on, hang on a minute." The fat one stood, tugging at her short skirt so it would cover her bare ass as she walked. She teetered down the steps in her perilously heeled boots, taking a girl with her on each arm. "We said we'd take you."

THE TRIO LED HIM to the house beside the one he was most interested in. At the front desk he asked for Blossom, just as the girls had told him to. He was led up to a tiny attic room that stank of sweat and sex and where he waited in the only chair while the pickled old woman went to collect the girl.

She entered with a practised catwalk, one flimsy, strappy shoe in front of the other. She stood in the middle of the room with her hands resting on the top of her ass cheeks and her elbows pointed back. She too was too young for much in the breast department.

"Eugenie?" Seth said from where he sat, feeling as though he should look away or something.

"You're s'posed to call me Blossom." Her hands dropped to her sides. "Do I know you?"

Seth shook his head. "I'm here about Edgar."

"How much do you want?" She sighed and slumped into the young girl that she was. "What'd he do now?"

"He's your brother?"

"Yeah." She nodded. "What'd he do to you?"

Seth stood. If he had a hat he'd take it off, or make some other gesture of propriety. But he was in a brothel, so what did it matter? She probably hated Edgar's guts and would be glad to hear he'd rotted from the inside out with the bloodsick.

"He died."

"No." She crumpled to the floor in such a rush that Seth couldn't have caught her if he'd tried. "No! He's not dead! That's a terrible thing to say!"

She was crying now, the kohl around her eyes quickly making a muddy mess of her face.

"Shh." Seth steered her toward the bed. "Keep your voice down."

"No!" She slapped at him. "I won't! Not after what you said. You're lying. You're terrible. Let me go!"

But Seth couldn't let her go in this state. She'd make a commotion, draw the madam's attention.

"You must be quiet!"

But she cried and cried, her wails getting louder the more out of breath she became.

"I'll pay you to shut up!" Seth offered. "I don't want to sleep with you. I just came to tell you about Edgar and to tell you where he is!"

"My baby brother," she moaned. "What happened?"

Seth told her.

"I want to see him," she spluttered between sobs. "Where is he?"

"There's nothing to see. It's been too long." Seth felt a surge of guilt. Could he have come sooner?

"I don't care! I want to see him!"

Dache wouldn't let her, Seth was sure. Still, if it would shut her up, he would tell her where to go. "Do you know the city well?"

She didn't, but she knew it well enough to find her way to the warehouse with the help of the fat girl from the porch. He told her to ask for Dache and then he left her there, curled up in a tiny ball in the middle of the bed, weeping.

SETH CREPT DOWN what once would've been the service stairs when the house was in its glory days. He'd only known to look for it because every Keylander home had a set of wide stairs with carved banisters at the front of the house for the family and guests and another, narrower set at the back for servants and staff. He passed a couple of girls perched on the landing in their negligees, smoking dust pipes. They glanced up only briefly and then went back to their game of double-handed Seduce.

Seth took the stairs all the way down to the cellar, where the kitchen looked warm and inviting, with steaming pots of something on the stove. It was likely just gruel, but it was hot and smelled like cardamom. There was just one cook, and she was asleep in a chair by the stove, her dust pipe dangling loosely in her hand. She was snoring. Seth quickly scanned the floor for irregularities that might indicate a trap door or a hidden set of stairs. Nothing.

He checked each room, all of them cluttered with the detritus of girls. Underlinens strung up to dry, stockings hanging like cobwebs from bedposts and chair backs, jars and cakes of makeup all in a jumble on the dresser tops. He pocketed a small pot of concealer and kept moving.

Perhaps he'd have better luck next door. He made his way up to the main floor then sauntered purposefully past the old hag and out the front door. Two of the girls were still on the porch. The fat one was not.

"She working?"

The two nodded in tandem.

"What's next door?"

"Boys," the one said.

"If that's your thing," Dreadlocks added.

Seth fought the urge to snap at her and crossed to the other porch. He went past it, as if carrying on to the corner. Then he deked around the side of the house, keeping his back close to the wall and his eyes peeled for a cellar door.

He found it, halfway to the backyard. It wasn't locked, but the wooden door was so rotten he probably could've pulled the lock off without much effort.

Once inside with the door pulled shut, Seth lit a candle lantern he'd brought with him. He stepped carefully around breaks in the boards and over steps that had crumbled away entirely. The room was a shooting gallery, with mattresses and rusty needles and strips of leather to bring up veins. A body was slumped in the corner, and by the stench and the drone of flies Seth could tell it had been dead for some time. Maybe that's why no one else was around. Giving it a wide berth, he felt for an exit. The door he found resisted when he tried to open it, but he shoved his shoulder against it and eventually it gave with a loud crunch. He was in a hallway now. He waited to see if anyone had heard the door's protests. No one came.

The basement layout was similar to the one next door. There was a kitchen, but it wasn't in use. Either the boys in this house didn't eat or weren't going to eat any time soon. Seth checked the basement rooms. They were empty, or were piled floor to ceiling with old furniture and broken bric-a-brac. The boys must have to work around the clock in this house, with nowhere to sleep except the filthy beds they worked in. He would send Amon back, with some of the kids who'd come from here, to see if any of the boys upstairs wanted to join BAT. In the Keys being bent was a sure ticket to persecution, but after all his time in the Droughtland he didn't give a toss. Besides, most of the boys who came from up here claimed not to be bent. They said it had just been a job, that they weren't queer at all. No matter. He needed soldiers, queer or not.

IT TOOK NEARLY an hour of rooting around to finally find his way into the underground system. The door, when he found it at last, was two nondescript planks at the back of what had once been a coal room.

When he pulled the narrow door shut behind him he found himself on a creaking set of rotting wooden stairs leading down into the darkness. Seth tested his weight on the first stair and then descended just as carefully. When the stairs ended he was standing on one side of a wide concrete tunnel, a murky stream running down the middle of it that stank as bad as any alley-end used as a toilet up above.

Seth leaned against the curve of the wall to collect his thoughts. If he headed due west for twenty-two kilometres he should end up right below Commander Regis's camp on the outskirts of the city. Seth had a rotating BAT regiment keeping an eye on it as best as they could. Apparently Regis was holed up there, waiting for something. But what? Did he know Seth was in the city? Did he know about Seth's army? Or was he here to destroy the circus now that everyone knew who they were?

Seth pushed himself away from the wall and walked along the edge of the ribbon of filthy water, holding his lantern ahead of him to light his way. He couldn't try to guess what was happening in the world around him, with Regis, or Eli, or Edmund. He could only move forward, one step at a time, toward his own goal. Seth hesitated with that thought.

Part of his mind wanted to stay with the task at hand. But another, larger part wanted to move past that, to the bigger picture. To the future, where Seth ruled and the Group of Keys was no more.

It was a gigantic idea, with no end to the obstacles and, equally, no end to the glory. His heart thumped gleefully. He wanted it all. Everything. He wanted to rule the Keys *and* the Droughtland. He wanted to break the barriers that divided the two and create a world shaped by his ideas. He could do it. He could handle it. He was the perfect and only candidate. A mother from Triskelia and a Keyland Chief Regent for a father. If anyone was meant to unite the two worlds, he was it. He'd be the first leader of the new world.

But right at this moment he just had to keep walking, and so he did.

21

かふ

Halfway to Triban, before the Triskelians were due to meet their weapons shipment, the night bandits came. Eli had been sleeping in his bedroll under one of the caravans when he'd awoken to the pounding of horses' hooves on packed earth. He shook Nappo and Teal awake and the three of them watched, silent and terrified, as the bandits circled the group.

Trace and Anya were sleeping in the caravan above them, and Eli could hear the slightest creak.

A voice broke the night. "We've got you surrounded!"

All Eli and the brothers could see were the horses stamping about, kicking up the earth.

"Women and kids in a group to the right," the voice continued. "Men to the left. Hands up!"

Suddenly, from the back of the caravan, the barrel of a shotgun appeared. Teal scooted back with a gasp, but it was only Trace, handing down the gun. Eli knew how to use it now, and so he took it, feeling its cold heft in his hands.

Don't. Do not take a life.

"Like we practised." Trace's whisper came out of the dark. "Wait for the whistles."

Those bunking under the caravans were supposed to open fire, on the count of ten, after the last short whistle sounded signalling that everyone was armed and ready.

Nappo nodded at him. "Whistle, Eli."

There is no excuse for murder. Violence is not the answer.

Eli tried, but his mouth was too dry. "I can't. You do it."

Nappo sounded the short whistle, which anyone could confuse for the coo of an owl, until they noted all four, one from each caravan.

"Everyone out!" the bandit in charge hollered, obviously clueing in to the fact that something was up. "Don't do anything you'll regret."

Three, four, five . . . Eli counted to himself.

"Cooperate and come out now, and there won't be no blood spilled!" The bandits' horses stamped their hooves as if sensing the shift in the air while the four Triskelian gunners prepared to open fire.

Eight, nine . . . Eli shimmied to the edge of his cover, cocked his gun and pointed. *Ten.* He closed his eyes and pulled the trigger. The three others fired too, gunshots pealing into the night, ripping away the suspended quiet and sending the night bandits' horses into a panic. Across the clearing one of the bandits howled and dropped, quickly scuttling away on his butt, dragging one leg. The others started firing back, but only two of them had guns. The rest fled. Eli forced himself to keep his eyes open and this time he aimed with purpose, straight at the one who was raising his gun toward the caravan where Sabine and Zenith and Celeste were bunked.

No! This isn't the answer!

Eli pulled the trigger. The bandit arched his back, let out one cry, and fell to the ground.

"Get his horse!" Gavin yelled as Trace leapt down from above the boys.

"We'll be back!" the last bandit yelled as he galloped away. "You're all dead!"

Trace ran for the spooked horse and grabbed its reins just as it was about to bolt.

"Head count!" Jack yelled, banging the wooden sides of the caravans. "All clear. Everybody out!"

Eli did not look at the man he'd shot as he crossed the camp and took his position at the edge of the clearing, in case the bandits returned. Gavin did the same in the opposite corner, as did the two other gunners behind them. Eli wasn't shaking. He wasn't even breathing hard.

He was calm.

And full of remorse.

He'd just taken a man's life.

And it felt so wrong.

Horribly wrong.

He tried to reason with himself. He'd killed that man back in Triskelia, hadn't he? With the machete? If not the one, then the other—perhaps both. Or maybe he'd only wounded them. Was that different? Not really. Eli's life had been threatened then, and now too. Still, was that a reason to murder? He urged the logic forward. He *did* have to kill the bandit. He'd been about to open fire on his grandmother and Sabine. And Zenith!

Eli glanced over his shoulder at the man's body.

Is his life worth less than Zenith's? Sabine's? Mine?

A realization hit him with the force of a mean right hook. The voice was his own. All this time he'd thought he was going crazy, but it was his own self talking to him, a higher kind of self. He could think of it only as his highers speaking through him, through his heart, his mind, his reason.

Eli had taken a life.

Who am I to take a life? It's not up to me.

But life was, after all, a series of costs. It would've been too costly to let the man live only to have him kill Sabine or Zenith or Celeste, or any one of them for that matter, and so he'd had to die. Didn't he?

No. The violence must stop.

Eli felt as he had when he'd finally learned to read. One day the letters were just so many black ants marching across the page and then suddenly they'd formed words and out of the words, ideas. This is what he felt like now. Enlightened. The violence must stop.

So this is what destiny felt like.

The head count went on behind him while everyone tearfully clung to one another, celebrating the fact that no one had been injured. Only, someone had. The bandit. He was dead. He had a family too, no doubt. And Eli had taken their father, or husband, or son from them with no less violence than the Guard had used to slaughter all of Triskelia and the Colony of the Sicks.

Was it true that some lives were worth more than others? That some murders were okay while others were not? Eli turned in a stunned circle, suddenly seeing everyone as having a variable worth. These people, his family, were worth more to him. Had his mother been worth more than his father? If he'd had a choice, would he have had his father die in place of his mother?

He would, he realized. And that was so wrong.

Eli stood there, half paralyzed with the power of his revelation and the questions that came with it.

"Thank you, Eli!" Sabine rushed him with a hug. "Trace told me everything. That you saved us. Well done!"

"I killed a man."

"But you had to."

"Did I?"

Sabine read his expression but didn't understand it. Her fingers went to the medallion at her throat. Eli did the same, but the absentminded gesture was the only thing they shared in that moment. Eli looked away, his thoughts racing.

"Nana is making tea." Sabine stood beside him and looked into the forest, trying to see what had captured Eli's interest for so long. "What have you been looking at?"

"The inside of my brain, as it happens."

"What does it look like in there?"

"It's a jumble of questions, as a matter of fact."

"Like what?"

"Like, when, if ever, is it right to kill?"

"When you have to. To protect yourself and the ones you love," Sabine said. "Why are you being so philosophical about it, Eli? You did what you had to do. You did what was right."

"No." Eli shook his head. "I did what was expected of me. There's a difference."

"You're just acting like this because this is your first time killing someone," Sabine said with a world-weary tone. "It'll pass."

"It's not my first time. At least, I don't think it is. And how do you know it will pass? You've never murdered anyone."

"No." Sabine tugged at her medallion. "I haven't. And what you've just done isn't murder. It was self-defence."

"You don't know what it feels like."

"No, I don't." Sabine kicked at the dirt, frustrated. "But let me tell you, you better get over this . . . this philosophical bullshit. There's lots more ahead, Eli. You've got to know that. It's the one sure thing."

"Not if we make a choice not to kill."

"That's not possible!" Sabine put her hands on her hips and frowned. "*You're* the one who showed up in Triskelia wanting to get things started. Well, now they are, and you're going to chicken out? Are you that much of a coward! Think of everyone who died back home. Think about them! You think we're going to make a difference without using violence? We tried that, Eli, and it got our people slaughtered!"

Eli's inner turmoil settled, as if it had been a dust cloud stirred up in the flurry of the bandit attack. Calm returned.

"We all have to answer to our highers when we die."

"Shut the hell up, Eli." Sabine spun around. "You don't know what you're talking about. The Keyland is going to answer to us, I'll guarantee you that much. Come find me when you've regained your sanity, or even just a portion of your backbone."

Eli let her go. He didn't want to argue with her. Not right now. Beyond her, Jack was kneeling beside the dead man's body.

"Jack! Wait!" He jogged over to him. "What are you doing?"

"Taking his boots."

"No."

"Why not?" Jack untied the laces. "They'll fit someone."

"Leave him!" Eli pushed him away.

"Never mind his things, Jack." Sabine appeared as Jack was about to shove Eli back. "Let Eli have this one."

"Are you okay, Eli?" Jack squinted at him as Eli retied the bootlace.

"No, he's not." Sabine pulled Jack away. "But he will be. Come on, leave him alone."

"I killed this man." Eli grabbed the arms of the fallen bandit and met Jack's eyes. "Say what you will, but it's no different from what someone did to Charis or Zari."

"What?" Jack lunged for him, grabbing his collar and shaking him. "How can you say that?"

Eli didn't struggle. "No different, Jack."

"Don't you let Trace hear you talk like that." He gave Eli another shake. "What's gotten into you, man? He was going to kill us! You saved us from him!"

"I took his life."

"Come *on*, Jack." Sabine pulled at his arm. "Let him go. Now."

"He's all yours, Eli." Jack let go with another shove and backed away. "You want to waste a perfectly good pair of boots and the rest of this bastard's shit because you've suddenly been struck by the highers, go right ahead. Knock yourself out, asshole."

"Please, Jack." Sabine took his hand. "That's enough."

They left him alone. Eli grabbed one of the bandit's ankles under each arm and hauled him out of the clearing and into the woods.

Alone with the body of the man he'd murdered, Eli didn't know what to do. He had no shovel to dig him a grave, and didn't know any words to say, yet he felt compelled to honour him somehow. He raised his eyes to the stars above and prayed. *Highers, take this man's soul. Help him ascend. Bring his family peace, and let them know they're not the only ones to grieve his death. Forgive me, I have done wrong.*

Eli sighed. He rolled the man into a dip at the base of a tree and buried him as best he could with twigs and leaves and loose brush. Then he built a cairn to mark the grave and went back to the fire where everyone left him alone, giving him a wide uneasy berth as they prepared for another day's travel on the road to Triban.

22

∼✦∼

Seth made his way along the dank, musty tunnels beneath Triban. He was right. He was alone down here, hadn't seen another soul in hours. When had they last been used? Was it possible no one knew they were here? That over the centuries the tunnels had slipped into extinction as the city's utilities fell into ruin?

As he sloshed along the shallow trickling creek of muck he thought of all the uses for such a tunnel system. It was his, after all. Finders keepers.

And then he heard voices.

Ahead a ways, but getting closer. Seth backed up, searching the walls for a ladder, an alcove, somewhere he could hide himself. The voices grew louder. There were two of them. Seth cut his light, flattened himself as best he could against the curved wall, and held his breath. Maybe three. But wait. They sounded young. He steeled himself. They sounded like children, and besides, he had the guns and the wherewithal. They were probably just dusty puppies, kids so kited they could only manage to stumble from one crime to another in pursuit of the drug that made their homeless, starving, exploited existence barely tolerable.

Three candle lanterns appeared out of the darkness, two glowing much lower than the third. Seth stepped into the middle of the tunnel.

"Halt! Who goes there?"

The three strangers' faces came into his light.

"No one special," the tallest one said. "What do you care and how come you sound like some pompous ass? 'Halt? Who goes there?' Who even says that?"

"S'cuse us," one of the smaller ones said. She was maybe five years old, wearing a thin dress and nothing on her feet. The taller one put an arm protectively across the little girl's shoulders. She was about Seth's age, with a stuffed backpack and a bag slung across each shoulder. Another, smaller child clung to her pant leg, his thumb jammed into his mouth.

"We'll be on our way, mister high and mighty," the older girl said. "And don't think of trying anything. I can kill you with my bare hands. Just you try me."

"What's your name?" Seth asked, not ready to let them go just yet.

"Rabbit!" piped the little girl.

"And I'm Effie and this is Bear," the older one said.

"Rabbit?" Seth held out his lantern to get a better look at the smaller children. "Bear?"

"They didn't have names. I let them pick their own." The girl adjusted the weight on her shoulders. "Look, if you don't mind, we got to get going."

"What do you mean they didn't have names?"

"I found them. No family, get it? No names. Sewer kids."

"Down here, you mean?"

"Yes, down here. Where do you think I mean?" The girl let out a frustrated humph. Rabbit stuck her hand in the filthy stream, fished out a broken comb, and stuck it in her pocket. "Rabbit, come on. Let's go."

"Are there others down here?"

"Of course."

"I'm Seth," he called after them.

"So hi, Seth. And bye, Seth." The girl started walking. "We'll be on our way."

"Wait!" Seth told them about the warehouse. "I feed everyone, and it's safe at night."

"Sure," the girl laughed again. "And then you sell the babies into slavery and the girls have to lie on their backs all day while you rake in the money. That's how it goes, right?"

"No." A flash of memory, the Droughtland girls with their short dresses and the blank stare of starvation, resignation. "No. It's not like that. I help people. I have an army."

"You. An army? Sure."

"A special kind of army. I take in boys who—"

"Right." Effie lifted Bear onto her hip and put a protective hand to his brow. "We don't need your help, Seth-whoever-you-are."

"I can take you too." He didn't take on many girls, but was starting to more and more now that the numbers were so large. They were good for kitchen work, and cobbling together uniforms, and for cleaning, and some of the scrappier tomboys even showed talent in fighting and weaponry.

"I don't want to be your exception, thanks." The girl laughed again, and then their splashing footsteps and chatter faded as they headed down the tunnel the way Seth had come.

He wanted to ask her about the sewer. More specifically, about the sewer children. He could bring them into his army. All of them. Who knows how much that would swell his numbers? He let the trio go. There would be others. Amon was right: there *was* a world down here, just not as populated, but still there for him to put to use.

Seth continued down the tunnel, picking up where he'd left off counting his paces. He'd learned to do it in the Guard, and by his calculations he was nearing the outskirts of the city. He climbed up the next ladder and tried the manhole. It wouldn't budge. He went along to the next one and pressed up on it with his palms until it gave. Seth slid it sideways just enough to pop his head out. He peered into the daylight, diffused and yellow from garbage fires burning in the city. He was halfway down a narrow, empty lane, so he took the opportunity to climb out and take stock.

The buildings were bombed out at this end of town, the result of a gang war that had started, gone on, and ended all within two weeks. Both sides had their hands on rare explosives, supplied by the same dealer, who was connected to yet a third gang that wanted the first two obliterated. Gang one and gang two had levelled the territory they were fighting for, along with each other, and so the third gang took over without a fight. But that was before the Guard had shown up and taken out gang three in a short-lived gun battle. They hadn't stood a chance.

Seth was in the right area. Commander Regis had set up camp on the other side of the bombed-out borough. That was smart, having the crumbling buildings and surrounding wasteland act as a sort of demilitarized zone between his camp and the violent rumblings of the inner city. No one dared wander here. Why would they? It was too close to the Guard, and besides, there was nothing left to loot or scavenge.

Seth also knew from his boys that Commander Regis had patrols in these parts, and snipers hidden in the abandoned buildings. He found a stick and tied a white cloth to it, one he'd brought for just this reason.

It didn't take long before a shot rang out, blasting a tiny crater out of the dirt at Seth's feet, narrowly missing them. Seth waved his white flag.

"Don't shoot!"

"Halt!"

Remembering Effie, Seth let out a quiet, sardonic laugh. And waited for the rest.

"Who goes there?" the man shouted.

"A trader!" Seth hollered back. "I have cigarettes!"

"Move, and you're dead. Two more guns are trained on you right this minute."

Seth's heart pounded as he heard steps descending nearby stairs. His plan would work only if he didn't know this Guardy. Or the others, if there were others.

The sniper appeared and stopped well away from him. Seth didn't recognize him, or at least not yet.

"Hand 'em over." The sniper gestured at him with his gun. "Throw them on the ground."

"We haven't talked about price yet." Seth shrugged out of his backpack, keeping his hands visible.

"Yeah, we did. When I fired at you, they suddenly became free." The Guardy laughed.

"Oh." Seth kept his hands up and his shoulders hunched.

"So dig 'em out, throw them my way and then back off, and if you're lucky I'll let you leave and if you're not so lucky I'll shoot you in the back. Sound good?"

Seth kept his eyes down and nodded.

"Go on, then." The sniper gestured at him with his gun again. "Let's see what you've got."

"I'm gonna have to use my hands, mister." Seth waved his truce hands.

"Yeah, yeah. Whatever." The way the man didn't look around him, not even once, meant one of two things. Either there were other snipers and he knew better than to give away their locations with a telling glance, or there weren't and Seth had only to overpower this one lone fool.

"Oh, ugh." Seth would take his chances with the latter. "Oh, I don't feel so good," he mumbled, and then keeled over, face down into the dirt, his eyes closed, his backpack clutched to his chest.

"Shit." The crunch of gravel told Seth that the sniper was coming closer. "Great." Again, he didn't call or otherwise summon anyone else. This might be way easier than Seth could've hoped for.

"Gross," the sniper muttered when he got close enough to see the skineater scars. He used the barrel of his gun to push aside Seth's hair to get a better look. "Disgusting."

The sniper wouldn't want to touch him, not with the scars. He backed away in a hurry. But he'd be back. The cigarettes were valuable enough for him to take a chance.

Seth cracked one eye. The sniper had his back turned to him and was looking for something in the rubble. Seth could take him out now with a bullet, but he'd rather wait. He closed his eye when the sniper returned, a length of rebar in one hand. He approached Seth at an angle, trying to fish the backpack away from him, but Seth held fast.

"Let go," the sniper muttered. "Let go, you rat bastard."

Seth clung tight, as if he'd seized in that position.

The sniper was forced to come closer, gaining better purchase on Seth's hands. He worked the sharp rebar under one of his palms. Seth braced himself, the pain of the metal as it sliced his skin surprising him. He had to act now, because in this same second the sniper was realizing that Seth wasn't out cold.

Seth yanked the rebar, pulling the sniper to him and at the same time kicking his legs out from underneath him. In one graceful motion Seth was sitting atop him, his knees pinning the sniper's arms to the ground, his hands clutching the man's own gun.

"You really wanted those cigarettes, huh?" Seth let a drop of blood from his cut palm fall onto the Guardy's cheek. "Even after you saw my scars."

"The sick!" He thrashed in the dirt. "Get it off me!"

Seth packed the sniper's mouth full of gravel to shut him up. The man coughed and gagged, the veins in his neck bulging out.

"Now get up." Seth stood. "You run, I shoot."

"You're making a big mistake." The Guardy gagged the words out as he got back onto his feet, wiping the blood away with his sleeve.

"Hands up." Seth poked the gun at the back of his head. "Into that building."

Seth led him into a bombed-out storefront, its shelves emptied by looters and its windows long since smashed.

"Take your clothes off."

"They're coming for me right now. We have a signal." The Guardy turned, his hands still up. "You should just run. They'll kill you!"

"I doubt anyone is coming." Seth leaned against a toppled display case. "Strip."

"They'll kill you," the sniper repeated, but he didn't sound so sure now. He slowly unbuttoned his shirt and pulled it off.

"Faster."

"If you think you'll get away with this—"

"Ah, shh." Seth put a finger to his lips. "I was so enjoying the quiet."

The Guardy got rid of the rest of his uniform, and then started to peel off his underlinen.

"No thanks." Seth shook his head. "I'm not bent, and I don't want your shit-stained panties." As Seth collected the uniform the man flinched. "Don't worry . . ." Seth gestured for him to get onto his knees.

From there he shoved him onto his front and tied his hands together behind his back. That done, he bound the man's ankles and cinched them up to the knot at his wrists. "I'm not going to kill you."

Throughout it all the sniper barely struggled. Take away a Guardy's gun and you take away his bravery. Not like Seth's boys. They didn't need weapons to feel brave. They'd scrap to the death with their bare hands. Unlike the Guard, his boys had nothing to lose and everything to gain.

"No, but we'll kill *you*," the sniper said with a sudden swell of confidence. "Any second, they'll come for me!"

"There aren't any other snipers on this block, are there?" Just then another gunshot cracked into the afternoon, far off. "And you do target practice on rats and stray dogs, so the gunshot won't summon them."

"Who are you?"

"Seth Edmund Maddox, son of the Chief Regent of the Eastern Key." He hadn't claimed that title in so long that it sounded odd now.

"He's Chancellor East now," spat the sniper. "Shows how much you know."

"Oh, and how did that come about?" Seth pulled a strip of cloth from his pack. "Would you like to tell me before I gag you and leave you for the dogs to chew off your tiny dick?"

"Chancellor East the Ninth had a heart attack."

"Or my father murdered him and made it look like a heart attack." Seth secured the gag across the man's mouth. "He's good at that sort of thing."

The man mumbled something through the gag.

"Oh, sorry." Seth tugged it down. "Did you have something else you wanted to say?"

"Your father wants you dead. That's why we were sent to Triskelia. To kill you and your brother. So you wouldn't make any more trouble for him."

"Hmm. Is that right?" Seth retied the gag, this time tighter. He pressed the gun to the man's temple. "And so you murdered thousands of innocent people just to bulldoze your way to me and my brother? And still you failed?"

The man let out a muffled cry. His eyes started tearing. He shook his head violently. Seth cocked the release and shot a bullet just above the man's head. It slammed into the wall, dusting the man with plaster. Seth's ears rang from the blast.

"And still no one will come, because what's another bullet going off out here?" Seth kicked the man. And then he kicked him again. He was thinking about Edmund and how he wished he could kick his father like this, hogtied and crying for mercy from behind a spit-soaked gag. Seth kicked and kicked hard and the Guardy cried out from behind his gag until he could cry no more and only lift his tired, pained eyes and plead for mercy that way.

Seth kicked him once again. That hadn't been part of the plan, but sometimes things didn't work out that way and sometimes Seth couldn't resist the urge to do something he knew was wrong. Sometimes wrong felt fantastic, like right now. Seth kicked him one more time and then made himself stop before he killed the man.

THE REST OF THE AFTERNOON did progress as planned. Seth stashed his pack and donned the Guardy's uniform, which felt so very familiar and yet so strange. It used to make him feel important, but now he thought only of finishing his task and getting back to his army.

Seth waited for nightfall, then caked his face with the concealer to hide his skineater scars. He left the storefront and the bound Guardy and sauntered down the middle of the street, rifle slung across his chest, heading for the compound. He stayed out of the pools of light cast from the lanterns at each side of the gate, and with a touch of his fingers to his hat in the most familiar of salutes he was let in without a single question or a second glance. He'd have to be quick, before anyone recognized him or noticed his scars despite the makeup. Ignoring the nerves chewing up his stomach, he strode purposefully through the compound, noting the number of tents and hence the number of men Commander Regis was holding up at the edge of Triban.

Commander Regis was not an original man, for the camp was laid out like all Guardy camps, with the Commander's quarters in the middle, for safety and to place him at the centre of it all. Most of the camp was packing it in for the night, dispersing to their bunks, letting the fires settle into embers that burned just enough for the night watchers to warm their hands in the wee, cool hours. Seth could not have timed his mission more perfectly.

Regis's tent was dark.

Either he was inside, asleep, or he wasn't there at all.

A Guardy stood at the entrance, so Seth strolled right on by and stopped instead at the rear of the tent. He pulled his knife from his boot and sliced the canvas with one swift tear. He hesitated. No one stirred. Not from inside, and not from the front. Seth crouched and let himself through the rip in the canvas.

He kept very still, letting his ears and eyes adjust to the tent's darkness. The air was practically electric with endless and terrifying possibilities. What if he was caught? What would they do to him? Would Amon manage BAT? Would he try to come for him? Or would Regis take him back to the Key to answer to his father directly?

A faint snoring rippled across the foul-smelling tent, where one bedside candle wavered in the stale air. A fart resounded, much louder than the snores. And then a sleepy sigh. A sleepy *girly* sigh.

Seth shook his head, angry with himself. He hadn't expected Regis to have company. He should've anticipated that. He crawled on his belly, elbows first, to the end of the bed. He lifted his head up, but only enough to see which side of the bed the girl was on.

There were two girls, with Regis sandwiched in the middle.

Seth gave himself a swift mental kick in the pants, but then before his nerve waned he crawled to one side and covered the girl's mouth with his hand. As she woke with a fright he whispered, "I'm a Triskelian. Be silent! Trust me."

She stared at him, wide-eyed and terrified, but then she nodded. Seth pointed at himself, gesturing that he was going around to the other side. He woke the other girl the same way, and after a brief wordless struggle she too relaxed, once the other girl had taken her hand across Regis's belly and nodded at her to comply.

Seth had been so looking forward to beating Regis to death with his bare hands. Now, considering the circumstances, that was out of the question.

Seth pulled his gun, pressed it to Commander Regis's temple, and woke him mid-snore with a jab to his skull.

He sat up, confused, swatting groggily at Seth's gun before dawning recognition etched shock across his face. The girls tumbled out of the bed and onto the floor, gathering their dresses and clutching them to their chests.

"One word and I splatter your brains all over these lovely young companions of yours." Seth kept his tone firm even as he pulled out his other gun and set it under Commander Regis's chin. "Understand?"

"Seth, listen to me." Sweat beaded across Regis's eyebrows. "We can make a deal here. Your father wants to see you. I can bring you to him."

"No, he doesn't," Seth whispered, despite his urge to scream. "He wants me dead! Just like you did. And he sent you to kill me and Eli and all of Triskelia, correct?"

"No, no. It's all a terrible misunderstanding. He's coming to the Western Key for the legislature. I can take you to him. He only wants to know that you're safe and well."

"Don't give me that bullshit." Seth jabbed the gun hard against his temple. "You have no power over me any more. And in a moment, you won't have power over anyone else either."

"Seth . . . think about what you're doing. Think!" If Commander Regis was feeling any fear he didn't show it, except for a slight flush across his cheeks. He had the calm look of someone who trusted implicitly that all would turn out for him in the end. The look of someone not accustomed to things going awry. "We can make a deal, you and I. I can give you a job, as a spy. You're perfect for it!"

"You're Seth?" one of the girls breathed. She pulled the other girl to her and whispered something.

"Yes, I'm Seth."

"The one who looks after all those boys?"

"Yes." Seth glanced at the girls. They'd pulled on their clothes and were huddled together, frightened. "And if you want to do your part, you can tie his hands and gag him."

"Now Seth, *think*." There it was. Fear. It was in his eyes now. "Think about what I can offer you!"

Commander Regis did not put up a fight as the girls bound him. Seth hoped he would, to justify what he was about to do. It was as if Regis was waiting for Seth to come to his senses or for his men outside to come to his rescue. There was no hope of rescue, but Seth had certainly come to his senses all right.

He'd waited a long time for this moment.

Seth told the girls to cover their eyes. And then, before he could think any more about it, he pulled his knife from its sheath and cut the Commander's throat from ear to ear.

A strained gurgle, and then silence. Seth dropped the knife. His hands shook.

"Keep your eyes closed and don't breathe a sound," he whispered to the girls, his eyes locked first on the blood seeping from the Commander's neck and then on his eyes fixed in the flat stare of death. "Keep your backs to the bed. You don't want to see this."

Seth didn't want to see it either, but he had seen it. And even in the near dark, with just the one nervous candle and the moonlight cutting in from the screened vents above, it was gory enough.

"Tell them Triskelia is responsible for this, but don't tell them it was me," he instructed the girls as he fumbled around the tent, his heart pounding. He helped himself to Regis's gun, knife, binoculars, machete, and medals while the girls trembled, crying quietly. He gave them directions to BAT's headquarters and then tied their hands and gagged them too so it would look as if they'd all been overpowered. Then, with his hands shaking and Regis's medals jingling in his pocket like so much small change, Seth retreated the way he came and sauntered out the gate, for all the world a soldier heading for his night shift.

Seth had hidden his pack not far from the hogtied Guardy. He wasn't going to look in on him, but Seth had made a fatal mistake, and now a change of plans was in order to correct it.

He'd told the Guardy his name. He shouldn't have. He hadn't thought it through, and as he chided himself for his sloppiness he found the man where he'd left him. The Guardy mumbled desperately through the gag, his eyes wide. He'd pissed himself earlier, and that's all Seth could smell as he cocked his gun and shot him once in the head. With a jerk the man died, and with him Seth's identity as Regis's killer. It wasn't that Seth didn't want or need the credit for assassinating Regis, but he needed to use it as a fulcrum when the time was right.

Minutes later in the pitch-black, dripping quiet of the tunnel system, he let the fear and excitement and horror descend at last. The weight of it brought him to his knees in the muck, where he retched over and over again, his stomach seizing with great clawing cramps. Steadying his breath, he struggled to regain some composure.

Finally he started for home, counting his paces from zero again. The fear and horror were gone. The excitement was not. He'd done it! He'd assassinated Commander Regis right in his own bed, in a tent right in the middle of the largest grouping of the Guard he'd ever seen! Seth really could accomplish anything. This mission proved it.

23

Eli took his sister aside the morning after the night bandit ambush
and told her he'd realized his destiny. It was to bring a peaceful
end to Keyland rule. He would free the Droughtland using
nonviolent means, and he wanted her to be a part of it.

While she listened, Sabine stared at him. Was he ill? He hadn't been
the same since the massacre, and while none of them had, he was among
the most profoundly affected. Especially if he was talking like this.

"At first I thought I was hearing voices," Eli explained. "But I wasn't!
It's the highers, guiding me to this conclusion."

"That qualifies as hearing voices."

"No. No, you don't understand—"

"That's for sure."

"The voices are *me*. My soul. My conscience. It's my conscience telling
me what's right and what's wrong."

Sabine folded her arms. "So your *conscience* has decided that it's
morally and spiritually wrong to save your people and free an entire
nation using minimal force?"

"It's like an epiphany," he told her. "It *is* an epiphany. Have you ever
experienced that? Have you ever not known something until all of a
sudden you've known it forever?"

"No." Sabine let out a long, tired sigh. "Oh. Eli. You haven't either.
This isn't an epiphany at all, this is you, suffering from everything you've
been through. This is post-traumatic stress of the biggest kind. We're all

sick from it in our own way, but you . . . you should listen to yourself. If you try to spread this . . . this *gospel* of yours . . . no one's going to listen. They're going to think you're insane. Because it *is* insane. And maybe *you're* insane. But we can take care of you. Just . . . just take a break, okay? Just . . . do nothing for a while."

All the time she was talking Eli had been smiling and shaking his head. "I'm not crazy, Sabine." He took her hands. He remembered when he first met her, he'd thought she was so strong. But now her hands were cool porcelain in his grasp. He didn't want to see them bloodied. He didn't want to see her soul bloodied. "You have your destiny, I have mine. That's just the way it is."

"No, Eli!" She pulled away. "You're crazy."

"Sabine, where does it stop? Each violent act gives birth to another, out of revenge, retribution, retaliation."

Sabine shivered. Those were the same words that kept ringing in her ears. *Revenge. Retribution. Retaliation.*

"So where does it stop?" he asked again. "When will grief just be grief and not a call to arms?"

"Easy," Sabine spat. "When justice has been served and the Keys demolished and the weather freed so that the Droughtland can become a livable place again, when people can grow food to feed their children, when villages are sustainable for the first time in hundreds of years, when there's no Guard to fear, no Keys to be oppressed by . . ." She hesitated. "I could go on. Want me to?"

"So that we can be like the Middle East? At war forever? So that generations of children will know nothing *but* war?"

"You're making this bigger than it is, Eli." Sabine hugged herself. "I'm just me and you're just you, and it's not any bigger than that. We're just trying to do what's right, that's all. The uprising is happening with or without us. I'm just trying to shape what already *is* into something better. The massacre set it off. I'm trying to make sure it doesn't get out of control. There's nothing mystical or mythic about it. This has nothing to do with the highers."

"You're wrong."

"No, Eli. *You're* wrong." Sabine's expression darkened. "The Keys can't go on. They must be stopped. And I know my part. You clearly don't know yours."

"I do know mine."

"Right." She glanced away dismissively. "Your *epiphany.*"

"Don't mock me, Sabine."

"Then don't say stuff that makes you sound like a maniac. Now, come on. We have to get going. I can't sit here and debate you all day."

"I won't take up arms."

"Fine."

"I won't do it, Sabine. And I'll ask others not to too."

"I've had enough of this, Eli." She looked her brother in the eye, searching for some give. There was none.

"And so have I."

The two held each other's stare for a long moment, until Sabine broke it. "I'm worried about you."

Eli nodded. "And I'm worried about you. Not only your life, but your soul too."

"I love you, Eli." Sabine hoped her expression didn't give away her alarm at his behaviour. "But I'm not going to stand around and listen to this any more."

Jack called for them then. The caravans were moving out.

Sabine held up her hands in defeat. "I just can't."

"I understand."

"No, I don't think you do." The last words caught in her throat. She turned away as the tears started.

"How else will it ever end, Sabine?" Eli called after her. "*How?*"

SABINE WIPED HER TEARS AWAY. What had happened to Eli? She needed him now. She wanted to confide in him, tell him she was scared that they'd all be dead soon and with nothing to show for it. Scared that this was all an exercise in futility. If overturning the Keys was at all a possible task it would've been accomplished a long time ago. How many other dusty little attempts had failed? How many others had already died trying?

Sabine's effort wouldn't be a part of history, it would simply *be* history, over and forgotten, just a teensy blip in the creaking, massive story of the world.

"Sabine!" Toby ran up to her, dragging Teal behind him. Toby was the youngest among them now. She'd wanted him to stay at Cascadia, but Yvon had come with them, along with Gavin and Jack, and the three had made it clear they wouldn't be separated from Toby and would take full responsibility for his safety. "Make Teal ride with me and Gavin and Jack," Toby was saying now.

"I don't want to." Teal yanked his hand back. "I'm riding with Nappo and Eli."

"There you go, Toby." Sabine was glad for the distraction. Children's squabbles were refreshingly simple. "I can't make him ride with you just because you want him to."

Toby growled and bared his teeth. He added a bark for good measure.

"He's a dog sometimes," Teal explained. "I think when he doesn't know what else to do."

Toby jumped around Teal, snapping at him.

"I don't want to ride with him, Sabine."

"And you don't have to."

"I don't?"

"No."

"Oh." Teal furrowed his brow. "Nappo says we have to do what you say, and that we have to ask your permission for stuff."

"Not stuff like this, Teal." Sabine grabbed Toby by his sweater and held him back as if he really was a lunging, vicious dog. "Only important stuff."

"Well, it's important I don't have to ride with some kid who thinks he's a dog." Teal picked up a stick and threw it. "Go on, fetch!"

Toby turned his puppy eyes up to Sabine and whined. Sabine rolled her eyes and let go. Toby ran after the stick, but Bullet beat him to it. And now Eli was at her side again.

Sabine didn't know what to say. The two of them watched the dog and boy fight over the stick.

"This is all hopeless, isn't it, Eli? I don't even know how to handle a boy who thinks he's a dog, and another who thinks he's a grown man."

"It's not hopeless," Eli said with conviction. "And I'm not crazy. I just have different ideas from you." He walked over to Toby and Bullet and wrestled the two of them apart. He tossed the stick for Bullet and held Toby, thrashing and barking under his arm. "You're not a dog, Toby. You're a boy." He held on to him until the thrashing stopped, and then he set him on his feet. "There. Are you back?"

Toby nodded. "I just wanted to ride with Teal."

"Ride with me instead," Sabine said.

"Really?"

"Sure." She led him to the caravan and lifted him up.

"Yay!" Toby clapped his hands.

THE DRIVER STEERED Sabine's caravan into line, passing the cart Nappo was driving. Eli sat beside him while Teal nestled behind in the open box with a group of others, wrapped in blankets and leaning against sacks and crates of supplies. Catching Teal's eye as Sabine's caravan passed, Toby waved like royalty through the curtained shutters from his cushy seat beside Zenith.

"See? Even better!" he yelled as Teal gawked at him enviously. "I get to ride with the leaders! An' you don't even have a roof. Na na na boo boo," he sang.

Zenith pulled him away from the opening, gave a little wave and a nod to Teal, and then pulled the shutters closed. Teal sat back, a smug look replacing his jealousy. Zenith would be giving Toby one of her lessons, and that was punishment enough. Nappo reached back and whacked his little brother upside the head.

"What'd I do?" Teal yelped.

"You know," Nappo said. "Who made you such a meanie, huh? Toby's just a little kid and he looks up to you and it's your job to teach him what you know, not toss him off like he's some little mutt."

Teal tried not to smile. "But he wants to be a dog."

Nappo lifted his open hand again as if to whack him once more.

"Sorry!" Teal covered his head. "Okay, okay."

"Next time he asks you for something or wants to hang out with you or even just wants to watch you stare at a rock, you let him. We have to take care of each other, Teal."

"Yeah, okay."

"Come up here."

"But I said yeah!"

"And I said come up here."

Teal bit his lip and climbed over the bench to sit beside Nappo. Nappo pulled him onto his lap and passed him the reins.

"Really?" Teal gazed at the worn leather. "I can do it?"

"Not like that." Nappo rearranged the reins across Teal's dirty palms. "Like this, so if the horse get spooked you won't lose your fingers."

"Okay." Teal held the straps as if he'd been handed the key to the universe. "Like this?" he whispered.

"Perfect." Nappo put his arm around his little brother. "And I'm serious. We have to take care of each other out here. Blood rellies or not, we're all family."

Eli watched the brothers, feeling a terrible, overwhelming sadness. If Nappo died, who would raise Teal? Sure, all of Triskelia had a hand in raising its children and the orphans they gave shelter and guidance to. But this . . . this tender interaction between two family members wasn't replaceable. And if Teal died Nappo would be forever bereft. There was no healing such hurt. And moments like this, easy and important, would never happen again between the two.

This was life! Moments just like this. Eli wanted it preserved. All of it. He couldn't bear the thought of any more death. They'd all suffered so much already. There had to be a better way.

Nappo gave his shoulder a light punch. "You alive over there?"

Eli nodded. He wished he could talk to Nappo about all that was racing through his mind these days. But he knew better. Nappo wouldn't understand. Just as Sabine hadn't.

"I'm just tired is all," Eli said. It was true. He was exhausted. He just wanted to sleep and then wake up and have it all be over. Just the thought of all that could lie ahead for them was enough to send him into a blissful, ignorant stupor.

Maybe it was time to leave. Take one of the horses and go off on his own. Or back to Cascadia to be with Mireille and do peaceful work, manipulating the clouds and bringing the rains to the people.

That's it! The rains.

It was as if a plume had been set off in his mind, releasing the vapours that would finally bring the storm. He had an idea, but he'd have to think it through before he moved on it. The question right now was whether he should carry on with the others, or go back, or leave entirely and find his way on his own.

He felt a responsibility to the group, to Sabine and Celeste and Zenith especially. And Nappo and Teal. Could he leave them? The three boys had made it to Triskelia together. They were tight in a way that could hardly be described. Brothers, really. Nappo was right. It didn't matter if they were related by blood or not. They were bound by life, and that was more valuable than blood.

When it felt right, Eli would leave. And if it didn't start to feel right, he'd have to make a hard decision. Be with his people, or go it on his own.

Not yet. It isn't the time to go yet.

Part of him wanted to break away right now, take a horse and take off. But a larger part of him knew that his place was with these people right now. His people. He knew he sounded off his rocker, but he couldn't deny what he knew in his heart to be truth. He would champion peace, even if it meant doing so from the eye of the storm.

24

W here was Nappo? Tasha had been looking for him forever! And not a clue, or a hint, or a tip, or a lead, or anything like what happens in happy-ending stories of true loves lost and reunited.

She stood at the side of the road, her belly a great big bulge, her thumb stuck out for a ride. It was raining again. She didn't know what was worse, the parched, barren earth of the Droughtland east of the mountains, where water was scarce and the heat deadly, or this ceaseless damp from rogue fronts and natural weather.

She'd fashioned a sort of hat out of a broken crate and a length of fraying rope, but it kept only the worst of the rain off her face. She wasn't exactly the picture of glamour, drenched and bedraggled and bloated as she was. The only coat she had was too big and missing one arm. What would Nappo say if he saw her now?

She'd come to the painful conclusion that she had to give the baby up after all. She'd hidden the pregnancy from her parents, so this is what she'd do: find that couple with the roadhouse, stay there until the baby was born, give it over, and then go home. She didn't see herself as a particularly responsible person, but this did seem the most responsible thing to do, all things considered. She'd like to be more responsible, if only it wasn't so dull.

She nodded to herself as her thoughts careened ahead. Yes, she'd give the baby up. It was a noble, selfless, kind, wise, nurturing thing to do.

Maternal even. And then she shook her head. No. It was *her* baby. What would she tell Nappo if she ever did find him? Uh, hi, we had a baby and I gave it away like a puppy.

What would he say to that?

Passersby looked at her strangely.

"What?" She flung her one covered arm out, the rain flicking off the oily material. "What're you looking at?"

Across the road an elderly man chuckled at her from under his little tarp. He was selling ratty old shoes from a pile, cobbling a pair balanced on his knees.

"And what're *you* looking at?"

"You, arguing with yourself." He worked the sole off one of the shoes with his knife. "Looks a bit kooky."

"Well." Tasha moved her hands from her belly to her hips. "That's nice, making fun of a pregnant woman. Aren't you a saint."

"Saint or no," the old man shrugged, "I could set you up."

"Thanks but no thanks." Tasha glanced down the road. Why wouldn't anyone stop? She was pregnant after all. She tried her other thumb for good measure, and then stuck out both, as if to indicate her desperation. "I've already got somebody who's taking the kid."

"I meant your boots." He gestured with his knife.

"Oh." Tasha leaned over, but her belly was in the way of her feet. She knew the state of her boots, or rather the lack of it, without looking anyway. Worn through in several places, and laceless since she'd strung her cloth sacks together to carry over her shoulders after losing her back-pack and most of her belongings in a Seduce game gone ever so wrong. "I don't want some skanky-ass shoes you yanked off some dead bugger, thank you very much."

"I'd give 'em to you for free, missy."

"Why?" Tasha squinted at the old man. She waddled across the road, tucked herself out of the rain, and frowned at his heap of crusty footwear. "Are they really from dead bodies?"

He shrugged. "Does it matter?"

"No." Tasha shuddered. "I guess not."

"So pick a pair." The old man sorted through a crate of soles beside his bench, looking for one to fit the shoe he was working on. "And not some silly, pretty ones, because what you need is some plain old practical things you can get some good wear and tear out of."

Tasha put down the red dancing shoes with a sigh.

"No ring?"

"Who gets married any more?" Tasha tried to sound nonchalant about it, but the words caught in her throat as she thought back to her sister's wedding. The party, the dancing, the heap of presents. That's when she'd met Nappo for the first time. "No one cares about that stuff."

"You care," the old man said. "I bet you got the dress picked out and the music decided, don't you? I bet you were marrying your dollies to each other since you were wee."

"So?" Tasha couldn't help it. She teared up. Seemed like she was always crying these days. Must be the baby making her funny.

"You and the father together?"

"I'm looking for him. He doesn't know."

"What does he look like? I'll keep an eye out. Lots of folks pass by here."

"Taller than me. Brown and lean. Chocolate eyes with golden flecks. Skineater scars, but he's so handsome you wouldn't notice."

"Good choice." The old man nodded as Tasha selected a thick-soled shoe that laced up past the ankle. "Lots of support."

Tasha sat on a rock and tried them on. "They fit."

"They're all yours, sweetheart."

"Really? No strings attached?"

"Just the laces." They shared a grin.

"Well, thank you." No one had been so nice to her in such a long time that part of her wanted to hunker down and stick close to this strange, kind grandpa forever. "Thanks, mister."

"You take care of yourself. And the little one."

Tasha put a hand to her belly. The baby was kicking. She took the old man's hand and put it there. Startled at first, he relaxed into a grin.

"Gonna be strong, kicking like that."

"Like her dad."

"What if it's a boy?"

"It won't be," Tasha said. "A woman knows."

The old man laughed. "Does she."

"I should get going," Tasha said, an eye to the road. "Traffic's picking up. Maybe someone will stop."

"Good luck, missy."

"Thanks again for the shoes," Tasha called over her shoulder as she headed back into the rain.

IT WAS ANOTHER couple of hours before a wagon stopped. It was covered, even the driving bench. Tasha climbed up, delighted to be out of the rain. It was a family, or appeared to be. A dad, a mom, a grandma, and a pile of children. As they rolled down the road, Tasha counted. Nine kids in all. All quite little, the oldest maybe ten or so.

"All yours?" Tasha asked, feeling the silence keenly.

"No." The woman managed to make the word sound exhausted. "And don't think for a second I'm taking on yours either." She pointed at her husband. "He's got a thing about orphans. Can't pass 'em by on the road."

The man kept his eyes forward.

"Ask him why he can't just leave 'em be."

Tasha blushed, wishing she'd never brought up the subject.

"Go on, ask him." The woman prodded Tasha's arm with a bony finger before turning it back on the man, whose shoulders had slumped. "Tell her, then."

"Can't just leave 'em," he muttered. "What would the highers think?"

"So we take 'em and drop them off in Triban? Like that's any better?" The woman guffawed. "This is why I usually leave him at home. I got the backbone. I drive on by. Nothing we can do if the babies are half dead. They'll just meet their highers sooner than later."

"I could probably take one off your hands." Tasha was already holding a little baby asleep in her arms, her little fists balled up, her lips cracked, cheeks scabby with bug bites. "I know a couple looking for a baby."

"He's all yours." The woman flapped a hand at her.

"It's a girl," Tasha muttered, adjusting the scrap of cloth around the naked baby. Her whole body was covered in the bites. And there was a bruise on her belly, and a cut not healing so well on one spindly leg. "If you'd bothered to check," she added under her breath. "We'll get off here," she said louder. "If you don't mind. Please and thanks."

The rain had finally stopped. The man slowed the wagon and helped Tasha down. He lifted the children down too, so they could stretch their legs and pee at the side of the road while his wife sucked on her pipe and the grandma snored, a string of drool dripping off her chin.

TASHA FOUND THE ROADHOUSE after another half-hour walk in her new comfortable shoes with the baby in her arms. She was just a little thing but grew heavy after a while, and so Tasha was thankful when she saw Cletus repairing a railing out in front of the long, squat building.

"Mister Shea?" Tasha called as she neared.

"That's me." Cletus took a minute to place her. He shook his head as she held up the baby, asleep and looking angelic, even with the red spots on her face. "I don't . . . who's this?" He took the baby and brought her to his face, inhaling the scent of her, despite her filth and the sour breath of hunger. "We can't just . . . Rachel!" he yelled for his wife. Rachel came onto the porch, followed by a dark little boy who looked just like Pilar, with the same black curls and chubby cheeks.

"Tasha?" Rachel took the little boy's hand. "What are you doing here, dear?"

"I'm not giving you my baby." Tasha's hands found her belly, almost subconsciously. "But I brought you one, and you can have her, so long as I can stay here until my own comes, free of charge."

Rachel and Cletus shared a look.

"I know, it's asking a lot," Tasha added. "But I'm betting you're good people, and I'd go home but it's so far away and I get tired so quick now and I just want to sit down a spell and not worry for even just one, stinking day."

The little boy ran to Cletus and begged for a look at the dirty little package in his arms.

"And whose baby is this?" Rachel took the baby and knelt so that the boy could get a peek.

"We get to keep her?" he asked.

Another look passed between Cletus and Rachel. "We'll see, Devi."

"There's no one else for her," Tasha said. "The people I got a ride with found her. They said she was just sat under a tree in her nappy and nothing else."

"The poor dear." Anger flashed across Rachel's normally generous, kind face.

"They had more they were looking to get rid of, but they were all crustier. And she was the youngest."

"What did you pay for her?"

"All I had, plus a tipper of dust." Tasha didn't even have to take a minute to make something up. She blurted out the lie as if she'd been keeping it in her cheek like so much chewing tobacco. "It wasn't *mine*," she added as an afterthought, not wanting them to think she was dusting. "I was muling. Now I'll have to hide from the dealer. He'll be after me to pay him back."

"We'll reimburse you, of course." Rachel straightened. "We won't know if she was born kited or not." She gently pinched the baby's arm. "She's certainly dehydrated, for starters. Let's get her inside and cleaned up."

"Can I carry her?" Devi asked.

"Once we've given her a bath, you can sit on the couch with her and give her a bottle, okay." Rachel and the boy disappeared inside with the baby.

Cletus and Tasha stared at each other for a moment, until Rachel popped her head out from inside. "You're coming in, aren't you? Devi wants to show you your room." And then she disappeared again.

"Guess that settles it." Cletus picked up his hammer. "See you at supper."

25

⋙

Allegra had the baby, finally, and at home as planned. Edmund had been set to leave despite her being in labour, but then Commander Cho had taken him aside. Edmund didn't know him well, but since this was the man who'd oversee his security while in the Droughtland he was willing to hear what he had to say. And when Cho told him that everyone thought it strange that he'd leave his wife just before she gave birth, he'd consented to wait.

Edmund stayed well away though, not wanting to relive what were now twisted memories of his other children's births. He locked himself in his office and brooded, wincing as Allegra's screams carried down the stairs and echoed in the hall.

In late afternoon the birthminder sent word that the baby was a boy, and healthy, and that Allegra was asking for Edmund to come to her now. Edmund braced himself, taking the stairs slowly.

He hadn't wanted more children and had hoped he wouldn't have to worry about it. Allegra, sickly as a child, had grown into a frail, narrow-hipped beauty not built for childbearing. She'd even had mumps! And while Edmund didn't make it his business to know or understand the goings on of women's reproductive health, wasn't that supposed to cause infertility?

And he certainly didn't want another boy. Not that he wanted a girl, either. Apparently he already had a daughter, except that he didn't think of her as his child, if she in fact existed at all. Never met her, never likely would. Simply put, he did not want this new child, daughter or son.

He sighed at the top of the stairs. The baby was crying, the fresh squall exclusive to red-faced newborns. The boys had been so very wee they'd had to stay at the hospital for almost two months under the careful watch of the birthminder and her staff. When he and Lisette had brought them home they were like two small kittens, sleeping and mewling and stretching out their tiny paws. He'd felt love then. He had. Despite how everything had turned out, he'd loved them then.

He stopped in the doorway to Allegra's room and felt a brief wash of shame as he looked at her propped up in the bed. With her cheeks flushed and with no makeup she looked even younger than her twenty-one years. He really was old enough to be her father. The shame left him though as soon as he laid eyes on the baby cradled in her arms.

"Come, darling," Allegra said when she noticed him there. "Come meet Edmund Junior."

"Hmm." Edmund sat on the edge of the bed and kissed her on the forehead. He shook his head when she offered the baby to him. "Let's not call him Edmund."

"But we agreed . . ." Allegra looked up from admiring her baby to give Edmund a quizzical look. "Little Eddie."

"I think we should honour your grandfather by calling him Charles."

"Oh." Allegra stroked the sleeping baby's cheek with a finger. "I don't know, Edmund. Maybe Charles could be his middle name? I so wanted him to be named for you."

"No. I do not want him called Eddie. Absolutely not."

Allegra glanced up, surprised at his tone. "Are you going to say hello to your son?"

The baby sucked in his lower lip, his eyes darting under closed lids, his brow furrowed. What little hair he did have swirled in blond whorls at his crown.

"He'll have curls," Edmund said. "Like you."

Allegra smiled. "He's got your nose."

Edmund put his fingers to the baby's forehead, gently coaxing away the furrow there. Despite everything, this child was far, far too young to be worried. That would come with the years. Undoubtedly. It was a strange time to welcome a child into the world, and it was a strange world to welcome him into.

"We're leaving at dusk."

"Oh, no . . ." Allegra reached for his arm. "Please, stay just one more day, Edmund. To be with your family."

Edmund lifted her fingers to his lips and kissed them. She smiled, eyes lowered shyly. He could play the part, if not feel it. What was the difference then?

He shook his head, summoning a sad dampness to his eyes. "We've already pushed it by waiting these last two days for the baby."

Real tears streaked Allegra's cheeks. "It's not fair."

Edmund kissed her once more, and then stood. "We'll hurry back."

"The baby will be almost two months old by then."

"Well, if we'd planned it better," Edmund said.

"You know there was no planning involved." Allegra wiped the tears from her eyes. "Don't pretend it could've been any different from the way it is. Don't patronize me. It's happened this way. So be it. But Phillip should be going, and you should be staying home, with me and the baby." The tears grew heavier as Allegra remembered her dead cousin. "It's all so wrong!"

"I'm sorry about Phillip," Edmund said. "You know I am. Had I known he couldn't handle the pressure, I never would've had him as Chief Regent." He paused. "But what's done is done."

"Send Nord then!"

"You know he is not fit to represent the Key."

"Then get rid of him altogether! What's the use of having him around at all?"

"It's more complicated than you know, my dear."

"Then tell me what's going on, truthfully." Allegra shifted the baby to cradle him along her other arm. "I want to know, Edmund. Everything has been so awful since Nord came. Losing dear Phillip. And you've been so distant. Is it me? Have I done something to anger you?"

"No. You're perfect." He rested a hand on her shoulder. "When I get back, I'll tell you everything."

"You won't." Her smile was wistful as she stretched up for one more kiss. "I know you won't, but that's okay. Just come back to us. Be safe. Hurry home. Charlie will be waiting for his father."

Edmund hesitated. This woman knew what it took to be a wife, how far to push, and more importantly when to let go. He kissed her, lingering generously. "I love you, Allegra." He didn't really feel an overwhelming affection for her. More of a satisfaction that he'd filled a position with the right candidate, but he said it to calm her, and it worked.

Allegra beamed. "And I love you, Edmund."

"Hello, Charlie." He kissed the baby's forehead. "And goodbye, son, until I come home."

"Charles Edmund Maddox." Allegra brought the baby up to her face and nuzzled him. "Welcome to the world."

AS THE CARRIAGES pulled out that evening, Edmund wondered what kind of world Charlie would grow up in. Would he ever know of his half siblings? As the convoy made its way out of the Key and into the treacherous vastness of the Droughtland he fell asleep, his children on his mind, even the girl, whoever she was. Wherever she was.

The convoy encountered the first protesters within the first hour out of the Eastern Key. Nord hollered out the order to open fire before Edmund had even opened his eyes from his nap. Three minutes later and eleven Droughtlanders were dead.

"What have you done? Are you mad?" Edmund blew the gold whistle that hung from his neck three times. "Cease fire! Cease fire!" The volley of gunfire stopped abruptly, screams and shouts peppering the air.

"I give the orders!" He grabbed Nord's collar and yanked him out of his seat. "No matter what twisted impression you have of yourself, you are not my Chief Regent because you're fit for the job. Don't ever forget that! Ever!"

"You want to let those scum get away with it? The disrespect? The lies?"

"Don't you dare speak of respect." Edmund gave the orders for the convoy to carry on at full speed across the plains, leaving the dead and injured Droughtlanders behind. "Don't you dare. They were unarmed! Those protesters are as much an annual event as the legislature itself! We don't waste bullets or time or energy on them."

"Everyone in the gardens was unarmed when you ordered the bombing." Nord twisted free. "That's the price of war, Edmund. You of all people should understand that."

"You don't know anything about war."

"And you do?"

"I have studied the art and science of leadership and government all my life!"

"I'm a Keylander too, Edmund, let's not forget. I grew up in the Keys, maybe not as upper class as you, but still. I know for a fact you've never been afraid for your life. Have you?"

"It has taken centuries to secure our way of life."

The two of them were jostled back into their seats as the carriage lurched around a bend.

"And all it will take to undo it is for the Droughtlanders to rise up," Nord said.

"What are you saying?"

Nord folded his beefy arms across his chest. "It wasn't smart, levelling Triskelia."

Edmund laughed. "When we stop to change the horses, I want you out of my carriage. You might be able to hold on to your post with the most heinous form of blackmail, but I do not have to be in the presence of your profound ignorance."

"You've unleashed something, Edmund. All I'm saying—"

"There's been nothing. They rolled over and took it from behind, just like the social whores they are. And now there's been barely a peep from the few survivors."

"Uprisings in the markets, the villages, that's nothing? And you call what's happening in Triban 'barely a peep'? You didn't wipe out the rebellion, you bloody well gave birth to it!" Nord nodded slowly. "You had a good thing going, with Triskelia quietly doing nothing in their little corner of the continent. Until you shook it all up with the ambush."

"They were uprising even then."

"They were not. They hadn't set foot outside that compound en masse for decades! Except for the circus. And you never knew the circus was just a bunch of Triskelians coming and going in and out of the Keys, right under your nose!"

"I won't carry on this conversation with you." Edmund picked up a book and flipped through it, dismissing Nord. "In fact, I won't grant you purchase of any kind."

"You will. And you do." Nord laughed. "You hate the fact that you may have started the war yourself, don't you?"

"There is no *war*. There has to be an enemy in order to have a war, not some figment of the imagination. And that's all Triskelia is now that we've taken care of it."

Nord said nothing for a while. Then he leaned forward, his elbows on his knees. "I've spent time out here, Eddie. You haven't."

And there, right there, is the reason Edmund would not consent to his son being named for him. Nord had ruined it. Edmund fixed him with a vicious glare. "Such a shame that your time out here didn't kill you."

"Well, it didn't. It made me stronger. And now I'm here to tell you that the entire population of the Droughtland is your enemy. Millions and millions of people, Eddie. With nothing to lose. Think about it."

"As Chancellor of the Eastern Key, I strongly suggest you stop talking."

"And as your Chief Regent, I strongly suggest you get a grasp on what's really happening. The tea party is over, Eddie."

Edmund leaned back, putting as much space as he could between him and this leech of a human. How had things come to this? He could not believe he'd ever felt love for Lisette, not with the dredging hate he felt for her now. This was all her fault.

26

※

Part of Seth wished he could have stayed and watched the aftermath of Regis's death, but his curiosity didn't have to endure
long. The two girls from Regis's bed showed up at the barracks
a week later.

"No one came until morning," the one called Melinda said. "And then
all hell broke loose, especially when we said it was Triskelia. We was
hustled away pretty quick. They kept us for two days, separate from each
other. They was asking us questions, but seeing as we didn't have to make
anything up except not knowing who you are, they let us go, because it
all checked out in their books."

"Thank you for coming to me." Seth stood. "You and—?"

"She's Daphne. She's shy."

"Well, you and Daphne can spend as long as you want here, as our
guests."

"Guests?" Daphne murmured.

"You mean, we don't have to put out?" said Melinda.

"No. You don't."

The girls shared a grateful if somewhat skeptical look.

"So what's next?" Amon asked, his eyes locked on Melinda, a stupid
grin plastered to his face.

"Ori and Finn can show them to the girls' wing, that's what."

Seth had lost track of how many were in his army now. He'd added the
girls' wing when they'd started showing up despite the word around

Triban that it was for boys only. Of course he bunked them separately, not like Triskelia with their mixed dorms and frank ambivalence regarding the obvious results. Seth did not need rampant venereal disease or dumb-eyed infants complicating matters. When he'd gotten back from the Guardy camp Amon had told him they'd had to evict the poppy den at the end of the block to make room for all the people flocking to them.

"It was harder than I thought," Amon had admitted. "There was a riot. We had to kill two people."

"But now we have the space we need," Seth said. "The difference with our army is that we know bloodshed is necessary. This is no Triskelia."

"There's no Triskelia any more anyway," Amon said.

"There will be again." Seth wanted to add, *We're rebuilding it*, but he left it at that.

"Everyone lost someone in the massacre," Amon mused. "Or knew someone who did, or had been treated at the Colony, or was just waiting for Triskelia to save them. It's like they don't have anything else besides us now. It's like, we're it, you know? Now that Triskelia is gone."

"It's not gone," Seth said. "It's dormant."

"What?"

"Never mind, Amon."

TEN DAYS FROM NOW the Night Circus would perform at Triban's coliseum, bringing with them Triskelia's precious Zenith. Inky posters had appeared on lampposts and bulletin boards, and everywhere Seth went people were talking about it. Some had given up the pretense of referring to Zenith as Auntie, now that the Guard knew who she was. Others, though, still clung to the custom.

Auntie is coming!

Zenith will make things better.

It's only a front . . . they're really going to storm the city.

No, it's a circus all right. Just a circus.

We don't need a circus! We need food, and guns, and the Guard dead and buried. Auntie will make it happen at last!

What is the Guard up to anyway? They've hardly budged.

It'll be a showdown when the Night Circus rolls in. Blood'll spill, you watch.

That's not Zenith's way.

It has to be now. After what they done to us, all those souls lost in the massacre.

Triban won't let the Guard take the circus.

You don't think so?

I know so.

We're being led to slaughter. Just like at Triskelia.

Those were just a few of the sentiments Seth overheard as he made his way down to the coliseum to see what was happening. To be safe, he wore a hooded jacket and kept to himself as he observed the hustle and bustle of the preparations well underway. Seth watched from the second-floor roof of the building across the street. He could see in a ways, through a portion of wall that had been bombed out long ago or had simply crumbled from disrepair.

The squatters had been kicked out, and a crew was going over the building with mops and brooms while another bunch lugged in rigging through entrances manned with armed security. He squinted at each figure but recognized no one. Not yet, anyway, and not from that distance.

It wouldn't be long before the Triskelians knew about the Boys' Army of Triban, if they didn't already. Would they believe he'd had nothing to do with the ambush and that he'd killed Commander Regis? Would they join him?

One thing was certain: he wouldn't join *them*. He had his own ideas and the manpower to tackle the Guard himself. He'd amassed more of a force to be reckoned with than Triskelia ever had in their decades of playing at rebellion and swinging from trapezes like monkeys.

He recalled the night of the circus back in the Key. He and his friend Maury had set the pigeons on the acrobat. Just for laughs. When the kid had actually fallen to his death, it's true, Seth had been thrilled. Both to watch it happen and in the aftermath, beholding Quinn's bashed-in head and the dramatic puddle of blood. He'd do it again.

It wasn't that he didn't value life, or feel bad when someone died. It was just that he had his head screwed on right about its not being as big a deal as most people thought. Once you're dead, there's nothing else. That's it. Sure, no more joy or satisfaction, but no pain or despair, either. So what?

Some people had to die as part of a larger agenda—so much larger that he doubted anyone else had really grasped it. But Seth had a clear understanding of his little part in it. And of what needed to happen.

He'd killed Commander Regis. And now, to achieve his larger goal, one more death was in order. Zenith's.

It did make sense, no matter now often he challenged himself to argue the opposite. She was Triskelia's leader, and he needed her out of the way. It was a matter of housekeeping, when it came right down to it.

If only the Droughtlanders treated the elderly as the Keylanders did, tucking them out of the way when they turned sixty-five. Zenith would've been well gone if that was the case. But she was hanging on, old and useless, leading her cliquey little utopia and not the rebel power most Droughtlanders believed Triskelia to be.

Seth left his hideout and returned to the barracks, his plan forming. He passed duos of his boys on almost every block. They straightened when they saw him, offering him tidy, abbreviated salutes.

There was room for only one leader, and that leader would be him. And until he stood at the top, triumphant, he'd take out anyone in his way. It was an unfortunate reality, but Zenith needed to go.

He wasn't stupid, though. He wouldn't let anyone find out it was him. He'd make it look as though the Guard did it. He could play the same game as his father, and that's what made Seth the ideal leader. He could play the good guy and he could play the bad guy, and by mastering both roles he'd succeed where everyone else had failed. Zenith was too good. The Group of Keys was altogether evil. Seth would come up the middle. He knew when each sort of power was required, and how, and by combining the nuances of both good and evil he would enjoy the dominance he knew he was destined for.

It was like a game of chess. There could be only one king on either side, and various pawns had to fall to make it happen. As he saw it now, Edmund was king on behalf of the Group of Keys and Zenith was king for the rest of the sorry lot. Seth needed her off the board so that he could battle Edmund. Sure, millions of chess games were playing out in wars all over the planet, but Seth was interested only in the board he found himself on. Zenith had to go. Not only would her death free the way for a new leader, it freed the way for a new Triskelia. *His* Triskelia. The true and righteous one that would do the work and spill the blood to become a superior nation. With that achieved, Seth's possibilities were boundless.

Zenith's time had long since passed. The world was in the midst of a revolution, and with that came a tumultuous reality in which hard things and wrong things sometimes become the right thing to do. And the right thing to do, the good thing even, was to kill her. It was almost merciful, if he really fiddled with the logic.

He would tell no one. Especially not Amon, who had a soft spot for the old bat and would never go along with the plan. This would be Seth's task alone. The entire city was excited that Zenith was coming. Auntie would do this and Auntie would do that. Triban had an inflated and wholly inaccurate opinion of their beloved Auntie.

Seth just did not get why they held her in such esteem. She never did anything! She just sat around quilting blankets for new babies and handing out forgiveness like so many candies in a jar on her sewing table. What kind of leader is that? Not a leader at all.

The only person he had to inform of his plan was his father.

A COUPLE OF DAYS LATER he and Amon retreated to the only quiet spot in the compound, Seth's attic rooms at the far north end.

"I'm going away for a while," Seth said. "But I'll be back in time for the circus. The regiments have all got their orders. Just keep putting them through the motions until I get back."

"Where are you going at a time like this?" Amon lit a cigarette. "And what for?"

"It's to do with Regis. That's all I can say on the matter."

"You can't go back out there, Seth!" Amon let out a breath of smoke. "They've brought in double the men now!"

"I'm not going there."

"Then where?"

"I can't say." Amon called Zenith "Zen Zen." He was one of her favourites. Seth couldn't tell him anything that might give his plans away. He glanced at Amon now. "Amon, I need you to be honest with me."

"Of course."

"Are you still dusting?"

"I told you I quit that," Amon said, his voice low and steady. "Ages ago."

"Are you on anything else?"

"After all I've done for you." Amon took another drag and shook his head. "You don't trust me."

"I do. I just have to be sure. There are almost five thousand people under our care, Amon. If I'm going away and leaving you in charge of it all, I have to know you'll be able to handle it."

"I'm clean."

"Not even hash?"

"Nothing." Amon shook his head. "I swear."

"Good."

"Tell me what you're up to, Seth. I'm your sergeant. I need to know these things. What if something happens to you? I won't know where to look."

"I'm sorry, Amon." Seth shook his head. "It's not safe to tell anyone. But when I come back things will be different."

"What about when the survivors come?"

"I may be back by then. If not, I'll be back soon after."

"How long will you be gone?"

"I can't say."

"You just want us to sit tight the whole time?" Amon stubbed out his cigarette and lit another. "The Guard isn't going to stay on the outskirts forever. They're up to something. They're going to want revenge for Regis's death."

"They don't know it was me, or I hope they don't yet. I'll be back before they advance nonetheless."

"How do you know?"

"Trust me, Amon." Seth tucked his compass and a spare knife in the top of his pack. "I don't want the boys to know I'm gone, so just tell them I'm in strategy meetings."

"They'll see you on the street."

"No, they won't." Seth cinched the pack tight. "Keep everyone safe. We'll need each and every one of our boys ready to fight when I get back. That's when it'll all come together at last. If the Guard won't make the first move, then we will."

"Tell me what you're planning, Seth." Amon gripped the cigarette between his fingers but had forgotten to smoke it. "What's really going on?"

"I'll tell you when the time is right. Trust me."

He hadn't said it like a question, but all the same, Amon nodded. "I do."

"All right then. Be safe." Seth settled the pack on his shoulders. The stub of ash from Amon's cigarette dropped to the floor. This seemed to knock Amon out of his stun. He took a final drag and then squashed it underfoot.

"You be safe too. I'll take care of everything here, Seth." Amon got the door for him. "Don't worry."

"I won't," Seth said, but only for Amon's benefit. He would worry; he worried about everything. But if he allowed himself to worry about the one thing he was about to do he'd chicken out altogether.

Halfway to the Western Key Edmund got word about Commander Regis's assassination.

"Still think there's no uprising?" Nord hadn't stopped grinning since they'd been told. "Still think there's no opposition? Some 'figment of the imagination' killed your top man in his own bed?"

"Did you have something to do with this?" Edmund glared at Nord. He was dressed in the suit Edmund had arranged for him before leaving the Key, his shoes polished, his hair slicked back. Edmund had kitted him out in the finery expected of a man of his position. But he hated him. And even the right clothes didn't make him look the part. He'd never be a real Chief Regent; it was like giving a mangy dog a bath and then calling it a purebred.

"Nope. Although I wish I did. The man was a pig."

"'No, sir' would have been sufficient." Edmund sighed. "But I suppose you have some bright idea about what I should do about it. Pray, do tell."

It occurred to Nord that he should've been thinking about it, "strategizing," as Edmund always said. But he hadn't thought about it. So Regis was dead. So what? He was an arrogant prick at the best of times and a sadistic one at the worst. Few tears would be shed, that was guaranteed.

"I'll give it some thought." Nord leaned back as the carriage met a smoother stretch of road. "For right now, a nap is in order." He glanced at Edmund. "Sir."

27

The caravans slowed to a stop in the night. Sabine pulled back a curtain to see where they were. A roadhouse outside Triban, the lights inside promising warmth and welcome, the glow of the city in the distance a menacing glimmer. She glanced over at Zenith, who'd fallen asleep sitting up, her silver hair mashed against the wall, a dark spot of drool on the pillow Sabine had tucked there. Sabine put a hand on the old woman's knee and shook her gently.

"Zen Zen?"

"Hmm?" Zenith opened her eyes. "What's that, child?"

"We've stopped."

Eli popped his head in. "Allies. We're spending the night."

"A real bed!" Sabine rubbed her hands together. "Delicious!"

"That's nice, dear." Zenith closed her eyes again. "You bring me back some."

Sabine sighed and shook her awake again. "No Zen Zen. We're staying the night here, in real beds, and there's food. Come, let me help you in."

Eli opened the door and pulled down the steps. "Jack's going to stick close to you and Zenith. I don't know about this place. Trace says it's okay, but I'm not sure. This close to the city, there might be trouble."

"I can take care of myself and I can take care of Zenith too." Sabine took Zenith's hand and helped the bewildered matriarch navigate the steps. "Go on, leave us, Eli. Besides, what would you do if there was trouble anyway? Pray? Like that'd do any good."

"That's not fair," Eli said. "I'm trying to—"

"Oh, that's better." Zenith breathed in the night air. "That wakes an old woman up. I do believe I've found my appetite too."

Sabine frowned at Eli and then offered Zenith a smile. "Good. I thought I'd have to show you straight to your bed, you were so snoozy."

"No, no." Zenith reached up to straighten her hair. "I must look a sight though. Be a dear and help me put myself together. Redo my knot?"

"No one cares what you look like Zenith," Eli said. "Let Nappo show you in. I need to speak with Sabine."

"*I* care what I look like, child. And don't speak to me with a sigh in your voice. You are so much like your grandpapa. It's quite tiresome."

Eli backed off before he got snapped at by her. Mention of his estranged grandfather got him thinking about Pierre. Where was he? It was as if he'd walked off the edge of the earth that night when he left Triskelia. Celeste never spoke of him, either. What did she think?

Sabine tidied Zenith's bun and then offered her an arm as they climbed the front steps of the neatly kept building.

Zenith looked up as a woman emerged from inside, her arms open. "Auntie!"

"Rachel, my dear!" Zenith embraced her. "I didn't recognize your place in the dark. What a treat!"

"You know . . ." Eli leaned in to whisper to his sister while Zenith was distracted. "You could at least return the respect I have for you. Or at the very least not make snide remarks in front of people. Especially Zenith."

"Give it a rest, Eli."

"And who's this?" Rachel hooked her arm with Zenith's and grinned at the sibling. "Twins?"

"This is Eli, and Sabine."

"We've met before," Sabine offered. "I was about six. I remember coming here on the way to the city. You had the best potato chowder and biscuits."

"I still do, come in." She helped Zenith up the last step. "We have a new baby, Auntie. Wait until you meet her."

ELI LET RACHEL and Sabine go on ahead with Zenith. He waited for Nappo and Teal, who were locking up the horses for the night.

"Who's going first?" he asked as the brothers approached.

"Gavin's going to take the first watch," Nappo said. "He says he's not hungry."

"I'll bring him out some food anyway. He's got to be hungry."

"Why do you care who's on watch anyway? It's not like you're going to do it." Nappo gave him a sideways look. "Not now."

"Sure I will. I'll take my turn."

"But what if something happens?"

The others had been talking about Eli since he'd killed the bandit, and so Eli had attempted to explain himself to Nappo. It had not gone over well.

"What do you mean?" Eli said, knowing exactly what Nappo was getting at but not knowing what else to say. He hadn't thought that far ahead on this particular issue.

"How would you handle it? Throw flower petals?" Nappo's tone was harsh. "Say, oh please, mister bad man, don't be so mean. It's not nice. Be a dear and go away."

"I don't know," Eli said, honestly. "But I'm willing to take my turn nonetheless."

"I don't know what that's worth," Nappo said as they entered the crowded roadhouse, the heady aromas of ale and cooking spices drawing them in. "Maybe you should skip it. I'll do double if you want," he offered as an apology for his sharpness.

"Okay." Eli was humbled. He hadn't thought it all through, but Nappo was right. What *would* he do? "Thanks. I'll make it up to you."

"Smell that!" Nappo took a deep breath. "Make it up to me by buying me a plate of that roast rabbit with plum chutney."

"You can tell that just by sniffing the air?" Eli scanned the dimly lit room for Sabine. She and Zenith and Celeste sat at a table against the wall near the back, with Jack standing guard nearby. A line was forming away from the table, roadhouse guests wanting to bring both salutations and concerns to Zenith.

"Look at that," Eli said.

"She's our leader, Eli." Nappo sniffed the air again. "Of course people flock to her, that's the point, isn't it? I think I smell chicken!"

The crowd was closing in around Sabine's table. She stood to keep order, to keep space around Zenith.

"I'm going to go help," Nappo said. "You get on finding us some food."

Nappo pushed his way through the crowd and set himself up opposite Jack. He folded his arms across his chest and donned a stone face.

All of a sudden a scream erupted from the other side of the bar. Nappo pulled his gun from his waist and took aim.

"Put that away in here!" Zenith slapped at it. "What are you thinking, child?"

A very pregnant girl let her tray of drinks drop to the floor. She waved her arms, standing on tiptoe to clear the crowd.

"Nappo!" Tasha waddled through the throng as fast as she could. "Nappo, it's me!"

She threw herself at him. Nappo let her cling to him, his confusion obvious in his wide eyes and oh-shaped mouth. "Uh, hi."

"I've been looking for you for ages!" Tasha turned her cheek against his chest and sighed. "Ages and ages. I left as soon as I found out."

"About?" As soon as he said it he remembered the drunken affair, or bits of it. Several nights at a party that seemed endless, with her hanging off his arm and sitting on his lap and cooing in his ear. She'd been fun, he remembered. "The Foothills!" he said. "Tasha, right?"

"Yes. Tasha." She pulled away from him. Her smile faltered. "You don't remember?"

"Oh, I remember. I do. Tasha . . . the breadminder's daughter. How's your dad?" He stared at her, or more specifically at her taut, round belly poking out her apron. "What's that?" he pointed at it.

"Oh, Nappo!" Tasha grabbed his hands and mashed them against her tummy. "This is your baby."

"Tasha, help me out here." The colour left his face. "I don't get it."

"You're going to be a daddy!" Tasha flung her arms around his neck, her belly wedged between them. "Now that I've found you we can get married and have the baby and go back to the market and you can work for my dad and we can have that house between my parents' and my sister's places!"

"Married?" Nappo teetered back. "Baby?"

Eli clamped a hand on his shoulder. "Steady there, pal."

"Sit, sit." Tasha steered him into a chair. "Have you come far? Where have you been? Did you miss me? Did you think about me all the time, because I've been thinking about you every second of the day, and I can't believe I've found you at last. Have you been looking for me too?"

Nappo swallowed. He eyed Eli, who was nodding, eyes wide, indicating that he do the same. Nappo nodded.

"I knew it!" Tasha hugged him again, her boobs pressing into his face. "I just knew you were looking for me too." She smelled like roast rabbit.

"I'm starving," Nappo muttered into her cleavage, bewildered.

"Oh! Of course you are!" Tasha pulled away and planted a wet kiss on his lips. "I'll go get you a great big platter of food. You wait right there. Don't move. Don't you get lost on me again now that we've found each other." She put her hands on her hips and sighed. She surveyed the crowd who'd been watching the reunion. "Love does have a way of surviving, doesn't it?"

The others smiled awkwardly, sympathetic eyes on Nappo, who had a dumb stare pasted on his face, his mouth slack. He managed another single, small nod, which seemed to pacify the girl.

"I'll be right back." She peppered his cheek with light kisses and then planted another big one on him before heading into the kitchen.

Eli parked himself between his stunned friend and the crowd, who now resumed their wait for Zenith.

"Congratulations," Eli said under his breath. "Way to go, daddy."

"Shut up." Nappo rested his head on the back of the chair. He draped an arm across his face and groaned. "What am I going to do?"

Hardly a minute later, Tasha hurried back with a tray of hot food and steins sloshing with each step.

She set the tray down and handed one to Teal. "Juice for you, little man. You're going to be an uncle! What do you think about that?"

Teal scrunched his face up in a frown. "Who *are* you?"

"You remember me, Teal. From the Foothills Market? Remember?"

"Sure." He threw a glance at his older brother, who was attempting to sit up and look alert. "I guess."

"So . . . Tasha." Nappo took a long pull on his ale. "How've you been?"

"I'll tell you. Now, you just eat." She set a plate of rabbit in front of him, and as he dug in she told them about surviving the massacre at the mountain camp and how the Guard had been looking for Seth.

"We didn't know about that. Hang on a second." Eli stopped her. "The others should hear this too."

Trace held back Zenith's admirers while the little group excused themselves to a private room. When Trace rejoined them, Tasha started her tale again.

"So the Guard knew Seth had been at the Foothills Market?" Zenith said. "And Eli too?"

"We heard about that tragedy," Celeste said, her face pale. "But we didn't know it was the same regiment who came for Triskelia."

"The Guard could've been on to Seth the whole time," Sabine said with some reluctance. "They could've followed him from Triban, even though we thought they hadn't."

"It could have been anyone." Zenith sighed. "Any number of the thousands who've come and gone from the Colony. It could've been one of us."

"Like Amon," Trace suggested. "In one of his dust stupors."

"Or even Pierre," Celeste murmured. "Perhaps they have him somewhere. Maybe that's why he didn't come back." She started to cry.

"Grandpapa will find us." Sabine put an arm around her grandmother. "He's fine. I'm sure he is. We would know. Even if he was captured we would have heard. I'm sure of it, Nana."

"I don't know, Sabine." Celeste shook her head. "I just don't know."

"It was only a matter of time." Zenith nodded for a top-up to her tea. She stirred in a fat spoon of honey before speaking again. "It has been only luck that we've been sheltered from the Guard for this long."

"Not luck!" Eli said. "Faith and trust. People trusted Triskelia to help them and in return they kept silent about the location. I crossed the continent and no one gave up the location, not ever, not even once. They would only say it was west. No. *No.*" Eli shook his head. "I don't believe it was a Droughtlander who revealed the location. I think it was Seth."

"There's no way we can know that for sure, child."

"Well," Eli shrugged, "is that any harder to believe than anyone else giving it up? That he left that night because he knew? Because he knew all along? Because he was in with Commander Regis?"

Tasha looked up at the mention of his name. "Who?"

"Commander Regis," Sabine said. She did not like this girl. Not one bit.

"He was the one on the mountain," Tasha said. "But he's dead now, so that's one bugger out of the way, isn't it?"

All eyes turned to her. Tasha grinned. "You didn't know he's dead? I don't know why not. It's been all the talk. I'm surprised you haven't heard."

"So tell us now," said Sabine. "Get on with it."

"I will. Don't get your knickers in a knot, honey."

"Look." Sabine bristled. The sooner they could get Tasha out of the room, the better. "Just tell us what you know."

"Don't think you can talk to me like that." Tasha's eyes narrowed. "What have I ever done to you, huh?"

Sabine's patience was quickly thinning. She glanced at the others and could see they felt the same. Poor Nappo looked downright sheepish, as if it was his fault Tasha was sitting with them in the first place. And it was, so he could go right on feeling guilty.

"Tell us or don't tell us," Sabine said. "We can find out from someone else. You can go now."

"And who the hell are you?" Tasha pulled her chin back defiantly. "Nappo? Are you going to let her talk to me like that? Huh? Are you?"

Nappo winced, her voice pinching his nerves. He put his head in his hands. "You should probably just go, Tasha."

Tasha glared at Sabine. Sabine glared right back.

"You people are snobs!" Tasha spat on the floor. "I come in here, willing to help, and you all shut me out like I'm some kind of idiot. The hell with all of you! Come on, Nappo."

Nappo just shook his head. "Tasha—"

"Don't even, Nappo. Just come with me. Now!"

Nappo stood. He stuck his hands in his pockets and kept his eyes on the floor and followed her out of the room. At the doorway, he turned back and shrugged. "I'll find out about Regis. She'll fill me in."

"And then some," Sabine said. "Good luck, my friend."

"Nappo!" Tasha yelled from the bar. "Are you coming?"

WITH NAPPO OTHERWISE OCCUPIED, Eli went outside to take his turn watching the caravans and horses. It was unlikely that anyone would try anything here, with the roadhouse so busy and everyone knowing who the caravans belonged to, but still, if needed, he'd holler for help.

After a while Sabine came out. She handed him a mug of tea, clambered up beside him on the driving bench of Zenith's caravan, and told him what Nappo had relayed about Regis. There was more to it than just his death. Rumour had it that Seth had killed him on behalf of Triskelia. That he had an army in Triban. Of boys. Thousands strong, with a hold on the city that both baffled and impressed its citizens.

"And we're walking right into it." Eli left the tea untouched. He had a sick feeling, a churning in his guts that told him terrible, terrible things lay ahead.

"You think he'd do any harm to us?"

"I don't know." Eli bet that Seth was in his height of glory, playing war with a bunch of other boys. "He's powerful. And capable of anything. Whatever you can imagine and worse. Or better too, I guess, depending on what direction his moral compass is pointing at any given time."

"Then you believe he has one."

"Everyone does." Eli tipped out the tea. "There's just no one force pulling them."

"Not the highers?"

Eli let a derisive breath out his nostrils. "You suggest that, after mocking me?"

"I don't want to argue with you, Eli."

"Me neither."

They sat quietly for a few moments, looking off toward the glow of the city in the distance.

"How far away are we?" Eli asked, shifting the topic to safer ground.

"A couple of hours. Give or take."

Another silence drew itself out like a tired sigh. They couldn't avoid the hard topics. Not when it was all they were thinking about.

"What would you have us do, Eli?" Sabine toyed with her medallion.

"Retreat," Eli said. "Let Seth do whatever he had in mind with his troop of tin soldiers. Let him take up arms while we take the higher path and come up with a peaceful solution."

For a moment Eli thought she was giving his words serious consideration, but then she shook her head.

"I wish you were on my side, Eli."

"I am! I just don't want anyone else to get hurt. It's wrong, and it will never end."

Sabine stared at him, as if seeking answers behind his eyes rather than in his words. "You want to know what I honestly think about your take on it all?"

Eli nodded, bracing himself.

"I think you sustained a head injury and your pacifist babble is the fallout."

Eli looked at his knees. He set his hands there and nodded slowly. Then he got up and jumped down from the bench.

"I'm going to bed, Sabine. Good night."

"Eli!" Sabine called after him.

"What?" he snapped.

"Stay. Argue with me," Sabine implored. "Be real!"

"I'll tell you what's real. Or what will be shortly. The end. The end of this tenuous peace, with violence threatening to break out at any moment. There's an electricity in the air. Even in that crowd in the roadhouse, wanting to see Zenith. You all think they adore her, and sure, some of them do, but I know that still more resent her. For everything that happened. If we go to Triban very few of us will come out alive, whether we do the circus or not. That's what's real. I know it in my gut as sure as if it's already happened and I'm looking back on it like some terrible memory."

"You can't know the future."

"But I do. I know it."

"None of us knows what will happen."

"And I'm telling you that I do."

"You're feeling the same anxiety we all are," Sabine said. "These are strange times, Eli. Nothing comes easily any more. Not life, or sleep, or love, or peace. Or battle."

"Is that some of your leader speak?" He could hear the edge in his voice. He didn't want it, but he was frustrated and wanted her to know how serious he was. "Look, Sabine. I don't want to be right, but I know I am. I know it."

"Listen Eli, first you say you've turned into some kind of pacifist. Okay. I get that. But now you're some kind of psychic too? Your crazy voices have some kind of crystal ball?" Sabine laughed. "Is that it? And even if you can see into the future and it's full of death, what are you going to do about it anyway?"

"You can believe in our connection, back in Triskelia, but you can't believe this?"

"I don't know what to believe." There was fear in her voice taking over the bitterness. "I just don't know any more."

Seth had mapped enough of the sewer system to know that the safest way out of Triban was due south. He'd stowed a preciously rare bicycle down there, with saddlebags stocked with supplies, and although he'd hidden it well he was surprised to find it undisturbed. He had another one stowed farther down, just in case.

He rode quickly through the slick of foul water, the back tire kicking it up, spraying his backside with muck. He wished he'd thought to rig up a tail guard, but with his mind on other matters he didn't think about it for long. Gone were the days when he worried about things like looks and dressing sharp and smelling good, or even being dry and warm and fed.

As he rode his thoughts turned once more to Rosa. He hadn't been with a girl since, and didn't want to. He wanted Rosa back. If only he had the time to look for her. If only he knew where to start.

The distance passed quickly, as did the road under him once he'd heaved the bike out of the tunnel and pedalled around the outskirts of

Triban, circling back northeast. He didn't want to stop for fear that he'd lose the bike to bandits, and so he barely looked up as he passed the road-house where his siblings lay in bunk beds, Sabine up top and Eli down below, each restless in their sleep.

As Seth rode by Eli was dreaming of him. Only his brother was in pieces, blown apart from the blasts at the ambush. He was wandering around with one leg and a crutch, the other leg, bloody and blue, slung over his shoulder like a cut of meat, one arm gone from the elbow, the other gone altogether and a great big hole blown in his head. A wake of tiny toy soldiers marched in formation behind him, guns drawn.

"Brother," Seth called to him in his dream. "I am not dead."

It was dark in the dream, so Eli lifted his torch to get a better look. He stepped over the wee soldiers and lit the hole in Seth's skull. Eli peered in. There were more toy soldiers in there, marching through a rainstorm, lightning and thunder and winds cutting across the muddy ground.

The dream woke him up with a jerk. His hand was tucked under the chain of his medallion. He nearly broke it, disoriented and lurching out of slumber. His clothes were drenched with an uneasy sweat.

He was suddenly and tremendously afraid. He pushed off the covers and stood up to peek at Sabine.

"You awake?" he whispered. She stirred but did not answer. He wanted to talk to her. He wanted to tell her about the dream. He considered shaking her awake but then thought better of it. He tucked himself back in under the covers and gripped the medallion as he fell back into the strange and bloody dreams that plagued him so.

The Western Key was a three-day ride northeast from the city of Triban. The walled enclave spread out, long and narrow, along a valley rich and pungent with forest that flourished in the near-natural weather systems.

There'd been murmurs, though, about weather espionage and coveted secrets, cloudseeding techniques the Western Key wasn't sharing with the other Keys, either from greed or malice.

It was also the largest Key on the continent, given its generally temperate climate, and perhaps for other reasons too. Seth got off his bike at the top of the treed hill that sloped down to the Key. He stayed hidden in the shadows of the forest, far enough away not to be sighted by the Guards who patrolled the perimeter, strolling back and forth along the top of its walls.

There was also talk that the Western Key was deliberately increasing its population with plans to one day dominate the Group of Keys. That they were hosting the legislature this year was a strategic but dangerous move. It was as if they were saying, See, we have nothing to hide, all the while crossing their fingers behind their back.

Seth leaned against a tree and squinted at the Key. His muscles ached from pedalling and his lungs were sore from the last uphill chunk of the ride. He uncapped a flask of water and took a ponderous sip. The legislature was due to start in two days. Seth capped the bottle and got back onto the bike. He'd skirt south and then east of the Key, far enough away to remain out of the Guard's sight. After the events in Triskelia and the recent attempt on its own walls, the Key had bolstered its forces. Seth had heard about the two groups of dusted renegades who'd made a sloppy rush at the walls. Disorganized and barely armed, they'd never posed a real threat.

Seth would, though. In good time.

28

⚜

Zenith's carriage led the convoy into the city, carrying the matriarch and Sabine, Jack as bodyguard, and Eli, who'd insisted on staying close to his sister despite their argument.

It was immediately obvious how much things had changed. The last time Eli had been in Triban no one had known who the Triskelians were. But now the entire city was waiting for them. It was as if Triban had woken up from a long sleep and was now as bright-eyed and angry as any city as wretched and wronged as Triban should be.

Surely both the Guard and Seth's supposed BAT, as they'd learned his army was called, also knew of their arrival. But as he peered out the caravan's window at the sea of people who'd gathered to greet them Eli saw no evidence of Guard activity, not uniformed anyway, and no sign of boy soldiers either.

He watched the spectators carefully. Were some Guard and others BAT? Undercover? Lying in wait?

A frenetic aura danced above the jostling mob. Eli could almost see it light on their shoulders as the caravan slowly made its way through the throng. It really did seem as if the whole city had come to mark their arrival. People of all ages pushed and shoved each other, maintaining an unsteady clearing just barely wide enough for the carts to pass. They carried banners and waved streamers and bleated on horns or shouted themselves hoarse over the cacophony of equally disorganized musical tributes staged along the way. There was a dangerous frenzy to it all. It unnerved Eli. He told Zenith so.

"They've been energized," Zenith said. "By grief and outrage. They've become a source of brilliance, and have flooded the shadows that sheltered us for so long."

The crowd surged forward suddenly, swallowing up the road and forming an unruly, feverish swarm corking the way. The carriage started to rock as people pushed against it, hammering the sides with their fists, chanting.

"*Now or never, now or never, now or never! Triskelia forever!*"

Jack unsnapped his holster, his hand hovering above his gun.

"No." Zenith put her hand over his.

"These are our people, Jack." Sabine braced herself as the carriage shook. "We need each and every one of them, and we need their anger and defiance."

"*No more bread and circuses!*"

Zenith shook her head. "They don't understand."

There were footsteps on the wooden roof of the carriage, and then Trace's voice lifted above the crowd. "Stop!"

"*No more bread and circuses!*"

"Your leader is in this carriage, my friends. She has come to the people."

Sabine's eyes widened and the colour drained from her cheeks. Zenith took her hand. "He means me, child. Don't worry. I wouldn't set you on a path you couldn't yet walk."

The angry chants simmered down into a curious chatter, and then the crowd boiled up again, only this time with a more generous tone. *Zenith! Zenith! Zenith!*

"We are here for you!" Trace shouted. "Please, welcome us in the fashion we deserve, as your leaders and as survivors of the Triskelian massacre at the hands of the Keyland Guard!"

Eli and Sabine watched as the crowd roared. The Droughtlanders of the city were filthy, their faces creased in anger and hunger and the spiky-eyed high of dust. Several fights broke out within the jostling tangle and some were pushed to the ground.

"They'll be killed!" Sabine turned to Zenith. "We have to do something!"

Zenith shook her head. "We mustn't interfere. Their anger and lack of control is too much for us right now."

Ze-nith! Ze-nith!

"They want you." Eli pulled away from the window as the crowd closed in.

Trace leapt down from the roof as others from the Triskelian convoy joined him, forming a human fence between the crowd and the carriage.

"Back up!" he hollered. "We don't want to have to use force!"

"And that's why the massacre happened!" a wild-eyed man in the crowd screamed. "You're just a bunch of cowards!"

Zenith stood. "I'll speak to them."

"No!" Sabine, Eli, and Jack all said at once.

"Come with me," she said. "You can keep me safe, and in doing so you'll realize you don't need to." And with that she opened the door of the carriage, emerging onto the top step. The crowd fell silent, assuming a hot, tenuous calm.

Eli and Sabine helped Zenith down the steps. Bullet skulked behind Eli, too overwhelmed to assert himself in any way.

It's her!

It really is!

And then the chants again. *Zenith, Zenith, Zenith!*

With Jack in front and Eli and Sabine forming a tight bracket around her, Zenith made her way into a storefront where she asked to be led to the second-floor balcony. The astonished storeminder showed them the stairs and then followed them up, offering dried goods and firewood and precious bric-a-brac to the woman he'd only ever heard of in whispers and pub stories. "No need, child." Zenith stepped out onto the balcony. "But if you have a glass of potable water, I wouldn't say no."

The storeminder hurried away to do her bidding, leaving the small group to behold the crowds below. From up there they could see the crowd stretching endlessly along the main thoroughfare and spilling down alleys and side streets. In the near distance a crude effigy of the Western Key's Chancellor dominated the horizon. It didn't look much like him but you could tell who it was meant to be, what with the big nose and the two rows of tiny, gleaming teeth filling his grin. Posters and placards bobbed above the crowd, most with at least one spelling mistake, but the intent was clear.

Wer is our revolushun? read one. *How many mor wil dy?* read another. Amidst it all were countless small Triskelian flags with the intricate triangle symbol like so many wide eyes staring back at them.

"Are they for us or against us?" Sabine could not look away from the crowd as the chants grew louder. It was as mesmerizing and beautiful as it was frightening.

"They may not know themselves," Zenith said.

"I don't like this." Eli scanned the buildings across the street. Some windows were open, crowded with still more spectators; others had scraggly curtains pulled across or were dark beyond. Perfect for snipers.

"Either way, the people are ready now." Zenith waved to the throng below. "They are ready to be our army."

"We're sitting ducks here," Jack said amidst the roar. "No doubt there's Guardy spies all over the place, and just because the camp up the hill hasn't budged doesn't mean it won't any moment. This place is about to blow, and I'm not sure we'll fare so well. We have to get out of here, Zenith. Sabine, you understand . . . forget about the circus."

"Jack's right," Eli said. "It's beyond that now."

"No. We're going to put on the circus, as much for ourselves as for them." Sabine waved to the crowd too. With the din from the chanting thundering in her ears she raised her voice just to hear herself. "And besides, we want it to blow, don't we?" She let the question hang there for anyone to answer.

"If by 'blow' you mean rise up," Zenith said for everyone. She put a hand to her brow, the better to see the crowd, what with the sun. "If by 'blow' you mean erupt, like a volcano."

"Or not," Eli said. "More likely 'blow' as in blow up in our faces and we all die."

"We could all be dead by tomorrow at this rate," Jack said. "This crowd isn't safe, Zenith." His hand still hovered at his holster.

"Sometimes numbers are what matters," Sabine said. "Right now, we need the masses, healthy, happy, or not."

"We need their anger, their defiance," Zenith added. "They've finally realized they have nothing to lose. We spent years trying to convince them with words, until we understood they would have to find it within themselves to rise up."

"So all this time, Triskelia has been waiting for a tragedy?" Eli said.

"It could have been a plague, or a year with no rain at all," Zenith said. "We weren't willing to orchestrate anything of the sort, not like the Keylanders."

The crowd was done with admiring Zenith. The noise died down a little, as if it were a shifting wind. Now they wanted more.

Speech! Speech!

"They won't be able to hear you." Sabine waved at the crowd again.

"The ones who can will share the message." Zenith steadied herself at the railing with one hand and accepted the glass of water from the storeminder with the other. "Thank you, mister."

"No, no, no, thank *you*," the man gushed, bowing as he backed away. "Such an honour, such an honour!"

"Don't drink it yet, Zenith." Jack grabbed the storeminder's arm. Taking the cue, Bullet's hackles went up. The dog lowered his head and growled. It occurred to Eli that Bullet might be more useful than he was in these uncertain times. The thought depressed him. "That water better be fit to drink," Jack said. "Or you *will* be sorry. I'll make sure of that."

"Only the best," the man urged. "I promise you."

"It better be." Jack gave him a slight shove as he let go.

Eli brought Bullet to heel, his depression shifting into shame. He felt like a prisoner of himself, held captive by his own ideas despite how illogical they may seem.

There wasn't an ounce of grace or peace in sight. Only uncertainty, fear, and danger most of all. They were exposed up here on the balcony, an easy target for anyone with the inclination and the firepower. Eli watched the far buildings, paying close attention to the dark windows and all their possibilities.

"Droughtlanders, people of Triban . . ." Zenith projected her voice with a strength and firmness Eli would not have thought her capable of. ". . . Triskelians." At that, the people within earshot erupted in cheers, infecting the rest of the crowd, who didn't even know what they were cheering for. "Meet your new leader. She is called Sabine. And she will be at your side as we do what is necessary to reclaim our freedom."

Sabine blanched. She, Eli, and Jack shared a confused look. What was this? Why such a sudden, unplanned introduction?

"I'm not ready!" Sabine exclaimed as Zenith took her hand.

"Sabine will guide us to justice," Zenith continued as if she hadn't heard her. "Sabine will accomplish all that I have failed to do in my lifetime."

Sabine wanted to back away into the cover of the building, but Zenith's light touch on her shoulder felt as heavy as gold. She could hardly move. She lifted a hand in front of her face, not waving exactly but just holding it there, as if keeping it all at bay.

"Zenith!" Jack said. "What are you doing? Now is not the time to—"

"We have come to you now," Zenith went on, "to unite as one and begin the revolution we have all been waiting for. It is time to topple the Group of Keys once and for all!"

The crowd roared. But this time it did not die down. It swept across the masses, kicking up a renewed frenzy as it did.

"This isn't safe." Jack put himself between Zenith and the rail. He pushed the old woman inside and ordered Sabine to follow. She couldn't move. Eli finally yanked his sister away from the rail. "We have to get out of here. Now!"

Below them the chaos was crowning as the heap of debris at the base of Chancellor West's effigy was set alight. The flames licked up the structure and then leapt out into the crowd, igniting a young woman's scarf as she fled. She fell to the ground and was quickly engulfed, her skirts going up in a whoosh of fire.

"Inside!" Eli shoved his sister. As he pulled the balcony doors shut behind them he could hear the burning woman's shrieks, and then the screams of countless more as the blazing effigy collapsed into the crowd, catching a veranda on the way down and setting that building on fire.

Incensed and terrified, the people scrambled to disperse but only slowed the process with all their shoving and fighting and trampling one another.

Downstairs the storeminder huddled behind the counter, an impressive club in one hand, a knife in the other.

"You should stay inside." Eli steered Zenith and Sabine toward the back room as Jack stood guard at the door. "Until it settles out there."

"Absolutely not." Zenith turned on her heel and headed straight for the front door. Jack tried to stop her, but it just wasn't in any of their natures to defy Zenith. "We will not be separated from our people any more," she said, her hand over his on the knob. "And we will not shy away from a nation expressing their frustration. This is exactly what we need to harness."

"Please don't go out there, Zen Zen." Jack put his other hand flat against the door, holding it shut. "Please?"

"Let me go." Zenith tugged. "Now."

Jack relented, backing away as she opened the door.

In the street a riot was in full swing, with store windows being smashed, people falling under the melee, fists flying. Trace and Gavin and the others had surrounded the convoy of caravans and horses and were standing calm and steady. Even amidst the chaos, no one meddled with the Triskelians or their property.

When the crowd edged too close Jack led the way back to the carriage. No one touched them. It was strange. Eerie. Punches came within an inch. Men, locked together in rage, tumbled at their feet but did not collide with them. It was as if the tiny group were shielded by an invisible barrier. Eli glanced up at the blue sky above, wondering if it was the highers keeping them safe.

You do believe. Faith is good.

"It's because they know we're all they've got," Sabine shouted over the din, as if reading his mind.

They climbed back into the carriage as flames claimed the rest of the block nearest the effigy.

Trace leaned his head in. "What now, Zen Zen?"

"Ask Sabine." Zenith settled into her seat and pulled a blanket across her knees. "I am quite done."

"We need to get sand on that fire lest it take the whole city." Sabine barrelled ahead of her fears. "Summon the fire brigade. Until they get here, try to find someone who knows where the sand stores are for these blocks. And have Gavin and Yvon move us to a safer spot."

"Do you want to go back the way we came in?" Trace asked.

"No." Sabine shook her head. "We're not leaving. We'll stage as close as possible while keeping a somewhat safe distance."

"Here we go, Sabine." Trace slapped the side of the carriage as if it were the flank of a horse. "Let the games begin!" He disappeared into the fray, the excitement in his eyes unmistakable.

Moments later the carriage was moving. When they stopped again they had parked down the street by several hundred metres but still right in the middle of it, as if announcing their commitment, their bold witness.

ELI WATCHED THE ACTION from inside the carriage, feeling cowardly and unsure of himself. Should he go out there? Try to calm them?

Be still.

But, he argued, he wasn't afraid. He felt protected, and he was certain that it was more than a feeling. He believed it was fact. Surely this immunity was meant for something?

You will be safe, so long as you make the right decision.

He would test that right now. Ignoring Sabine's protests, he climbed onto the roof of the carriage. Up there he could keep an eye on the fire raging in the distance and keep watch from all sides should anyone try to approach.

A crank siren pealed out from a few blocks away, summoning Triban's exhausted fire crew as great pillars of black smoke churned out chunks of charred debris that sounded like wind chimes as they skittered along the road in the gusts generated from the fire. Oddly musical, it was a strange accompaniment to the screams of the unfortunates falling under their own frenzied stampede and the war cries of others raising fists and weapons to the nearest perfect stranger who had done them no wrong. These were a miserable people in a ruin of a city, and if Zenith thought any good would come of aligning Triskelia with Triban she was dreadfully mistaken. And now it all rested on Sabine.

SEVEN HOURS LATER and three whole blocks had burned to the ground. The fire had been subdued thanks to the fire brigades and the paltry trickle of water afforded by a patched-together hose hooked up to an exhausted well. When the fire chief had shown up he'd swung valiantly into action, spacing the sand carts at intervals, organizing civilian brigades, and directing his men—armed with only axes and sledgehammers—to knock down the buildings on either side, creating a gap in the fire's fuel and a point from which to battle its flames. It had worked.

The crowd had thinned, fleeing the blaze, the brutality, and—in a spectacular show of cowardice—the call to help quell the fire and uphold the peace. Sabine had left Eli at his rooftop lookout with instructions to call for backup if anyone threatened Zenith's safety while she cobbled together a triage area behind the Triskelian convoy, enlisting a handful of Triban's more charitable citizens to see to the wounded.

Now that the area was safe again, Eli climbed down. He checked on Zenith. She was fine, seemed quite unfazed in fact, even shooing him away when he asked if she'd like him to stay on guard for her.

He found Jack first. He was speaking with the fire chief not far from Zenith's carriage.

"I can't thank you enough, Chief." Jack clapped the man's shoulder in a gesture of appreciation. "You run an amazing crew."

"We have over a thousand members," the chief said. "Unofficially. We don't see all of them all the time, of course. People have their struggles . . . they step up when they can. Good men, the lot of them. And that's saying something in this city."

"Well, again. Thank you. And I know we'll want to take you up on your offer. How do we find you?" Jack wiped his face with an already sooty handkerchief. "Do you have a hall of some kind?"

Eli hung back. Were they to join forces with a bunch of Triban ruffians? He appraised the Chief. He was filthy, of course, covered in soot and sweat. But he had a strong jaw and carried his estimable bulk with a convincing assuredness.

"One main hall, and then several spots around the city where we station the sand carts and equipment." The Chief described the location of the hall, using a pencil and a space of wall to draw a map. "I'd need a few days to get word out to the men."

"About what?" Eli's curiosity got the better of him.

Jack shot him a look. "Not now, Eli."

"I can't guarantee anything," the Chief went on as if Eli wasn't even there. "I'll be honest about that. I don't keep tabs on my men or their allegiances or lack of 'em. But you need us, I'll make sure we show up."

"And we appreciate it. It's clear we can't use the police, what's left of them," Jack said. "Can't tell who's in the back pocket of the Guard."

"I won't pretend my men are angels, but the police are far worse." The Chief shook his head. "I wouldn't know where to begin to sort out the corrupt from the even more corrupt."

Down the street a fireman whistled for the Chief. "I'll be in touch," he said as he backed away. "I know where to find you."

"And I you now," said Jack. "Thank you."

The Chief lumbered over the rubble and out of sight. Jack tapped the map on the wall.

"Copy this, then cover it up." With that Jack walked away, his clothes soiled with soot and mud, his blond hair caked with it. He disappeared behind Zenith's caravan, toward the triage area.

Eli stood still, wrestling with his pride. Who was he to boss him around? He ran after Jack and grabbed him by the arm.

"Let's get something straight."

"Don't go there, Eli." Jack pulled away, leaving Eli's hands filthy. "Do as you're told."

"I'll do as Zenith tells me, as Sabine tells me. But not you. We're peers, Jack. Kindly treat me like one."

"Then kindly act like one, asshole, and not like some higher-hugging imbecile!" Jack stalked off, carefully stepping around casualties, lined up and supine, and toward where Gavin was kneeling over an elderly woman who was struggling to breathe.

ELI TOOK IN THE SCENE before him. Sabine and Gavin had set out three canvas tarps on the road, and just by looking Eli knew which one was

which. The walking wounded congregated on the first, the worse off on
the second, where they were being attended to, and the near dead and
beyond help on the third, where Celeste was holding the hand of a burn
victim, his skin blackened, his scalp bloody. Eli watched, transfixed, as
the man's chest rose slower and slower and then not at all. Celeste set his
hand down, wiped her own, draped a shirt over his face, and moved on
to comfort the next.

Eli's eye wandered back to the second tarp, where Sabine worked
alongside a girl with a thick dark braid. Sabine was picking glass out of a
woman's palms while the girl bandaged up the arm of a boy clinging to
the woman. Eli recognized the girl at once.

It was Rosa. The girl who'd travelled the Droughtland with Seth and
then left him once his atrocities were revealed. The girl Seth had loved.

She looked up and saw him there. She offered a slight lifting of her
mouth in acknowledgment, but that was all. It wasn't a smile. Rosa went
back to work and did not look up again.

Eli approached them and waited silently until they were finished.
Rosa stood.

"Eli."

"Rosa," Eli said. "How've you been?"

"Good, I guess. Good." She moved along to inspect an old woman
with a swollen ankle that angled badly to one side. She knelt down and
cut away the woman's sock. The old woman winced as Rosa felt along the
bone. "I think it's broken, Auntie."

"I thought as much." The old woman nodded, her eyes tearing up.
"I heard a crack when I fell."

"We'll get it sorted out," Rosa said. "Don't you worry." She offered the
woman a willow-bark tablet to chew on. "I'll send someone to wrap it,
and we'll find you something to use as a crutch."

"Where have you been all this time?" Eli trailed her to the next
patient.

"In Triban."

"Have you seen Seth?"

She shook her head.

"Do you know where he is?"

"In his warehouse compound, I'm sure."

"So you've heard the rumours?"

"Heard the rumours, seen the soldiers. As hard as I struggle to find much good to say about your brother, I will admit that the city is getting safer with his boys on the streets. That doesn't mean I want to have anything to do with him. Let's get that straight." Rosa pulled a bandage from her kit and spread a rank-smelling paste onto it. "So if you're here to try and get me to forgive him, or take him back, or anything like that, I'll tell you now. It isn't going to happen. Not after everything. You tell him that."

"I haven't seen him since the night of the massacre."

"No?"

"No."

"Oh, dear. Listen to me. I'm sorry, Eli." Rosa's expression softened. "I can't even begin to imagine how awful it must've been for everyone. And here I am going on about my petty slights."

"We're still trying to figure out if Seth had anything to do with it."

"Eli!" Rosa levelled him with a defiant glare. "How can you even think that?"

"This, coming from you?" Eli's eyebrows arched in surprise. "After your anti-Seth speech just now?"

"It wasn't *anti-Seth*." Rosa secured the poultice on the patient's leg with a strip of cloth. She stood, hands on her hips. "My relationship with Seth aside, I said BAT was good for Triban, didn't I? Gets boys off the streets, straightened out, fed, clothed. Gives them a safe place to sleep. Keeps them out of trouble. And most of all, gives them something to be proud of. And that's all your brother's doing. Does that sound like the actions of someone who plots massacres? BAT's the best thing to happen to Triban in a long time, I'll have you know."

"Right. BAT."

"The Boys' Army of Triban."

"Yes, I know what it stands for," Eli said. "So, you know all this but you haven't seen him?"

"You think I'm lying?"

Eli shrugged. "I don't take anything for granted these days."

"I'll tell you what I told Sabine." Rosa prepared another poultice and placed it on the patient's other leg, where the skin was taut and white from a severe burn. "His district starts about forty blocks south of here. You can't miss it. He's got boys on every corner. In twos. With guns." She sighed as she caught Eli's expression. "Don't ask me where or how he got them. I don't know. And no, I haven't seen him. Ever since I found out it was him, I've made a point of staying on this side of the city."

To quell further questions, Rosa put Eli to work, carrying her supplies and following her instructions to pull or hold as she set bones or to pass her this or that from her kit. It was well after dark by the time everyone was triaged and packaged up as best as was possible. Those who'd perished were loaded up and removed by the deadminders, for a fee, and when Gavin and Jack had transported the last of the wounded to safe shelter the Triskelian convoy continued their journey to their final destination. The coliseum. Rosa rode with them, in the carriage with Eli and Sabine. Exhausted and wary, the three spoke little, and did not mention Seth at all.

29

$\sim\!\!\diamondsuit\!\!\sim$

Seth caught sight of his father's group of mounted Guards and armoured carriages when it was about a day and a half out from the Western Key. He rode parallel along their route as best as he could, sticking to the far side of the ridge and checking only every hour or so that they were still within range.

As he rode he couldn't help but think about how things used to be. Not that long ago he might have been travelling with his father himself, either as apprentice to the title or as member of his advisory board or even as Guardy. His life in the Eastern Key seemed like a dream now, whereas back then a life out here would have been unimaginable.

But this life was real now, and he really was about to do something he might not even live to regret. Nonetheless he carried on. This was his only chance to confront his father.

But what if it went horribly wrong and Seth didn't make it back to Triban? Would Amon abandon BAT and return to a life of dust? Turn it over to the Triskelians to make his boys into circus pets? Or would he hold on to it and make something of himself?

Seth could speculate all he wanted. It made no difference. The future would unfold even if he weren't around to participate. If that were the case, Seth rather hoped to be killed, swiftly . . . execution style. He didn't think he could stand being taken prisoner, spending who knows how long, if not forever, in a barren cell. He'd go mad. He pedalled along, his resolve strengthening as his muscles worked. If he were captured, if his plan failed, he'd do everything in his power to end his own life.

He crested the ridge again. The convoy had gained on him. He took a moment to pull his mask over his face and then pedalled hard and fast up the next ridge. He'd have to do it soon. When a slope lay ahead he coursed down it, revelling in the dry rush of wind in his ears. If he died today it would only be sooner rather than later. What would he regret if his father's men put a bullet into him before he could speak his piece? Not his time out here. Not joining the Guard.

Rosa.

She was his single regret. Not meeting her, but how he'd treated her. How it had ended between them. That would remain his one true regret. As for everything else, he was at a kind of peace with himself. He genuinely was, and this surprised him so much he almost laughed out loud. His trials at Triskelia really must've worked, because he felt a kind of clean he'd never felt before. It made sense, really. He was as ready to confront his father as he'd ever be.

Before he could change his mind he steered off his course and careened through the sage and dirt, heading straight for his father's carriage. In an instant, twelve guns were pointed in his direction.

"Edmund Rutherford Jeffrey Maddox!" Seth shouted it out like a skip rope chant, hoping the Guards behind the guns would take a moment to wonder why this stranger knew Edmund's full name.

"Hold your fire!" The one with the Commander stripes shot an arm up into the air and slowly brought it to his side. A signal for the gunmen to wait.

"Edmund Rutherford Jeffrey Maddox!" Seth shouted again.

"Stay where you are, hands in the air, or we shoot!" the Commander yelled as the carriages and horsemen lumbered to a stop, the dust sweeping up around hooves and boots and carriage wheels. Seth stopped too, far enough away to be heard, near enough to be shot.

"Edmund Rutherford Jeffrey Maddox!" he hollered. And then again, at the top of his lungs, almost frantic. "Edmund Rutherford Jeffrey Maddox! *Edmund Rutherford Jeffrey Maddox!*"

"Silence!" The Commander guided his horse forward, rearing back when he spotted the skineater scars on Seth's bare arms and legs. "Stay back!"

Under his mask, Seth grinned. As if he'd do anything other than what he was told, especially now with even more guns trained on him. It was working, though. So far, so good. Seth kept his hands in the air as the Commander signalled for one of his men to come forward. He said something to him out of earshot, but soon the Guardy was approaching Seth. He crept forward, one arm cocked, the other steadied atop it, pistol in hand. When the marksman was in position, the Commander gestured for the others to lower their guns.

"State your business!" he bellowed from his safe distance.

"No sudden moves," the marksman murmured. "Keep nice and still, asshole. Or I shoot."

Seth nodded.

"State your business!" the Commander repeated.

Seth kept his eyes on his father's carriage. The curtain was pulled aside and someone was peeking out. Seconds later the door opened and Edmund himself stepped down into the dirt. Seeing his father again brought on a hot rush of panic. What was Seth thinking? Weak at the knees and with his mouth suddenly bone dry, his hands started to drop.

"Keep them up!" The marksman gave the air a practised, intimidating jab with his gun. "That's the first and last time I warn you."

Seth stuck his hands up again. He closed his eyes and reminded himself why he'd come and what he'd already gone through since seeing his father last. This calmed him enough that he could work up some spit to wet his mouth and finally speak.

"I have come to talk with Chancellor East," Seth managed. "I have a message for him, and him alone."

"Mask, sir?" the marksman yelled over his shoulder to his Commander.

Before Commander Cho could speak, Edmund answered for him. "He'll leave it on."

"Sir!" the Guardy barked. "Yes, sir!"

"Him," Seth murmured, stunned at the sight of the man who'd held court over his will for so many years. He'd been ready to sacrifice anything, do anything to win Edmund's approval. Now he was no longer in awe of him.

It was shocking to realize that his father was just a man. Nothing more. Seth felt a surge of confidence, a burst of determination. "I want to talk to him."

Edmund stood by his carriage, hands clasped behind his back, staring. Seth was too far away to see his expression, but by his movements, or lack thereof, Seth was sure Edmund knew it was his son shouting his name. Did any of the Guardies recognize his voice? Or put two and two together to wonder if it was him? Seth tore his eyes from his father and surveyed the entourage. He didn't recognize anyone, or not as far as he could tell.

"On guard!" the Commander shouted. The other Guardies launched their weapons back into position. "Hold!" Commander Cho dismounted and approached Edmund just as someone else climbed down from the carriage.

It was Nord.

Seth tried to make sense of it. What was he doing with Edmund? And why was he in his carriage, and not in uniform, and why, most of all, was he behaving so familiarly with him, leaning in to be a part of Edmund and the Commander's discussion?

Nord?

Seth's confusion made his eyes water. He blinked, the wetness blurring the sight of the two of them head to head with the Commander at the carriage. If he could he'd rub his eyes, but he didn't dare let his arms down.

Finally, the Commander stepped away and shouted. "Douser!"

The Guardy wearing the douse pack came forward. As he primed the pump Seth squeezed his eyes shut, readying himself for the bitter solution to rain down. And rain down it did, a shower of the stinking stuff covering him in a slick.

"Can I wipe my eyes?" he asked with them still shut, burning as the solution leaked its way in.

"Negative," the marksman said. "Keep your hands up, eyes shut."

Seth stood still. He could hear the Guardies repositioning themselves. He knew this formation. He'd been a part of it several times himself. When he was allowed to open his eyes he'd expect to be surrounded, a line of the lowest-ranking Guards forming the inner circle, the higher-ranked the outer.

"Keeping your eyes shut," the same Guard was saying now, "strip."

Seth pulled off his hat and shirt, and then his shorts. Down to his underlinens, he hesitated. Once naked, they'd know he was a Keylander. Keylanders were cut. Droughtland boys were not.

"I said strip!" the Guard yelled, the click of his safety releasing. "That means everything!"

"Enough," Edmund spoke. From a distance still, but a nearer one. "He's acceptable as is. You can wipe your eyes."

Of course he meant Seth. He knelt, feeling for his shirt in the dirt. He lifted it to his face and wiped his eyes without removing his mask. The douse still burned, but it was an improvement. Shaming, though, to be put through the same protocol as any lowly Droughtlander, when not long ago it was he himself on a healthy Guard horse, going through the same motions.

Seth opened his eyes. Edmund looked the same as he always had. He'd expected him to appear changed somehow, but he didn't. Perhaps it was because Seth himself was so changed, covered as he was in sick scars and so tanned he looked naturally darker skinned. His hair was shoulder length, blonder from the sun, and his body leaner and more muscular than it had ever been. His father, on the other hand, was the same pasty, gangly man Seth had always known.

Edmund stood three metres off, considered the minimal safe distance for interacting with diseased Droughtlanders. Nord stood beside him, the cheekiest grin Seth had ever witnessed plastered on his wide face. Nord knew who he was. No doubt about it.

"Put your clothes on," Edmund said. While Seth did as he was told, Edmund ordered the Guard to retreat. They fell neatly out of their circles and regrouped about thirty metres away, well out of earshot. Nord had his gun out though, levelled at Seth with the safety off.

"Been a while." His smirk stretched out into a kind of smug grimace. "Figured you'd be dead by now."

"Shut up, Nord," Edmund said. He kept his distance and stared at his son. "What on earth could you possibly have to say for yourself?"

"I could ask you the same thing."

"You've been ill."

"Obviously." Seth laughed. "You can thank Commander Regis for that."

"Hard to thank a dead man." Edmund paused. "Who killed him?"

"I did." From his pocket Seth retrieved the pouch with Regis's medals and tossed it across the distance.

"I see." Edmund pulled on a leather glove and inspected the contents of the pouch. "Then it could be said that you did thank Regis, in your own way." Edmund cocked his head to the side and fixed Seth with a look that almost resembled pride. He threw the bundle back. "Why are you here now?"

"I have information you want."

"At what price?"

"I want a position."

"Look at you!" Edmund laughed. "You're covered in the scars of the skineater sick! You cannot come back. Absolutely not. And as far as any Keylander knows, you died months ago, and if not then, then in Triskelia."

"I don't want to come back." Seth spoke low and evenly, resisting the urge to spit at his father's feet. His heart argued against his ribcage, pounding with equal parts rage and impatience. "I don't ever want to be a part of the Keys again. I want recognition as leader of the Droughtlanders. I want talks. I want a treaty. I want negotiations. And if not, then I want a war. A fair war. A war between nations, not between lion and mouse."

Nord laughed. "But you like cheese, Maddox."

"Don't use his name," Edmund hissed.

"What is he doing with you?" Seth gave Nord a derisive nod.

"I'm Chief Regent, asshole."

"And a brilliant one at that, I'm sure. Congratulations." Eyebrows raised, Seth looked at his father.

"Blackmail," Edmund said. "You can imagine the details."

"Eddie, come on. You're not going to listen to his bullshit, are you?" Nord waved his gun as if dismissing Seth's very presence.

"The Droughtlanders are stirring like never before." Seth kept his eyes on his father. "The uprising has already begun. And you know we outnumber you."

"*We?*" Nord lowered the gun. "Let's go, Edmund. This is insane."

But Edmund did not move. He folded his arms across his chest and tilted his head back just so. "I'm listening."

"We would not be the first father and son in history to be enemies," said Seth, speaking quietly. "It is a story told over and over. But I can offer you power, Father. And I know you love power. We go to war, the Keys and the Droughtland are dismantled, we come out the leaders of the new world. At which point we both win, despite the struggle and expense to get there."

"Foolish and reckless." Edmund was shaking his head. "And I already have power. No. I'm not interested."

"Finally," Nord said. "Thank you."

"Either you agree to this or we launch the revolution with your assassination and by levelling your Key. It will happen, Father. I'm offering you a business proposal. Don't think of it as anything less or more."

"Why should I believe you have any power out here at all?" Edmund's anger slipped past his guarded exterior and darkened his eyes. "You're not one of them. Why should they follow you?"

"I would think that Commander Regis's assassination would be demonstration enough of my capacity to do battle. And you're wrong, Father. I'm more one of them now. You said yourself I can't go back, not with the scars, no matter how ignorant the Keylanders' beliefs about sicks are. I'm not contagious. I haven't been since two weeks after I contracted it. You know that. But the Chancellors like to keep everyone scared, don't they? That's how you lead. That's how the Group of Keys has always kept their power. You make your people afraid of the unknown. *My* army is motivated by pride and determination and respect."

"Army?" Again, Edmund looked almost proud.

"Nearing five thousand strong."

"You're bluffing," Nord said. "Where are they?"

"In position." Seth kept his gaze steady on his father as he answered Nord. "Elsewhere. I came on this mission alone. As a gesture of goodwill, indicating my honourable intention to play by the rules of war."

Edmund returned his son's clenched-jaw glare. "Rules of war, you say."

"You're full of shit," Nord said. "I could pop you off right now and that would be it. End of discussion. We carry on our merry way. Come on, Edmund. Let me knock him off. He might be your son, but he isn't really any more, is he?"

"Seth is dead to me." Edmund did not break his stare.

"Good. Then let me make that happen, once and for all. He won't give you any more trouble." Nord raised his gun. "It will be my pleasure to put this maniac out of his misery."

Catching Nord by surprise, Edmund took the gun easily. "You'll do no such thing."

Unarmed, Nord didn't know what to do. He glanced over his shoulder.

"Do not summon them," Edmund said. "We'll be finished here soon enough, and the Guards' involvement will only complicate matters."

"You're going to do it yourself?"

Edmund ignored him. He raised the gun and peered at his son through the scope. "How do I know this is genuine? If I deign to consider your proposal, how will I know you mean what you say?"

Seth almost sighed with relief. He and Edmund had just turned a corner together. Alone. Now his heart beat with excitement, along with the remaining and very real fear that came with looking down the barrel of a gun held by his own father no less.

"The Triskelians are regrouping in Triban as we speak. They're about to stage a performance. The Night Circus is and always was a part of Triskelia. Did you know that?"

"It has come to my attention. Since the attack."

"Massacre, you mean?" Flashbacks of the gore threatened to upset his composure. And the memory of being trapped, with Ruben's dead arm. And then—

Edmund shrugged. "An emotional word best left out of matters such as these."

"I cannot believe you're even having this discussion." Nord shook his head. "You are both completely mad."

"I will assassinate the leader of Triskelia. That is how you will know that I mean what I say." Seth found an upsurge in bravado and clung to it gratefully. "And our agreement will be sealed."

This clearly impressed Edmund. A small smile brightened his face.

It wasn't as much of a sacrifice or challenge as it sounded, but Edmund had no way of knowing how feeble a leader Zenith was, how old she was, how past her prime, how ineffectual. How useless. It would be more of a mercy killing, really. Zenith would be far more powerful in death than she ever was in life.

"Ah." Edmund raised a finger. "We do not have an agreement yet."

"She'll be in Triban for the performance," Seth went on. "The Triskelians are calling it a fundraiser, but I know they're planning something much bigger. I don't know what, but I can find out. If we have an agreement, when you have word of her death, that will be the official launch of the new battle. Between you and me."

The smile flattened into a smirk. "It will be short-lived."

"Don't be so sure." Seth shook his head. "I can make a life of opposing you, Father."

"You think highly of yourself."

"He's the worst kind of snob," Nord interjected. "Confidently wrong."

"If you want to be a real leader, you have to have a worthy adversary." Again Seth ignored Nord, directing his words at his father. "One of the most basic rules of war. You aren't a leader right now. You're a bully in a field of rabbits, that's all. Where is the pride in that, Father? Where's the challenge?"

"Perhaps I'm not interested in a challenge."

"I may not know you very well, Father, but I know you well enough."

"Do you know yourself well enough?"

"Leave that to me."

"Come on, Edmund!" Nord kicked the dirt. "Enough of this philosophical shit."

Edmund lowered the gun and let a long moment draw out like spider silk between them. When he spoke again it was slowly, as if choosing each word for its individual weight.

"What if I told you that it was you who led us to Triskelia, Seth?" This wasn't true—sole blame rested with the informant who'd since been transported to the Western Key in the wake of Regis's assassination—but for now he wanted to knock a little power out of his son. It worked.

Those words were a sucker punch to the gut. Seth actually gasped. He shook his head. "I didn't! It wasn't me."

"What if it was? And what if the Triskelians knew it? Do you think anyone out here would take up arms for you?"

Seth told himself not to rise to the bait. Edmund hadn't said anything that proved it, and Seth was sure that he and Amon hadn't been followed on their way to Triskelia. His father could be bluffing. Seth glared at him and said nothing.

"How is your brother?"

"I wouldn't know."

"I see."

"I doubt it." Seth felt himself shrinking, becoming his father's son again instead of his capable opponent. He darkened his glare with a furrow of his brow. "I do know he feels nothing but hatred for you."

"Present tense. He's still alive then. Ah, *family*." Edmund rolled his eyes. "How nice for you." He thought about mentioning Allegra, and the baby, but decided against it.

"He may have survived. He may not have. The way I said it reveals neither." All this cagey banter was frustrating Seth and his skin was itching and burning from the douse. He was spent. "Look, deal or not, Father?" How much did his father already know and wasn't letting on about? "If so, then I need to be on my way. If not, you're still going to let me go, aren't you?"

"True."

"Because you can kill your wife, but not your son?"

"I did not know she was there," Edmund said out loud what he'd assured himself over and over since that fateful day. "But it did work out for the best, I won't pretend that it didn't. If she had been exposed she would have been executed anyway, and I would have lost my position." Edmund was building a house of cards with his words. "Surely a man of war—such as yourself—understands complex and difficult decisions. Your offer to kill the leader of the Triskelians, for example. I'm sure you've thought about the impact, both in your favour and against it."

Seth started to shake his head. Zenith was different. She didn't have children, and she was so old death would take her soon anyway. But he wouldn't argue the point. He wanted this to be over now, before he betrayed his plan and told Edmund about Sabine. It was tempting, just to spite him. But then, maybe Edmund knew about her already too.

"Whatever lets you sleep at night," Seth said.

"Go." Edmund spat the word at him. "We're done here."

"We're on?"

"We'll meet again, I am sure." Edmund wouldn't look at him now. "In the meantime, you do what you need to do."

Seth climbed onto the bike. "Is it a deal?" he persisted.

"Time, and thought, will tell."

"Don't give me that cryptic bullshit," Seth said. "If I do this—if I kill her—I *will* consider it a sealed deal. We *will* be at war."

Edmund said nothing more.

After an awkward wait, it was Seth who broke the silence. "Mark my words, Chancellor East. We will be at war."

Still Edmund said nothing.

Without a goodbye, Seth pedalled up the hill he'd come down, feeling the heat in his thigh muscles as he sped to put safer distance between all the guns that could still take him down. He did not stop, not even after he'd cleared the crest and was heading down the other side. He pedalled as fast as he could. Seth should have been tired from cycling for so many hours, but instead he felt as if he could go on forever, which is exactly what he planned to do.

EDMUND HELD ON to Nord's gun as they returned to the carriages. Commander Cho fixed Edmund with a concerned, quizzical look.

"Get us moving," Edmund said. "As for the stranger, he was never there. The encounter never happened. Matter of state security. Understood?"

"Yes, Chancellor."

"Be sure your men understand the gravity of the situation. Their allegiance in this matter is imperative."

"Sir." Commander Cho saluted Edmund as he climbed back into the carriage. "Yes, sir."

The Commander figured that the masked Droughtlander was an informant who had important intelligence that simply could not wait until the next time he was due to meet his Keyland contact. Commander Cho passed this version of events on to his Guardies, knowing they'd demand an explanation for the special treatment the vermin had enjoyed.

Soon the Keylanders were on their way again, with not far to go until they could rest at last. The Guards were so looking forward to it after such a long trek that they gave not another thought to the Droughtlander. None, not even the Commander, had met either of Edmund's boys. Edmund had selected them for that very reason. He was glad for his caution now, despite the logistical nightmare it had been to clean that particular slate.

Inside the carriage was another matter entirely. Nord fumed across from him, angry most of all that his gun was still in Edmund's possession.

"I could shoot you right now," Edmund mused, using Nord's gun as a baton, as if his words were a symphony. "I could say it was a struggle, and that I grabbed your gun and had to protect myself. You know all about coverups, don't you, Nord?"

Nord said nothing. He crossed his arms and levelled Edmund with the fiercest glower he could muster. "You've got me. I'm the mouse to your cat."

"Exactly. Call it natural selection. And so you won't blame me if I do."

Keeping his eyes on Nord, Edmund suddenly banged frantically on the carriage walls, yelling, "Help! He's trying to kill me! Help!"

"Edmund—"

Edmund fired the gun.

With a choked warble, Nord's head knocked back as the bullet punched through his skull and out the other side. He was dead instantly. Reeling, Edmund held his breath until his eyes watered and his lungs rebelled and breathed for him anyway. As the carriage stopped and the Guards rushed to investigate Edmund had to fight to keep the relief off his face and to play up shock and horror as Commander Cho ushered him out into the daylight.

30

☙

The coliseum was heavily guarded by Triskelian supporters, both armed and unarmed. The self-appointed protectors, each standing two metres apart, formed a human wall around the enormous building that now exerted such a powerful draw. Travellers had come from all directions and had set up camp right in the streets and along the boardwalks. Some lanes were blocked entirely with tents.

It was taking quite some time to snake a route to the coliseum's entrance.

"They're not all here for the circus," Eli said. "Do you think?"

Sabine surveyed the crowd from the carriage window. Mostly men, few women, and hardly any children.

"No." A rush of excitement goose-pimpled her arms and coloured her cheeks. "I think they're here to fight alongside us!" She put a hand on Zenith's knee. "Do you think so?"

Zenith's eyes fluttered. She'd been sleeping. "What's that?"

"Never mind." Sabine flung open the shutters and leaned out, wanting a clearer view of the people she'd be calling on to take up arms. "There's so many!"

Jack joined her at the window. "We'll arrange for a group to find out who out here has weapons or fighting experience. Find out where they've come from. I'm imagining a lot of them are survivors from the Colony of the Sicks, or had loved ones there."

They weren't encountering the same frenzied greeting as they had on their way into Triban. The air was much more sombre here. The crowds of men and boys lining the streets were eerily quiet, watching them pass with grave expressions and then returning to their Seduce games or fire pits.

"Hardly any girls," marvelled Rosa.

"If I was one of them you can guarantee I'd be out there," Sabine said, wondering privately and not for the first time how a young girl like her could lead a mass of bitter, angry, grieving, tired, and somewhat sickly men and boys to war. "There's no way I'd stay behind to change diapers or scrounge for something to put in the stew. Not a chance. Everyone should be here. Not just the boys and men. Are girls that cowardly?"

"No." Eli had held his tongue until now. "They're that smart. Most of them."

With an exasperated sigh, Sabine swung her head around. "Keep it to yourself, Eli. Or else take off now. Go back to Cascadia or something."

"I might." He didn't say it spitefully. It really was something he was considering. "After the circus. Before the fighting starts."

Sabine gave him a cool look. "If that's the order of the events, even."

"That's what you're planning, isn't it?"

"You saw what happened earlier, Eli." Sabine pulled the shutters closed and took her seat again as the convoy—carts and horses and all—was escorted through an enormous entrance, down a wide echoey hall, and right into the main arena. "I can plan, but there will always be that unpredictable element impossible to factor in. But except for knowing for sure that we can't know everything, I'll plan as best as I can."

Eli left the subject there as the convoy stopped and everyone got off. He helped Zenith down from the carriage and held her elbow as she stepped unsteadily forward. Her cheeks were flushed and her forehead glistened with perspiration.

"Are you okay, Zen Zen?"

"I wouldn't mind sitting down." She barely whispered it. "And perhaps something to drink?"

Eli whistled for one of the men unloading the carts to bring a chair. Eli settled her into it, reluctant to leave her alone. He stood by her, watching his sister hustle the others into action. Sabine glanced back at Eli and Zenith, giving them a little nod, which Eli took to mean he should stay put.

"You don't think your sister can do it," Zenith said with some effort.

"No. I don't."

Yes, you do. You just don't want to admit it.

"You do, though," Zenith said. "You just don't want to admit it."

"All right," Eli said. That was just too much. "Can you read minds?"

"No." Zenith shook her head. "No. But I have lived a long life and know a thing or two. I know how to read even the subtlest of clues."

Eli told her about the voice. He told her everything. That he couldn't take up arms, that he knew there had to be a better way to make things right. He told her he was worried he'd gone crazy. He told her he thought the voice was from on high. That he was speaking to his highers, and them to him.

"Perhaps that is so," Zenith said matter-of-factly. "And why not?"

"Is it normal?"

She shook her head, and then was caught off guard by a fit of coughing. "But who knows what normal is, anyway?" she said, her cough easing.

"Sabine thinks I'm crazy."

"So will Seth. That is your challenge."

"Seth?"

Coughing again, she nodded. "When you are together again . . ." she paused to take a shallow breath, ". . . all three of you," another wheeze, "I want you and your siblings to come see me at once. Just the three of you. Promise me?"

"Sure," Eli said. That wasn't likely going to happen any time soon. "Let me fetch you that drink, Zenith. Tea?"

TEA FETCHED AND ZENITH SETTLED, Eli stood back for a moment to take it all in. Triban's coliseum was much larger than the Eastern Key's, but it was in rough shape. Whole sections of seats had been ripped out and the concrete steps that climbed the stands all the way up to the patched and sagging roof were cracked and crumbling. It was getting dark, and as they unpacked all around him Eli couldn't make out much else outside the pools of light from the torches that had been hung at intervals along the cavernous walls. The circus rigging was already set up though, and this surprised him.

When Jack passed, Eli asked him about it. "This didn't all come from the ruins, did it?"

"Some did. A lot of the scaffolding was salvaged. But some is from a warehouse we keep in Triban," Jack said. "And some was brought in from a training camp south of here."

Again it struck Eli how little he knew about the world he moved in. "There are other Night Circus troupes?"

"Not exactly," Jack said. "But there are three training camps, and we do rotate people in and out fairly often. After tours and such. Not now though." He hefted a crate of costumes they'd brought down from Cascadia out of the cart. "Not now."

ZENITH HAD FALLEN ASLEEP AGAIN, her empty mug loose in her hand. Eli squatted and took it from her, setting it down at her feet. He put a hand on her knee and tried to wake her. When she didn't stir easily, he changed his mind.

She does not have long, Eli. Not long at all.

Eli nodded. He put his hands on his own knees, pushed himself up, and went to find Trace to carry her to bed.

Trace was directing the unloading of the two arms shipments into a windowless room off one end of the arena. When Eli explained that he needed someone to carry Zenith to her room, Trace left one of his men in his stead, with instructions to keep the room under armed watch at all times. He followed Eli back to Zenith, who was still sound asleep. The flush on her cheeks was gone now, replaced by an unnerving pallor.

"Go get Rosa," Trace told Eli after taking one look at the old woman. "Zenith? Wake up!"

She didn't stir.

"She didn't look like that when I left her—"

"Just go!" Trace lifted Zenith into his arms as Eli scanned the dimness for Rosa. "Tell her to hurry!"

Trace jogged across the arena with Zenith in his arms. As the others took notice of the commotion they fell in behind, fretting and asking what was wrong with her. Someone else found Rosa. She came running, put the back of one hand to Zenith's brow and the fingers of the other at her carotid before barking for water to be boiled and for Trace to follow her to the room she'd been setting up as an infirmary of sorts.

Seth arrived back in Triban the day after the Triskelians' calamitous welcome. He rode past the burned-out blocks, still smouldering, and stopped at the first two BAT soldiers he found. They stood at attention and saluted him. Seth let a moment pass before setting them at ease. They both started talking at once, describing the crowd, and the riot, and the fires.

"The flames were enormous, Commander Seth!" the one boy said.

"And people were running everywhere, getting trampled and shit—"

"Mind your language." Seth surveyed the two. He did not know their names, but they wore the red vests of new recruits. Seth was thankful for the vest idea, and for the girls he had scrounging the material and sewing them, the two from the Guardy camp among them. He thought he recognized the taller boy, but he wasn't sure.

"Sorry, Commander."

"Did you see the Triskelians yourself?"

"I did!" the taller one said. "Auntie was there, even!"

"Zenith, you mean."

"Yeah, and your brother and sister too. All three of them were on that balcony right over there, with some blond guy who had a gun."

Seth didn't know what to wonder about first. That these two brats knew about Eli and Sabine, what Zenith had said or done, or how the Triskelians had come by guns. He'd assumed they'd lost what little fire-power they had in the ambush. He kept his expression even and turned to the shorter boy.

"And you? Did you see them too?"

He nodded. "I can't believe the two what look like you. It's really something."

"Yes. It is."

"How come you never said you were a Triskelian?"

What to do now that it was all out? He'd have to work it in his favour. But how? He frowned at the boys. "What are your names?"

"Singh," said the tall one.

"Blake," said the other. They wore matching expressions of dismay.

"I have over five thousand boys, Blake. Singh." Seth glanced up at the balcony they'd pointed out. "I can't possibly remember everyone's names. Now, tell me about the one with the gun."

"Wasn't just him," Blake said. "They all had guns."

"Not on the balcony," Singh said. "Just the one guy. He was blond, tattoos on his arms. A bunch of them that stayed on the street had guns though. Good ones too."

"And did they say anything up on that balcony?"

"Auntie did."

"You mean Zenith."

"Not s'posed to say her name, are we?" The boys shared a look. "In case Guardies are listening."

Seth smiled. "I think that quite all of the cats have been let out of the bag, Blake."

"Commander?" Blake looked at him, confused.

"A figure of speech. What I mean to say is that there isn't any reason to keep her identity secret any more. So. It was Zenith on the balcony."

"Yes, Commander."

"And?" Seth gestured for Blake to keep talking. "She said . . . ?"

"That the revolution was starting, and it was time to rise up and start kicking the shit out of the Keyland Guard—"

Seth held up a hand. "Zenith said no such thing."

"Maybe she didn't say *shit*," Blake emended. "But that's what she meant, right, Singh?"

"Yeah, and that we have a new leader."

This did catch Seth off guard. He quickly revisited the conversation with his father. He'd said he'd kill Zenith, right? He replayed as much of it as he could remember, and was sickened to have to admit that he'd committed to killing the *leader*, implying whoever that was, and not necessarily Zenith.

"Who's that?" Seth kept his tone level.

"Your sister." Blake's tone clearly suggested that Seth should've known that already.

"And I did know that," Seth said hurriedly. "I just wanted to be sure the correct information was being shared. Thank you, boys. Back to your post."

"Commander Seth," the boys said with a salute in place of goodbye.

BACK AT THE BARRACKS, Blake and Singh's story was corroborated by countless boys and then by Amon himself, who hadn't been there but who'd taken it upon himself to collect as many eyewitness accounts as he could in order to distill some facts.

The Triskelians were camped at the coliseum, and yes, Zenith *was* with them, and *had* announced Sabine as the new leader of Triskelia.

They were still planning on putting on the circus.

They were armed. Not sure with what or how many.

The actual Triskelians were few in number, but they'd had who knows how many willing bodies join them along the way. And more were waiting for them upon their arrival.

Yes, it was Zenith and Jack on the balcony, along with Sabine and Eli.

Word had spread faster than the fire that Seth was their brother, and now everyone thought BAT was Triskelian and had been all along.

Seth listened quietly, not saying anything for a moment. Most of it he could take in stride, but he didn't know what to make of *Sabine* being leader. He wouldn't do anything to harm her, that was a given. So then what? He'd made a deal with their father, and had to show something for it. He'd given his word.

As Amon started talking again, Seth let the words slip over him while he concentrated on the bigger problem. Slowly, an idea formed. If he went straight off, did away with Zenith that very night, he could perhaps still claim that he'd fulfilled his end of the bargain. Keylanders didn't know that the Triskelians had no "transition of power" ceremony of any kind. He could tell Edmund that he'd done it before Triskelia's leadership was officially passed to Sabine. Besides, even Edmund wouldn't want his daughter assassinated by his own son, whether or not Edmund was aware of Sabine's existence. Would he?

That thought was shoved aside by the very idea of Sabine as leader of Triskelia. Sabine!

If he'd joined the survivors earlier, would Seth have been the one given the power? It should be him. What did Sabine know about leadership? Tactics of war and defence? Logistics of running an army and orchestrating manoeuvres? Nothing! She'd been raised in the circus, for crying out loud. The *circus*!

Seth put up a hand to interrupt Amon's excited reporting. "I'm exhausted, Amon. I'm going to go to bed."

"Absolutely. You must be tired," Amon said, although he had no idea where Seth had gone, what he'd been up to, or how much energy he'd expended. Amon was just glad to have him back. It was stressful being in charge. He didn't like it much. "We'll meet with the others in the morning?"

"Yes."

"I wonder who's with them? Do you think Zen Zen will see us? Listen to our side of things?"

"I'm tired, Amon."

"Right, sorry. Good night then."

"Good night."

Once Amon had gone, Seth gathered a small pack, donned a hooded sweater and changed his clunky boots for soft leather-soled ones, doused the lantern and slipped out the window. He dropped to the ledge as quietly as he could and then crept along its narrow width to the corner, where he shimmied down the rusting pipe to the street below. He'd brought the bicycle all the way into the big room on the main floor earlier and now he wished he'd at least thought to have left it in the anteroom instead. He couldn't collect it now, not without being noticed. Keeping to the shadows and the alleys, he made his way on foot.

Bunks had been set up for the Triskelians in several of the unused rooms down the musty halls leading off the arena. They couldn't stay in the boardinghouse Triskelia normally used and where Eli had first met Anya and Charis. The Guard had found out about it, and Morley, the old man in charge of its comings and goings, had disappeared almost two weeks earlier. A week ago his freshly dead body was returned and posed at his desk behind the little window at the entrance. A clear message.

The group would sleep at the coliseum instead. But no one was asleep that first night, except for Toby who was curled up on a bale of canvas. Everyone was gathered on the main stage waiting for Zenith to wake up, except Celeste, who would not leave Zenith's bedside. The rest kept a solemn vigil, for Rosa had been honest with them. It was not likely that Zenith would make it through the night.

Sabine went back and forth, checking on the small group in the sick room and reporting back to the others.

On one of these visits, she took a moment to sit with Eli on the stage.

"That's why she announced you as leader like that," he whispered, apropos of nothing. "So suddenly."

Sabine leaned in. "You think she knew?"

Eli nodded. He was just about to tell her that he'd known too, but then two watchmen called from the main entrance, their torches bobbing in the dark as they approached.

"Sabine!"

She stood. Nearer now, she could see that the two were escorting a third person between them.

"What is it?" she called. "Who do you have with you?"

The others stood, all curious.

"Your brother!" one of the men reported. "He wants to see you."

SETH KEPT WISELY SILENT, letting the watchmen do the talking. He'd planned on sneaking in and doing the chore, but as he neared the coliseum Seth's ears could not help but tune in to the rumours rippling through the camps, from fire pit to fire pit, circling Seduce games as if shuffled right into their decks.

Zenith is dead!

No, fool . . . she's just sick. She's fine. They've got a lifeminder and all.

I heard Auntie is at death's door.

Well I heard she's already dead and they're keeping it secret, so's we don't get upset and start a riot, like what happened with the fires.

That can't be, I saw her when they first got here, her up on the balcony, fine as anything, saying the girl is the leader now.

Auntie is dying!

Auntie is dead!

You can call her Zenith now, idiot, everyone knows who she is. No secret no more.

End of an era, friend. End of an era.

IT WAS THE END of an era, but more importantly it was the beginning of another. Seth's. Sabine and Eli could only stare at their brother, and he at them. Seth spoke first.

"I did not have anything to do with the ambush on Triskelia, or anything leading up to it that may have jeopardized the safety of Triskelia or the Colony of the Sicks."

Trace hopped down from the stage and put his face in Seth's.

"What'd I tell you about coming back, eh?" He sent Seth stumbling with a shove. "I said no way were you ever welcome back, right? You deaf? Stupid? You want me to beat the crap out of you? Is that what it would take for you to get the message that you're not welcome here?"

"Wait! Trace, leave him alone." Sabine jumped down too. "We need him. We need his army."

She forced herself to put aside her doubts about Seth, her anger. Zenith lay dying in the sick room. There was simply no time right now.

"How is she?" Seth scanned the sad faces on the stage and then settled his gaze on his sister.

"Not good."

"I'm sorry to hear that." There was more behind those words. Sabine could tell.

"Come with me," she said. "We need to talk."

"I'm coming too." Eli jumped down.

The brothers locked eyes for a moment.

"Still wearing your medallion." In a daring move, Eli lifted Seth's and then let it drop. "Think that's appropriate?"

Seth had pulled it out at the entrance, as further confirmation of his belonging inside, as if his lineage wasn't enough. The two men guarding the door hadn't so much as glanced at the medallion; they'd let him in on looks alone. Neither had ever seen triplets before, and it so unsettled them that they hadn't thought to question him about his intentions.

Seth hooked one finger under the chain around Eli's neck and pulled the medallion out of his sweater. "As appropriate as it is for you to still be wearing yours." He closed the medallion in his fist and gave it an almost imperceptible tug. A flood of resentment washed over Eli and his own hands formed fists. He raised them.

Seth cocked an eyebrow. It was a come-on to fight, an instinctive reaction between brothers. But now was not the time. He shook his head. "Don't, Eli."

Let it go. Be calm.

Eli shook out his hands. "I'm coming with you." As they walked toward the sick room he told them about Zenith's request that they see her together and his promise to oblige.

"How would she know that I'd come?"

Eli shrugged. He wouldn't tell Seth about the voices, the unspoken knowing. Not ever. Not if he could help it.

HALFWAY TO THE SICK ROOM, Sabine told Seth about Rosa. Seth slowed his pace, falling behind his brother and sister by several steps. They stopped.

"Will she see me?"

"I don't know." Sabine shrugged. "And I don't really care. This isn't about you."

Seth was having a hard time holding on to his focus. Back in the company of his siblings he'd lost some of it, and with the prospect of seeing Rosa he lost the rest of it. He didn't care about his promise to Edmund. Not in that moment anyhow. Besides, if Zenith was going to die anyway it would all work perfectly. He might have to help her along, though. Like Ruben. It would be merciful, and so not murder at all. That it was unfolding this way served as proof he was doing the right thing. Get rid of Zenith, and then take over for Sabine. He was certain she wouldn't mind. Surely a girl like her would be thrilled to shrug off that much responsibility. One thing at a time, he coached himself. Right now, that was Rosa.

AS THEY CAME into the room Rosa was wringing out a cloth and placing it across Zenith's forehead. Rosa was just as he remembered. Beautiful, her movements graceful for all their domesticity. She looked up, taking several moments to register Seth's presence. Her hands froze and her face fell. Before turning back to her patient she said quite firmly and to no one in particular, "I don't want him in here."

"Seth!" Celeste rose from her stool and rushed to embrace him. "You're here!"

"Nana, good to see you." He awkwardly returned her hug, his attention all on Rosa. "You are well?"

"I am! Oh . . ." Celeste ran her hands down Seth's arms and clutched his wrists. "And it is so good to see you, Seth."

"We need a moment with Zenith, Nana," Sabine said. "You and Seth can catch up later."

Celeste's look shifted from joy to skepticism. "Whatever for?"

"Trust me, Nana." Sabine steered her grandmother toward the door. "Please."

Rosa was not so easily convinced. "I stay."

"We need a private moment with her."

Rosa shook her head as she busied herself around Zenith. "No, you don't. Not him."

ROSA'S SUDDEN FLURRY of activity was meant to distract her from the shock of seeing Seth after so long. She was confused about how she felt. Part of her wanted to slap Seth while another part wanted to pull him to her for a kiss. She ignored the latter and focused on her anger.

"Rosa," Seth said, and then again, because he had no other words. "Rosa . . ."

"Stay away from me," she growled.

Sabine gripped Rosa's arm. "Leave us alone with Zen Zen. Just for five minutes."

Rosa focused on Sabine and nodded. "Okay." She didn't look at Seth as she passed him on the way to the door. He couldn't help but reach out, catching her hand. She wrenched it away, gave him a scathing look and rushed out into the hall, where they could all hear her crying and then Celeste's soft voice comforting her.

"Stay," Eli ordered when Seth took a step toward the door. "There's time for that later."

THEY STOOD AT HER BEDSIDE, Eli and Sabine on one side, Seth on the other.

"What's the point?" Seth finally asked, breaking the uneasy silence. "What are we doing?"

"She wanted it." Eli's tone was short. "That's the point. You would deny her last request? Are you in a rush to get back to your great big army?"

Seth sneered at his brother. He was just about to volley back when he suddenly felt Zenith's fingers close around his wrist.

"Zenith!" Sabine said as Zenith opened her eyes. "Go get Rosa, Eli!"

Zenith shook her head. "No," she said. It was barely a whisper. "Stay."

Eli helped her take a sip of water.

"You three are our salvation." Zenith licked her lips. "There is power in the trinity."

"Rest, Zenith," Sabine urged. "We can come back when you're feeling better."

"No." Zenith gestured for the siblings to come closer. "I will die tonight—"

"No, you're going to be fine." Sabine pushed Eli as she spoke. "Go get Rosa!"

"No! All of you stay." Zenith sucked in a breath, exhausted from the protest. "Listen carefully." She reached for Sabine's hand. "You will be the mind of the revolution." Zenith took Seth's hand with her other. "You will be the body." Seth and Sabine locked glances across the bed. Zenith let them go and reached both hands toward Eli. He took them in his. "And you, child, you will have the most challenging role. You will be the soul."

The three of them looked from one to the other. None of them had to say it. They knew it. *Felt* it. That visceral connection none of them had experienced fully since Triskelia.

"Eli." Zenith's breath caught in her throat. "Sabine. Go now."

Watching Zenith struggle for breath, listening to the rattle as fluid leaked into her lungs, Sabine started to cry. Zenith really was dying. Sabine wasn't ready for it. She wasn't ready for any of this! She leaned in and kissed Zenith's sunken cheek before stepping aside to let Eli do the same.

"Thank you, Zen Zen." He backed away, feeling inadequate and helpless, like he should do more for her, pray for her, hold her hand at least.

Sabine and Eli closed the door behind them. Rosa leaned against the wall there, alone now, covering her face with her hands, weeping.

"I don't want to want him back," she wailed. "But I do!"

"Oh, Rosa." Sabine put her arms around her and nodded for Eli to leave them.

"Is Zenith okay?" Rosa said between tears. "Should I go in?"

Something in Sabine's gut told her to wait, and so she asked the same of Rosa.

"IT'S ALL RIGHT, SETH." Zenith fixed her watery eyes on him. "I am ready."

"But—" He shook his head, knowing what she was referring to without a doubt. "But I don't need to. Not now."

"Then do it for me instead of for yourself, child."

"No." He pulled the stool up to the bed and sat. "I'll wait here with you. I can tell Edmund a lie. He doesn't have to know." He spoke to her as if she'd known his plan all along, and perhaps she did. She'd known that he would come, after all.

"Please." Not a request, but an order. "Don't let me suffer."

He didn't want to do it though. She would die before the night was out. Wouldn't she? But what if she didn't? What then?

"You can't know." The rattle in her chest was worse. "It's like drowning."

"I don't want to," Seth said as if he were a five-year-old refusing to put on his boots.

"Please, Seth." She closed her eyes.

He carefully considered what she was asking of him. He could do it. He'd done it before. He'd done worse. Perhaps this *could* be the merciful death he'd been trying to convince himself it was. He reminded himself that he'd left the barracks mere hours earlier with the plan to kill her.

That he would do it for his own gain but not because she wanted him to infuriated him. He was a coward. A real man would do it.

Seth turned on the stool. There was a pillow on the next cot. He lifted it, feeling the heft. Gripping it with both hands, he held it above Zenith's face. Her eyelids fluttered and her lips tinged with blue as her breathing grew more laboured.

Without resolve, he placed the pillow over her face and pushed hard. She barely thrashed. It was over quickly. Not like with Ruben.

Seth carefully eased the pillow away. There was a dark spot of damp where her mouth had been. He turned the pillow over, more horrified by that wet *O* than anything. He gave the pillow a shake, as if dislodging her last breath from its feathers, and then set it back on the other cot. Zenith's mouth was parked in a dreadful yawn. He put a finger to her chin and lifted her jaw shut. He didn't need to close her eyes. She hadn't opened them again.

He sat with her for a long moment, feeling neither relief nor guilt, and then he went to tell the others that she'd gone.

31

꙳

When Edmund reached the Western Key he went directly to the Justice Hall to meet the mysterious prisoner who'd led the Guard to Triskelia and provided so much intelligence about the rebels. He wanted to see this man for himself, this stoic relic of a rebellion that had never amounted to anything and was now decimated beyond repair. Most importantly, he wanted to know how much the man had divulged about Lisette and his children, and to whom. Only Regis, as Nord claimed? Or did others know?

Escorted by a Guardy who walked ahead of him, square-shouldered and expressionless, he made his way through the corridors that led to what turned out to be the infirmary.

"Has he not recovered from the interrogations?" Edmund asked of his companion. He'd read Regis's file, seen the menu of measures he'd used to extricate the information. Sensory and sleep deprivation, pain manipulation, shaming and humiliation techniques, beatings, starvation. This Pierre Fabienne—or so he said his name was—had been difficult to break. As usual, Regis had noted in the file, it came down to the fingers. Chop one off and they start talking. If that didn't work immediately, as in the case of this man, keep going. Regis had chopped all four fingers and a calloused thumb off one hand and then had positioned the cutters at Pierre's crotch before he finally cracked.

"Touch and go, they say," the Guardy who was now letting him into the man's room said. "Figure it was a heart attack a couple of weeks ago. And a stroke shortly after. Wore him out, Regis did."

"But not before he got what we wanted," Edmund said.

"I wouldn't know. All top secret. Since Regis was killed the man hasn't said a word. We took him here only after the assassination, before they set up Vance to take Regis's place."

This Vance. Could he trust him with his secrets as he'd trusted Regis? He'd have to tread carefully. Try to find out if Regis had shared any of his intelligence with him. He'd meet Vance later. He was on his way in from the far side of Triban, where the Guards were holding their position until the Chancellors decided the next course of action. At the moment, Edmund was just one of the larger group of leaders, all of them wrestling with the quiet tension of command. But if Seth meant what he said, and did what he said he would, that might all change sooner than later. Edmund's pulse quickened as the thrill of it all settled into his blood.

The room was dim and cold, with one filthy window high up the damp back wall, the cot practically swallowing the patient in its yawning sag. Edmund took a deep breath to calm himself and then made his way to the bedside of the shrivelled old man who blinked up at him, the right side of his face drooping as if earnestly trying to retreat.

"We're going to take you back to your people soon," Edmund said with false brightness. He rocked forward on the balls of his feet, his hands clasped behind his back. "What do you have to say about that, Mr. Pierre Fabienne? How do you think they'll treat you knowing the depths of your treason?"

"I . . . didn't mean . . . for this," Pierre slurred. He'd been holding on for this moment ever since he'd heard them talking about Edmund coming. He'd worked a piece of coil loose from the mattress with his one good hand and held it in his fist underneath the blanket now. He wanted to hurt this man who'd kept his beloved daughter from him, who'd ruined his family and soaked his life with the heavy rain of loss.

"What's that?" Edmund leaned a little closer. "I believe the stroke you've suffered from has affected your speech." But he'd heard him, and understood him. He was only playing with him now.

"I told him . . . everything." Pierre struggled to get the words out. Edmund straightened a little when he detected the French accent, as if hearing a piece of bad news. "They know *everything*."

"Regis, you mean." Edmund solemnly hoped his secrets had died with the corrupt Commander. "They say you haven't talked since."

"He knows it all. About Lisette. He knows your wife was a Triskelian. You are finished." Pierre slowly pulled his hand, slightly sluggish from the stroke, to the edge of the blanket. "They will punish you."

"I don't think so. The man you told everything to is dead." Edmund shrugged. "And I was given your file. I'm keeping it very safe, you see."

"Then you know Lisette was my daughter."

"Mm-hmm. So you claim." Again, Edmund's tone was bright. "Which would make you my father-in-law, wouldn't it? If you're telling the truth."

"You have my things still?"

"They're around somewhere, I'm sure. Why?"

"Her opal ring . . ." His voice petered out. "Lisette's."

"I know the one." Edmund's voice betrayed him. He hadn't really believed this was Lisette's father, but he was startled by the mention of the ring Lisette had so cherished.

Pierre took his chance now. He dragged his hand out and thrust the rusty coil at Edmund's face, aiming for his eye. Although he didn't expect to mortally wound him he did want to injure him, make him hurt, even just a little. But he missed entirely. Edmund grasped Pierre's wrist and held it, squeezing, until Pierre let go of the coil. It clattered to the floor. Edmund kicked it under the bed.

"I see she inherited your foolishness, if not your looks."

Letting loose a primeval groan, Pierre thrashed in the bed, his wrist still in Edmund's grip. He'd failed everyone—his wife, his daughter, his people. Ever since he was told of the massacre he'd been invaded by shame and horror at his weakness. It was like a cancer, and he wished only that it had killed him by now.

WHAT DID KILL HIM, just hours later, was one bullet expertly shot by a marksman in an executioner's hood. They didn't make Pierre get up from his bed, and instead dragged it into the courtyard and shot him there so they wouldn't have to clean up the infirmary. Pierre's body was rolled into sackcloth and bound with rope and loaded into Vance's cart and left there while Vance gave his briefing to the Chancellors gathered at Government House.

Listening to the updates—the Triskelian survivors setting up their silly circus, the gathering of Droughtlanders in Triban in anticipation of being led into action, this boy army everyone was talking about—Edmund carefully assessed the other Chancellors' reactions to his presence. Aside from comments about his unfortunate run of Chief Regents as of late—*Hard to find someone up to the task these days . . . Can't know who will betray you . . . Times like these*—nothing seemed amiss. Letting out an involuntary sigh of relief, Edmund concluded that Lisette's identity as a Triskelian was still a secret. Regis and Nord had known, and Phillip, and they were all dead. Did anyone else know? Vance, perhaps?

Time would tell. And time would punish too. Unless he could keep hiding the fact that his children were aligned with the resistance his hold on his position was tenuous at best. He'd need Vance as an ally. What would be his price?

Edmund had only a few moments alone with the new Commander of Regis's men. He couldn't dare explain everything, and so he told Vance that his sons were embedded as spies in an action so covert that the other Chancellors didn't even know the boys were still alive. He instructed Vance to find Seth and to leave Pierre's body with him. He even told him what to say when he did, hoping all the while that Vance wouldn't question any of it.

"I'll reward you for your discretion," Edmund said as Commander Vance's men fell into formation around him. "Be assured, you will be rewarded."

"Sir," Vance said, and that was all.

He and his men left with Pierre's body and fresh orders as the Chancellors and their Chief Regents adjourned to their billets to get ready for the evening festivities. Once his trunks had been brought to his rooms at the estate of the Key's Chief Financial Officer and the footmen dismissed, Edmund sank into the armchair by the window and poured himself a stiff drink. The last time he'd visited this Key he and the then Chancellor had been guests of Chancellor West himself, put up in the five-room guest suite on the top floor of his estate. Edmund took a generous sip of his drink and tried not to let it bother him that his status had clearly taken a slide downward.

32

⚜

With Rosa's help, Celeste and Sabine washed Zenith's body with soft cloths and water perfumed with sandalwood. It was a solemn chore, done with great care and gentleness. They didn't speak, nor did they cry. They lifted her limbs and handled her with the same tender grace as if she'd been a newborn receiving her first bath and not her last. The group in the stadium was holding these hours close to them, suspended in time. No one took the news outside. Not yet.

Trace broke down several wooden crates and built a coffin and a lid to fit. It was lined first with straw collected from a nearby livery and then with the softest blanket the group had among them. Zenith wouldn't have wanted them to use anything more, nor to fuss over the coffin. Not at a time like this, with the city a powderkeg at the end of an already-lit fuse.

Sabine, well aware that Zenith's death might launch the city into a catastrophic tailspin, wanted to keep it from the people for a little while longer, even as the others started murmuring about the inevitable. Seth wanted to send out the news immediately so that they could get on with things and deal with the consequences.

"Better action than just sitting here, waiting," he argued while Sabine urged him not to leave. "The people have a right to know. Who are you to keep it from them?"

"I'm the leader," Sabine said. "And I say it's best to keep it quiet, even for just a day or so."

All Eli wanted to do was to honour Zenith appropriately. He could hear his brother and sister squabbling, but he wasn't really paying attention to their words. He was envisioning the service he would conduct for her. There would have to be a viewing first. It might take days for Zenith's admirers to pay their respects, but they'd have to allow it. And then a service. Open air, so that all who wanted to could attend.

He interrupted Sabine and Seth to tell them of his plan, so sure was he about its necessity.

They listened, and after a pause Sabine shook her head. "No. Eli, there's no way we can do something like that now. Not with things as they are. Of course we all want to do right by her, and it would be wonderful if we could, but I'm afraid it's just not realistic."

"No way," Seth agreed. "That would just be asking for trouble—an event like that would be a target. Not only for the Guard, but for any whacko who wanted to do something stupid."

"We're doing it." Eli would not lose this battle. He hadn't stood up for much, but he would insist on this. "Seth, you can put your boys to work on securing the area and monitoring the attendees. Sabine, you can take the chance to speak. It needs to happen. It will happen. Zenith deserves this. So do her people. Let me do this *one* thing. It's all I ask."

Unable to come to a consensus, the siblings took the dilemma to the larger group. Trace and Jack and Celeste were on Eli's side, as were all the others. Only Sabine and Seth were awake to the likelihood of what was about to happen. The others were heavy-limbed with the stupor of grief.

After much begging and pleading, all of which annoyed Seth, he gave a small nod of assent in Sabine's direction when she looked for it.

Then Sabine spoke, a knot of grave concern forming in her gut. "I'll agree to it." This was it. This would be the catalyst for a world about to tip off its axis and plummet into galactic darkness. "But we'll do it quickly. Everything must be abbreviated. There's simply not the time to honour her in the way we'd all like to. I'll allow three days. Start to finish. Including the viewing."

Even before she was finished talking, Seth was making ready to leave. "I'll organize the boys," he said. "I'll try for the quickest turn-around possible."

"Before you go, Seth," Sabine said and then turned back to the tired group gathered in front of her. "I want it made clear that Seth is to be obeyed. He's supplying us with a trained and compliant army, and as they are under his command in battle, so will we. Whatever your feelings are about him personally, I expect you to set them aside and listen to his commands in the coming days."

Their uncertain expressions lit by the warm glow of the lanterns, the others listened. No one spoke. She looked at Trace, waited for him to challenge her, but he just sat at the back of the group, arms folded across his chest, his glance set stubbornly aside. Her respect for him swelled in that moment. She would thank him later for his concession. She turned to Seth now and bade him leave. Finally, she gave formal permission for Eli to get things underway.

"What about the circus?" Jack asked just as everyone was about to disperse.

"It's still on," Sabine said firmly. "After."

Suddenly a rumble was heard from outside, the sound of hooves and cartwheels battering the cobblestones, voices raising in protest and quickly silencing again. It wasn't dawn yet. What was going on? The siblings and the others—except for Celeste, sitting vigil with Zenith's body—hurried to the street entrance, stepping outside and seeing what those camped around the coliseum were seeing.

It was Vance and his men, making their way back to the Guard camp by cutting straight through the city, drawing its tensions taut as if pulling back the band of a slingshot. It was an awesome spectacle: a thousand armed Guard parading silently through the street, each one steadfast and stern, made bigger by the armour protecting their backs and chests, armour Seth had never seen before.

Vance knew exactly where Seth was. It wasn't hard to find things out in Triban, no matter how the Chancellors might pretend otherwise. "Embedded" or not, Seth's presence in the city was no secret.

The phalanx of Guard didn't stop as it passed directly in front of the coliseum, but it did slow enough for Vance himself to kick off a large bundle from his cart. Exquisitely timed, it bumped to a stop at the feet of the Triskelians. Since it was clearly lifeless, no one rushed to unwrap the body from its crude shroud.

"A gift. From the Chancellor of the Eastern Key," Vance called over his shoulder as he was swept out of sight with the troops' steady advance. "Here is your traitor."

It happened so fast that no one noted the thin expression of surprise Vance could not keep from his face upon seeing the Chancellor's other son, and the girl. There had been no mention of a girl. What was he to make of it all? What was Chancellor East up to?

No one moved or spoke until the last Guardy was out of sight. Bullet didn't even bark once, sneaking just one furtive sniff at the bundle. It was as if the city and its people had been entranced, knowing that whoever dared break the spell would ignite the first moments of a war that had no end in sight. While Sabine was grateful beyond words for the city's unspoken compliance, Seth fumed beside her.

"If we'd known they were coming," he said, "we could've—"

"Just go now," Sabine said as Eli kneeled to reveal who had been delivered to them. "Gather your troops. We haven't much time."

Eli cut the ropes and carefully slit open the sackcloth to expose Pierre's gaunt face, whiskered and bruised, bloody around the mouth.

"Get Nana," Eli said.

The Triskelians circled around him stared down at the wan face of death, transfixed by shock and confusion.

"Someone go get her now!" Eli shouted.

When still no one moved Eli ran to find her himself, the medallion Pierre had made for him bouncing against his sternum. As he sprinted out of the flat light of the creeping dawn and into the lingering darkness of the coliseum he felt as if he were running head first into the blackness that lay ahead for them all. He would need his highers now. They all would, as their souls battled for peace at the expense of their lives.

Interview with Carrie Mac

July 2006

What initially inspired the Triskelia series?
The seed of it was a recurring dream I'd have of a world like Triskelia. It was such a rich, fascinating world . . . I'd fall asleep each night hoping to dream about it. Other inspirations include the Cirque du Soleil, the political and social state of the world since September 11, 2001, the science of cloudseeding, and the Maddox family.

Where are the Keylands/Droughtland?
It is a global situation, with the story set in an imaginary North America of sorts.

How far into the future does the story take place?
Is it the future? Or is it an alternate world? There's no reason why it couldn't be either one . . . or something else entirely.

Could you briefly explain the history behind the Keylanders?
Human plagues and livestock diseases, global warming, water commodification, corporate and civil war, and overpopulation are just some of the factors that contributed to the state of the world when the Group of Keys was formed by the ruling class.

As a kind of global cleansing, and as a way to protect themselves, the Keylanders used biological warfare to decimate the world's population to a more manageable number. Very little infrastructure survived with so few people left to manage it. The Keylanders had been prepared for the loss of labour, but not for the long-term impact. Slowly material goods degraded, and nothing replaced them since there was no labour to produce them. The Keylanders adjusted by erecting walls to keep out everyone else.

Within the safety of the walls, the Keylanders only had to worry about one thing—water. And so they perfected the art and science of cloudseeding—redirecting the weather patterns so that any precipitation would fall on the Keys, leaving the land between the Keys parched.

The land between became known as the Droughtland, and the people struggling to survive in it, the Droughtlanders.

Did the plagues (the sicks) occur naturally or were they man-made?
A "sick" is a crude reference for any of the illnesses that are rampant in the Droughtland. Right now, we have a detailed understanding of all the ills that plague us because of a vast supply of information and research. Imagine losing all that information. All we would have left would be symptoms. Imagine AIDS, but not knowing how it is transmitted, or if you have it . . . or the avian flu, or tuberculosis, or hepatitis. Take away the internet, the medical texts, the doctors, the researchers, the funding, and then let the illnesses run rampant, and you'll get the state of things in the Droughtland. Yes, biological warfare was used by the Keylanders historically, but it is no longer necessary, as so many of the sicks are rampant enough on their own.

The initial impression is that the Droughtlanders are a weak, impoverished people struggling to live on scarce resources. However, there are a number of feasts in the marketplaces, and a few things such as the splendidly ornate costumes worn by the circus performers. How did the Droughtlanders happen upon these things?
Some things are left over from before, but the Droughtlanders are master crafters, traders, barterers, scavengers, and thieves. There are fallen and abandoned cities to pick over and markets to trade at. Furthermore, each Droughtland village has a specialty they are known for, whether it's creating pottery, or weaving, or raising chickens. There is industry in the Droughtland, but it is low-tech. For example: the Night Circus costumes are rebuilt from old clothes, Triskelians' shoes are shared and often cobbled, and day-to-day wear is constructed from common fibres and is worn to the point of falling apart. We humans are tremendously creative and resourceful, especially in times of need.

What is the significance of the French used in the book?

In the Droughtland, all manner of languages are spoken—English is the language of trade. When the Group of Keys formed, the roots of Triskelia also formed, within the Night Circus, which is inspired by the savvy and brilliant (and francophone) Cirque du Soleil. I combined this history with the idea that where there is oppression there is resistance. I simmered this into a culture of people who are natural resistors, and who would raise their children with similar values and strengths. Triskelians are a people who have maintained their identity and autonomy since the Group of Keys was formed. Because they were a strong, unified French-speaking community to begin with, they remain so now.

What brought you to the decision to include poppy dust addictions and other vices in the story?

It made sense to me because oppression, and the accompanying poverty, often send people looking for something to make life seem better, or to at least to make them feel something other than debilitating hopelessness and despair.

How does the story relate to the world in real life?

Our world is barely hanging in there right now, what with all the countries struggling to thrive amidst foreign occupations, economic devastation, sickness, and civil or tribal warfare.

The story was heavily inspired by my thoughts and confusion about 9/11. For example: 2,752 people died as a result of the 9/11 attacks on American soil, yet to date, an estimated 56,000–62,000 Iraqi civilians have died as a result of the occupation and war there. As North Americans, are we supposed to value the lives of those who perished in New York *more* than those in Iraq? Are some lives worth more than others? And what about the global death toll due to starvation and malnutrition? And the millions of HIV/AIDS orphans? Or the half a million children who died in Afghanistan as a result of thirteen years of foreign sanctions exercised by the Western world?

Have you incorporated suggestions from young readers into the next two
books of the trilogy, and if so, how did you work them into the story?

I have. The manuscript for the first book was read by two groups of teenaged readers, who all had endless opinions about what should happen next. There were very heated "debates" at these two book clubs, about who was good and who was evil, who should be killed off, who should conquer, and who should fall in love with each other. I listened carefully, asked lots of questions, took copious notes, and I have been influenced by their feedback as I work on the next two books in the trilogy.

As I get further into the story, I often refer back to my notes from the focus groups. Some of their ideas were way out there, and my suggestion to them is that they should write a sequel too!